Shell Game

BENNY LAWRENCE

Mindancer Press

Bedazzled Ink Publishing Company • Fairfield, California

C000001959

© 2013 Benny Lawrence

All rights reserved. No part of this publication may be
reproduced or transmitted in any means,
electronic or mechanical, without permission in
writing from the publisher.

978-1-939562-08-1 paperback
978-1-939562-09-8 ebook

Cover Design
by
TreeHouse Studio

Mindancer Press
a division of
Bedazzled Ink Publishing Company
Fairfield, California
http://mindancerpress.bedazzledink.com

For Quicksilver, inevitably.

A cloud was on the mind of men, and wailing went the weather,
Yea, a sick cloud upon the soul when we were boys together.
Science announced nonentity and art admired decay,
The world was old and ended,
                              but you and I were gay...

~ G. K. Chesterton

People talk about a time that seems as distant as a dream,
When the stars all spiralled backwards, and the rivers ran upstream,
In the middle of the war that brought our nation to the brink,
Back when nothing ever worked out in the way that you would think.

PART ONE

I CLIMBED ABOARD
A PIRATE SHIP

Narrated by Lynn

CHAPTER ONE

HE SAID, "MY name is Hasak, and I am going to rule these islands."

She said, "My name is Darren, and I am going to punch you in the nose."

And this she did. Blood bubbled out juicily from Hasak's nostrils, dribbling down his chin and fouling the front of his second-hand chain mail shirt. He staggered backwards, smashed his head against the lintel of the nearest hut, and toppled. And that was the end of another would-be overlord.

The village where I lived was nothing special—just a bunch of mud huts and a fishing skiff or two. And yet four raiding parties had invaded it in the past three days. The first set of raiders took all the young men, the ones with the muscle to work the oars of a warship. The second set took all the men older than twelve and most of the women as well. The third set took what food was left: sacks of flour and jugs of oil and piles of dried fish. The fourth set wasn't very impressive. A few men with old armour and rusty weapons. All of them, even their leader Hasak, had a sort of mangy hangdog look about them, as if they didn't really believe that they would get away with what they were doing. But they still rousted us out of the huts, all ten of us, and half of them held us at sword point next to the drying posts while the other half rooted around the village, looking for something they could use.

All of Kila was like that, back then. It was over a decade since the murder of the last High Lord. The civil war was in full flame, and the noble houses had stopped even pretending to make alliances. The islands had become a patchwork of tiny realms and principalities, whose borders shifted daily. Every minor noble with a pint-sized navy was scheming for control. That meant daily assassinations in all the larger towns and bitter sea battles over the trading routes. Out in the poorer parts of Kila, where I lived, it meant that marauders were common as ants. If you woke up in the middle of the night to the sound of scratching in a nearby hut, it was an even bet whether it was a raider or a rat. It wasn't a good idea to go and check.

I don't know if I can explain why we were all so calm when Hasak arrived. It's true that, by the time he came, we had almost nothing left to lose. But that doesn't necessarily matter, you know. I once saw a woman go manic, attacking a soldier three times her size with nails and teeth, because he had taken the last thing she owned: a battered baking tin. She did pretty well, too. The soldier who had tried to rob her walked away with one ear less than a person really needs to function.

But that all happened later. When Hasak came, as I say, we were all very calm. I remember a sword somewhere near my throat, and the hand of the raider who was holding it shook so badly that it scratched skin more than once. But that didn't bother me. I had been through worse.

Even the smaller children didn't cry. I can't tell you what all of *them* were thinking. All I can remember, myself, is a kind of dullness. I'd been through this kind of thing time and time and time again, I knew how it always ended, and I knew that nothing was going to change this time around.

But that was before Darren showed up.

We had our backs to the harbour—that's why we didn't see her ship arriving. I did see a sort of red flush in the corner of my vision, but it didn't mean anything to me. *These* days, of course, everyone knows that she's coming when they see the red sails. But back then she was just getting started. It wasn't like it is now, when you can make a chill settle over a crowded tavern by whispering her name.

She didn't look like a conqueror when she walked into the village, either. More like a shipwrecked sailor hobbling back to civilization after years on a desert isle. All her crewmen looked the same way; it was the combination of faded, salt-crusted clothing, weather-lined skin, and sunburn. They looked like they hadn't had a good night's sleep in a month.

And yet. There was a *something* about Darren, even in the beginning, that I now find very difficult to describe. It wasn't the cutlass (though I did notice that) and it wasn't the muscles (though I noticed those even more). She moved in a way I found interesting, sort of steady and purposeful, as though a howling gale could whip over the beach without making her lose her footing. For a sailor, though, that wasn't so strange.

I think what really caught my notice was her expression when Hasak drew himself up and issued his challenge. It seemed to translate, roughly, to, "Oh, fuck this shit. " I'd been thinking something along much the same lines myself when Hasak appeared, but I hadn't been able to *do* anything about it.

Darren, on the other hand, could punch him on the nose. And she did. Her face barely changed when her knuckles crunched against bone. After Hasak staggered and fell, she shook her hand out while giving a long, meaningful look around. The rest of Hasak's men apparently remembered all of a sudden that they had very important things to do elsewhere. They headed fast for the trees, abandoning their leader where he bled by the huts.

We villagers were left behind with Darren and her salt-crusted mariners. They were the fifth bunch of raiders to conquer the village in three days, and I was beginning to get a little sick of it all. You'll have to bear that in mind if you want to understand why I did what I did next.

DARREN FORGOT ABOUT Hasak's men, even before the last of them were out of sight. She finished looking around, spat thoughtfully, and then said, "Regon."

That was clearly an order, because one of her sailors—brawny, but short—detached himself from the group and made a quick tour of the huts. Meanwhile, Darren leaned against a drying post. Her hands were in her trouser pockets. Her eyes, grey-blue as her woolen shirt, were fixed on the thatch of a nearby roof, as if it was the only thing in the area worth her attention.

That irritated me. So did the casual way that Regon was turning over baskets and raking through wreckage. And so did the way that the ten of us were tamely standing there, waiting for him to finish.

"He won't find anything," I spoke up. "They've already taken it all."

Darren gave me a cursory glance, and then dismissed me as Regon came jogging back to her side.

"Bare as a whore's arse," he reported. "There's not enough here to get them through the month, let alone the winter."

"That's what I said," I pointed out.

Now her gaze settled on me again. "You. Are you in charge?"

I wasn't, but it struck me that I might as well be. I was older than anyone else left in the village—anyone except for Klea and Aegle, both of whom were too ancient to do anything other than mutter through toothless gums. So I nodded.

"You'll starve if you stay here, you know," Darren said.

The irritation was building. "If that bothers you, then you could give us supplies."

She nodded absently. "I would, if I thought you would be able to keep them. But you'd lose them as soon as another raiding party showed up. So I'm going to take you somewhere else. Someplace safe. Have your people pack whatever they still have. Then we'll get you on the ship."

"Like hell you will," I said.

A number of the children looked at me in surprise. To be completely frank, I was a little surprised myself. But more than that, I was tired of being bullied. So I took a step forward and crossed my arms and stuck out my jaw and said again, "Like *hell* you will!"

It sounded better the second time. Even so, I was expecting a few snickers from the watching sailors. I didn't get them. Regon gave a small, tight grin, but it was one of painful understanding more than anything else. On the other hand, I now had Darren's full attention.

"I'm not a slaver, kid," she said. "Nor a murderer, nor a rapist. I know there's no proof, and you'd be an idiot to trust me if you had any better options. But you don't. I'm your only chance. So even if you're scared—"

"I'm not scared," I answered, "and I don't give a good goddamn whether you're a murderer. We're not getting on that boat."

There were murmurs around me. The other villagers seemed to disagree. Darren jerked her head at them. "You stay here and you'll die. All of you. You realize that?"

"That's not the point. It's our choice whether to stay or go. You've got no right to make it for us."

"You've got no right to make it for *them*," Darren pointed out, with maddening accuracy.

"Fine. *I'm* not coming with you."

Darren looked impatiently at the sun, checking the time. "I'm not forcing you, I'm *offering*—"

"So leave me alone."

The skin of her cheeks twisted into a small, rather bitter, smile. "No. Sorry. I don't let people die for stupid reasons."

"Well then," I answered.

We stood for a few moments, assessing each other. I was trying to think of a way out of the impasse when that little maverick part of my brain took over and announced, "I'll fight you."

The children's curious looks turned into stares of open shock.

Darren, too, seemed flustered. "You're a kid."

"I'm twenty," I retorted.

She drew her cutlass, slowly. I got the sense that she was doing it to give herself time to think. "Do you know how to fight?" she asked at last.

"No. Well, not really. I've fought fish. I mean, I've killed fish. I mean, I've fished. This is a fishing village," I explained.

The doubtful crease in her forehead was turning into a deep trench.

"Oh, come on," I said, trying to encourage her. "Just fight me."

"What do you want to fight with?"

"Swords. What else? Crochet hooks?"

"Do you *have* a sword?"

"Of course I don't," I said impatiently. "You'll have to lend me one, won't you?"

The silence after I said this lasted a good few minutes.

"I'll tell you what," she said in the end. "Why don't you take mine?"

"Oh, no, I couldn't possibly—"

"No, no. Really. I insist."

"All right."

Our hands met briefly as she passed the cutlass over. Her skin felt cool and dry and rough and made me shiver a little. To take my mind off of that, I gave the cutlass a few experimental swings. It made a very satisfying *swish* as it sliced through the air. I nodded, then did my best to imitate a fighting stance.

"I'm ready," I said, and then I thought of something and looked back over my shoulder.

"Don't try to interfere," I announced grandly to the cluster of villagers behind me. "This is my battle."

Klea muttered something through a gummy mouth that might or might not have been agreement. Either way, it didn't matter much. Nobody was going to interfere; that much was plain. The younger children actually took several steps backward, clasped their hands behind them, and dug into the sand with their toes.

Darren was waiting, her arms resting at her sides. I took a deep breath and then aimed a slash at her stomach. I expected her to dodge it, and she did. What I didn't expect was that her hand would dart out to grab my wrist and give it a single hard shake. The cutlass clattered from my grip.

"Surrender?" she said. And then she said something less polite when I seized her ear with my free hand and twisted as hard as I could. She grabbed my other wrist and forced it down, so I lunged for her shoulder with my teeth. She swore again, this time in a yelp.

Darren didn't want to hurt me, of course. That was her handicap, and I made her pay for it as I twisted a hand free and went for her ear again. But now she was done playing. She locked her legs behind mine and bent them. That threw me off balance, and when I staggered, she knocked me to my knees. I butted backward with my head. Darren dodged that, and then bore down with her full weight, until I was lying full-length on the ground with her body sprawled on top of mine.

She was panting. I could feel it in the way her breath hit the back of my neck. "What is *wrong* with you?" she hissed in my ear.

"I'm sick of being pushed around, that's what's wrong with me!"

I bucked, trying to throw her off. She gave a frustrated grunt and shoved me down again. My lips scraped against the sandy dirt, and I spat grit.

"Look," she said. "Just *calm down* and I'll let you up."

"You let me up and I'll kill you."

I sort of snarled when I said *kill*, and was pleased with the result. To me, it sounded suitably terrifying. Darren just gave a snort, clearly unimpressed, so I went for her with my teeth again and this time got a mouthful of something soft. I clenched my jaw, forcing my teeth as hard into the flesh as I could, then twisted my head from side to side and tasted copper blood.

When she swore that time, she used words I had never heard before. I paused to listen, hoping that I would remember all of them later.

She was hissing with pain as she tried to tear her arm free. When I hung on, she gave me a quick cuff on the side of the head. I let go immediately. It didn't really hurt, but I thought that I had made my point.

"Captain," I heard a sailor say. "Hate to interrupt you, but . . . tide's changing."

Darren lay still for a moment, her breathing heavy. Then she leaned down on me hard with her uninjured forearm. So that she could get a hand loose, I supposed. There was the rustle of cloth as she rummaged in a pocket, and then a cord slipped around my wrists and tightened. Her weight came off of me, and I scrambled to my feet, but she kept a firm hand on my bound wrists. A few of the sailors were wearing sly grins, but those disappeared when Darren glared.

"All right," she announced. Breathless, but trying to get things back on track. "Someone take her on board. I'll deal with the others."

The stocky sailor named Regon came forward (a little gingerly, I thought) and took hold of the cord that bound me. Darren edged away from us fast and stooped to retrieve her cutlass. She ran her thumb down the length of the blade, checking to see whether I had nicked it. Not even looking at me. All too ready to put me out of her mind. I wasn't prepared to tolerate that.

"Hey!" I said, stomping on the ground.

She flinched, her face almost pleading. "What?"

I jerked my chin in Regon's direction. "Tell him to tie me to the mast."

Darren's eyebrows flew up her forehead. "Tell him to do *what*?"

"Tell him to tie me to the mast," I repeated slowly.

Her mouth opened and closed twice. "You *want* to be tied to the mast?"

"That's not the question," I said, in my most reasonable tone of voice. "The question is, do you want me running around your nice orderly ship like a lunatic? Knocking over barrels and throwing wineskins overboard and trying to bite your fingers off? The only sensible thing to do is to tie me to the mast."

"You wouldn't do that," she said—with more confidence than she felt. I could tell.

I grinned nastily. "Wouldn't I?"

Her face was an interesting study, right then. There was disbelief, but then as the seconds passed, she began to believe that I was serious. And then she realized that the tide was turning and that she didn't have time to sit around and debate the issue. She made an intriguing sound, something in between a moan and a snarl—I was to hear her make that sound quite a few times in the coming days. Then she threw up her hands.

"Fine," she said. "Fine. Have it your way! Regon, you heard her. Tie her to the goddamn mast. Tie her to anything she wants to be tied to. Tie her to the *anchor* for all I care. But get her on the damn boat, *now!*"

Then she strode off, nursing her bleeding arm. The village children scampered at her heels like puppies. Regon tried to lead me away gently, but I set my heels in the dirt so he had to yank me along. Within fifteen seconds, the cord was biting into my wrists and I'd stubbed a toe and my back was aching and my knees were scraped where I had knelt on the path.

And I couldn't figure out why I felt so fantastically happy. I filed that away as something to think about, once I had the time.

REGON WAS TIGHT-LIPPED to begin with, but we got quite chummy while he was tying me up. We talked about our favourite knots, and about fly fishing, and the weather and the best way to cook oysters. Everything but the war, really. I think that we were both sick of discussing it.

The small boat moved steadily back and forth between the ship and the shore, ferrying crew and passengers aboard. The other villagers climbed onto the ship, clutching a few possessions under their arms—Klea and Aegle had old shawls and pots and pans; the children had broken toys, shiny clamshells, that kind of thing. All of them looked at me sidelong as they walked by the mast. Regon had done a careful job. Rather than twisting my arms back around the pole (which we agreed would be too uncomfortable), he had lashed me there with a few turns of rope around my waist, and then tied my hands in front of me. I was sitting cross-legged on the deck, the sails shielding me from the worst of the sun.

Darren boarded the ship last, looking surly, and stomped across the deck to the spot where I sat. I squinted up at her. Her left arm, the one I had bitten, was heavily bandaged. I wondered whether someone had stitched it up, and, if so, whether they used a sail needle.

"Hello," I said.

She gave me a long, unfriendly look, and then dumped a bundle on the deck next to me. "These are your things. We picked them up for you."

"That was very thoughtful," I said. Because it was.

She looked at my tied hands, and her expression softened. "I just want to help, you know."

"I know." I did.

"So . . . can I let you loose now?"

I smiled at her again, less savagely than before. "That's up to you. Do you mind me running around the place like a maniac, foaming at the mouth, and doing my utmost to knock your entire crew into the drink?"

Darren blew out a breath, running a hand through dark shaggy hair.

I shrugged, as best I could, considering I was tied to the mast and all. "I did warn you, you know."

"You warned me," she repeated. "You know something? Fine. I don't have time for this. We need to get moving."

"Go ahead. I can't stop you."

She still looked uncomfortable, but then the breeze freshened. All sorts of interesting things happen on ships when the wind gets stronger. Masts and booms groan disturbingly and sails ripple out and sailors go bouncing all over the place trying to do twenty things at once. Darren forgot about me immediately.

"Teek!" she called. "Hoist up the small boat, then weigh anchor. I want to be across the strait by sundown tomorrow; we're too damn exposed out here. Spinner, find something to feed those kids. Not too much. The passage might be a little rocky and I don't want to have to swab out the entire hold."

She took the tiller herself, and she was so absorbed, I don't think she noticed me staring.

WHEN THE MEAL was ready, someone brought me a portion. The soup was watery but there were scraps of mutton in it, a taste I'd almost forgotten. I cradled the warm mug as I sipped. It was getting cold.

As I was tipping the dregs down my throat, a *clamp-clamp-clamp* of boots on the deck told me that Darren was stalking back over to the mast. Then there was a *shring* as her long knife came out of its sheath.

"Hey, hey," I objected, as she knelt down with the blade in hand. "I know I haven't been making things easy for you, but murder is kind of a drastic solution, don't you think?"

"Just shut up and hold your arms out."

I pulled back, trying to wrench my wrists away from her. My mug went clattering to the deck boards as we wrestled. "You're not cutting these ropes."

"Yes, yes, actually I am. You're a kid. This is insane—Waugh!"

"Waugh" was Darren's reaction when I bared all my teeth and snarled at her. At the same time, she cringed a full foot back, out of biting range. I think that when I bit her earlier that day, I'd managed to leave an impression. So to speak.

"Look, time out," I said. "You're new to this. I understand. But it isn't complicated. You can't let a prisoner roam around your ship. Not when she's trying to kill you."

Darren made a small, exasperated noise as she sheathed her knife. "I don't *care* if you try to kill me. You're the size of a badly-nourished kitten. The worst you could do is give me a couple of flesh wounds and bruise my self-esteem. Here I am, trussing you up, treating you like an assassin, when you should be in the countryside somewhere, with a farmer's wife force-feeding you pie."

Her eyes wandered as she spoke, and that's when I drew back my heel and kicked her in the pit of her stomach. Not hard.

She gave a little *whoosh* and sat back, blinking. After a second she asked, "What the hell was that for?"

"For getting maudlin. I'm not a kitten."

"I just meant that you're tiny."

"Hey," I said defensively. "I could still be an assassin. Do you know how many assassins are short?"

"Um—what?"

"A *lot*, is the answer." She didn't seem convinced. I lowered my tone to a warning growl. "A hell of a lot."

"Kid—" Darren pulled herself back up to her knees.

"You've got to be careful, you know. It's when pirates get overconfident that they end up dead. You know what kills most pirates?"

"I'm not a—"

"Monkeys," I intoned darkly. "You wouldn't expect it, but monkeys are much better with knives than most people realize—"

She made that noise again—half moan and half snarl—as her hand clamped over my mouth. I could feel the fingers quiver next to my skin. She was fighting to keep her temper in check.

"Why are you acting like this is a game?" she asked hoarsely. "I'm not a pirate and you're not a prisoner, and you have to get a grip, kid, because captivity and helplessness aren't funny. It would only take me an instant to cut your throat. The world is not a safe place for people like you. Do you understand that?"

I moved my head to the side, just slightly, and as I had expected, she let me go right away. *Wimp.* The wind was cooler on my face where her hand had been pressed against it.

"Let's say I do understand that," I said.

She spread her arms—*well?*

"Darren, captain, sir, whatever—I'm on a ship that I don't know how to sail, being taken I don't know where. I'm helpless. If you want to cut my throat, I'm not going to be able to stop you, whether I'm tied to the mast or not. Are you really saying I'll be safer if I don't talk about monkeys?"

Her jaw worked a little as she thought about that, but all she said was, "It's usually safer to do as you're told."

I snorted. "That doesn't make you safer. It just proves to everyone how helpless you really are. Trust me, I know."

That was more than I had meant to say. I closed my mouth with an audible snap before anything else could escape. Darren's eyes were on me, thoughtful, and I bit my lip, waiting to see whether she would probe any further. I had revealed too much already, and if she asked the right questions . . .

But one thing you could say for Darren, even then—she didn't like to go after people's secrets. With a sigh, she shifted her gaze to the pine wood of the mast above my head and stared as though nothing else in the world mattered more. When she spoke, her voice was quiet. "I could just as easily tie you up below decks."

The relief was so strong, I had to blink twice before I could concentrate again. And blink twice more before I realized the total insanity of what she was suggesting. "All the others are below decks, right? The other people from my village?"

"What? Yes."

"Then they could untie me."

She raised her eyebrows, not getting it. "Um—yes. I guess they could."

I sighed. "Then it wouldn't be a very good strategy to tie me up below decks, would it?"

There was a long pause. By then, the sun was setting. Darren's brooding face was half yellow and half pink.

At last, and with a hint of desperation, she asked, "Is it all right to give a prisoner a blanket?"

I thought that over, carefully. "I think so."

"Would you like a blanket?"

"Yes please."

She came back with one after a brief disappearance. It was rough wool, and, like all the other cloth on board the ship, it was greyish blue. Did they get a special deal on grey-blue dye, I wondered, or was there an entire herd of grey-blue sheep running around naked somewhere?

Awkwardly, Darren folded the blanket around me, tucking the edges between my body and the mast. I smiled up at her. "Thanks."

"You're welcome?" she answered. With a last bewildered look, she headed below.

I WOKE HALFWAY through the night, when the wind rose. Wavelets were slapping the side of the ship, sending cold briny mist through me.

The blanket was sodden. The knots that bound me had swelled in the wet and were digging into flesh. I was trying to decide whether to scream for help when I heard Darren trudging up from below.

She knelt down beside me and felt my chilly cheek. "This is ridiculous. I'm taking you down."

Under the circumstances, that didn't seem so wholly unreasonable, but I hedged. "You could take me to your cabin?"

"I don't *have* a cabin," she said, as she picked at the rope on my wrists. "How big a ship do you think this is?"

"Damn." I bit my lip. "Do you have barrels? Crates?"

"Ye—e—e—ss . . ."

"All right. So go down to the hold and stack some crates around a corner, and that can be your cabin. And you can bring me down to that."

There was a little choking sound, but her face was invisible in the dark. I couldn't point with my hands tied, so I nodded at the steps that led below.

"Go on. Get to work. I'll be here when you're done."

And, staggering a little, as though she was drunk, she went.

IT TOOK DARREN an hour to shift things around in the hold. The ship was a small trading vessel with a shallow draft, square-rigged on the foremast and mainmast. It was light and manoeuvrable, but it didn't have much in the way of living space. There was no captain's cabin. There wasn't even enough room to hang a hammock for each sailor. If the weather had been a little warmer, then Darren and her eight crewmen would all have been sleeping on deck. As it was, they were crammed together in the open hold, along with water barrels, boxes of biscuit and dried meat, a tiny brazier for heat and light—and now the refugees from my village as well. Any time anyone moved in the close-packed space, they trod on someone's foot or rammed someone's skull.

Darren told me all this, with some exasperation, as she brought me down to the tiny corner she had cleared behind a stack of biscuit boxes.

"You're more trouble than anything else that's ever been aboard this ship," she said, guiding me behind the wall of boxes. "And I carried cobras once. *And* they laid eggs."

"Poor baby," I told her, or, rather, I told her "P—p—p—poor b—b—b—baby." My teeth were chattering so hard that I thought they would splinter.

Her complaints broke off. She looked at me with sudden concern. "You're soaked."

I didn't try to shoot out another smart-ass remark. I just glared at her.

"Gods on high, I'm a moron," she said, the self-reproach returning to her voice. "Wait here a moment."

She disappeared. My legs folded beneath me, and I flopped to the deck, feeling my wet clothing ooze into the wood. I wanted to call out to her and ask what she thought she was *doing*, leaving a prisoner alone and unguarded, but the thought of saying anything made my jaw tremble faster. I curled into a tighter ball. My sopping tunic squelched.

Darren was talking when she came back in, her arms full of blankets. ". . . I should never have left you up there in the cold. I mean, you're obviously out of your gourd, and I know you asked for it, but that's no excuse. I should have—"

"C—c—c—captain?"

"Yes, what?"

"B—b—b—b—blankets."

"Oh, *damn* it!" she said, and stooped to wrap one of them around me. She sounded disgusted but I could tell, even before she said another word, that the disgust was for herself rather than for me. "Look, warm up a second, then we'll have to get your wet things off. I mean, I won't get them off, you'll get them off, I'll leave you alone to—" She glared through the decks at a heaven she couldn't see. "Blast and bugger and damn. I'm so bad at this."

"At what?" The dry blanket was making a difference already. I could feel my fingers again.

"At—you know. Helping people." She grew awkward. "Never mind."

She was flustered, and I didn't want her that way, so I quickly changed the subject. "How many spare blankets do you have lying around?"

"Not enough. That one's mine. The other one is Regon's."

"He didn't need it?"

"He's not big enough to stop me from taking it, so it worked out fine." She sounded better now. "Are you going to get difficult if I ask you to take your wet clothes off? I'll get out of the way."

Get difficult, she said, and I felt a bit annoyed. Hadn't I been difficult ever since the moment we met? Lord knows I was trying hard enough. How much could one woman give?

"I'll take my wet clothes off," I said. "But you should find a rope."

"Oh, what *now*?" The desperation was back in her voice.

"Well, you have to tie me up again."

"Why, in the name of *every* god in creation, would I need to tie you up again?"

"Just think for a second, captain. You're going to be sleeping next to your prisoner. What if I decide to cut your throat in the middle of the night?"

"Who the hell said that I'm sleeping next to you?"

"This is your cabin. Of course you're sleeping next to me. So you need to take precautions—"

"Precautions."

"—precautions, to keep control of your vengeful prisoner."

"My *unarmed* prisoner—"

"—don't forget naked—your vengeful, unarmed, naked prisoner."

Even in the dim light, I saw her tear at her hair. "I brought you a spare tunic! What kind of sick bastard do you think I am?"

"You're a pirate," I explained patiently.

"I told you, I'm *not*."

"You sail the seas, kidnapping maidens from remote villages and tying them to your mast. Call a spade a spade. You're a pirate. You operate in piratical fashion. And if you want to keep on operating much longer, you can't be so trusting all the time." I thought about patting her tanned cheek, but it seemed too soon. "Go get the rope. I'll change while you're gone. Don't take too long, though. You look tired."

THAT WAS THE first day. Darren, I learned, snored like a bull calf, and I made a mental note of that as one more thing to address when the time was right. In the meantime, I just draped a blanket over her face.

I lay, head propped up on one arm, watching her, as snores burbled from underneath the blanket, and I thought about the next step, and the one after that, and the one after that.

CHAPTER TWO

TO ANSWER THE obvious question: No, I did not know what I was doing. Not exactly, anyway. Maybe it would have been different if Darren had sent a carrier pigeon to my village before she arrived, announcing her intention to show up and punch people in the face. If she'd done that, maybe I would have found a few quiet hours before she came to sit and think about how I would use the opportunity. As it was, I had to improvise.

You could say that I was making it up as I went along. I would prefer to say that my plan was a work in progress.

THINGS GOT INTO a pattern pretty quickly and stayed that way for the rest of the week-long trip to the mainland. I spent my nights down in the tiny, improvised cabin. Darren slept there too, in the short stretches when she wasn't on watch. She seemed afraid of brushing against me, though, judging from the way she kept her back pressed against the biscuit boxes that formed the cabin wall. For that entire week, I don't think she touched me once while we were sleeping. That was an incredibly good score, considering that we were sharing a space about the size of a rowboat.

It was an uphill job, I can tell you, trying to convince Darren of her responsibilities as a pirate with a prisoner. Left to her own devices, she would have let me romp all over the damn place unsupervised. Of course, I wasn't about to put up with that.

Regon helped. After I threatened him a sufficient number of times, he unearthed a short, broken length of anchor chain and an old padlock, and he improvised a fetter for my ankle. During the day, I was chained to the mast, and during the night, I made Darren secure me to a deck support in the cabin. She winced each time I held my foot out to her, but at least she wasn't arguing any more. Probably because she was too busy.

Looking back, I can see that we had a fairly easy crossing. The wind was strong and steady; the trading ship, with its light cargo, sliced effortlessly through the waters of the channel. But I didn't know much about sailing back then, and to my inexperienced eye, it looked like we were always on the verge of disaster. Darren and her crew were never still for a moment. Every hour of the day, from dawn to dawn, they were charging to and fro, frantically hauling at things and letting things go and pulling some things on deck and throwing other things over board. If there was ever a lapse in activity, then there would come a cry from a man on the masthead or another on the aft castle, and they would all charge off again.

On top of that, all of the children from my village had voracious appetites, and most of them had weak stomachs, and none of them ever managed to get to the rail on time. The crew was forever sluicing down the deck after their accidents. The children who weren't sick spent their time chasing after rats, or investigating interesting smells, or shrieking complaints when they were told they couldn't go swimming. Yes, the crew had a busy time.

It made me tired just to watch them, as I sat comfortably on deck, shaded by the sails. I used to rest my chained ankle out in front of me. A dozen times a day, Darren nearly tripped over my leg as she barrelled purposefully from one side of the ship to the other.

"You need more sailors," I suggested to Regon, halfway through the crossing. I'd persuaded him to take a break through the simple expedient of threatening to murder him in his sleep if he didn't take a break, and he was leaning against the mast beside me, sharing my shade.

At the words "more sailors," Regon huffed out a tired laugh. "Nice thought. Not going to happen, though."

"Why not?"

"Because . . . because it's not going to happen, that's all."

"Don't tell me she can't afford to hire more. She's a noblewoman, right?"

Regon stiffened. "Who the hell told you that?"

I raised an eyebrow at him, surprised at his reaction. "For the sake of the living gods, she's the captain of a trading ship. It doesn't take a leap of logic to figure out that she's a noble."

"Some trading ships have peasants for captains."

"Oh, please. I've seen Darren use a sextant." (It was well worth watching—her utter focus as she stared at the sun.) "How many peasants get the chance to learn navigation?"

Regon paused, the sudden sick pause of a man who just gave away too much information, and knew it. "Oh, damn," he gulped.

That didn't make any sense. "Why is it such a big secret?" I asked. "She's probably . . . what, a younger child from one of the great trading houses? And she went rogue during the war? Started running cargoes for herself rather than her daddy? That's got to be a dead common story these days."

"It is," Regon admitted reluctantly. "But Darren . . . is . . . well, it's different with Darren. I can't tell you any more."

"Why not?" I said casually. "Does she have a price on her head, or something?"

Silence. Dead silence, electric with panic. Ever so casually, I angled myself so I could see Regon's face.

"So she's been banished, huh?"

The alarm on his face told me everything I needed to know.

"Do you have *nothing* to do, Regon?" Darren panted, as she charged across the deck again. "Really? Honestly? Because I'm sure I could find some use for you, if I made the effort. For one thing, the ship needs a new anchor and for another, we're almost out of fresh meat."

Regon shot to his feet and hurried away from me without a backward glance. He might as well have hung a sign around his neck that said I TOLD THE PRISONER SOMETHING I SHOULDN'T HAVE in giant bleeding letters. Fortunately, Darren was no more perceptive than usual that day.

"What about you?" she asked me. "Getting bored?"

"Not particularly," I told her as I studied my ten brown toes.

"Kash was thinking of trying to cook tonight," she said. "Brave man. He could use someone to seed the raisins for duff. And there are fish to scale."

"Ah, but I'm your helpless prisoner, remember?" I said. "Prisoners don't work. Unless they're slaves. And I don't think you're tough enough to make that kind of arrangement stick."

I gave her my special insolent stare and waited. The moments crawled as she looked down at me, lips parted, trying to decide whether to speak. For a second she glanced away, and I thought she was going to give in, but finally, *finally*—about *time*—her face hardened all over, and she spoke with a snap in her voice.

"Prisoners don't have to eat, either," she said. "I've been damn patient with you, kid, but it's time for you to give something back. I'm sending Kash up here. You do what he tells you."

I wanted to give her a proud hug, but I just grinned instead. "You've got it," I promised.

She stared. "What? That's it? You're not going to argue with me for an hour? Or tell me to hit you over the head with a hammer?"

"You're underestimating yourself. You can be very commanding when you try. Where are those fish? Point me at them. Point me fishwards."

Darren kept shooting glances at me for most of the rest of the night. She watched when Kash and I were scaling the mess of perch. She watched while I cajoled different members of her crew to come and sit with me while they were eating, first Regon, then Spinner, then Teek. Perhaps she suspected that I was pumping them for details, gradually piecing together the story of her life: her early years, her career as a merchant captain, everything right up to the day she was exiled. But if she did suspect, she didn't interfere.

WHILE I'M AT it, I might as well set the record straight. It's not true that Darren was banished because she was caught sleeping with a woman. No matter what you've heard.

She was a noble, after all. And when nobles marry, it's to forge alliances and spawn heirs. Love doesn't come into it, of course, but neither does sex. The idea of "saving yourself for marriage," that quaint mainland invention, is unknown on the islands. For the great houses, youth is the time to sow your oats, to get all that kind of thing out of your system. Result: no Kilan noble in history ever went to marriage as a virgin.

That's true even for the first-born children of the noble houses, the precious heirs, destined to rule their respective families and maintain the bloodline. So it's all the more true for the younger sons and daughters, who are put to work captaining the merchant ships almost as soon as they can count. *They* grow up surrounded by sailors and sailor-talk, doxies in taverns and dock-front whores, and since their lives are a hard grind day to day, they indulge in cheap pleasures every chance they get.

And they're not shy about sleeping with their own sex, either, at least when nothing else is on offer. What else would a captain do when he's becalmed for a week in the dead centre of the ocean, with forty other men around, and only a ragged memory of the last time he saw a woman's breast? And everyone knows what's going on when a young countess, cloistered in her father's house and waiting for marriage, takes a "favourite" from among her serving girls. No one even blinks an eye when they emerge from the brat's private bower horribly late for dinner, pink and giggly and staring at each other's navels. There's nothing shameful about taking what you want, if you're a noble. That's just part of life. As long as it's done with gusto and bluster and sheer cheek, nobles can admit to wanting anything.

Darren's father Stribos had been notorious in his own youth, as I learned later. "A woman for duty," he always said. "But a boy for pleasure, and a goat for ecstasy."

So you see, no one would have batted an eye if Darren had rutted every whore in the shipyards, chased servant women around the halls, or even if she had thrown a peasant girl on the banquet table and spanked her in full view. At the very worst, it would have been seen as a rough joke. A bit immature perhaps, but all in fun for a person of her rank.

No, Darren was banished for falling in love.

"WE WAS GOING overland," Teek began softly.

He was leaning against the mast beside me, all his attention apparently fixed on the rope yarn he was spinning between calloused fingertips. He spoke as if he was talking to himself, and it was sheer coincidence that I happened to be in hearing range.

"This is three years gone, back when the captain still bore arms in her father's service. She had a tip, like, that there were sable skins going cheap upcountry, and we was going like blazes before someone beat us to the market. We got there first and bought 'em damn near out. A fortune in fur, for the price of a wagon of apples. But everything started going wrong, like, on the way back to the ship."

I'd spent several hours convincing Teek to tell me this part of Darren's story. He was taciturn and stolid, nothing like Regon, whose tongue ran away with him if I gave him a little encouragement. But I found Teek to be a better informant. For one thing, Regon swore that Darren had never made a mistake in her life, and would carve huge chunks out of his own memories if they seemed to show otherwise.

Teek went on. "Captain had spent every coin she could on sable, leaving just bare enough to feed and supply us on the way back home. A gamble, that. She lost. Seemed the whole country was trying to slow us down. Winter shut in fast. There was a mudslide and we had to detour, then Regon, he got sick, and one of our mules broke its leg. Thing after thing. Tried hunting but there was nothing around but half-starved squirrels. Captain cut our rations but she had to beef 'em up again when bandits closed in and we barely had the strength to wield a sabre. We was two weeks going upcountry, and we'd spent seven coming back and we was nowhere near the coast. Ah, if you'd seen us. Ribs like washboards and the hunger-glitter in every eye, and we had to pull the wagon of furs ourselves, because we'd eaten the other mule. But then we happened on a valley."

Teek had suffered badly in the hungry time. I could tell that from the way his chin wobbled when he told me how they were finally saved. The valley was shielded from the worst of the bitter weather, and it held a thriving town which had no shortage of anything. Teek's chin wobbled worse as he described cheeses the size of wagon wheels, and hams that must have come from pigs as big as oxen, and mammoth tubs of butter and deep cream puddings.

"The captain, she was near to screaming," Teek went on. "She was hungry as any man there. Hungrier, for she'd pushed herself harder. And it was all she could do not to fling herself at the nearest string of sausages. But the trader in her was raving at the thought of what she'd have to pay for it."

"I thought you were out of money."

"And so we were. But we had the furs. Any village that knew its business, seeing starving men, would've taken our wagon and tossed us some stale loaves and the heels of the cheeses. I knew that, we all knew that, but we were past caring. All but the captain. She couldn't bear the thought of suffering like we'd suffered and having nothing to show for it at the end."

I was already getting riled up at the thought of the blackhearted villagers. "Those bastards!"

He chuckled, knotting the end of the yarn. "Ah, but it didn't happen that way. Because *she* was there, you see."

"She?"

Teek's eyes swept the deck, searching for Darren. She wasn't there, but even so, he lowered his voice. "Name of Jess. She worked as a beekeeper in summertime. Got the honey for the village from a few dead trees. But in the winter she also kept a bit of a school, and she helped with birthings. This and that. What I mean . . . they all listened when she spoke. And she spoke *loud* when the whisper first went round that they could get our sable for a biscuit and a half-cup of sack. She spoke loud and not a one stood against her. They took us into the inn that night and gave us such a supper that we could have rolled the rest of the way home. Didn't ask for so much as an acorn in return."

"That's a bit better," I said, relaxing.

"Bit better? I'd say so. Captain gave 'em a fair payment in fur, of course. We stayed a week and the inn was full so the captain went to sleep on the beekeeper's floor. And they went about the village together and they talked 'til late. You could see the lamps in Jess's windows burning well after dark." Teek paused a second, brooding. "Might ha' been the food after all the starving, but it seemed to me that the captain was happy as she'd ever been, and she's not the happy sort."

"You don't say," I murmured. "So what happened?"

"We went home. Loaded the sable, sailed it to market, sold it, made a hell of a profit. Captain's father was pleased as could be."

"Yes . . . but what about *Jess*?"

"Coming to that," he said, unhurried. "Now, I don't know everything, because I wasn't always shipping with the captain. Spent some time serving alongside one or another of her brothers. But I was with her enough to see things changing. She began to find excuses, like, to head to the mainland. Happened more and more often that she'd come back from a voyage with crocks of honey in the hold. And a stunned sort of funny sort of a grin."

I smiled myself. "So then what?"

His face darkened. "She got her courage up—the captain, I mean. Invited Jess to visit the House of Torasan. Her house. To meet her family. Damn fool move, or a damn brave one. Both."

"Did her family know?" I asked. "About the two of them?"

"You could hardly have missed it, the way they looked at each other. But her father, her older brothers . . . they could pretend, you understand? They could pretend not to see. Few times she tried to tell them and they cut her off before she spoke three words. Gave her the if-you-know-what's-good-for-you speech. Well, the writing was on the wall, the choice she had to make. And she made it. Middle of a state dinner, with nobles from all over Kila tittering at the tables, she called Jess up to dance. Then kissed her full in front of her father's throne."

I pumped an arm in the air. "All right!"

Teek sighed. "Then she went straight to her room, she and Jess, and they grabbed what they could, knowing they only had as much time as it would take for the ink to dry on the banishment scroll. They were 'bout halfway done when the soldiers came and threw them out the front gate. She was left with almost nothing. The clothes on her back and a bag of copper."

"Then what?"

"Ah, well, then, the captain went to the dockmaster, and she'd done a good turn once for his son, so he wasn't too quick to desert her. There wasn't much he could do, but the captain managed to talk him out of an old trading ship, a wreck of a thing lying on the beach." Teek glanced around at the ancient deck. "She and Jess patched it as best they could, and then together they sailed it away from the islands. They came safe to Jess's valley, and there the captain retired from the sea. Helped Jess make honey."

"That's nice," I said fondly, pleased with the happy ending, before I realized . . . "Hey, wait. What happened?"

Teek put down his coil of yarn and propped his chin on his doubled-up knees. He followed a gull with his eyes as it screeched its way along the bottom of the horizon. "Land soon," he commented.

"Teek, tell me what happened next, or for the love of sweet mandarins I will tie your thumbs in a knot."

Teek's face stayed impassive as he stared out to sea. I was taking a breath, ready to make a new and better threat, when the voice spoke right beside my ear. "I left her."

My head spun. Darren was crouching beside me, her jaw tight.

"Is that all you wanted to know?" she said. "Fine. I left her. That's the end of the story."

Teek gave me a pleading, warning look. I ignored him. "But why?"

Darren didn't answer. She stood and contemplated the sky, with what appeared to be loathing. "Teek, relieve the helmsman," she said eventually. "And if any overpowering need to tell stories should strike you while you're back there, let me know so that I can whack it out of you."

Teek hurried to the helm, bowing his head as he went past Darren. I didn't blame him. She was properly angry this time. It hummed off of her in hot red waves.

I pulled myself up, so that I didn't have to crane my neck to look Darren in the face. "I made him tell me."

"Oh, I know." Her voice was dark and icy. I pressed on anyway.

"You have to realize, you're a pirate queen now. A public figure. Your life is going to be an open book. If you can't—"

"Shut up." She spat out the words like they were poisonous. "You damn idiot kid." She raised her voice, roaring to the whole crew, "Land bloody ho, you stupid bastards!"

Sure enough, there was a green fuzz along the horizon. Trees.

She gave me one of her quick angry looks. "Shut up and sit down and don't get in the way. Or if you think you're a slave, find something useful to do. Either way, stop distracting my men."

I studied her back as she stalked off. It was rigid with fury. I had touched a nerve. About bloody time.

"She doesn't mean it," Regon told me, apologetically, as he reached over me to make a rope fast.

"She does mean it," I said, flopping back down into my comfortable position. "But that's all right. I was being obnoxious."

"Oh, it's not you. She's always like this when we're going into this harbour."

"Why?"

"You'll see."

I SOON FOUND out why Teek had been summoned to the helm. The ship was heading into a long inlet with high cliffs on either side. The water was studded with rocks and shoals, jagged points carving up the surface into a thousand broken mirrors. It looked like a sunken graveyard, and any half-sane person would have backed gently out and sailed the other way. Darren's fingers, rattling irritably on the railings, betrayed her nervousness, and even Regon looked a bit uncomfortable. But Teek was stone-faced, almost bored, and his hand was sure on the tiller as he wove the ship between spiky chunks of granite. I still found Teek sort of dull compared to Regon—and Darren of course—but there was no denying that he had his uses.

The cliffs gave way to shores of soft sand as we neared the inlet's end. Forest surrounded us on three sides—oak, aspen, and alder. This was waste land, empty, untenanted. Yet—I blinked—there on the coast was a dock, roughly built from large logs to which the bark still clung. It was big enough for one fairly small ship to lie at anchor, that big and no bigger.

I put two and two together. Darren was the only one who used this harbour. The dock had been built for her to use.

And yet someone knew she was coming. Beyond the dock, I could make out tents pitched in the shelter of the trees, and ox wagons, and smoke from cooking fires. Someone here was ready for her.

The "someone" turned out to be a small woman with freckles across her nose and a searching, intent expression. Her hair was pulled back in a single dark braid and her hands rested in her pockets as she waited on the beach for the ship to moor. I looked back and forth between her and Darren, who was now leaning against the rails, her face sour and grim. They couldn't have been much more different. Where Darren was long and lean, this other woman was short and sturdy; where Darren was tanned and tough, she was softer, her face winged with laughter lines. She was dressed in a tunic and trousers of brown russet wool—anyone could see she was a landsman—where every salt inch of Darren screamed of the sea. Yet there was the same strength in both of them, though, when their eyes finally met, it was Darren who looked away first.

Regon was a short distance away, gulping from a flask. I reached to the full length of my chain and tugged on his shirt. "Is that Jess?"

He finished swallowing, sighed, and offered the flask to me. I took a pull. What was inside tasted something like sour apples and something like tar. It made my lips tingle and I licked them again and again.

"Not Jess," he answered at last. "That's Holly. Jess's wife."

CHAPTER THREE

HOLLY AND HER people had known that we were coming. Maybe they had a lookout posted to watch the inlet. However they did it, dinner was ready by the time we moored. A large cauldron waited at the far end of the dock, and the smells wafting out of it made the smallest children roll and squeal. More landsmen, dressed the same way as Holly, ducked into the tents and brought out wooden bowls and spoons. They lifted the children down from the side of Darren's ship, one by one, escorted Klea and Aegle down the gangplank, and took them all off to be fed. They did it so matter-of-factly, it was plain that this was a well-oiled routine.

Regon tried to unchain me so that I could go with the others, but I beat his hands away and we had a brief, whispered fight. We had to keep our voices low so we wouldn't attract the attention of Darren, who was still prowling around like a wounded cat. In the end, he gave in, left me where I was, and tossed me a chunk of dried beef. Huddled by the mast, I nibbled it, listening to Darren and Holly. They were pacing up and down the dock as they talked, and I could hear the tension in Darren's voice. She was making a mighty effort to be civil.

"Only ten this time?" Holly was saying. "The war must be over."

"You know better," Darren growled. "There are only ten because their village got shredded and I didn't get there in time to help anyone else."

"I was kidding. Humour? Levity? Remember how that works? No? Well, there's one good thing. Jess and I can find places for ten without too much trouble."

They wandered out of hearing range, and as I waited for them to come back, I wondered idly what kind of "places" Holly and Jess were finding for Kilan refugees. I'm a realist, or a cynic, whatever you want to call it, so my first theory was that the pair of them were making money hand over fist selling cheap labour to silver mines and brothels. But I found that I didn't really believe that. There was something about Darren that made my inner cynic shut up and sit down, and Holly had the same kind of quality. Call it, I don't know, *soundness.* Most people I had met in my life were like rotten logs, who crumbled into maggots and dust as soon as I rapped them. Darren had yet to crumble, though, no matter how hard I rapped, and I was beginning to suspect that she might be solid all the way down to the heartwood.

The voices came nearer again. It was Holly talking. "You'll want to load the supplies first, won't you?"

The beach next to the dock was lined with boxes and coils of rope, sides of beef and barrels of oil and wine and even chickens squawking their protests in wicker baskets. Darren and her crew ate surprisingly well while at sea. Now I knew why.

"I've told Jess before," Darren snapped. "She doesn't need to do this. I'm not going to starve if she stops feeding me."

Holly didn't seem insulted by Darren's crust. "We know that you do important work. Is it so strange that we want to help you?"

"You do enough. I'm not asking for anything else."

"Of course you're not asking. You never *do* ask."

Their footsteps kept coming closer. Too late, I realized they were heading up the gangplank. I took one quick look around—there was nothing to hide behind, so I just stretched out in a casual sprawl. Then I plastered my most innocent expression over my face. *Who, me? Eavesdropping?*

Darren stopped dead when she saw me. Then she gave a slow, measured sigh. "You just don't give up, do you, kid?"

"I'm sure I don't know what you're talking about," I said, twitching my ankle so that the chain clinked on the deck.

"It's not what you think," Darren said to Holly, whose posture had gone rigid all of a sudden. "I'll explain later."

"In the meantime," Holly said, a bit too calmly, "introduce us."

"What? Oh, right. Holly, this is—" She paused. "Well, I'll be damned. Kid, what *is* your name?"

I clinked the chain a little faster. "Really, captain. You should know the name of someone you've been sleeping with for a week."

I could almost see crystals of frost forming in Holly's hazel eyes as she trained them on Darren.

"*Not* what it sounds like," Darren said frantically. "Let's just sort out the cargo and I'll explain." Grabbing Holly's arm, she hustled her back to the gangplank, but spared me a look over her shoulder. "I'll deal with *you* later."

"Promises, promises," I muttered, and settled in for a nap on the sunny deck.

I WAS WOKEN by the tramp of boots on the deck beside me. Not sea-boots—there were hobnails clicking against the planks. Instinctively, I snapped my knees up to protect my stomach, but there was no need. The footsteps came to an abrupt halt beside me, and a soft hand touched my shoulder.

I blinked upwards. Holly crouched there, a bundle under one arm.

"So let me get this straight," she said. "You're her hostage, right? Or her prisoner? Something along those lines?"

"Yes," I said, maybe a bit more defensively than necessary. "And if you're here to try to talk me out of it, you might as well get lost. I'm having a hard enough time dealing with *her* insecurities. I don't need you to get in on the act."

Holly smiled wryly. "To be frank, I think you deserve each other. No, I'm not here to talk you out of it. I just thought you would need a few things if you're going to be on the ship much longer."

She placed her bundle on my lap. Blinking with confusion, I unfolded it. An old ivory comb and a small neat pocketknife sat at the centre. The bulk of it was clothes—a couple of linen shirts, a woollen overtunic, loose trousers, a warm cloak. All in shades of brown and deep cream and russet red; all well-made and sweet-smelling. Nothing like the rough, slapdash, oh-well-that's-good-enough outfits that Darren and her crew wore.

"They're mine," Holly said apologetically. "I didn't have the time to make anything new. But you're about my size. If you tell me just what you want, then I can run you up something of your own, and you can collect it the next time Darren's ship comes in."

I found my voice at last. "Why are you doing this?"

She held a shirt up against me, to check the fit. "I know a thing or two about Darren. And I'm not a complete novice when it comes to dealing with women, either. I know what you're trying to do. It may work out or it may not, but nothing else has worked with her up to this point. By the way, do you have a name?"

I never really know when a casual question is going to stir up the old dread inside me. This one did. My stomach twisted. "Not one that I want to keep."

She studied me. "What are you running from?"

"Nothing," I said automatically.

Holly didn't bother to tell me that I was lying. There was no need; we both knew it. She simply held my gaze.

"I don't want to talk about it now," I whispered, in answer to her wordless invitation. "Thanks, but . . . I'm not ready. I don't think I could get the words out."

"Well, all right." She was reluctant to let the subject drop, I could tell, but as she re-folded the clothes into a neat stack, she contented herself with asking, "Darren's treating you properly?"

"You know Darren, you said. What do you think?"

Holly smiled, but it was a little sad. "Darren's noble to the bone. She's got to try to get over that, or it's always going to hold her back in life."

"I know. Oh, how well I know. Don't worry, it's on my to-do list."

"Well, then. Is there anything else I can get for you?"

"No, I think I'm set. Actually, no. Wait." I sat up straight as a thought struck me. "While we're on the subject of names . . . do you think you could give me one of those?"

Her eyebrows shot up. "Are you sure?"

"Yep. You don't need to agonize over it for hours. Just pick one. Something in your own language. I need something that doesn't come from Kila. Something new."

This was sheer impulse, but it made sense to me. I hadn't needed a name on Darren's ship so far—there weren't any other women chained to the mast, so no risk that I would be confused with anyone else—but the crewmen couldn't keep calling me Hey You forever. Holly didn't seem surprised in the least. It was the first time I encountered her ability to take strange things in stride, and I've often been grateful for it since.

"How about 'Lynn'?" she said after a few minutes' thought.

Lynn. I tasted it, assessing it. Not much of a name. Not much of an anything. It sounded brief, clipped, and empty. But maybe that was exactly what I needed. After all, I was shedding my entire identity so I could build a new one from the ground up. "Lynn" was a blank, unmarked name, a kind of cipher. Perfect for someone who was starting from scratch.

"Lynn," I said, trying it out loud. "Yes. That's fine, that'll do. Thanks. I'll keep it. What does it mean, by the way?"

Holly smiled again, a real smile this time. It showed little white teeth. "It means, 'Kid.'"

THE SHORE MADE Darren restless. She paced up and down endlessly while the supplies were being loaded, and though she didn't yell at her crew, she kept making hurry-up noises under her breath. In spite of that, sundown was approaching by the time the men stowed and lashed the last barrel. Though Darren was plainly itching with the need to be gone, she was too much of a sailor to risk the rocky inlet in the dark. Grudgingly, she told the crew that they would spend the night in the little cove.

Regon and Kash made up for the lost time by unshipping the rudder and scrubbing it clean of barnacles and dangling wisps of seaweed. As they worked, Darren stomped around and around them, giving lots of advice that they clearly didn't need.

"Talks a lot, doesn't she?" Holly observed—we were watching from the ship. "Darren always has to manage everything. I think she believes that the sun won't rise in the morning unless she's there to supervise the process. Here, have some more cider."

"She's a noble." I shrugged, as she refilled my cup. "You're not Kilan, so you might not understand. It's how they're taught to think of themselves. *Blood is right and blood is rank . . .*"

"*Blood alone is rulership,*" Holly said, finishing the old saying. "I've heard that. Sometimes, Darren needs a gentle little reminder that things don't work that way around here."

"I can imagine." I raised my voice. "Darren, will you leave those poor men alone? They've got it under control!"

She glanced up at me, irritated. "I'm making sure that—"

"You're just stepping on their feet." (By now Regon and Kash were hiding their smiles.) "Give them some room."

Darren folded her arms crossly, but she also backed off. As she wandered further down the beach, I could hear her muttering something about checking the stores.

Holly and I watched her go.

"I've never really understood it," she said presently. "The Kilan obsession with bloodlines, I mean. It doesn't seem to make any sense."

"It doesn't make the tiniest little bit of sense," I agreed. "But that's how it is."

"So impractical, though. We have nobility in this country, but they don't have the blood mania to the same extreme. Is it true that a Kilan lord can be deposed for not having any children?"

"Dead true. It happens all the time. There are always a bunch of second-rank aristocrats, younger sons of younger sons, looking to knife their way to power. You know what they say? They say that a noble without children is half a corpse. And not just because he's a target for every assassin who wanders through the neighbourhood. Kilan lords believe that descendants make you immortal, and without them, you're not even really alive." A breeze touched the aspen, and I shivered. "Is there any more of that cider?"

She refilled my cup again and left the bottle in my reach when she'd finished pouring. "But why do they have so *many* children? Take Darren—she has more than a dozen siblings."

"Because nobles get a lot of work out of their children. They use them as merchant captains, army fodder, wedding bait . . . everything but mousetraps. Darren was one hell of a moneymaker for her father, or so I'm told, so he must have been well and truly pissed when he banished her. Bet he regretted it later."

Holly finished her drink and overturned her empty cup. "Is it very dangerous for Darren to do what she's doing? I mean, going back to the islands after her banishment?"

"Yes," I said flatly. "She's an exile. In the eyes of the nobles, she isn't even human. They could do anything to her and still be within the law. Kill her. Sell her. Paint her green and show her at fairs. Anything."

Holly let out a long sigh. "She doesn't say anything, but I know she's afraid. The last time she was here . . . six weeks ago . . . she staggered down the gangplank once the ship was docked and she wouldn't say a word to me. She just sat in one place and stared until dark. Then she asked for brandy and drank until dawn. Regon told me they had a close call."

"What kind of close call?"

Holly gave a helpless laugh. "You may find this funny, but Darren doesn't really choose to confide in me, for some reason. Maybe you'll have better luck."

Darren's restless prowling had taken her near the stern of the ship, and something there caught her attention. She squinted, then backed away and took a good look. Then she marched back towards us with purposefulness in every taut line of her body. "Kid?"

"It's 'Lynn.' And yes?"

"You want to explain why my ship has the word 'Badger' painted in giant letters on the stern?"

"Oh. Did I forget to tell you? That's the ship's name now."

"You *named* . . . my ship?"

"A pirate queen's flagship needs a name."

"My only ship. My *only* ship. Not my bloody flagship. And what the hell kind of a name is *Badger*?"

"It's the ship's name. Obviously. Look at this ship. It is clearly a *Badger.*"

"How do you figure?"

"It came to me in a flash of inspiration. Don't question the creative process. Anyway, Regon agreed with me."

She threw up her hands and wheeled around. "Regon, you're part of this . . . this conspiracy?"

"Well, someone had to help her with the painting," Regon said reasonably, tossing a barnacle over his shoulder. "She couldn't reach. Being chained to the mast and all that."

"She told you to paint Badger on the ship, and you just trotted off and *did it*?"

"Don't be silly," Holly said. "He had to wait for Lynn to write out the letters for him. And then he had come to me to get the paint."

The noises that Darren made right then sounded like a kettle that had been left too long on the fire.

"You people better watch it," Darren said. "Who the hell do you think's in charge here, anyway?"

She tromped off with the last tatters of her dignity.

Holly waited until she was out of earshot. "She hasn't figured it out yet. Has she?"

"Give me time," I protested, stretching luxuriously. "It's early still."

"True, but I find it's better to get them over the hump as soon as possible. Now, how about some of that soup? It's getting a little chilly."

IT WAS VERY late when Darren came to our makeshift cabin, and her eyes were red-rimmed with drink. She unbuckled her cutlass and set it on the floorboards, her movements slow and deliberate, as though she didn't trust her own hands. I sat up in my blankets and waited.

At last, she said, "You know that we're leaving tomorrow."

"So?"

"So . . . you need to get down on shore."

Frustrated, I tugged at a fistful of my hair. How long was this going to take? "I'm your chained, helpless prisoner," I pointed out for the sixtieth time. "How am I supposed to get down on shore?"

She rubbed her temples, and I knew she was getting a headache. "Well, what if I decide to be merciful just this once, and let my helpless prisoner go free?"

"Oh, I don't think you'll do that," I said absently, tugging at my hair again. There seemed to be a bit too much of it. It was shaggy at the back. "I need a trim here. Lend me your dagger?"

She drew it without thinking, and then there was the shade of a smile. "Isn't it a bad idea to give a dagger to a slightly-deranged captive?"

"There, now. Who said you were unteachable? You'll have to cut my hair for me."

Darren lifted her hands. "I'm not going to do that."

"Why not?"

"Because I might stab you, that's why not."

"Come on, I trust you."

"I don't care whether you trust me, accidents happen. Besides, you don't need your hair cut. You hardly have any of it to begin with."

"I like it short."

"You look like a boy. But if you *insist*, I've got some scissors around here somewhere."

Darren rooted around—it took her a minute or so. The shears that she eventually produced were long and blunt and rusty and looked about six times more likely to kill me than her well-sharpened dagger, but she seemed happy with them, so I let it pass. I scooted around so that my back faced her. She braced a doubled-up knee against me, to get leverage, and I leaned into it.

"I mean it," she said, between deliberate snips. "Even ruthless, pitiless pirates have their good days. I could decide to let you go."

I cocked my head thoughtfully. "You could, of course. But you're the pirate queen. The captain of the formidable *Badger*. Even if you're feeling merciful, you can't do anything that would chip away at your fearsome reputation."

"Hold still. I nearly chopped off your ear. And even pirate queens let prisoners go sometimes, I'd think."

"Hey, which of us is the expert on pirate queens? Besides. By now I'm so bitter about my captivity that, if you ever let me go, I would probably just raise an army of deranged ex-slaves and come after you. And kill you elaborately when you least expect it."

"Hold still, I said." She grabbed the top of my head in one work-roughened hand. "Someday you're going to have to tell me what you're bitter about. How do you kill someone elaborately, anyway?"

"Well, I have a few ideas. One involves marmalade."

"Does it?"

"It does. Another incorporates ten under-ripe mangoes and a rat on a stick. You said 'someday,' by the way."

The snipping stopped. "I never—"

"You said that I have to tell you someday what I'm so bitter about. And I will. But someday isn't today. Good thing that I'm not going anywhere."

There was the familiar sigh, and then she brushed wisps of hair from the back of my neck. "I still don't see why you want it so short."

"Because I like it short."

"Oh, for the love of—just *look* at it."

She held out one of the larger locks, and I studied it gravely. "Yes," I agreed, after I felt I'd given it all the attention it deserved. "Yes, that is my hair."

"It's so pale," Darren said. "It looks like . . ."

She paused, and I knew from her frown that she was concentrating deeply, summoning up every ounce of poetry in her soul. "It looks like *wheat* or something."

"Look at you, spouting compliments to captives," I said. "That's a pirate, all right."

She smiled in spite of herself. Then she looked down at her hands.

"I know you," I whispered. "You're not the kind of woman who would pick up a slave girl on a whim. And you're not the kind of woman who would just throw one away, either. You're not going to let me leave."

SHE WASN'T THERE when I woke up. I'd gone to bed braced for another argument, expecting her to have an eleventh-hour change of heart. It would be just like Darren to stick someone else with the job of getting me off the ship, while she went and lurked in the bushes until it was done. But Holly wouldn't be Darren's stooge, I hoped, and Regon and Teek were both at least a little bit afraid of me. Kash and Spinner, more than a little. If Darren wanted me gone, she'd have to do the dirty work herself.

So I didn't panic as I looked around the empty cabin. I combed my hair, drank some water (Darren had left a flask), and then did a few deep breathing exercises, waiting for the combat to begin.

But minutes later, I felt the *thrum* beneath my hand where it rested on the planks, and the next moment, my heart was leaping in my throat. That was motion. The *Badger* was outside the narrow inlet, sweeping full-sailed through the open seas.

Regon peeked through the doorway. "Are you decent?" he asked dutifully.

"You're supposed to ask that before you look in, you know," I pointed out, as I tossed the blankets aside. "Where's the captain?"

He stooped to unlock my ankle chain. "It's her turn at the tiller. She wants to know if you're so cowed and terrified that she can force you to help with the cooking."

"Good question," I said, and pondered. "Is she looking very ruthless today?"

His smile, in his brown face, looked like a crease in an old saddle. "I've never seen her so ruthless. Really, she must have been practising."

"Then I'm duly cowed. Let me get at the supplies and I'll see if I can make a duff that tastes a little better than Kash's boots."

That turned out to be a busy morning, but Regon found the time to talk to me once more, while I was scouring out the breakfast pots.

"You know," he said, "I think it's good that you're staying."

"Thank the captain. I had nothing to do with it."

CHAPTER FOUR

THE WEATHER WAS worse on that second crossing, and we were heading into the wind, but everything around me was so fascinating that I barely noticed.

It only took me a week or so to get the hang of the cutlass. A cutlass is designed to be easy to use; it's basically a big butter knife, except that you can kill people with it if you happen to want to. Within a few days, I could make it swing and whistle through the air in a manner most gratifying. Darren would stand by, looking either tolerant (if she was in a good mood) or disapproving (if she wasn't).

"All of this isn't going to help you in an actual battle," she would say. "If you really want to be able to fight, I mean *really,* then we need to build up your arm strength."

"But where's . . . the fun . . . in that?" I would pant in reply. "Watch this, I'm going to do the stab-behind-the-back thing."

Things had gotten into a pattern between us, more or less. Darren had argued that by now, I had to be so terrified of her that I wouldn't try to escape during the day. I had agreed, after due consideration, so now I was only chained up at night. That left me free to prance around the deck wielding Darren's weapon whenever I wanted, which made a nice change. Before long, though, I discovered something much more interesting than the cutlass.

Darren had a habit of staring out at the horizon pensively, in the rare moments when she wasn't busy. (It was on my list of things to fix, but I didn't expect to get around to it any time soon. There were much more urgent concerns.) When she was standing and staring, her hand often slipped into her pocket and pulled out a coil of thin leather cord, which she would wind around her fingers or tie into elaborate knots.

That was the cord she had used to bind me on the day we met. Somehow, I didn't think that Darren kept a leather cord in her pocket just on the off chance that she would meet a strange woman who wanted to bite her, so the situation required further research. One night when she was sleeping, I filched the thing from her pocket to have a little look-see.

There was a full moon that night. The dim blue glow trickled down from the galley stairs and through gaps between the warped planks. I positioned the cord in the best of the light. It was braided sinew (from a bear,

I later discovered), smooth and shiny with use. Uncoiled, it was a few feet long. At either end, a small bone bead kept the braid from unravelling. I tugged at the ends experimentally.

Darren's voice came sleepily from the blankets. "Not for playing."

I tugged at it a few more times anyway. It was incredibly strong. "It's a garrote, isn't it?"

"Mmm-hmm."

I made a loop in the sinew and imagined slipping it over a man's head. He would start to suffocate as soon as you drew it taut, but you could kick him in the back of the knees to hasten the process. Then when he fell, his full weight would be added to the force of the pull. This garrote wasn't wire; it wouldn't cut the windpipe right away. But it was a weapon that you didn't have to be a muscleman to use. The garrote could focus your strength, or make up for strength you didn't have. You could wield it to defend yourself or to kill.

Darren propped herself up on one elbow. "Lynn, please."

I coiled the cord carefully and handed it back before I flopped down beside her. "Teach me to use it?"

Her eyes had slipped shut again. Groggily, she shook her head. "It's not like a cutlass. No way to practice with it safely . . ."

"How did you learn?"

"Used a post," she yawned. "Padded post."

"So we'll set up a padded post. Honestly, do I have to do all the thinking around here?"

Darren didn't answer. Her chest rose and fell. Then she said, "Why do you want to learn to fight?"

"Well, if the ship gets boarded . . ."

"If this ship gets boarded, we're all dead."

There was anger, but again, she was directing it at herself, not at me. I waited, and the next words were halting.

"I'm scared shitless every time I leave that harbour. Every time we head back to the islands. Every time . . ."

I waited long minutes, motionless, but there was nothing more. She slept, or more likely, pretended to sleep. I didn't see any prospect of doing that myself, so I filched the garrote from her pocket again and practised tying knots.

OF ALL OF darren's sailors, Spinner was the one I got to know best. He was the youngest of them, maybe even slightly younger than I was, though he didn't know his actual age. Looking at the rest of Darren's crew, you saw grizzled faces, muscles like tree roots, and hands so rough that they could have been sharkskin gloves. Spinner, on the other hand, was slim and smooth as a peeled switch, with wispy hair and skinny wrists. His voice was flute-like, even when he was cursing.

On any other ship, torturing Spinner would have been a popular form of recreation. On any other ship, men would have been lining up after dinner to kick him around the deck. On the *Badger,* for some reason, no one ever seemed to notice that there was anything different about him. All the sailors called each other dirty bastards and sons of whores in a completely impartial way, no offence meant and none taken.

I got the rest of Darren's story from Spinner, what there was of it. It didn't take long to tell. Six months after Darren went off to the valley with Jess, she reappeared in a port town on the mainland, one of those places that survives by selling drink and women to Kilan sailors. When she rolled into town, Darren had a single battered ship, a fierce expression, and a mission. She was looking to recruit.

I actually slapped my face when Spinner explained this to me. Dumb, dumb, *dumb.* As an exile, a criminal, Darren wasn't entitled to any protection under Kilan law. Even a commoner could kill her without facing punishment. With that hanging over her head, it was simply heart-stoppingly *stupid* for her to walk into a tavern filled with sailors she didn't know. It made about as much sense as drenching yourself in gravy and then prancing up to a dragon's den with a sign around your neck reading PLEASE EAT.

"It worked out," Spinner said. "She found Regon almost right away, and he's her man, from his skin to his soul. They've sailed together more than half their lives. He stashed her away in a dark room, and he went out and found the rest of us. We'd all served under her before."

"But why was she recruiting in the first place? What did she want to do?"

Spinner shrugged. "Honestly? I think she's still figuring that out. Defend the Weak. Protect the Helpless. Save Kittens. Really, we're just wandering from place to place until we find something to do."

I'd been afraid of that. It was very noble, and all, but it wasn't the wisest strategy imaginable in a time when there was a warship on every other wave.

The *Badger*, being a little two-masted trader, was not the kind of ship you'd choose for travelling across a war zone, if you had any options. It was too light for ramming, too small for grapnels, and though Darren's sailors knew which end of a cutlass to hold, there were too few of them to fend off a serious attack. Darren's only choice, if trouble came calling, was to try to outrun it. Outrunning trouble is one of those strategies that works until, all of a sudden, it stunningly, devastatingly doesn't.

"Holly said that you had a close call a while back," I told Spinner, fishing for details.

He nodded. "The captain's father put a price on her head when he learned that she was back in the islands, making trouble. The captain's got this cousin. Distant cousin. Bounty hunter. Totally insane. She almost caught up with us when we stopped to take on water. We got away, but that night, the captain worked her way right to the bottom of a beer barrel, tankard by tankard, and she didn't speak to any of us for hours."

Darren didn't speak to any of them, I realized, because the narrow escape had forced her to acknowledge what she must have already known: sooner or later, her luck would run out. Any band of marauders with a few hours to kill would consider the little *Badger* a juicy target, even if they didn't know that it was captained by an exile. And if they did know . . . well.

It was just a matter of time, and Darren knew it.

Her men knew it too, so I couldn't figure out why they were following along so tamely. They had all sailed with Darren for years before her banishment, that was true. But was that enough of a reason for them to keep heading straight into the centre of the storm? Were they like Darren, possessed by some kind of stupid guilt that made them incapable of looking after themselves? Were they just do-gooders at heart? Or did serving on the *Badger* offer opportunities for profit that I hadn't yet seen?

"Why the hell do you follow her?" I asked Spinner. "What's in it for you?"

He scratched his beardless chin for long moments before he responded. "I dunno."

Which made me suspect that I'd been overthinking the whole thing.

DARREN SHRUGGED WHEN I told her what Spinner had said. "If I were a better person, I'd send all of them somewhere safe."

"Send them somewhere safe. Right. Because it's not like they could choose to leave on their own. That's just crazy talk."

"They won't leave me. Not unless I force them to go. Most of them have served the House of Torasan all their lives. A noble whistles, they jump. That's how things are."

"They love you."

"Oh, piss off."

She was tense that day.

She was tense most days. As we worked our way deeper and deeper into the islands, she was just getting worse and worse. She slept badly, and almost never sat still for an entire meal. Halfway through, she would pause in mid-mouthful, as if the bread or beef or beans had suddenly rotted on her tongue, and push her portion away, and wander off. The rest of us would look at each other, and then return our attention to our food.

It wasn't bad food, either. By then, I was cooking more often than not, since I still wasn't up to some of the harder work shipside. But Darren never finished. Teek and Regon would divide her share between them.

We were three weeks into the journey by the time Darren decided on our destination—one of the granite isles over on the far west side of the archipelago. The idea was to start at Isla, the largest village, and work our way along the coast, picking up whatever unfortunates we could find. When we had a full load, we'd ferry them back to the mainland, to Jess and Holly and their protective hands, to their valley full of peace and plenty. It was a longer trip than Darren had tried before, but the need was getting desperate on that side of Kila. War galleys were being sunk by the dozen and as fast as they sank, new ones were launched to replace them. Galleys need crews, so anyone with a pulse was at risk of getting conscripted as a rower. Teek and Regon had stories of the things they had seen: seven-year-old boys chained to oars, old men being dragged from their beds as they begged to be allowed to die at home, families murdered over a few dried fish.

During the day, I mostly managed to keep Darren distracted. One evening, though, I caught her vomiting over the rail when she thought no one could see. I know what it looks like when you vomit from sheer terror. There's a lot of bile in it.

I brought her some water. She took the cup from me and stared blankly at the ripples on the surface.

"You must think I'm an idiot," she said abruptly.

"Well . . . frankly . . . yes. But you're the very best *kind* of idiot." I tugged at her sleeve. "Come on. Bedtime."

AFTER DARREN CHAINED me up that night, she paced up and down the tiny cabin, two-and-a-half steps either way.

"All right," she said at last. "How about I take your shoes?"

I was getting dizzy, watching her. "What will that accomplish?"

"If I take your shoes, you can't run. Hard to run without shoes. You'll be stuck on board where the decks are smooth. So I won't ever have to bother with chaining you to anything." She nodded, satisfied. "I think that'll work. Don't you think that'll work?"

There were a few seconds of silence.

"Don't you?" she asked, crestfallen.

"It's a good plan," I told her, as gently as I could. "It's a very good plan."

Her shoulders sagged. "But?"

I lifted a bare foot and wiggled my toes at her.

"Oh cripes." She sank down and raked her fingers through her hair.

"It *was* a good plan," I said, still trying to reassure her. "You're getting better at this."

"You don't wear shoes? Ever ever?"

"Fishing village, remember? It's not as if the nobles came through distributing footwear."

"Mpmph."

"It wasn't your fault."

"I *know* it wasn't my fault."

"Well, don't be embarrassed. You'll think of something."

We lay alongside each other in the comfortable dark. There were sailors sleeping just a few feet away from us, on the other side of the cabin wall. Somehow, it was easy to forget about that. Somehow, I could believe that we were worlds away from the rest of the human race.

Darren sighed, and then mumbled into her folded arms. "It's not too late, you know. For you to leave, I mean."

"Helpless prisoner. *Helpless prisoner,* captain. Do I have to explain all over again how this works?"

"Give the bullshit a rest, just for a second. You know that I don't have a hope in hell of surviving another six months."

"If you really believe that, then why are you doing this?"

"Gods on high. Some days, I don't even know anymore."

"Liar. You know perfectly well why."

Slowly, not making any sudden movements, I reached out and laid a hand between her shoulder blades. She twitched, but she didn't flinch, so I rubbed her back gently, up and down, up and down.

"Did you ever hear the story of the Clever Lass?" I asked, once her muscles loosened.

"Yes. No. I don't remember. What's it about?"

"It's about a farmer's daughter who attracts the attention of a wicked king. The wicked king, being wicked and all, sets her a bunch of impossible tasks. If she fails at any of the tasks, she has to marry him. If she performs them all, then she's free."

"Hang on." Darren lifted her head. "Isn't it the other way around? If she performs all of the tasks, then she gets to marry the king?"

"Hey, I'm telling this story. Besides, my way makes more sense. Who wants to marry someone who spends all their time thinking up impossible tasks? 'Darling, will you pass me the toast?' 'Not until you solve the toast-passing puzzle, strumpet!' No. That would not do."

"All right. Fair enough. How many impossible tasks are there?"

In the version of the story I'd heard, it was seven, but that didn't seem intense enough. "Sixty-three," I improvised. "None of them gave her any trouble, though. Not until she came to the last one, which was the very worst."

"And what was that?"

"It was this. The king told the Clever Lass that she had to come to his castle the next day. But she couldn't come in the daytime, nor in the night-time, and she couldn't be walking, or riding, or driving in a wagon. She couldn't be clothed and she couldn't be naked, and she had to bring him a present which wasn't a present."

"I don't think I remember this part."

"You should. It's the best part of all. The next day, at dawn, the Clever Lass strips down to her skin, and then she takes a fishing net and she wraps it around herself. She catches a bee and traps it between two plates. Then she gets a goat, and she puts her right leg on its back. And she goes up to the castle like that, hopping on one foot while the goat walks beside her. As soon as she gets into the king's throne room, she lets the bee escape from between the plates. A present that isn't a present, you see."

Darren turned her head towards me. "How the hell could a person even do that? Fishing net? Goat? Hopping? While juggling plates?"

"I don't know how she did it. Maybe she'd been practising for just such an occasion. Or maybe she had a natural talent when it came to shenanigans involving goats."

"Was there a point to all this?"

"I just like that story. Does there have to be a point? All right. All right. I guess I'm just saying, impossible things aren't impossible. They require some additional imagination, that's all. And you have to accept the fact that you might end up looking like an idiot."

In the darkness, I heard her inhale. It was a deep, steadying breath, as though there were things she wanted to ask me, if she could only summon the courage. Instead, with a sudden jerk, she rolled over, ending the conversation. "We have to be back on deck in four hours. You think you can keep it down and let me sleep?"

"I don't know. Let's find out together."

"Just shut up, Lynn."

"Yes, Mistress."

"Stop that."

"Or what?"

"Or . . . oh, just shut up."

"Of course, Mistress."

"Don't push your luck."

WE REACHED ISLA the next morning.

If I have a special talent, it's this: I can sense trouble. I might not be good at getting out of the way once I've sensed it, but at least I know that it's coming. And *I knew,* that day, what we were going to find. I knew it before the charred husks of huts showed up against the green of the horizon. I knew it before a thing that looked like a whale skeleton reared into view—the shattered bones of what once was a granary.

I can tell you the way it looked; that's easy. What I can't really describe is the stench—choking, acrid, but with a horrible sort of sweetness. That's what people smell like when they burn, and once you've smelt it, you don't forget.

The final touch was the dead seal that had washed up on the village beach. It slapped heavily on the damp sand as the tide rolled it a few inches forward, a few inches back. Gulls, tearing at the eyes, hopped daintily whenever the carcass moved beneath them.

I stood with my elbows on the rail, chin resting on my cupped hands, contemplating the corpse of the village. Sometimes a dead town can be revived. Survivors straggle back, bury their families, replace the thatch of the huts, mend their nets, and get on with things. That wouldn't happen for Isla. The massacre had been too systematic, the destruction too complete. No one would live in this boneyard again until a century's worth of trees grew and fell and rotted to soil above it.

Around me, the men were moving. Monmain and Kash, sombre as gravediggers, let the anchor chain rattle out, bringing the *Badger* to a halt in the calm water. Spinner tottered up from the hold with an armload of cutlasses and passed them around. Regon, who hated fighting, nevertheless shrugged his way into an ill-fitting sword belt, muttering as he cinched the leather tight around his middle.

Darren had her back to all of this. She was by the rail, trying to lower the small boat, working both winches by herself and generally making a mess of it. I understood Darren too well, by then, to be confused about why she wasn't asking for help. I could read it in her bent head and the tightness of her back muscles. She was trembling on the edge between screaming and bursting into tears. I shifted my weight, about to join her, but Teek and Regon got there first. They took over the lowering of the boat, and Darren moved a few steps away, staring out at the horizon as if she had caught sight of a particularly interesting cloud.

Once the small boat hit the water, she was the first one down the ladder. The rest of the crew joined her, one by one. When Kash, the seventh, climbed in, his weight pushed the gunwale of the small boat almost level with the sea. Regon shook his head in warning at Spinner and me, the only ones left on deck, and pushed off from the *Badger* with his oar.

Spinner and I exchanged glances.

"Don't tell me that they're going to look for survivors," I said. "Don't tell me they think that there could *be* survivors."

He shrugged. "The captain's like that. Don't worry, it won't take them long."

"No," I agreed. "But we might as well keep busy."

I had stolen a set of bone dice from Darren the night before, and now I took them from my pocket. "Come on, have a seat. Do you know how to play koro? Never mind, I'll teach you."

THE SMALL BOAT came clanking against the *Badger*'s side before we were done with our second round of koro. Spinner was quick on the uptake but he'd never played before, and my mind wasn't on the game either.

Darren practically rolled over the side, her chest heaving like she was a half-drowned swimmer. At some point, in her pain and rage, she had bitten her own arm, and a trickle of blood was making its way unhurriedly down from the puncture marks. She went straight for the tiller and gripped it with both hands. To try to stop herself from hitting something, I guessed.

Without warning, she drove her own head against the wood, three times—*crack, crack, crack.*

I started forward, unthinking, but Regon caught my elbow.

"What happened?" I whispered fiercely. "I wasn't going to let her go in the first place, but I thought she'd be all right with you."

Regon gave his head a single, grim shake. "She was all right. Until we found the villagers."

"You found the villagers?"

"They were in the well."

"They were in the . . . oh."

"The ones we pulled out of there, all their fingers were broken, so we figure they were thrown down alive. Drowned or suffocated while they were trying to get out."

"And you let her see?"

"Couldn't stop her. It broke her, though. All at once, she just hit bottom. I don't know if anything can bring her out of it. Apart from a damn good bollocking."

Darren was still folded over the tiller, her whole torso wrenching in silent sobs—or maybe she was just gagging.

"Well, then," I said, "a bollocking she shall have. See if you can keep the others out of the way."

I GOT HER down to our cabin. It helped that she wasn't really paying attention to anything, just staggering in a red mist. Once we were down there, I propped her up against a stack of crates and tried to start the conversation. "So, Mistress—"

All at once, she came to life. "Shut up."

"Not one of our more successful missions—"

"—shut up," she went on without pause, "shut up, don't say anything, don't say one goddamn word, dammit, dammit, dammit, dammit—"

"I will not shut up," I informed her. "See, you need to hear this and apparently no one else dares to say anything. You are doing this wrong."

"I know I'm doing this wrong!" Darren roared. "There's a well full of broken people back there because I'm doing it wrong!"

"You weren't there. You couldn't save them, because you weren't there. And right this very minute, someone else is being killed because you aren't there, and every minute for the rest of your life, guess what? There will be someone else, somewhere, being killed, that you can't save, because you won't be there. And that's never, ever, ever going to change. Can you cope with that or not? Because, if you can't, you won't stay sane." I drew in a fast breath, bracing myself. "That's why Jess is still angry."

"Do *not* say that name."

"Jess understands why you left, Darren, she does. Everyone who knows you that well and loves you that much understands. Jess *knows* that you're too damn *noble* to let people hurt when there's something you can do to prevent it. Jess *knows* that you can't sit safe in the valley, surrounded by peace and happiness and crocks of honey, while your own country burns. If you hadn't left, the guilt would have eaten you from the inside out."

Darren's fist crashed into the wall, and then she winced and cradled her hand. I let her take a second before I went on.

"Jess understands. She *does*, Darren. So does Regon. So do I. So does everyone. You couldn't have made a different choice and continued to be yourself. You had to come back to Kila." I paused. "You really did a number on that fist, didn't you? Give it here."

Darren must have been dazed; she let me take her hand and inspect the shreds of skin dangling from her raw, bloody knuckles. I clucked impatiently, found a handkerchief and wrapped it.

"But here's the thing, Darren," I continued. "Jess understands why you can't spend your life with her. But she is royally, mortally pissed that you are just going to throw that life away."

Mechanically, Darren pulled her hand away from me. "I'm not—"

"You *are,* Darren. Never mind the fact that you throw yourself into every suicidal situation you can find. You won't even give yourself *permission* to live. No matter what you do, who you help, you twist yourself in knots—you *hurt* yourself, *Darren*—thinking of the people you *didn't* help."

"I never do enough," she said. Her voice was hoarse, from a throat scraped raw. "It's never enough . . ."

"You cannot save all of Kila by yourself."

"After everything I've been given, it's my damn responsibility to—"

"You cannot save all of Kila by yourself!" Now I was screeching. "You stupid, beautiful, heroic, sulky, overgrown child, you cannot!"

I broke off, my chest heaving, and rubbed my face with the sleeve of the linen shirt that used to belong to Holly. Darren's eyes were wide and baffled. From the deck, there was total quiet, where there should have been creaking and grunting and swearing and the bark of orders, and I wondered how many of the men were listening in.

Once I'd caught my breath, I went on. "You do as much as you can with the tools you have. If you want to do more, you have to *be* more."

"Be what?" she said, sarcastic and kind of rude. "A pirate queen?"

"Sure," I said steadily. "You *could* do that, you know. You could capture other ships, larger ships, warships, and build a fleet. Recruit renegade sailors to defend you as you go about your good works. Loot the flotillas of rich merchants to provide for the poor. You'd end up in some morally suspect situations, no question, but you could also help more people. You might even help end the war. Or you can just keep pottering around in the *Badger,* with men you know and trust, helping out here and there. It's up to you, but whatever your decision, don't beat yourself over the head with it. You don't have to take the world on your shoulders, just because you're a noble."

It actually seemed to be sinking in. She let out a long sigh, and I suspect that a few unhelpful thoughts and emotions went out with it. Her eyes closed, and her face became almost mild. And I felt my guard slipping. That was a mistake.

"What did you do while we were gone?" she asked, as if she was changing the subject.

"Nothing really. Spinner and I played a game."

"I saw the dice. Knucklebones?"

"No. Koro."

"You can play koro," she said.

"Of course I can play—" I began without thinking. Then I stopped. The bottom dropped out of my stomach.

Shit.

Darren's eyes were open just a slit. "You can play koro, the Game of Kings. And you can read, and write. Well enough to spell *Badger*, at least. And you don't mix up your pronouns and you don't swear every time you open your mouth. You're awfully well-educated, Lynn. At least for a peasant girl who grew up in a fishing village in the middle of nowhere. There are things that you're not telling me."

A million panicked voices were yammering away inside my skull. I had only moments to think of a distraction, and the one that I came up with probably wasn't my best ever.

"Hey, look," I blurted, pointing behind her. "Pie!"

Dead silence.

Well, that didn't work.

"Really, there are all kinds of possible explanations," I said, talking a little too fast. "Maybe I'm not a peasant at all, did you ever think of that? Maybe I was born to a rich merchant family in Kafiru and was educated along with a nobleman's daughter. Maybe the civil war started when I was thirteen and my parents smuggled me out to a distant village in the care of a faithful retainer. Maybe the faithful retainer eloped with a fisherman's wife of loose morals and took all the money and abandoned me there."

Darren was inspecting my face as though there was writing there that she had to decipher, one word at a time.

"Maybe I'm just a really smart peasant," I concluded. "*You* don't know."

"You are . . ." Darren started in wonder, and then shook her head and started again. "You are a very strange little person, do you know that, Lynn?"

I shrugged. "But you wouldn't have it any other way, right?"

"I wouldn't go quite that far," Darren said slowly. "But I don't hate it. I definitely don't hate it."

If you considered the words alone, it was a lukewarm invitation at best. But, as always, with Darren, the trick was to figure out what she wasn't saying.

Without giving myself the time to think about it, I closed the distance between us. She only took one step back, probably because that step took her up against the cabin wall. But the panic on her face seemed like the *good* sort. I assume you know what I mean when I talk about the *good* sort of total, mindless fear.

"Lynn," she said softly. "Are you—"

Are you sure? Are you serious? Are you really about to do this? No matter.

"Yes, yes, yes I am," I answered, slipping my hands into her trouser pockets. "The question is, are you?"

She blinked.
She licked her lips.
She didn't move.
That was enough of an answer.

This would have been a much better distraction, I realized, belatedly, once my lips were on hers. But I only dwelt on it for a moment, since other matters now required my full attention.

CHAPTER FIVE

AS YOU CAN imagine, I overslept the next morning. When I first woke, the hold was hot and damp rather than cool and damp and I judged that it was about noon. The blankets beside me were empty, but the depression where Darren had rested was still warm to the touch. She had left the bed not very long ago. I grinned into the blankets, turned over, and went to sleep again.

This time, my sleep wasn't nearly as pleasant. There were strange sharp-edged dreams that rattled back and forth in my brain, pictures that didn't attach to each other—bitter-green fish with teeth like icicles, men with rats instead of hands. The visions all blended and fell, blended and fell, rolled over me in a great crushing wave, and I was left somewhere dark and airless, with one thing, one thought thudding at my mind like the beat of a drum: *They will find you, they will get you back, they will find you, they will get you back* . . .

The heat was more oppressive, now. The heat was terrible.

"Leave me alone," I could hear myself saying, "damn your blood, can't you just leave me *alone?*"

"Wake up. There's no time."

My eyes snapped open. Darren was a blur of furious motion around the cabin, snatching up her cutlass, sheathing a long dagger in each boot. Each motion quick and precise, never a fumble. You might think it strange that she wasn't afraid, but there's always an air of unreality right before violence erupts. That five minutes before a battle are like the five seconds after you fall out of a boat, when you feel like you might just be able to walk on water.

As soon as she saw me looking, her hand flew to a pocket and came out with the key to my leg chain. She threw it down beside me and it bounced three times against the boards, *tink, tink, tink.*

"Get loose," she tossed at me as she raced for the stairs. "Hurry up."

Still half-asleep, I sat upright, groping for the key. I wanted to refuse, yell at Darren, demand an explanation, but then there came a roaring in my ears, as though I had suddenly recovered from deafness, and a wave of sounds crashed at me.

That hollow booming from the curved side of the ship . . . that was another ship alongside, bashing against us with every swell in the waves.

There were creaks and howls as the men from that ship poured onto ours, battle roars, the *shring* of cutlasses, and then a *thud* I could feel through the planks, as a body hit the deck hard. All of a sudden, I was wide awake, and all of a sudden too, Darren's suggestion didn't seem so completely ridiculous. I knelt down and fumbled with the chain on my ankle, but my hands were sweating and the key slipped from my grasp. I scrabbled on the bare planks, felt metal, but, the next second, felt it slipping sideways into a crack between two planks . . . and under my searching fingertips, it fell all the way through.

The key was gone. Unbelieving, I rattled the manacle on my ankle. It held firm, of course. I wouldn't have settled for anything less. I scooted along the length of the chain and yanked at the end where it was bolted to a deck support. Regon had promised me that it wouldn't come loose. Unfortunately, he was right.

I was beginning to wonder whether perhaps I had been a little bit stupid when a body came crashing down the stairs from the deck, landed heavily on its side, rolled twice and lay still.

It was Darren. There were two bloody slashes on her that I could see, one along the ribs and one on her shoulder, plus the bruises and scrapes from her trip down the stairs, and a swelling, gory lump on her right temple. But there was a quivering beneath her eyelids. She wasn't gone yet.

Yet. Yet. Shadows at the companionway paused, looking down at Darren's body, and then moved out of sight. The battle was still crashing away overhead, and whoever our attackers were, they had decided that they could deal with Darren after they brought down the rest of the crew. That gave me time. Perhaps five minutes. Five minutes to figure out how to save Darren when I was unarmed, chained to the deck, and half the size and weight of any of our attackers.

Blankly, I stared at the floor. There were footprints on it, Darren's footprints. The waves must have been high that day, wetting the decks up top, because, when she rushed around the cabin getting her weapons a bare quarter-hour before, she had left footprint-shaped puddles of seawater. A quarter-hour before, Darren had been upright and walking; now she was prone on the boards. In all likelihood, someone would tramp down in five minutes and casually stab her where she lay.

Those two pictures placed beside each other—Darren whole and walking, Darren prone and bleeding—nearly made me scream at the top of my lungs.

Yet it was those patches of sea water that gave me the idea.

It was absolutely and without question the stupidest idea I had ever had, and six months before, I would never have considered doing such a thing. Not to save my life. But this was Darren's life . . . and that, somehow, was different. I don't think I hesitated more than ten seconds.

I reached out and moistened my fingers in one of the salty puddles, then brought them to my face and scrubbed my eyes. Within a few seconds, my eyes were stinging viciously and though I couldn't check on the effect, I was sure that they were red and swollen. Next, I had to do something about my clothes, and as I tried to tear the sturdy cloth, I muttered curses that Holly's cast-offs were so well-made. It was taking too long, so I just ripped out the laces of the shirt, so too much skin showed.

Now, injuries. Here again, I didn't pause to think. I dragged three fingernails along the length of my face, from forehead to chin, leaving open scratches that were soon beaded by tiny drops of blood. I bit my shoulder close to the breast, not quite hard enough to break the skin, but the tooth marks looked deep and convincing.

I wanted to try for finger-shaped bruises on one wrist, but now the clamour on deck had quieted. There were shouts, some laughing voices, but none I knew and I wondered briefly how many of Darren's crew had died . . . but now footsteps were approaching the companionway again. No time for more artistic touches.

I was tearing up already, but just in case, I dipped my fingers in the brine again, and flecked a few drops on my cheeks, just below my eyes. Then I huddled on the boards, my arms crossed protectively over my stomach, and lay like a dead thing.

IT TOOK SUPREME effort not to look up as whoever-it-was tromped down the steps to the hold, but I managed it.

"She's still out," a man said.

"From that little tap?" a woman responded. "She always was a wimp."

The woman's accent was refined, cultured, with long drawling vowels. This was another noblewoman, then, the captain of the attacking ship.

"Want to wait for her to wake up before you finish it?"

"I don't think that's necessary."

There was a creaking step as one of them moved forwards. That was my cue. I let out a choking, terrified sob.

I wasn't prepared for how fast the woman moved. Half a second later, she was at the cabin doorway, bloody cutlass upraised. My panic wasn't all an act as I scrambled backwards, away from her, as far as the chain would allow; cowered against the side of the boat, and peeped at her from behind my fingers. She assessed me, and the tip of the cutlass lowered.

"Darren's got an on-board whore?" she asked lightly. "My, my, she has grown up."

I wet my lips before stammering out, "Is she dead?"

The other woman glanced over her shoulder. "Nearly. Oh, by the way—"

One second, she was nowhere near me; then her fist came out of nowhere, delivering a vicious cuff to the side of my head, and the pain was like red-hot pincers. My hand flew to my ear, cradling it, as her face loomed over me. "I am the *Lady* Mara, of the house of Namor. Don't let the formalities slide, just because we're on a boat."

The circumstances didn't bode well for my relationship with Mara of Namor in any case, but I think that I would have hated her—instinctively, immediately—if we had met in any other place and at any other time. It was the voice, the spoiled sweetness of it. That, and something about the eyes.

"I'm sorry, my lady," I said automatically. My teeth were chattering, in spite of the heat. "But—please—my lady, are any of her sailors dead?"

There was a flicker of interest in those eyes now. "Just one, unfortunately. The big one with ears like a monkey."

Oh, Kash. I didn't let myself show any sign of shock or grief as Mara continued to speak.

"We're not supposed to waste sailors these days. They're in short supply, or something like that. We're supposed to *conserve* them during fights. It makes things horribly boring. But now I'd like to know—"

There was a flash of that viper-fast movement again, and then she was holding my chin tightly between finger and thumb. "Just why exactly are you interested, little girl?"

I closed my eyes for a whisper of a moment, summoned up all the hatred and fury I'd ever felt in my first seventeen years of life, and forced it all into my voice. "I want them dead. I want them all dead. Especially *her.*"

She patted my cheek. It felt like getting slapped. "Be careful what you wish for, now. I'm going to kill her, yes, but you may end up looking back fondly on your time here. There are worse jobs in Kila these days than being chained to Darren's bed. Such as being chained to mine. And that's one of the few careers open to you at the moment."

I let a trickle of injured *hauteur* enter my tone. "But Lady Mara, you don't understand, you can't do that!"

She grabbed me by my injured ear this time, and I couldn't stop myself from crying out as she yanked it upwards. "What makes you think you can tell me what to do, scum?"

"But . . . that's . . . just . . . it," I pleaded, blinking the tears out of my eyes. "I'm not scum, I'm not a commoner . . . I'm . . . I'm like you . . ."

She let go of my ear. I hit the boards with a bump, my hands hovering protectively near my face.

"Talk fast," she said.

"I've been here almost four months," I said quickly. "She kidnapped me. That *horrible* woman kidnapped me." The tears were coming more freely now. Under the circumstances, it wasn't hard for me to make myself cry. My voice came out in a blubbering bawl. "She took me from my father on the northern isle. From Bero."

Mara's hands slapped down on my shoulders; her fingers dug in; she drew me close. "The House of Bain rules Bero," she rasped. "Are you trying to make me laugh? Everyone knows that the lord of Bain only has one child."

"That's me," I said, through rattling teeth. "I'm Ariadne. I'm his daughter."

THERE WAS SILENCE. I wondered whether she was going to laugh in my face. But then her legs straightened as though they had springs.

"Captain?" came the voice of Mara's crewman, from outside the cabin. "Everything all right?"

"Fine," Mara said, her eyes not moving from me.

"The pervert's moving around a bit here, you want me to finish her?"

"No!" I cut in hastily. "No, please, you can't."

Mara's hand twitched, and I flinched back, but she controlled herself. Even if she wasn't convinced, she couldn't risk inflicting any more damage on the heir to the powerful House of Bain. She had to content herself with saying, "I thought I pointed out that I dislike being told what to do. Besides, you want her dead."

"My *father* has to execute her," I said desperately. "Don't you realize what that pirate has done to me? I've been . . . I've been *sullied,* I've been *taken.* My father has to execute her himself to take the stain away. Please, he'll pay anything if you bring me back to him. But I won't be worth much unless you deliver her alive."

She studied me. "I have a contract to get rid of Darren. She's embarrassing her daddy. Now what do you think will happen to my reputation if I don't make good, hmm?"

"My father will get rid of her. He will get rid of her very, very completely. You must have heard of the dungeons on Bero. Nobody leaves that place unless they're wrapped in a burlap shroud."

Mara looked more thoughtful. "I took a deposit from Darren's father, though."

"Darren is of the house of Torasan," I said, with more than a little disgust. "Stribos is a miser and the bulk of his wealth comes from *salmon fishing*. My father Iason of Bain will take any fee you name, and triple it, and fill your ship with silver besides. Please," I said, gathering strength for the last appeal. "I am his only child. Without me, he's half a corpse."

There was a faint smile on Mara's lips. Her hand moved, and I flinched again, but she just ruffled my hair lightly.

"You stay put, now," she said. "Don't move a muscle."

She moved outside the cabin, and her steps creaked up the stairs, followed an instant later by the heavier step of the other sailor. I closed my eyes, slowed my breathing, and listened as hard as I could.

"If that girl is telling the truth," came Mara's oily tone, "then she's worth her weight in diamonds."

"Yes, but . . ." The man's voice hesitated. "Do you believe her, captain?"

"I'm not sure," Mara admitted. "Maybe I should check and see whether she can play koro."

THE VOICES MOVED further up the stairs, and away. Gingerly, I touched my ear—it *really* hurt, though I'd had worse—and then edged across the floor to Darren. Stretching the chain to its full limit, I just managed to reach her. Most of her injuries looked worse than they were. The only dangerous one was the bump on her head. It was fever-hot, and sticky with blood, but she'd live.

"Ow," she muttered.

My fingers froze. "Were you listening?"

"Yes."

"So this is your insane bounty hunter cousin?"

"That would be my insane bounty hunter cousin. She used to make family dinners total hell. Is it true, what you told her? About you and the House of Bain?"

I sighed. "No. And . . . yes. And no. It's complicated. Can we go with 'no' for now?"

"I met Lord Iason once," she murmured. "Didn't like him. He smiled too much." Her breath went in and out with a painful rattle. "I remember though . . . his hair. Very pale. Like wheat."

"Darren," I said firmly, "focus."

I hauled her into a sitting position and checked quickly for broken bones, then did my best to comb blood-stiffened hair away from her forehead. "You're a mess. Never mind. Are you listening?"

"Gah," she said, with a shake of the head. I decided to take that as a "yes."

"Darren, that barrel has oil in it . . . no, not that one, *that* one . . . the one I'm pointing at . . . would you look up, please? . . . thank you . . . yes, that barrel there. I need it. Get the bung out for me."

She blinked.

Oh, well. Sometimes pirate queens need a bit of extra encouragement, and don't we all? I took her face between my hands, carefully, and kissed both of her eyes. The sound she made was something like a squeak.

Then I turned her head to the side, careful not to touch the lump again, and spoke right in her ear. "Get on with it, Mistress."

Grey-blue eyes, wide and staring in the dark. Then, without warning, they narrowed. Focused.

Her boot-heel lashed out and struck the bung of the barrel. The bung shot back into the barrel's depths, leaving the bunghole open, and oil began to spill over the floor in long, slow *gloops*. I scooted over to the puddle, took a handful of the stuff, and carefully rubbed it over my ankle and foot. I took another handful and dribbled it into the space between the shackle and my skin.

Darren had the idea, now. "Flex your foot. Straighten it as far as you can."

I flexed and she took the shackle. "This might hurt," she warned.

"I know. Do it fast."

She yanked. There was a single wrenching second when I thought my tendons would all snap and the flesh rip, but then my greasy foot shot out of the cuff. Darren flew backwards, just managing to catch herself on her elbows.

We both froze, listening. There was a *creak creak* on the planks near the stairs, as though someone was hovering there indecisively. Mara was still dithering. We had a little time.

I helped Darren up again. She moved jerkily, wincing once she was on her feet. "I don't know how much use I'll be in a fight," she warned.

"You don't have to fight," I told her. "Just come here a second."

I plunged a hand in her pocket (she squeaked again) and pulled out the garrote. As I'd hoped, Mara hadn't noticed the thin coil of sinew when she disarmed Darren. I tied a careful slip-knot in it, as Darren had taught me, and then pulled the loop over my head.

I handed the end of the leather strip to Darren and watched her eyes widen as she realized what I was asking her to do. I hastily held up a finger. "Don't argue. Just try not to faint when we go up there."

Her hands were shaking. "Lynn, oh hell and damnation, this is such a bad idea."

"It'll be a brilliant idea if it works, and if it doesn't work then we won't be around to regret it. Besides, we don't really have a choice, do we?"

"I guess not," she said, and then she licked her lips. "You know . . . you remember that day, back in your village? When you told me that I didn't have the right to make the choice for you? Have you been getting your revenge on me ever since?"

"Nooooo," I said doubtfully, drawing out the word. "Or maybe I was in the beginning . . . but . . . choices are overrated, and I've always known that. Back when I was living in that godforsaken village, I had to make choices *all* the time. Where to look for food. Where to hide when the raiders came through. That sort of thing. But none of it mattered. Nothing I could choose to do would improve things, or save anyone, or change anything. I had plenty of choices, but I had no *control.* It's been like that all my life."

"And after I took you?" Her face was bare and inscrutable in the darkness.

"After you took me, it was exactly the opposite. Can't you see that?"

"I think so," she said slowly. "I think I do. So you don't want a choice about . . . well . . . whether to stay with me?"

"Let's say that I don't need one." I did my best to smile at her, though my throbbing ear was sending hot jolts through my head. "How about we get this over with?"

Painfully, she straightened her back. "Once we start with this, we can't stop for a break. It might get kind of intense."

"I can handle it," I promised.

She looked me over. "Yeah, you can, can't you? Her shaking hand brushed a loose hair from my cheek. "Guess I just need to worry about myself, then. Let's get on with it."

She wound the free end of the garrote around her left hand, and took my shoulder in her right. Then we headed up the stairs, Darren striding, and me stumbling on ahead.

THE SUNLIGHT WAS blinding—could it be much later than noon? At first, I saw nothing but a white glare and misty shapes moving up and down on the bobbing deck. Then things came into focus. Darren's crew, disarmed and bound, were kneeling next to the rails. Teek had lost half an ear, and Regon was bent over a stomach wound, but those were the worst injuries. Mara's crew was grouped around them. Mara herself leaned casually on the tiller . . . deep in thought, it seemed. Kash's body—huge, sprawled, leaking, horrible—lay propped against the mast. The rigging of the war galley lashed to the *Badger's* starboard side threw a spider work of shadows over the scene.

When I staggered and caught at the cord around my own neck, I wasn't acting. The swaying deck, the spray, the bright splashes of blood over the boards, made everything seem more than a little unreal—a dream of a dream, the memory of a memory.

Darren, fortunately, was on top of things. "Get back!" she roared, and the sound made every hair on my head stand erect. "I can cut her throat any second I choose. Get back! Drop your weapons!"

At least five men lunged forwards instead. Mara clearly hadn't briefed them on the situation. Just in time, her voice rang out, "Stand down!"

Her men were still instantly, recoiling. Mara walked forward herself, using the tail of her shirt to wipe blood from her cutlass.

"Well, well, Darren," she said. "This is unusual behaviour for you."

"I'll do it," Darren grated, and her hand twitched. "One pull, and your big payout is in two pieces on the floor."

"When you were a *child*, Darren, you wouldn't even hit your dog. When did you grow up and find your big-girl voice?"

Darren gave the garrote a vicious yank. Actually, she didn't put any extra tension at all on the cord around my neck. She had tied the sinew to her wrist, and she yanked at the slack dangling end. But I gave a strangled gasp at the right moment and it must have seemed convincing enough, because the mocking look fell from Mara's face.

"You piece of trash," Darren said. "You think you know anything about me? How have you been spending your time since the war began? Chasing down petty criminals for a copper a head? Begging my father for odd jobs and table scraps? You were a bitch when you were a child, Mara—nothing's changed, has it?"

For the first time, the smugness in Mara's eyes was gone. There was a tiny flame licking there.

"Big words," Mara said, "for someone whose only ship is an eight-man trader."

Darren laughed. "I don't have to prove anything to you, Mara. But you might want to bear something in mind. I made it past Iason of Bain's defences, made it past his whole navy, landed in his territory, and got out again with his daughter in my bed. Let's say that I have . . . resources."

"You expect me to believe—" Mara faltered, and that falter said everything. The story was, of course, ludicrous. The House of Bain, at the time, had the best coastal defences of any state in Kila. It still does, as a matter of fact. But every word from Darren's mouth carried conviction. It was her stance, her swagger, her . . . everything.

Darren laughed again. "You think I'm frightened of Iason? I don't do anyone's dirty work these days, Mara. You spend your time licking my father's feet. I am the pirate queen. And you've taken on more than you can handle."

Darren was doing so well that it was all I could do to not burst out cheering. Then she gave the cord another yank, and not cheering became easier.

"Now. Are you prepared to lose a windfall like this?" Darren patted my head again. "Because if you want her, you can have her. I can get a new one. You just need to let me and my men go on our way."

Mara barked a startled laugh. "I have to admit, Darren. Somewhere along the line, you developed balls of pure iron."

Darren shrugged. "I think it's a fair enough trade. She's worth a king's ransom, of course, but I took her for more personal reasons. And let me say, she doesn't disappoint. You might want to try her out a few times at first before you take her home. I'm sure you can convince her not to blab to her father."

This was getting a bit excessive. I was all for dramatic realism, but Darren was starting to enjoy herself too much. Pretending to flail against the tight cord, I found Darren's hand and gave it a hard pinch. She started to yelp, and had to turn it into a sort of evil laugh. "That's the deal, Mara. Are you interested? If so, you've got ten seconds." She raised her hand, holding the end of the garrote, to show what she meant, but she didn't apply pressure again.

The seconds ticked by. I could hear my own heartbeat.

"Very well," Mara said at last. "How do you plan on doing this?"

"First step's easy. Release my men."

Mara gave a short nod to her sailors, and several of them stooped down by Darren's crew. Sailors *never* cut ropes when they can untie them, so it was several minutes, as sweat-beads prickled on my forehead, before Darren's six surviving crewmen stood up. Regon was still hunched over his wound. He gave me a shaky smile, while a red ooze seeped between his fingers.

"Now back up," Darren ordered. "All of you. Back onto your ship. Mara, you'll be last, and you can have the girl as soon as you cross over."

One by one, they moved. Even Mara was headed obediently backwards. The plan was working, so far as it went . . . the problem was, as I was beginning to realize, that it went no further. If Darren didn't let go of me, then Mara wouldn't back off. If Darren did let go of me, she would instantly lose her bargaining chip. There would be nothing to stop Mara and her men from swarming back over the *Badger*. None of our sailors had the strength to put up more than a token resistance. Darren herself was already swaying on her feet.

This plan wouldn't accomplish anything. Mara, her hands raised, shuffling slowly back towards her war galley, knew that. Darren knew that too. I could tell when her hands suddenly sagged, as if all her remaining strength had left her, all at once.

Which meant—I swallowed twice, and my head felt light and dizzy and heavy all at once—which meant that it was time for something drastic.

"Darren," I whispered, my breath barely stirring the air, "can you hear me?"

"Yeah. Look, this is—"

"Doomed, I know. I have an idea. Loosen the cord and push me at Mara just as she's stepping over the side."

Mara's men were stepping over the rail, back to their ship, one at a time.

"Please don't ask me to risk your life." Darren's voice was tiny, desperate.

"I'm not," I assured her. After all, I wasn't asking. "Just . . . just trust me, all right?"

The sun beat down. Mara's sailors hopped the rails, one by one.

Finally Mara stood alone, Darren a few feet away, me between them.

Darren slid her hand between my neck and the cord. Slowly, she loosened it. A smile was creeping around Mara's face.

"Step up onto the rail," Darren instructed. Her voice was shaking, but not so you'd notice. Not unless you knew her well. "Step up, and . . . she's yours."

Mara stepped, adjusted her balance, held out a hand. Her nails looked like claws.

The loop of the garrote lifted up and over my neck. Darren's hand reached for my back, as though she was going to push me, but it was more of a caress. Her fingers were still shaking.

I stepped forwards, and Mara's hand closed around my wrist and pulled me up . . .

I'M NOT DARREN. Never have been, never will be. Sacrifice comes as easy to Darren as navigation, but Darren, you see, is noble. Noble in the real sense, I mean—noble in her core. For all her faults, Darren's inner nature was sound to the heartwood, completely free of any kind of meanness or selfishness. Most of her sailors were the same way, which was why they stayed with her in the first place. But that's not me.

Before I met Darren, I never felt any urge to suffer for other people. The idea would never have occurred to me at all. I did enough suffering on my own behalf. The world couldn't expect more of me than that.

For someone like me, someone who specializes in survival, sacrifice is a strange and unnerving concept. After all, it's about as far from survival as you can possibly get. It's suicide, with side benefits.

So why did I do it?

I guess I'd found a reason that made sense to me. I could still feel Darren's hand on my back. That was enough.

THE INSTANT MARA pulled me up to the ship's side, I grabbed her around the waist with one arm, then locked my knees behind hers and bent them. This was the move Darren had used two months ago to bring me down, and it worked on Mara just as well. Her balance was thrown; one foot came off the rail entirely. She staggered, one arm windmilling, and tried to jump down to the deck, but I held tight and pushed off with both legs. Together we slipped down the canyon between the two ships, bashing against the wood planks, and then into the water. There were shouts from above us, which I ignored.

Mara was lashing out, her scream a furious gargle. I snaked my arms around her and went limp, a dead weight, pulling us both under. The waters closed above our heads—a green milky spill with the sun bobbing on the surface. Our heads clanged against barnacled wood. Mara was tearing at my arms, striking at any flesh she could reach, but now even the blows seemed very distant.

It got darker, darker, darker, and my last thought was this. Sacrifice was surprisingly easy, with the right motivation.

CHAPTER SIX

THERE FOLLOWED A wonderful glorious time of nothing. It was soft and dim and peaceful, something like being dipped in black cream. But it didn't last. There was a terrible, crushing blow to my chest, as if a mule had kicked it, a boulder dropped on it; as if a bull had pinned me against a wall and was pushing, pushing, pushing. The black around me shattered into spiky pieces with razor edges that glittered before they embedded themselves at the back of my brain.

I was forced to take a long strangled breath, which felt like inhaling a million red-hot tacks. My whole chest bucked. And the next instant, the donkey kicked me in the chest again. I only managed to give a weak gurgling kind of sound in protest.

"Breathe, damn you, breathe, breathe, breathe—"

It was Darren's voice and she didn't sound good. Through the headache and the chest ache and the everything-else-ache, I tried to flop my hand a little to reassure her. My hand ached too, I discovered.

"Will you open your eyes, damn you! *Damn you*! Open your goddamn eyes or I'm not going to be responsible for what happens next!" She was still pounding on my chest (it hurt as much as ever) and her words came out in time to the blows. "You—stupid—bloody—idiot—KID!"

My chest was about to cave in. I made a huge concentrated effort and managed to pry one eye a slit open.

"Darren, stop, she's awake," came Teek's voice, deep and reassuring. Then his horn-hard hands were there too, gently prying us apart. "It's all right, captain. You can stop. You can stop."

She was breathing more heavily than usual. Had she been running, screaming, or crying? All three?

Without warning, she lunged, twisted her hands in my wet shirt, hauled me up, and gave me a bone-splintering hug that almost stopped my breathing again. Just as quickly, she let go, and I flopped back to the deck boards.

"*Ow*," I complained, opening my eye a little wider this time.

Her hands: shaking; her hair: wild; her eyes: wild; her tunic: damp and salt-crusted; her face . . . oh, this is pointless. You know. Or at least, you know if you've ever felt anything like it. It was the pure explosion of feeling, at least half madness, that makes you drunk and dizzy and elated and terrified all at once, and which, once felt, you want to feel forever.

She took my face gently between her hands, and that was it, that was the moment, when the game was up for Darren, formerly of the House of Torasan. She had been claimed, and she knew it, and she wasn't going to resist it any longer.

It had taken her long enough. But it was worth the wait. I let her ride out the emotion for a minute before I asked the obvious question. "Where's Mara?"

Darren made a thumbs-down. "Spinner and Teek and I had a little disagreement about who was going to go in after you. By the time we got in, it was over. She must have swallowed a lot of water, screaming that way."

"What about her crew?"

Darren glanced up, ruefully, and I followed her eyes. I've heard people say that the first step towards peace is learning to understand your enemy. There may be a glimmer of truth to that, but I personally think it's more accurate to say that the first step to peace is learning that your enemy has beer and is willing to give you some. Three open barrels stood side by side on the deck. Dozens of sailors, Darren's and Mara's alike, stood around in clumps, dipping cups into the deep brown brew. They were chugging, making loud satisfied *ahhhs* as they wiped their foamy beards with the back of their hands, smacked each other on the backs, and called each other glorious bastards.

"Mara had them on short liquor rations for the past month," Darren explained. "I think she was trying to save money. They weren't all that sorry to see her go."

Blood is rank and blood is right, blood alone is rulership . . . old habits die hard. With Mara dead, her sailors had automatically fallen in line behind Darren, the only other noble around. She might be an outcast, but she was a captain, she knew how to navigate, and she had beer. Plus, she was not crazy, which made her a big improvement on Mara in at least one respect.

It wouldn't always be this easy. We wouldn't always be fighting sailors with a batshit crazy captain. We wouldn't always be fighting sailors who fell so easily into the old patterns of power and obedience. We wouldn't always have this much beer. But it was a start.

"It's better than having them kill us all," Darren admitted. "But what am I going to do with them? What am I going to do with *that* monstrosity?"

"Isn't it obvious, Mistress?" I shaded my eyes and looked up the long masts of Mara's war galley. Heavy reinforced timbers, sharpened prow for ramming, grapnels for boarding . . . now *that* was a ship for a pirate. "That's the next addition to your fleet."

"It's not mine."

"Sure it is. You see any other pirates around here?" I took Darren's hand and let her help me into a sitting position. "You'll have to rename it, though."

"Oh, really?"

"Of *course* we do. Where's your sense of etiquette? I think we should name it after me."

"What?" She glanced at me sideways. "The *Lynn*?"

"I was thinking more along the lines of the *Idiot Kid*."

THE REST OF the day was work—inspections, interrogations, funerals, meals, inventories, even *accounting*. You'd be amazed how much math is involved in piracy.

It was a long, weary day, but after that long, weary while, Darren and I finally got to go back to our cabin together. Even then, she was brooding.

"You know, Ariadne," she began.

"Don't call me that," I said, cutting her off. "That's not my name."

"You know, *Lynn*, those sailors would all follow *you* if they knew that you were heir to the house of Bain."

I shrugged. "I'm not . . ."

Darren raised one eyebrow.

" . . . I'm not *really*," I finished, sort of limply. "I mentioned that it was complicated, right?"

"Is this one of the things that you'll tell me someday but not today?"

"Probably. I hope so." I flopped onto the blankets, wondering whether I did, in fact, hope that I could tell her one day. Telling people about that part of me was not something I had ever been interested in doing before. Well, whatever. I shrugged all that away, and asked, "Aren't you forgetting something?"

"What?"

I pointed to a length of anchor rope which I had brought to the cabin earlier.

Darren appeared bewildered. "What's that for?"

"This is for me. You lost the key to my chain. Which was pretty bloody careless of you, if you want to know the truth."

"*You* lost the key," she said automatically, and it was only after a second that she added, "Um, *what*?"

I held out my ankle. "Get knotting. And you'd better make it good if you don't want me to slip loose in the middle of the night. Show off some of that sailor ingenuity."

"Oh, you're not going to make me keep doing this . . ."

"You really don't know the first thing about being a feared and dreaded pirate, do you?" I petted her dark shaggy head as she crouched by my ankle, knotting the tarry rope around it securely. "Never mind. I'll get you there."

"*If* I don't go berserk and throw you overboard." She swivelled so that she could tie the other end of the rope to the deck support.

"No, I don't think you'll do that," I said serenely. "Besides, you won't have to keep me tied up much longer. It's just until we design the mark."

Her face came up, baffled. "Until we design the *what* now?"

"The mark. Your mark. The one you're going to put on me."

"Wait, wait, *wait*. Are you talking about a brand? Because there is no chance I'm branding you. Not a flaming chance."

"Damn right you're not branding me. Ow. You're tattooing me. But only after I've come up with the design. I wouldn't want a stupid-looking one."

"Lynn," she said, finished now with the rope, as she scooted on the blankets beside me. "Why the hell do you want me to tattoo you?"

"It just makes sense. It's the simplest way to keep me from escaping. You mark me so that if I run, anyone who finds me will send me back. So obviously I won't bother to run."

"Oh, Lynn . . ."

"What?"

"What happens next?"

She had never sounded so lost. Part of me wanted to stop everything, take her chin, force her to look at me, and explain. Explain how she worried about all the wrong things; explain to her why her guilt was needless; explain how I both understood what she wanted to be and knew what she could be . . . or I would never have bothered with her at all. I know you're tired, I wanted to say, I know you think everything rests on you. If you trust me, if you only trust me, I can make things get better, I will *make* things get better; I won't accept anything less.

But I wouldn't ask her to trust me that way. Not yet. Too soon. For the time being, I would just have to make explanations unnecessary. For the time being, I would carry the weight for both of us—and I would simply give her what she needed.

"I'll tell you what happens next," I said, taking her shoulder and easing her back with me onto the blankets. "You keep me on this ship for oh, at least a couple of years, until I become an expert sailor and a proven fighter. You capture more ships, and expand your fleet, and your fame spreads wider and wider. Eventually, after years in your service, I learn to believe in you and your cause, and, though I'm still bound to serve you, I become your most trusted vassal. Together, we turn your fleet into the most powerful fighting force in the east, feared by the rich and guilty and loved by the innocent. Admirals surrender as soon as they catch sight of your flag; entire armadas betray their leaders and flock to your command. In the end, you don't even have to fight to take the islands. Hordes of people demand that you take your rightful place on the throne of the High Lord, and they welcome you with cries of joy. And I'm at your side as you walk into the palace."

She looked at me . . . and she didn't roll her eyes, for a change. "Is that what's going to happen?"

As though the answer really mattered. As though I knew something she didn't.

I shrugged. "You tell me, Mistress. You're in charge, after all."

Then I took her by the back of the neck and pulled her towards me.

PART TWO

WHAT SHE SAID

Narrated by Darren,
formerly of the House of Torasan (Pirate Queen)

CHAPTER ONE

ALL RIGHT, I admitted to myself, ten minutes into my duel with Tyco. *I am losing.*

It's a bad idea to reach that conclusion in the middle of a fight. You make more mistakes when your confidence is rattled. Better to believe that you're a wizard, a sword saint, a god of war, right up to the moment when someone slits you up the middle and your entrails come boiling out.

But it's one thing to keep a positive mindset, and another to ignore the obvious. I hadn't even marked Tyco yet, while his big sabre had carved a long furrow along my side, and left a deep slash in my sword arm. He'd cut dangerously close to the tendon. I winced every time I tried to extend and even when I managed a thrust, Tyco batted my blade away with embarrassing ease. My own blood was streaming down into my right boot, making it *squish* when I took a step. We were beyond the denial stage. I was losing.

I'm not bad with a cutlass, but there's always someone better. I should have known that Tyco would be good. Before the war, he had been arms-master to the House of Namor, training young nobles in the ancient art of sticking pointy things into other people. Now that the governments had crumbled, and the seas had turned wild, he was showing the world all the exciting things that he could do with sharp objects.

Tyco's ship, the *Kraken*, had struck three coastal towns over the past month, with a speed and ferocity that left little but red-churned soil in its wake. Tyco led every assault. They say that he foamed at the mouth while he was fighting, and each time he impaled one of his victims, he let out a shuddering pant, as if he had just—well, *you* know.

And his crew was much the same. Many of the sailors that I fought in those days had been ripped from their homes and sent to the warships against their will. Oftentimes they would fall at my feet in mid-battle and beg to be allowed to surrender. But not Tyco's men. They fought with bared teeth, snarling like hounds; the hilts of their weapons and the hems of their shirts bore a crust of dried blood.

We'd been hunting them for weeks, always a step behind on their gory trail. But even beasts need to take on water, and we finally ran them to ground in a little cove where they'd landed to fill their casks. My new flagship, the *Banshee*, hooked Tyco's monster just before dawn. His crew managed to throw off the grappling hooks, but not before thirty of my best troops flowed over the *Kraken's* side.

Now, on the deck below, my sailors were slowly forcing back Tyco's wildmen. Near the bow, my quartermaster, Corto, was slicing up the *Kraken's* mate, his cutlass moving so fast that it looked like a tangle of silver wire. Amidships, Latoya was fending off three bandits at once with a length of heavy chain, making her weapon shrill as she whipped it through the air. Even skinny Spinner was holding his own. So what was the matter with *me*?

I wasn't the only one wondering. Tyco wasn't giving the battle his full attention anymore. Now he was toying with me, flicking his sabre in quick slashes that left my shirtsleeves in bloody ribbons. His grin was wide and ugly. When I lunged too far and overbalanced, he actually sent me stumbling with a boot in my rear.

That was just *rude*. I caught myself against the side of the *Kraken*, then tried to catch my breath.

"Funny," Tyco remarked, as he raised his sabre for the finish. "I expected more, from the pirate queen."

"You're not the only one," I muttered under my breath, and forced myself to lurch forwards.

I NEVER PLANNED to become a pirate queen.

But I also didn't plan to be stripped of my rank and title for kissing another woman in public. Nor did I plan for my homeland to get embroiled in the worst civil war since the days when dragons crawled the earth. And I definitely didn't plan to meet someone who would demand to be chained to the mast of my ship and then refuse to be let go.

Plans change, is what I'm trying to say.

MY ARMS WERE giving out. Each time I lifted my sword, my muscles burned like flaming ropes. I was done, and Tyco knew it. He slapped away my last desperate strike and pulled back ready for a thrust. I should have pivoted to the right, but I was so tired that my reflexes were nowhere. Instead, I gaped at him and tried to remember the set of heroic last words that I'd recently composed.

Then there was a flash of *something* in the air above Tyco's head, something fine and swift as a dragonfly wing. Tyco could have saved himself if he had reacted instantly, but he blinked, and that was enough. The next second, he stumbled, almost dropping his sabre, and a gargling noise forced its way out of his mouth. His eyes bugged madly; his fumbling fingers reached up towards his throat, groping at the thin leather braid that was throttling him.

The cord jerked even tighter. Tyco was dragged, still gargling, up to the tips of his toes—then came a *crack* as someone delivered a vicious kick to the back of his left knee. The big man staggered, then fell, and the girl standing behind him let out the slack on the cord, so he crashed face-first into the deck.

I lowered my sword arm in utter relief. But the words burst out of me anyway. "I ordered you to stay back on the *Banshee*, Lynn!"

"Did you, Mistress?" Lynn said vaguely, as she stooped to loosen the garrote from around Tyco's neck. "That's not how I remember it. I think you ordered me to lurk around and strangle any ape-men who tried to slice you in half."

"Oh, really?" I shook out my aching hand.

"Mmm-hmm. I heard you distinctly. And it turned out to be a very wise and far-sighted order, don't you think?"

Lynn peeled up Tyco's eyelid to reveal a blank white ball. Satisfied, she straightened, unhooked a flask from her belt, and tossed it towards me. "You ordered me to bring you some brandy, too."

That was more like it. I took three long gulps of liquor and the heat sang all the way through me, making my numb limbs tingle.

"Better?" Lynn asked, taking the bottle back.

"Much," I admitted. "You still shouldn't be here. Regon shouldn't have let you come."

"He didn't *let* me, exactly. He tried to be the voice of reason, but I threatened to belt him in the happy sack and he gave up. Then all I had to do was get over to the *Kraken*."

And how, exactly, had she managed that? I was afraid I knew. Lynn's pale hair was plastered back against her head and her clothes were sopping wet. I looked over my shoulder. Thirty yards of open water separated the two ships. "Don't tell me you swam."

"All right," Lynn said obligingly. "I won't tell you. Now can we get back to business? We are sort of in the middle of something here, you know."

As if my hearing had suddenly returned after a spell of deafness, I heard the sounds of battle swell up all around me—cutlasses ringing against bucklers, sailors howling for their gods or for their mothers. Battle. War. Bloody death. Right. Every inch of me stung, and I wanted nothing more than to curl up on the deck for a nap, with Lynn at my side. But that indulgence would have to wait. Reluctantly, I gripped my cutlass by its red, sticky hilt.

"Will you stay out of the fight if I order you to?" I asked Lynn, almost as an afterthought, and without much hope.

"Mistress, I *always* obey your commands." Lynn's eyes fastened onto

Spinner, who was in the middle of the crush of men, fighting a sailor a full foot taller than he was. "I might not hear you, though. I still have some water in my ears."

TO BE FAIR, Lynn did stay out of the worst part of the fighting. She made two darting sallies into the thick of things to throttle men whose attention was elsewhere, and she pulped some knuckles with a well-aimed belaying pin. But when things were finally over, with the last of Tyco's men gurgling on the deck or crumpling to their knees, she bobbed up before me as fresh and unmarked as a lady's handkerchief.

As usual.

"That could have been worse," she told me, as I leaned, gasping, against the *Kraken's* side. "We didn't lose as many as I expected. And you seem to have all of your important bits still attached. Are you in a lot of pain?"

I waved a hand, trying to look nonchalant. "No. I'm fine. I just need to catch my breath. Or crawl into a corner and die for a while. Finish up for me?"

"I hear and obey. Naturally." Taking my wrist, she guided my hand into place over the deep slash that Tyco's sabre had left in my arm. "Spinner will be by to stitch you in a minute. Keep pressure there until he comes."

She gave my hand a squeeze, turned, drew up her shoulders, and then walked unhurriedly to the forecastle, where Tyco still lay.

She was a study, the small person who called herself my slave. For the swim to the ship, she had stripped down to a linen shirt and open-kneed breeches. They were more or less dry by now, but they still made her look waif-like, especially since her feet were bare, and her hair close cropped. Weaponless, unarmoured, she looked utterly out of place amongst all that leather and steel. Yet she picked her way between the pools of blood with composure.

Lynn reached Tyco just as he was beginning to twitch and blink. "Latoya?" she called, nudging the big man with her toe. "I could use some help."

Latoya was a recent find—we'd picked her up in a raid down south—and she was worth her considerable weight in gold and cinnamon. She came from Tavar, that brutal stretch of sandy waste where you only survived by being good at just about everything. Latoya herself had been a hunter, a desert tracker, a circus wrestler, a camel-tamer, and a leatherworker, all before her twenty-sixth birthday. Eventually, she made her way north to the Ughaion River and spent a few years as a bargeman.

That was where we found her and convinced her that a life of piracy would offer more scope for her many talents. Near seven feet high and built like a granite cliff, she battled every kind of danger, from raiders to thunderstorms, with the same unflinching calm. She was also about ten times better than I was at the brain-twisting mathematics involved in navigation, which was something I was trying hard to be mature about, without a whole lot of success.

I had hired Latoya to be bosun of the *Banshee,* but she had quietly appointed herself as bodyguard to both me and Lynn and watched over us as if we were slightly stupid children.

Latoya coiled the chain she used as a weapon, draped it over her shoulder, and jogged up to Tyco. In one motion, she twisted his arms together behind his back, then forced him to kneel upright. It brought his face almost level with Lynn's.

"Tyco Gorgionson," Lynn began, "you were warned that this would happen."

He tried to struggle. That was pointless. Latoya held him still without even changing expression. When he found his tongue, he was as eloquent as men usually are in such a position. "You fucking bitch," he gasped.

"Ah," Lynn said, "a poet. If only you had decided to explore *that* side of your personality during the war."

Spinner appeared beside me, threading a needle with seal gut. "Don't get in my line of sight," I muttered at him. "This is going to be good."

Tyco still hadn't learned. He was trying to thrash his way out of Latoya's iron hold, and flecks of foam were appearing on his lips. His eyes rolled wildly until they fastened on me.

"I won't kill you, Darren!" he screamed. "You hear me? You won't be that lucky! I'll slice you up, and I'll do it in front of your little whore—I'll take your eyes, your fucking tongue, I'll—"

Lynn snapped then. She gave Latoya a nod, and Latoya hoisted the struggling man a crucial four inches higher. Lynn always kicked with her heel, not her toes, because she almost never wore shoes. But her technique was superb, all the same. With a quick snap of her leg, she applied her foot to the exact part of Tyco's groin where it would do the most good. He screeched, tears spurting.

"You have a thing about slicing people up, don't you?" Lynn went on when he quieted. "You did it just last week, to a girl of sixteen near Retlio, and my mistress had to sit with her as she died. My mistress couldn't even hold the girl's hand at the end, because you'd taken those from her too. Does that ring a bell? Do you remember that girl? Or have there been too many to count? You were warned, Tyco Gorgionson, you were warned. There's law in the islands again. One law. The law of my mistress."

Tyco twisted so he could look at me again. "You want to kill me, you fucking coward? Face me yourself!"

Lynn kicked him in the kidneys this time, and again he crumpled.

"Why are you looking at her?" Lynn asked. "*She's* not going to kill you. Why not? Because you don't deserve to have any bragging rights in hell. You won't be able to tell the other ghosts that the pirate queen sent you. You'll have to admit that you had your throat slit by a slave. A girl. The least of Darren's servants. Not much to boast about, is it, on the other side?"

Tyco's face had turned grey, and sweat ran down it freely. Lynn let him wait a few seconds.

"But my mistress doesn't make martyrs," she said. "And she doesn't kill dogs that she can tame with a stick. You won't die today, but I promise you won't enjoy what happens next. You're done, Tyco. It's over. Latoya, put him out for me."

Latoya freed one hand and gave a sharp rap to the top of Tyco's head. He thudded down to the deck, dropping, as so many men had dropped in the past year, by Lynn's feet.

"BEHOLD," LYNN SAID, as she returned to my side. "Finished."

"Almost," I agreed. I had my breath back now. "One more thing. Now the unpleasantness is over, can I have my garrote back?"

Her forehead wrinkled innocently. "What do you mean?"

I pointed. "That is *my* garrote."

She glanced at it. "Is it? I guess you put it in my pocket by mistake."

"You don't have pockets. You were wearing it wrapped around your wrist."

"I guess you wrapped it around my wrist by mistake. Really, Mistress, that was very thoughtless of you. I can't spend all my time lugging your weapons around."

I put out my free hand, the one attached to the arm that Spinner wasn't stitching up. "Give it back."

"Nah, that's all right," Lynn said, breezing past me as she wrapped the garrote back around her wrist. "I don't mind suffering a bit in the service of my overlord. Corto, get us underway. We should drop these thugs off before evening."

Corto automatically reached for the helm, but I glared at him. "I *do* still give the orders around here, don't I?"

Corto cleared his throat and waited.

" . . . get us underway," I muttered sulkily, and then winced as Spinner's needle dug deep. "Don't I get to do anything fun, now that I'm an overlord?"

"Not really," Lynn said. "I get to do the fun things. It's the paltry reward I get for my selfless service towards you."

"That, and you get to steal my stuff."

"That too."

She gave me a comforting pat on the shoulder and trotted away. Spinner let out a low whistle as he knotted off the thread in my arm. "You know. Sometimes you have to wonder where that girl comes from."

And that was the thing. I did wonder. I wondered every day.

CHAPTER TWO

IMAGINE THIS. YOU wake up, scratch, roll over, find yourself face to face with a sleeping woman, and realize that you have no idea who she is. How often does that happen to a person?

Well—actually, I guess it happens quite a bit. But those situations usually involve far too much wine, and maybe some mushrooms, and a number of slurred, drunken compliments, and, the next morning, an awkward race to find your trousers and escape before the sun comes up.

I, on the other hand, had woken up that way every day for sixteen months. I had woken up that way ever since the morning I came across a scruffy, half-starved girl in a burned-out fishing village, who challenged me to a duel, lost resoundingly, and somehow ended up as my slave rather than my passenger. Which definitely had never been the plan.

But plans, as I say, change.

I always knew that she wasn't ordinary.

I knew it just from that first encounter. Ordinary peasants don't mouth off to noblewomen like me. Ordinary peasants scuff their feet and tug their forelocks and hope not to be noticed. Whereas Lynn shoved her way to the front of the crowd and demanded attention. As if she was used to it. As if she expected it.

That was the first warning. But it got more and more blatant as the weeks wore on.

I don't think she ever realized all the signs she gave. It wasn't just the obvious stuff, like how she could read and write and clobber me at koro with only half her mind on the game. It was more the little things. The words she used, the way she walked; her fearless stare, her posture. However secretive she tried to be—and believe me, she tried—she couldn't hide her differences. Even when she was bound in iron fetters and dressed in rags, Lynn had the air of a lady about her.

A million times, I squinted at Lynn, imagining her with long hair and decent clothing. Dressed that way, in my mind's eye, she looked like any of the girls I had grown up with at the court of my father, Lord Stribos. And I couldn't shake the conviction that she must have grown up at court herself.

Then came the business with Mara. At the end of that long, confusing day, when I found myself still alive, if rather dented, I had no idea what to believe. In that desperate minute when my deranged cousin was about to slash me to fish bait, and Lynn stepped in to distract her, had she told a bare-faced lie or an even more bare-faced truth?

This was what it all came down to. It was just possible that the girl who called herself my slave was actually the Lady Ariadne of the House of Bain, heir to an absolutely obscene amount of wealth and power.

But if Lynn *was* Ariadne, she wasn't about to admit it to me.

I DID MY best not to pry, I really did. People end up on the sea for all kinds of reasons. A good part of the time, they're running from something. My own past involved a humiliating banishment and a painful break-up, both of which I was doing my best to forget when I met Lynn. She had made it very clear that she didn't want to be interrogated. So I told myself to let it go until she was ready to talk.

A good plan, that was. A sensible plan. Except for one thing. Lynn showed no sign that she would be ready to talk any time in the next century, and the waiting was driving me around the bend. I'm not a patient person, I admit it, but I think you would have been a bit edgy yourself if you were in my shoes.

I was born to a ruling house. In the law of Kila, I was as far removed from peasants as a ruby is from acorns. Yet there were other lords who were equally far above me in station. There were hundreds of Kilan nobles back then, but at any given time, there were only three or four families who truly mattered. And the House of Bain was one of them. It ruled the massive north island of Bero, which had the diamond mines and the best of the silver deposits. Its fleet was the best in the nation. You were a fool not to be scared out of your wits if you saw warships bearing its white banners.

Yes, it was a powerhouse, except in one crucial way. The lord of Bain, Iason, had only one child.

It was surprising, to say the least. For any Kilan noble, the highest and purest duty was to secure the survival of his line. Most lords would father as many children as their wives could breastfeed without being chewed raw, and then a few more for good measure. I myself had about fourteen sisters and brothers (they were hard to count, they moved around so fast.) It was insanely risky to beget one single heir. If Ariadne caught the plague or fell off a cliff, then Iason was finished, doomed to be toppled from his throne by the more ambitious of his dukes and generals. As the sole hope for the Bain legacy, the girl must have spent her entire childhood under heavy guard, swaddled away from everyone and everything.

So how had she gotten away from the castle on the northern isle? How had she ended up in the fishy little town where I found her? And what the hell was Iason doing about it now?

In the weeks and months after Mara's attack on the *Badger*, you can be sure that I kept my ears open. I never heard any rumours that Iason's single, precious daughter was missing. But of course, if you were a supreme lord who had lost your only heir, you wouldn't exactly announce it from the rooftops.

I could put it out of my mind for days at a time. When Lynn was stripped to the waist, scrubbing the deck with the rest of the crew, or taking her turn at the dirtiest jobs (no one else cleaned the head as thoroughly) it was easy to forget who she might really be. I could even forget about the hundreds of painful and creative things that Iason would do to me if he found out what I was up to with his daughter.

It was at night that I thought about it. Or, more correctly, in the early morning. That's when I would wake up and scratch and turn over, and come face to face with a woman whose true identity I just didn't know.

Sometimes, as she slept, I would ask her the same question I had asked her that day, in the darkness of the hold. "Is it true, what you said? About you and the House of Bain?"

And I would remember the only answer she had been willing to give me.

"No. And yes. And no."

ALL OF THIS probably makes it sound as if I did nothing during those months but fret and wring my hands and watch Lynn scrub the head. Let me assure you, I kept busy.

My transformation into a pirate queen was more than half accidental, but once it began, it moved swiftly. Mara's ship became the first of my war galleys. Only a few weeks later, we captured another while its crew was otherwise engaged. (A word of advice to my fellow mariners. If you don't want your ship to be stolen by pirates, don't let all your sailors saunter off to the brothel at the same time. I'm just saying.) Lynn named our prize the *Banshee,* and it became my flagship. And just like that, I had a fleet.

Not that it was easy. Every day seemed to bring a new impossible problem. For one thing, I had to find captains for all of my new ships— preferably, captains who wouldn't bash me on the head as soon as I turned my back. Trustworthy troops were in short supply back then, so I gave all the men of the *Badger* a crash course in navigation and began parcelling them out, one by one. Monmain became the captain of the *Idiot Kid;* Geraint took *Destiny*; Vair had the *Wheel of Time.* I could barely stand the thought of losing Teek, my best helmsman, but, in the end, I gritted my teeth and entrusted the *Badger* to him. I still had a strong sense of affection for the stinking little tub; at least I knew that Teek wouldn't sink her.

I refused to give up Regon, so he stayed on the *Banshee* as first mate, and I kept Spinner too, because he and Lynn got along so well. Other than that, my original crew was all gone to the four winds, and I was faced with the task of finding dozens—*hundreds*—of new sailors.

That was tricky. No matter what you've heard, and no matter what you think, the average sailor is not a gentle giant with a rough exterior and a heart of gold. It's an uphill job just finding a crew that can stay sober more than three hours a day. I chose the best I could find and kept order in the usual way, with screamed insults and threats and the judicious application of a very pointy boot here and there.

What I had truly dreaded was the task of keeping them away from Lynn. She wasn't the only woman on my ships, but she was the smallest, and the youngest, and she didn't go around the ship heavily armed. More than once, in some desperation, I wondered whether I would have to keep her in a small metal box to protect her from the others. But Lynn never allowed me to protect her. She had a sharp tongue and a level head, and a strong sense of pride, and she gamely took on the job of carving out her own place on board ship. She did let me show her what parts to kick on the human body to inflict maximum pain, but that was about the limit of what I was allowed to do.

Over time, things sort of worked themselves out. Some of my sailors got to like her, and some got to respect her, and the rest came to see her as a kind of mascot. It helped that sailors are the most superstitious people alive. (If you don't believe me, try getting one to change his lucky shirt before a raid. Just try.) As the months rolled on and we grew stronger, and richer, and better-equipped, Lynn became a talisman, the embodiment of our luck. Every time we took a new ship, my sailors would chase after Lynn to get her to name it. Sometimes she was enthusiastic and came up with names like the *Black Rush* and the *Wheel of Time*. Sometimes she was not, which was how we ended up with the *Name It Yourself This Time* and the *Oh, Sod Off*.

I still got the shakes every time we left a safe harbour and headed back to the islands. But Lynn always knew, and Lynn was always there. Sometimes it was very casual. She would just happen to be somewhere nearby, coiling a rope or scaling a fish or studying a chart. But she always knew when it was time to drift to my side and find a hand to hold.

And every time, I would whisper, "You know, I'm really not a pirate queen."

And every time, she would whisper back, "Do you honestly think that anyone can tell?"

THE *KRAKEN,* TYCO'S ship, was the twelfth one we captured for my fleet.

Capturing ships is simple enough. You run your flag up the mast, redecorate a little, let out a hearty "Huzzah!", and work from there. Capturing sailors is a much more complicated business. It's a real chore, trying to figure out what to do with them all. You can absorb some of them into your own crew, as long as you're good at picking out men who won't try to stab you in the back at the first opportunity. (I wasn't, but Lynn was.) No matter how many you recruit during the culling process, though, you're left with a surly bunch of backstabbers that you have to dispose of somehow. Tradition holds that you throw them overboard, but I had balked at that. Fortunately, as Lynn pointed out, the sea is crammed full of tiny little islands that work perfectly well as makeshift prisons. Added bonus—you don't have to feed or supervise the prisoners yourself. At the beginning of everything, I didn't like this idea much either, but, as Lynn said, what was the alternative?

I got used to it. Before long, I was flinging gangs of untrustworthy sailors onto desert islands every few weeks, and thinking no more of it than of tossing fish bones over the side.

For Tyco's men, none of whom I was prepared to take on, we'd selected a real winner of an island. Bare and rocky, with only two meagre clusters of trees. My sailors ferried the crew of the *Kraken* there just as they were—unconscious, or bleeding, or bound. I watched from the *Banshee's* aft castle. The beach was too distant to make out details, but I knew what was going on. Latoya and Corto would stick two knives into the sand so that the sailors of the *Kraken* could cut their bindings. Beside the knives, they would deposit a cook-pot, a flint, a saw, a spade, and a few sacks of seed. Next, Corto would explain things to the *Kraken's* crew. They could survive for several months on shellfish and the eggs of seabirds. If they wanted to live any longer than that, they would have to raise crops. If they worked like blazes, enriching the soil with bird dung and food scraps, then they would survive. Maybe.

I was out of earshot, but I could see the men of the *Kraken* opening and shutting their mouths furiously. It wasn't hard to imagine the kind of language currently being used over there. I used it often enough myself.

There was a sound behind me. That was Regon, softly clearing his throat.

"I've put a prize crew of ten on Tyco's ship," he said. "Carter's in command. They'll sail east, meet up with the *Idiot Kid*, and take the galley to the coast to be manned and overhauled."

"Fine," I said, breaking from my funk. "Did Lynn name it?"

"She did, yes," he answered slowly. "It's to be called, *One Law*."

It was a surprisingly solemn name for Lynn. I knew why. The history of the *Kraken* had been so brutal, I wouldn't have let her end it with some kind of joke. She understood that, even though, given her druthers, she probably would have named the ship the *Kumquat* or the *Up Yours, Tyco* or something along the same lines.

"Fine," I told Regon again. "It's your watch. Once everyone's aboard, set course for the Freemarket. We're low on supplies."

None of my men ever bothered to salute, and I'd have smacked them if they tried, but Regon gave me a wink and a nod that served the same purpose, and went to talk to the helmsman.

I took a last look at the barren island. Latoya and Corto were rowing back to the *Banshee* with long, slow strokes. Tyco, his shaggy hair in strings around his face, was staggering up and down the beach, screaming something that I was too far away to hear.

You'd think that a moment like this would make me happy—that there would be a little victory glow. You'd think that, at least, the blackness would lift for a minute, the heavy, choking blackness that had descended on me when I first heard about the barbarity of Tyco's raids. But it didn't happen. I was glad to be alive, I was glad we hadn't lost, I was glad Tyco was through, but I felt no real sense of triumph. There were thousands more like Tyco and I couldn't duel them all.

Besides that, I was cold, and hurting, and I stank. I flexed my arms and they moved awkwardly; my leather gambeson was stiff with congealed blood, and it stuck to the skin beneath. Sooner or later, I would have to haul up a few buckets of freezing, fishy seawater and try to scrub off the worst of it.

It wasn't an attractive thought. To put off the evil hour, I wandered into my cabin.

Gone were the old days of sleeping in the hold with my crew, hearing their every groan and snore and fart. The *Banshee* had a proper captain's cabin, practically big enough to swing a cat. After years of life on a small ship, it was a glorious thing to have a cabin with actual walls. It was even better because I wasn't alone in there.

As I had expected, Lynn was in the cabin already, curled up on the bunk we shared. The bunk wasn't big enough for one person in the first place, and it was ridiculous even to try for two, but Lynn was determined. And bendy.

At some point, Lynn had traded her wet clothes for a fresh tunic. It was sleeveless, so it exposed the tattoo on her right shoulder: a storm-petrel in flight, etched in lines of black ink. That was the symbol she had chosen as my personal mark not long after we met, and it was emblazoned on the *Banshee's* flag as well as Lynn's arm. It was a bit of an odd choice. A storm petrel is a little feathery black bird, not exactly the kind of thing that screams "pirate" in my book. I wasn't the one who had it carved into my skin, though, so I didn't see any point in griping.

Lynn wasn't the only one who wore my mark. Quite a few of my sailors had copied her. On a hot day, you could walk the decks of the *Banshee* and see black birds engraved into dozens of brawny biceps, shoulders, and chests. Lynn was not happy when she first found out about this development (I have never, repeat *never*, heard someone scream so long without taking a breath) but she got to accept it, eventually. It helped that her tattoo was the most intricate and detailed, each black feather crisply outlined. Some of the sailors' marks were so crude that they could have been random splodges of ink.

Now, as she sprawled on our bunk, Lynn was studying a paper of some kind.

"What are you doing?" I asked, hanging my sword belt on a peg.

Lynn looked up. "Checking the map. I try to keep track of which islands we've used. Not that that matters, does it?"

"What do you mean?"

She rolled the map and tossed it into the open sea chest that stood at the bunk's foot. "Well, when you say 'What are you doing?' in that tone of voice, it means that you know perfectly well what I'm doing but you'd like me to stop because you want attention."

"I never—"

"You always. But that's fine. I want attention too." She swung her legs off of the bunk. "So. Tyco's marooned, all's well with the world?"

"All is far from well with the world."

"All is slightly more well with the world."

"All is marginally less fucked up with the world."

"Keep a sense of proportion, Mistress. We're alive, and the night is yet young. Want to ravish me?"

I looked blankly at my stained and sticky hands. "Um . . . sure, I guess. Listen, Lynn—"

"'Um, sure, I guess'?" Lynn repeated, eyebrow arched. "You sweet-talker, you. No wonder you scored so much tail during your depraved youth."

I felt my cheeks flush. "I didn't really."

"I can't think why," Lynn said seriously. "And you can calm down,

Darren. I was just pulling your ever-so-pullable leg. I know what you need right now."

The blessed girl had a pail of hot water ready, and rags and soap. The laces of my gambeson had gummed together, and she began on the tricky task of coaxing them loose without cutting them.

When storytellers make up heroes, they imagine people who can fly, or chop off lots of heads very quickly, or walk through fire. Lynn's own magical gift was more miraculous than any of those and ten times as useful. She could give a complete bath to a filthy and reeking pirate queen using only a single basin of water. It took her full attention, and I closed my eyes as she worked. First she peeled off the clotted leather armour, then the ruined shirt, then the rest of my clothes down to the boots. Then she set to work on my body—scrubbing off the bloodstains with one warm cloth, wiping off the pink soapy liquid with another, slowing where the skin was gashed or stitched.

The steady motions first lulled me to a doze, making me sway on my feet. Then, as she worked her way over me again, this time with a clean dry cloth, they began to stir me up. She was taking her time with this pass, letting her hands trail over sensitive spots as if by accident. The cabin suddenly seemed very warm, and my breath rasped faster and faster. Once I gasped.

"Should I stop?" Lynn said, pausing.

"Sweet fucking mother of—NO!" I ground out, not quite coherently.

She resumed, slower still. "You're loving this," she commented, as she worked on one of my calves. "Not just the bath, I mean. You love having me serve you."

"What's that supposed to—" I began, and then I gasped again.

"I mean—Mistress—that you like being reminded that I belong to you. That you can go ahead and use me."

I probably would have said something in reply if I'd been able to breathe.

She wrung out the last cloth and set it gently in the basin. "This part makes you nervous. But it's so simple. You only have to ask. And you can ask for anything that you want."

She rose to her feet. Her hands hung loosely at her sides, and her eyes rested on my collarbone. Her posture signalled that she was waiting for instructions. Not demanding, or baiting, but waiting for whatever I decided. It was a very familiar stance. I had seen Lynn take it countless times, but more than that, I had seen servants standing before me in that way since the day I first learned what servants were. I don't know why the sight made my blood surge and my heart beat faster. Maybe it wouldn't have, if I'd been a better kind of a person. But it did.

"Take your clothes off," I whispered.

She must have been ready for that, because it only took an instant for her tunic to slither to the deck.

I had no idea who she was. But, times like that, I felt that I could wait a little longer to find out.

CHAPTER THREE

THE MOMENT AFTER I woke up the next morning, I felt a sense of such total peace and wellbeing that I thought I was about to float.

Two moments after I woke up, the pain crashed in. There was the sting of the sewn cuts, the web of scratches, the duller ache of the bruises, and then a throbbing in the muscles of my sword-arm, which I had overused the day before. Plus a throbbing in other muscles which I had overused the night before.

Three moments after I woke up, my brain came back to life. It started buzzing away with a kind of fizzy unease, circling around the mistakes I had made when we attacked the *Kraken*, listing all the things that I needed to accomplish that day.

Lynn was still sleeping, her right arm flung out of the bunk and dangling over open air, her left knee drawn up almost to her chest. She didn't look comfortable and I thought of waking her . . . but then she breathed deeply and a fold of her flimsy tunic fell back, exposing her chest. I recoiled.

When you're—you know—in the moment, you don't think about how these things are going to look when you're—you know—done. The marks were vicious, the colour of port wine, some of them as big as an apple. They started at her neck and worked their way downwards. In between were smaller scrapes, fresh and glaring, as well as (I groaned) bite marks. One bite was right underneath the storm-petrel tattoo, the symbol of my ownership. A band around each of her wrists was mottled red . . . oh gods, the ropes. I remembered putting each of those marks on Lynn—why was it so easy to act that way when my blood was up? I buried my face into the blanket before I could see anything else.

Why the hell do I do these things to her? I wondered. *Why the hell does she let me?*

WHEN LYNN WOKE, the first thing she did was to streeeetch, in one long motion, arching her feet down to the bottom of the bunk, and then shaking her whole body out. Her face bore the dreamy smile of someone who didn't have to get out of bed for at least four hours more.

"I dreamed about armadillos," she announced. "You might want to make a note of that. It's probably very meaningful. What's the matter?"

She *always* knew. I bit my lip.

"Darren," she said. "Spill. You brood ten times more than could possibly be healthy for a person of your size and weight. Let's have it."

Now, I am a person who knows how to talk. Back when I was a merchant captain, before piracy came into the picture, I haggled and bargained in half the major cities on the continent. On a good day, I could sell a man his own shoes and make him feel as if he'd gotten the better end of the deal. And I wasn't just a merchant, either. I acted as an envoy for the House of Torasan, representing it in councils and conclaves. I once critiqued a baron's tax policy so brutally that he dissolved into tears, right there at the table. Yet, somehow, when I try to have a conversation about *that kind of thing*, I always end up stammering and gulping like a half-wit child trying to recite the times table.

"I just . . . you see . . . well, Lynn . . . You know, sometimes, you know, it's the morning after, and we . . . you know . . . the night before, and it just makes me wonder whether I . . . you know, whether I . . ."

"This again." She rolled to face me. "For the thousandth time, Darren, you're just fine in bed, and you'll be even better once you learn to relax."

"It's . . . not . . . *that*," I said stiffly. "I just . . . mean . . . I want to make sure . . . Is this what you *want*, Lynn? Are you getting anything out of this?"

She didn't answer right away, but gave a deep sigh. Then she tossed the blankets aside and hopped out of the bunk. My heart plunged. "You aren't, are you? You're humouring me, or I pressured you somehow, or—"

"Hang on," she said, coming back to the bunk with a full wine cup. "I think you need to get at least a little squiffy if we're going to talk about this."

I took the cup, stared at the glassy gold surface. "Why?"

"Because you're shy. Take three good swallows, and then I'll answer you."

I had to force the stuff down. It was the godawful kind spiked with pine resin, and it had a bitter, oily tang. Lynn wiped a drop from the corner of my lip before she went on.

"Mistress, a good rule of thumb for the future. If a girl is yelling 'More, more, more' while clawing all the skin off your back? Odds are, she's getting something out of it."

I rolled my shoulders. Now that she mentioned it, my back did sting a little. "But—"

"Look at me, please."

She didn't wait; she lifted my chin gently with two fingers. "What did you and Jess do in bed?"

My eyes slid away, trying to find something to focus on that wasn't

Lynn's face. Is it normal to have to tell your new lover what you did with your old one? "The usual, I guess. She would . . . and then I would . . . and then we would . . . well, you know . . . together. It was . . . nice."

"I'm glad. Darren, listen. It's all right to want something other than nice."

Maybe the boat was about to sink, I mused. If not, maybe I could sink it. Anything to get me out of this conversation. Almost unconsciously, I looked around for a hatchet.

"Did you enjoy what we did last night?" Lynn continued, unmoved.

I found a fascinating piece of lint on the blanket to pick at.

"I'd like you to answer out loud, please. It'll only take one word. One syllable. Three letters at most."

It took a minute or so, but I *did* manage it. "Yes."

"How much?"

I snapped. "A lot. All right? A huge unhealthy whack of a lot."

"Thank you," she said solemnly. "So did I. So much that I'll probably go around the ship today wearing a large silly grin."

I snorted softly. Her hand found its way into mine. "We both want this, Mistress. We *both* get something out of it. We never do anything that I haven't agreed to. So what the hell is the problem?"

There was a loud, squawking chorus of voices in my head, which sounded something like seagulls and something like my maiden aunts. All of them seemed to agree very heartily that there was a problem. Then again, neither seabirds nor my elderly relations had a tendency to give good advice. My quick-witted, self-assured partner, on the other hand, did.

"I guess you're right," I said.

She tugged a lock of my hair. "I generally am."

Someone gave two sharp raps at the door. "Coming up on Freemarket, captain!"

FREEMARKET. I ADMIT, it makes me a little nostalgic to remember Freemarket. How to describe the place? Well, it wasn't exactly a market, and it sure as hell wasn't free. It was a mid-sized island, roughly in the centre of the Kilan archipelago. Back then, the whole island was carpeted by shops, taverns, and vendor-stalls, with a fringe of docks and harbours running the length of the coastline. The purpose of every single person who lived there was to separate you from your money as quickly and pleasantly as possible. You could buy literally anything at the Freemarket, from a boatload of salt to a lizard so big you could put a saddle on it and ride it down the street.

The prices there were as dizzyingly high as any you could ever hope to scream at, and the quality of the goods was nothing to celebrate—the ale was sub-par, the wine unspeakable. Yet it was always rammed with ships desperate to pour money into its coffers. Back then, you see, the market truce was still intact. Within the harbours of the Freemarket, you could dock next to a captain whom you'd cheerfully strangle on any other day, and both of you would still be intact the next morning. You could meet your worst enemy at a fish vendor's storefront, and both of you would nod your heads grimly and pass by without drawing a weapon. You paid for the truce through the nose, as you paid for everything else—a stiff tax to the harbourmasters and local watch. It was worth it for a chance to rummage through a cheese stall without forever looking over one shoulder.

It was about three years afterwards that the Freemarket burned. I don't remember the name of the man who did it, but that hardly matters. He was just one more bastard who thought that the world would be improved by a little extra fear and flame. I went after him, of course, but unfortunately for him, I wasn't the one who got him in the end. You offend a whole lot of people when you break market truce, and not all of them are as reasonable as I am. By the time I caught up with him, his own ship was burning, and he was nailed to the prow as a figurehead, his mouth and eye-sockets stuffed full of red-hot cinders. I couldn't get the smell out of my clothes for weeks . . . But I'm getting ahead of myself. Point is, all this happened when Freemarket was still whole, before some jackass with a barrel of oil and a burning torch decided that our lives needed a few extra complications.

IT WAS A bright, breezy, dew-fresh morning when Lynn and I came up on deck. Regon had already docked and moored the *Banshee* on the east side of the island, an easy walk from the shipwrights. Vendors' tents stood along the path, rippling in the light wind. They were of all colours from turquoise to lemon-yellow to scarlet to emerald, and carnival-bright banners streamed from their central poles. Smells came rippling from the food hawkers' stoves—grilled chicken, cumin, garlic, fresh-baked bread, honey, sun-warmed strawberries. I drank in the aromas, inhaling so hard that I almost fell backwards.

But Lynn was frowning, rubbing at one of her elbows. "We're in for bad weather today."

I frowned myself. "I thought it was your right arm that ached before a storm?"

"Actually, they both do. The right one is a little bit worse most of the time, that's all."

"Why is that, anyway? Did they get broken?"

"A long time ago." Lynn took a deeply suspicious look at the cloudless sky. "You should get on with it. Shopping isn't going to be nearly as much fun once it starts pissing down."

"Yeah, I'm going. Do you want to come with me?"

I said this very casually and waited to see what threadbare excuse she would produce this time around.

"I'd like to, Darren, but I should probably rest this." Lynn moved her sore arm limply. "I'm starting to get a headache, too. Not my day, I guess. You go ahead. I'll stay and watch things here."

I would like to pause at this point to share something about women that it took me a very long time to learn. If your girl tells you that she has a headache, she is sending you a message in code. The message is that she wants to play a game, and the game is called, "Figure out what is bothering me by reading my mind." If you fail to guess right, you lose. If you do guess right, you still lose, because you should have known that something was bothering her before she said anything. Either way, be prepared to set aside a couple of hours for back rubs and apologies.

Jess, who was my lover back in the dark ages, used to be very fond indeed of this game. Lynn didn't play it all that often, except when we were at the Freemarket. We'd made fifteen trips to the market in the past year, and every time, there was something. Sometimes it was a headache, sometimes it was cramps; a pulled muscle, sunstroke. Or she had to clean the galley stove, or she wanted a nap, or it was high time for her to organize my charts of the Outer Isles. Whatever it was, the outcome was the same: Lynn never put a foot on shore.

It had worried me in the beginning, but after fifteen repetitions, I'd sailed straight past *worried* to *annoyed,* and I was now in hailing distance of *just plain pissed.* I suppressed a sigh.

"Don't sulk," Lynn told me. "You can manage to buy a few barrels of biscuit without my supervision. I have full confidence. But just in case . . ."

I was wearing my good blue coat that day. A little swagger never came amiss in Freemarket. Lynn held me at arm's length so she could inspect me, adjusted the cloth here and there, did up a button that had come undone, and then carefully took me by the lapels.

"Lynn," I objected.

She ignored that. "If anyone recognizes you as an exile and gives you a hard time, what do you do?"

"Give them the hairy eyeball," I recited sullenly.

"And if that doesn't work?"

This was too humiliating for words. A few of my sailors were standing about smirking; Regon was leaning against the mast, hands jammed in his pockets, clearly loving every second. There were five men watching, and I made a mental note of their names, reminding myself to take the time to pound some respect back into them later. So what if Lynn tyrannized over me every now and then? It was still my damn fleet, wasn't it? *Me am boss.*

"Darren," Lynn repeated, in the don't-mess-with-me-I've-seen-you-naked voice. "What if the hairy eyeball doesn't work?"

I surrendered. "I find the nearest watchman and offer to pay him a week's salary if he makes my enemies bleed a lot. I can handle myself, you know."

"No, Mistress, you can't," she corrected me, with a pat on the cheek. "And you shouldn't be allowed to try. Take Latoya, and a squad of ten men, and don't sneak away from them this time."

Regon's smirk was diabolical by then, but it was wiped instantly off of his face when Lynn wheeled on him. "And *you.* Why are you still awake? Your watch was over hours ago. You think my mistress has the time to come and pick you up if you faint and pitch overboard? Get the hell to your hammock, *now.*"

He raised his hands in defeat. "I'm going. I'm gone."

"*Pirates,*" Lynn muttered, as Regon shuffled for the stairs. "If you had brains, you'd be dangerous." Then she cast another glance at the sky. "I'm serious about the weather, Mistress. You really should get going. And . . . be careful? Please?"

"I'll be careful," I promised. "Don't you worry about it. Just rest. Put something cool on your head, huh?"

"Why would I want to put something cool on my—" she began automatically, and then, too late, she remembered. "Oh, right." She laid a hand unconvincingly against her forehead. "Right, yes, I'll do that, right."

"HEADACHE!" I SNARLED, disgusted, as I strode into the market. "Does she think I'm a moron, Latoya?"

Latoya wisely chose not to answer that. Or maybe she was out of breath, since she was lugging a haversack of coins which was about as heavy as a good-sized pig. My other bodyguards were further back, moving casual-like through the crowds just in case anyone got too interested in me.

At the moment, the crowds all seemed to be busy with the Freemarket's other attractions. It was only ten in the morning, but the hawkers were already setting out lunch. Every stall held giant wooden trays crammed with food—tender lamb hissing hot on skewers, chunks of spicy sausage dusted with herbs, cherry pastries oozing with juice, sherbet cooled with crushed ice, candied nuts, golden rolls crusted with roasted onions. And then there were the drinks—red wine, white wine, plum wine, ginger wine, blossom wine, malt beer, spruce beer, cider . . . everything from syrupy cordials to a clear fluid which smelled like brimstone and tasted like lightning. All of which I ignored, since a single square meal at the Freemarket was more expensive than a banquet on the mainland. Even *water* cost money at the market.

My stomach was gurgling plaintively, though. To take my mind off that, I continued my rant.

"A headache isn't even a good excuse to *begin* with," I went on. "The fifteenth time around, it's pathetic. It's not like Lynn to be so feeble. And what's the point? Lynn likes food, she likes people, she likes bossing me around. Why wouldn't she want to come to the market with me?"

"She's afraid," Latoya said bluntly.

This made me grind to a halt in the middle of the street. I hadn't expected her to answer. Latoya was not a chatty individual. Most of the time, talking to her was like talking to a wall, with these two differences: first, walls normally don't wear trousers, and second, walls aren't secretly smarter than I am. I think. I hope.

"What do you mean?" I asked her. "Afraid of what?"

Latoya, not being one to use words when a gesture would do the trick, shrugged. I attempted to translate. "She's afraid of something but you don't know what?"

Latoya's eyelid flickered, sort of affirmatively.

"But how can you tell?"

Another shrug.

I sighed, while absent-mindedly fending off the hawkers who had come to swarm around me now that I was standing still. It was pretty easy to get rid of the perfume seller. He backed off at the first good snarl. The fish merchant turned out to be made of stronger stuff, though. I had to stomp on his feet to make him stop trying to stuff dried herring in my pockets.

"It would help if you could be a bit more explicit, you know," I said, once the fish merchant was in full retreat. "With, you know, words and things. Or you could use puppets, whatever. But the shrugging gets to be exasperating. Why is Lynn afraid?"

"It's none of my business, Captain," Latoya said. Which, by the way, was the longest sentence that had come out of her mouth in a month. "She's your girl, right?"

DAMN STRAIGHT SHE was my girl. Fine. Screw Latoya. I would figure this out all on my own. *Me am lover as well as boss. Me am love boss.*

I chewed away at the problem while we did business with the shipbroker. We weren't there long, but it was long enough to empty Latoya's haversack of money. To re-stock a ship in a war zone, it took a back-breaking load of hard-earned coin . . . or hard-stolen coin, in my case. Piracy had done a lot to fix my cash flow problem.

Before I got into the lucrative business of beating people up and stealing their stuff, I had to rely on Jess to supply me with ropes and paint and oil and wine and biscuits. She did it, out of the goodness of her land-lubber heart, but it was a relief to be free from her charity now. No need to grumble out ungracious-sounding thanks every time I saw her, while staring down at the toecaps of my boots so I didn't have to see her face. No need to suffer through those patronizing lectures, in which she told me that maybe she didn't have the right to an opinion now that we were through, but in her *personal* view, I was drinking far too much.

Oh, Jess still had a hand in things. Along with Holly, her new partner-type-thingy, she maintained my secret harbour on the mainland and found homes for some of the refugees I rescued. I was grateful for the help, but not dependent on it, not any more. That was one accomplishment that did give me a sense of triumph.

I didn't have much to do at the shipbroker's. Corto, the quartermaster, did the actual bargaining; Latoya inspected the goods and counted out the cash. My job was to stand with crossed arms and scowl, and add a little sneer every now and then, as I thought appropriate.

As I stood and scowled and sneered at the right moments, I pondered this new puzzle of Lynn and the market. What was there about this place that could possibly frighten her? We spent most of our time in one kind of mortal peril or another (nasty men with big swords, food poisoning, take your pick) so it was hard to believe that she would hide from a herring seller. But if she really was afraid of something around here, why didn't she tell me about it and send me off to beat it with a stick? Did she trust me that little? Or did she just want me to figure things out for myself? That was the only explanation that made even a particle of sense, considering the way she kept trotting out the same old shabby excuses.

All right. (I aimed a particularly savage sneer at a nearby longshore-man, and he gulped and ducked his head.) What about the market made Lynn afraid? What about it was different from the dangers we faced day to day? Well, it was on shore. But we visited islands and deserted coasts all the time. Lynn didn't exactly dance down the gangplank, but she didn't seem unnerved by the experience, either.

Was it the people?

I almost dismissed that theory. Lynn spent almost all her time with pirates, vagabonds, and roustabouts. The vendors and shipbrokers at the market were pushy, but at least they were respectable . . .

Respectable. My eyes shot wide open.

That was it. So simple. The Freemarket was the only place where we had the chance to mingle with Kilans who weren't criminals or paupers. At the market, you could rub elbows with members of the ruling class—wealthy merchants, or the nobles who served as captains on trading ships or war galleys. And Lynn wouldn't set foot on the island, because if she did . . . then *one of those people might recognize her.*

"Finished here, captain," Corto said, loping over. "Are we taking the boxes straight back to the ship?"

I pulled myself from my reverie. "*You* are. Take the others and get a move on. I'll follow shortly."

Corto put his thumbs in his pockets and waggled them worriedly. "Alone?"

There was no real risk that he'd disobey me—the Kilan commoner who can stand up to a noble is one in a thousand—but I snapped the words out anyway. "You heard me, you mutinous dog. If there's to be any more discussion, it'll be between you and a rope's end."

"Aye, captain," Corto said hurriedly. "Aye. Understood."

"Good," I snarled. "Move your carcass."

He moved, but as he moved, he muttered, "Your slave is going to kill us for leaving you."

"It'll be good for you," I called after him.

"What? Being killed?"

"It teaches humility."

Then I twiddled my thumbs and tried to look natural until they all tramped out of sight.

AS SOON AS the door swung shut behind Latoya, I picked my target. One of the shipbrokers was a little fat man with beady, calculating eyes. The perfect informant is easy to threaten and easy to bribe, and the little man checked both boxes, as far as I could see. I put on a suitably forbidding expression and ambled up to him, taking my time.

The merchant was busy flicking the beads of an abacus and muttering under his breath, and for the first minute he pretended not to notice me, but I could see the sweat beading at the back of his neck. At last, he deliberately, oh so deliberately, set down his stylus. "Is there something more that I can do for you, my lady?"

I laid both my palms flat on his counting table and leaned over. "I need to speak with you. Privately."

He didn't seem nearly as frightened as I would have liked. "My lady, I'm . . ." He coughed. "Well, I'm flattered, frankly. But I'm a married man, and—"

Oh, for the love of sainted trout. I got a good two-fisted grip on the front of his florid green shirt and hauled him up until he was standing on tiptoe.

"Ah," he said, talking more quickly, "ah. Right. I can see we aren't looking for love. But you do remember the market truce, right? And all the soldiers that enforce the market truce? The soldiers who will put your head on a stake in the harbour if you don't make an effort to be civil?"

That was true, and it severely cut down my options. I gave the merchant a little snarl anyway as I let go of his shirt, but it wasn't one of my best. Then I fumbled in the hidden pocket of my coat, grabbed one of the heavy red-gold coins that I kept there for emergencies, and slapped it into his chubby hand.

He glanced at it casually, and then, for just a second, his eyes flickered wide. Then he stowed it swiftly in his bulging money pouch and ushered me to a small office at the back of the building.

"What can I offer you?" he asked, broad and expansive, once we were back there. "Wine? Ale? Tea? I could send out for fig juice. Meat pies? Parsnip fritters! A girl? A boy? Or both at once? No? I could throw in some warmed oil. Perhaps a sheep?"

"Thanks ever so, but I would settle for a heaping bowl of you shutting up right now." I threw myself into a chair padded with wildcat hides. "All I want is information. What's your name?"

"Ballard," he said, inclining his head. "Was that the only information you wanted?"

Smug little ass. Moments like that, I felt a lot more sympathy towards all the thugs who wandered around casually gutting merchants. I pushed my feelings away, forced one of my uglier smiles, and asked, "What do you know about Lord Iason's daughter?"

NOT MUCH. THAT was the first fact that emerged, although he tried to hide it with bluster.

I waited impatiently as he waffled for five minutes, and then cut him off. "Everyone knows that Ariadne is his only child. Details, Ballard. What does she look like?"

"What does she look like," he repeated worriedly. "Well, of course she's been cloistered, she doesn't move in public, I've never seen her . . ."

"But you've heard things. Talk."

He pulled nervously at his lip. "Well, they do say that the Lady Ariadne takes after her father."

I had seen Iason of Bain only once, and that from a distance, at the wedding of my fourth cousin twice removed. Everyone had been half-mad with delight and terror to have him on the guest list, and for the entire week of festivities, he'd been surrounded by drink-stewards and dancing girls. Though I could still picture him vaguely, I didn't want to trust my memory on a point like this. "And what does Lord Iason look like?"

"Very fair, my lady," Ballard said. "Pale hair, pale skin."

I pictured the girl I had left on the *Banshee* this morning, her hair sun-bleached almost white. She was as tanned as any of my sailors, but the skin on the inside of her wrists looked like milk.

"Slight of stature," Ballard continued. "Short, for a man."

Lynn barely came up to my shoulder. I could lift her with one hand. "How old is she?"

Ballard counted on his fingers. "She would be twenty-one. There were great celebrations three years back for her eighteenth birthday. Perhaps you remember them?"

I didn't. Three years back, I was in the process of being exiled from my home for showing a bit too much affection to a certain lady beekeeper. Keeping up with current events was not a priority for me at the time. "Do you know anything about Ariadne personally? Her interests, her character?"

Ballard winced, thinking hard. "The only thing that comes to mind is that she's said to be—well, very outspoken. She has the stubbornness of a woman, so they say." He saw my expression and quickly rephrased. "A young woman, I mean. But I imagine that's changed in recent years. After her marriage, I mean."

CHAPTER FOUR

MY FEELINGS AT that moment? Well, imagine someone prying your teeth apart, forcing a stone the size of a skull down your throat, and then shaking you so that it bounced around in your stomach. That would be a fair approximation.

"Now that she's *what?*" I asked. With a surprising amount of calm, I think, considering.

"Married, my lady," Ballard said, surprised. "She was married shortly after she turned eighteen. To Gerard of Saupon."

Gerard? *Gerard?* I'd met that bastard. He'd spent almost a month on Torasan Isle, years back, during some kind of trade negotiation. He might have been the heir to a powerful house, but he was also a snivelling, useless boy, with a face like a flour weevil and a habit of groping every servant girl who walked within his reach. Eventually one of them got sick of it and threw him in the fish pond—for which she was soundly whipped, while Gerard watched and glowered. I couldn't imagine gallant little Lynn putting up with that moron for a second.

On the other hand, her father probably didn't give her much of a choice.

"She got married shortly after she turned eighteen?" I asked slowly.

"About three years ago, yes. But Gerard was killed some time afterwards. A riding accident, I believe. I don't recall exactly when. There were no children from the marriage." He squinted into the distance. "I don't remember hearing any news of the Lady Ariadne after that. Wait—no—there is something. If I recall correctly, she's now betrothed to the second son of the Lord of Oropat, but the wedding has been delayed for years. Some dispute about the dowry. Does that answer your question?"

I was still trying to cope with all the new information. Lynn, *my* Lynn, was married long before we met. Lynn was now a widow. Did she even know that?

"My lady?"

"That's all," I said, shaking myself from my stupor. "You can keep the change; you've been very helpful."

Ballard lifted his silly hat. "All my thanks, my lady."

I debated with myself for a minute, shrugged inwardly, and then grabbed his shirt again, pulled him in close, and gave him the most absolutely foul look that I could muster. "Don't go offering me any sheep the next time I'm here."

"I wouldn't dream of it, my lady," he said, gently detaching himself. "I wouldn't dream of it."

I WALKED SLOWLY on my way back to the ship, a sack of the more expensive and delicate supplies slung over my shoulder. As I walked, I tried to match up the dates. Lynn—Ariadne—was married to a spoiled princeling at age eighteen. By the time she was twenty, she was living in a miserable little fishing village without so much as a pair of shoes or a spare cloak to her name. When did she run away from home, and why?

It had to be Gerard, I decided. Marriage to Gerard would be enough to make anyone want to head for the hills, but especially someone as fiercely free-thinking as Lynn. Since she was the heir to the house of Bain, her prime duty after the wedding would have been to whelp as many children as she possibly could. No surprise that she balked at that, especially since every pregnancy would have begun with a conjugal visit from the Maggot of Saupon. That's what she was running from, but what was she running towards? Did she intend to spend the rest of her life in that squalid village where I'd found her? Surely not. Maybe she had something better in mind, but the war scuppered her plans by making it impossible for her to travel. She couldn't reach her real destination and got stranded in the wilderness. By the time I happened along, she was in real trouble, but she knew how to seize an opportunity when it came.

Obviously, her father Iason had kept it a secret that she was missing. Not too difficult, since, as his precious only child, Ariadne had spent her entire life in seclusion. And since her husband was dead, no one would think it strange that she wasn't popping out babies every year or so. To keep up the pretence that she was still at home, Iason had betrothed her to another idiot princeling, but he was finding excuses to put off the wedding. Dowry dispute, my hairy foot.

Iason must be looking for Lynn—he *had* to be looking—but he was doing it very, very quietly, to prevent any scandal. Unfortunately for him, Lynn really did know how to hide. First she buried herself in the poorest, most miserable village she could find, and then she re-invented herself as a slave girl on a pirate ship. Not exactly where you would look for a princess.

So Iason's meek inquiries wouldn't be enough to uncover his truant daughter. Sooner or later, all of Kila would find out that she was gone. When that happened, then it was just a matter of time before the childless Iason would be deposed and some other self-important twit would take his place. I couldn't force myself to care about that prospect. Iason's daughter obviously didn't.

Ariadne and I made quite the pair. An exiled noble and a runaway princess, turned pirate and slave. That was not something that happened in Kila every day. Or—well—ever.

The thought cheered me. I was back in the harbour by now, running a professional eye over every ship that I passed. The *Almathea* looked leaky, but that could be fixed with a good scraping and caulking. The *Silver Hind*, a large galley with a milky-eyed doe as its figurehead, was almost new. I like a ship that's weathered a few storms, myself. I wasn't just killing time by looking the ships over. Chances were, I'd capture some of them for my fleet in the months to come, so I was getting a head start by inspecting them in advance. I gave them all a piratical grin as I strolled past. *See you soon, my pretties.*

From a long way off, I could make out the red sails of the *Banshee*, and a small figure pacing restlessly in front of them. I checked my pace a little. I had forgotten that I would be in trouble.

Lynn clumped down the gangplank to meet me and folded her arms. "I know you have an explanation. I know it's going to be *thrilling*."

"I'm sorry, all right?" I said, as we boarded the *Banshee* together. "I know you were right about bodyguards, I just get edgy having people at my elbow all the time. I won't do it again."

"Hmph," she said, but she sounded mollified.

I took the opportunity to distract her further. "Report. Everything all right with the ship?"

"The ship," she said, "is well. A couple of thugs have been standing on the dock there, peering at us inquisitively and scratching themselves where they shouldn't. I put the harbour patrol on notice. And Regon had a rush of blood to the head and challenged Latoya to arm wrestle. I expect him to make a full recovery. Eventually. Oh, you bought apples."

"I bought apples," I confirmed, leaning over so she could snag one from the top of the pack. "Not giant rubies, as you would expect from the price of them, but apples. They better be damn good. Or I'll have to go back and snarl at the shopkeeper."

She was already halfway finished eating her first, but she paused. "Sorry, should I not have taken one?"

"No, it's fine. Just . . . take your time with it. Savour."

I slung the sack to the deck, took an apple for myself, and perched on the gunwale beside her. The water and sky were orange and gold. The tide lapped softly against the standing ships. Beautiful moments like that make me feel guilty, because I can never forget that I'm basking in nature's splendor while other people are dying in their own filth. I explained this to

Lynn once, but she, ever the pragmatist, pointed out that guilt was beside the point. It doesn't matter whether you've earned a beautiful moment, she said, just take strength from it if you can. If you don't love the world, she said, you won't fight for it.

I studied her out of the corner of my eye. She was eating the second half of her apple in slow, deliberate bites, licking drops of juice from her fingertips. That was Ariadne of Bain, I told myself—the heir to the most powerful house in Kila, with my mark of ownership tattooed on her shoulder, wholly content as she munched a piece of fruit. The idea should have terrified me, but instead, I found myself warmed. She had a world of other options, but I was the one she'd chosen.

"I'm sorry I had that panic attack this morning," I said.

She waved that off. "You have panic attacks at regular intervals, Mistress. It saves me the trouble of checking to see that you're still breathing."

"Yeah, well." I rolled my own apple between my fingers. "What does it . . . Why do you . . . I mean . . . How does it make you feel?"

I congratulated myself for getting the words out, but, maddeningly, Lynn came right back with, "How does what make me feel?"

"When I—you know—"

"When you tie me up?"

"Yeah."

She took a small, thoughtful nibble, her eyes on the horizon. "Cherished."

I grinned in spite of myself, but I aimed it downwards, towards the water. "You don't get scared?"

"Ah—no, Darren." She kept her tone as serious as possible, which wasn't very. I knew what Lynn sounded like when she was trying not to laugh. "No, pirate queen, for some reason I'm never scared of you. Go figure."

And why would she be scared of me? Even at my worst, I was twenty times better than Gerard.

I stretched in the warmth of the setting sun. My edginess was gone, my whole body languid and content. Lynn had given me a puzzle to solve, and lo and behold, I went and bloody *solved* it. Hadn't even asked for a clue. It looked like maybe I was kind of a genius, which was something I'd always privately suspected might be true.

All that Lynn had to do now was admit that I was right.

Right about then a shadow fell over me, blocking the warmth of the sunset. I looked over my shoulder to see a woman of my own height, dressed in the long split tunic of a landsman. Her amber hair—hair that I used to run my fingers through, once upon a time—was in a tight braid wound around her head, and she wore travelling boots rather than her usual calfskin shoes. She was clearly a woman with a mission, which was all fine and good, but couldn't she be a woman on a mission somewhere far away from me?

"Guh buh buh wah?" I stammered.

If you can think of a better thing to say when your ex-lover suddenly shows up aboard your pirate ship, feel free to share.

"Hello," Jess said. "Do you have a minute?"

"IT'S NO GOOD scowling at me, Darren," Jess said later, after she'd refreshed herself with three of my very expensive apples. "Whether you like it or not, Holly and I are part of this movement now. You've been sending refugees through the valley for years, and the numbers are getting to be more than we can handle. Darren, don't make faces, *please*. We're not giving up on you—we just need a long term plan, because the gods alone know how long the war will last. I want to join one of your ships for a while and see for myself the situation on the ground. Then I'll be better placed to help think of a permanent solution."

"How did you get to Freemarket?" I asked, just as Lynn asked, "Was Holly all right with this?"

"Holly agrees that it's necessary," Jess said. "Though, Darren, she did tell me to warn you that she's going to gut you with a clam fork if you let anything happen to me."

I acknowledged the threat with a grunt and a wave of my hand. I am used to threats, though I'll never understand why people always hold *me* responsible for everything.

"And I got to Freemarket on a cattle boat," Jess went on. "That was a mistake. I don't think I'll ever be able to look at sirloin the same way. Now, I know I didn't warn you I was coming, but all of us are adults. This isn't going to be a problem, is it?"

I was opening my mouth to say something along the lines of *Actually, yes it is, yes it really, really is, now that you mention it*, but naturally Lynn jumped in first. "It's fine. You can sail with us for as long as you want."

Jess did at least have the courtesy to look at me for confirmation. I sighed. "After all that you've done for me, Jess, it's the least I can do in return."

It was true, so I tried hard to mean it. But my sense of languid well-being was gone, replaced by the first twinges of a stomach ulcer.

JESS AND LYNN spent most of that evening catching up, while I sat nearby, sharpening my cutlass and feeling left out. It was slightly freakish, how well they got along. Every now and then people ask me about this, so I should come clean: I don't know how you can make your old lover and your new lover get along if they don't want to. And, for the record, I don't know how you can stop them from getting along if they do want to. Either way, you're probably out of luck. Grit your teeth and find a cutlass to sharpen. It does help work out the tension, a little.

I left Jess about a year before I met Lynn, and the breakup wasn't what you would call smooth. I don't think that "smooth" is an option when your lover catches you sneaking out of the house in the middle of the night, with your boots tucked under your arms.

I tried to explain that it was my duty as a noble to return to Kila and protect the peasants during the war. So my decision to leave her forever had nothing to do with my *personal* feelings.

That didn't go down well at all.

For the next month, my face sported a bruise the exact size and shape of a wooden spoon.

Later, Lynn insisted that Jess had forgiven me. Which I found very comforting until I realized that Lynn had reached that conclusion without once speaking with the woman.

The first time the two of them met face to face was early in my piracy career. This was when we were shipping in the *Idiot Kid*, and we had come to the secret harbour to restock. Usually, Holly would meet us there. But on that particular day, it was Jess who was waiting by the dock, and even from hundreds of yards away I could see the thunderclouds in her face.

My first impulse was to go and hide under a pile of fish guts and have the crew tell Jess that I'd been eaten by land crabs. I'm not ashamed to admit it.

But I was a captain, and a noblewoman, and a fearsome pirate, so I screwed my courage to the whatevering place and tromped down the gangplank. Then I got a close look at Jess, and almost jumped off the end of the pier to escape.

"Where is she?" Jess demanded, without any preamble.

"What?" I said, confused. "You mean Lynn?"

"Don't play games with me, Darren. I want to know what you're doing with that girl."

"What girl?" Lynn asked, popping up in that startling way she had. "You mean, the girl who has almost perfect hearing and doesn't like it when people talk about her behind her back? That girl?"

Jess inspected her through narrowed eyes, and I felt the heat rising to my cheeks. It was a warm day and Lynn wasn't wearing particularly much. And then there was the fact that she was at least ten years younger than both Jess and I.

Jess's lip curled with open distaste. "So. Heroics aren't enough entertainment for you anymore, Darren? You've decided to keep a concubine as well?"

"I . . . uh . . . ah . . ." I looked desperately at Lynn for help, and she squeezed my hand.

"Holly must have told you about me," Lynn said. "So I'm sure she also told you that I'm here because I want to be."

"Well, I know that you're not trying to escape out of a window. That doesn't make the situation all right."

"The situation," Lynn repeated. "What do you mean by 'situation,' exactly?"

"You know perfectly well what I mean."

"Oh, I know what you mean, but what's the sense in talking around it? Let's get the facts on the table. You have a problem with this because I'm Darren's slave."

Jess was speechless for ten whole seconds before she could collect herself. "This is sickening. How can you not understand that?"

"What are you afraid of?" Lynn countered. "This is Darren that we're talking about. She's not going to sell me to corsairs, or clap me in irons. Not unless I beg her to, anyway."

Jess clapped her hands on her ears. "I don't need to hear these details."

"You ask questions, you have to listen to the answers. That's how it works. Jess, look. I know you're worried about me, and that's very kind, in an infuriating sort of way. But you don't even know me. It's sort of premature for you to be judging my choices."

"Your *choices*?"

"You heard me."

Jess breathed: in, out. Tight, controlled. "Maybe we should talk without Darren listening."

"I'm pretty sure we shouldn't."

"All right. Fine." Jess drew herself up, her nostrils flaring, as though she was bracing herself to do something repulsive. "You love Darren. Well, I loved her too, but it didn't blind me to her arrogant streak. She has this idea implanted in her soul that she has to be better than anyone else. It's not enough for her to live as an ordinary human being. She has to work miracles and save nations and have adoring maidens grovelling at her feet in gratitude, or she doesn't see the point. And now here you are, deliberately inflating her ego. You're feeding all the worst parts of her." She sighed. "Maybe Darren didn't force you into this, but she knows better. She shouldn't have—"

"Shouldn't have what?" Lynn interrupted. "Shouldn't have allowed it? What should she have done? Forced me to do something different?"

Jess brushed that away. "You don't get it."

"Correction—you don't get it. And there are parts of it you don't need to get. You wouldn't want what Darren and I have, and that's fine. But you'll have to stop thinking of me as a victim."

"You really don't understand." Jess's voice took on that familiar patronizing note. "You don't even realize how much power you're giving up. Women like us, we so rarely get the chance to make our own decisions, to control our own lives. You have that chance, so why are you throwing it away?

"You want me to make my own decisions?"

"In essence, yes," Jess said. "I suppose."

Now she's in for it, I thought. Lynn's face was still solemn, but her eyes gleamed. I stood back and prepared to enjoy myself.

"Let's try a little experiment, shall we?" Lynn said. Clam shells littered the beach around us. She picked out three of the biggest, crouched, and set them side by side on top of a flat rock. "Darren, I need something small. Your ear cuff, the silver one?"

I pulled it off with a wince and tossed it to her. She slipped it under the middle shell, and shuffled them, sliding them around each other on the smooth stone.

"I know what this is," Jess said, bending over Lynn to watch. "I've seen hucksters do it on side streets."

"Beauty *and* brains," Lynn said approvingly, as she swapped the shells around one last time. "All right. So you know the point of this. Where's the ear cuff? And this is a crucial question, because that's the only piece of jewellery that Darren ever wears."

"It's the only thing I've found that isn't too girly," I pointed out, but neither of them paid the slightest bit of attention.

"Choose a shell," Lynn said.

Jess frowned, looking impatient. "I've told you, I know this game. I know it's a con. There's no point in choosing."

"But that's how the game works. So choose."

Jess glanced at each of the shells in turn. Her eyes flicked up to Lynn's, questioning, but Lynn just smiled pleasantly back at her.

At last, Jess set a finger on the middle shell. Then she looked at Lynn again. "It isn't there, of course."

"Of course not," Lynn agreed, as she plucked the ear cuff out of her sleeve. "Here you go, Darren—no, careful, don't drop it—oh, you're hopeless, let me." She clipped the thing back in place and patted my cheek before she turned her attention back to Jess. "You have choices in a shell game, but all of them are wrong. The thing you're trying to find is up the huckster's sleeve. So you can't choose the right shell—it's impossible."

Jess's voice grew sour. "I *knew* that."

"You *knew* that," Lynn repeated, "and you chose a shell anyway. I gave you three choices, and you knew they were all hopeless, and you knew you could never win that way—but you still played by the rules, because I told you to do it."

Jess was annoyed now. "Well, what could I have done?"

"First thing that comes to mind? You could have knocked me down, sat on my chest, and searched me."

"But . . . why would I . . ."

"To win. That's the point. The rules of the shell game say that you *have* to lose. If you want to stand a chance at winning, you have to change the rules. You have to reject the choices that you're given, and come up with some of your own."

An unbelieving smile was cracking Jess's face. "So what would you have done if I'd asked *you* to choose a shell? Would you have knocked me down and frisked me?"

"Something along those lines. Something that you wouldn't have seen coming. I might have distracted you with a naked dance. Pretended to be a rabid dog? *I* don't know. Whatever I did, it would have made me look insane to an impartial observer—like this fine, upstanding citizen here." She rubbed my arm. "People always seem kind of bizarre when they do something unexpected. But if you don't break out of the rules of the game, then the choices that you make aren't really choices at all."

Lynn stood up. "I'm going to go say hello to Holly. We'll probably get some supper started. This one forgets to eat if somebody doesn't make her."

"I know," Jess said softly.

"I suppose you would, wouldn't you?" Lynn agreed, and it sounded like a peace offering. "We'll call you for dinner in an hour or so. Assuming that I haven't seduced your wife and run away with her by then. I can be *very* convincing when I try."

She headed off into the trees, threading carefully between broken branches in her bare feet, and Jess followed her with her eyes until she was out of sight.

"I don't know if I'm convinced," Jess said slowly. "But I think I like your slave."

And from then on, they were friends.

Like I say—go figure.

WE HUNG A hammock for Jess in a quiet corner of the *Banshee*, and got to our bunk fairly late.

I woke an hour later to a distant rumble of thunder, and then the hissing of rain on the planks overhead. As usual, Lynn's aching arm had been right about the change in the weather. I lay with my head propped up for some time, but in the end, decided not to go up on deck. Regon could handle the *Banshee* on his own, no matter how foul the conditions. And I was drowsy, and warm, and didn't want to move Lynn's head from my shoulder.

But I did take the opportunity to unwind my garrote from her wrist, and stow it back in my own pocket.

The movement made Lynn stir and groan. I ran a finger very gently down her cheek. Lynn had calluses in all the same places that I did, but her face was soft as peach skin.

I thought about my girl living in the castle on the island of Bero. I wondered how long she spent with Gerard before she realized that she would have to break the rules in a very big way if she didn't want to wake up beside that rat bastard every morning for the rest of her life.

"When are you going to tell me the truth, Ariadne?" I asked her.

Her eyes didn't open, but her whole face contorted, as though she was about to cry. "Ar-i-ad-ne," she said haltingly.

She wasn't awake, that I knew. Lynn talked in her sleep, though it usually didn't make any sense. Just the other day she had sat bolt upright, her eyes blank, and announced solemnly, "But I don't *want* to be a sandwich."

Tonight things sounded more promising, so I held still and waited. I didn't know much about the ugly art of interrogation, but I was familiar with the old wakey-wakey technique, which involves snapping a question at someone just as you shake them to consciousness. I didn't plan to go quite that far with Lynn, but if she should happen to let something slip when she wasn't fully awake . . . well, that wouldn't be the worst thing, now, would it?

Lynn's lips kept moving, but for some minutes, only mumbles came out. Then she frowned and snuggled into me, and the words became clearer.

" . . . selling . . . glorp . . . in . . . big buckets . . ." she murmured.

Not exactly what I had been hoping for, but I tried to encourage her. "Sounds good, but where would we get that much glorp in the first place?"

" . . . probably . . . the pink one . . . but I'm not sure . . ."

"Definitely pink. It'll work with your complexion."

" . . . I hate my life."

I straightened up a little. "What did you say?"

Her eyes opened. "I hate my life," she said again.

My throat felt dry. "Why the hell are you saying that?"

No answer. She was staring straight ahead, her eyes glassy.

"Lynn, are you awake?

Still no answer. I passed my hand a few times in front of her eyes. Not a blink, not a twitch.

"Lynn . . . ?"

She was scaring me with that dead-codfish glare. I reached out a hand to grip her shoulder, but to my relief, her eyes slipped shut again, and she let out a long sigh.

Would she wake up if I touched her? I edged closer instead, my face inches from hers. "I hope you're all right," I whispered to her in the dark. "I hope I'm giving you what you need, because I'm just kind of guessing here."

Lynn murmured something.

"What was that?"

She went on murmuring, very fast and so quiet that it sounded like a buzz. Carefully, so carefully, I manoeuvred so that my ear was just above her lips. "IhatemylifeIhatemyhomeIhatemylifeIhatemyhomeIhatemylifeIh atemyhome . . ."

Over and over and over and over. There was no emotion in it—she recited the words so matter-of-factly that she could have been repeating a mathematical formula or a recipe for chicken stew. And yet, somehow, it seemed like the most honest thing I had ever heard her say.

I lay down beside her again, biting my lip. "Sleep," I told her uncomprehending face. "Sleep. It'll get better, as soon as you tell me the truth."

CHAPTER FIVE

I SLEPT BADLY after that, which made me crabby the next morning. Lynn herself seemed fine as we ate breakfast in our cabin, chatting breezily while I pushed my porridge around and around the bowl. She probably noticed my black mood, but if so, she didn't mention it. She talked about the news that Jess had brought us, and Kilroy's aching hip, and the watch schedule for the next seven days. Then she grimaced, as if remembering something, and tugged at one of the longer locks of her hair.

"I'm going to need it cut again soon," she said.

I grunted over the top of my cider cup. "You don't need to keep it *that* short. You're not a convict."

"We've been over this a million times. I keep it short because I like it that way."

"Whatever. I still don't understand it."

I expected her to snap at me, and truth be told, I kind of wanted her to. But instead, she glanced at the wall, her expression one of fierce concentration.

"Let's say," she began slowly, "let's say that hypothetically—I mean purely, totally hypothetically—let's say that once upon a time, someone *made* you wear your hair long. Wouldn't you want to cut it as soon as you got the chance?"

I pictured Lynn—Ariadne—in full court dress, with billowing skirts and hair that hung past her waist. I didn't like the image as much as I would have expected. It didn't seem like her, somehow.

"I guess," I hedged. "Depends who made me wear it long before."

What I had in mind was an overprotective father who wanted his only daughter to look like a girl. But that didn't seem to be it, judging from the way that she was fidgeting.

"Well, let's say," Lynn began again, "and this is all completely hypothetical, remember . . . let's say it was someone who liked to grab it."

"Grab what?"

"Your hair. My hair. Long hair. Whatever."

I can't be sure, but I think I gawked. "Who used to grab you by your hair?"

She held her hands up defensively. "We're talking hypothetically, remember? Purely hypothetically. You do know the meaning of the word, right?"

"Of course," I said haughtily, hoping that she wasn't about to ask me to define it.

"Hypothetically. As in, 'Let's say, hypothetically, that I was raised by baboons.'"

I was completely lost. "What does this have to do with your hair?"

She clutched her head and made a strangled noise. "*If,* and I say *if,* someone used to drag you around by the hair . . ."

"Then I guess maybe I'd wear my hair short, yeah."

"There. You see? That's all I was looking for."

She took a fierce swig from her cider cup, and then fiddled with the hem of her tunic, not looking me in the face. Bewildered, I tried to sort through what she had said. If someone used to drag Lynn around—hypothetical, my arse—then the culprit was probably Gerard. Not a nice idea, but not so terribly surprising, from what I knew of the man. Nothing to be ashamed of, either, so why couldn't she admit it out loud?

I set my own cup down with a clink. It was time.

"Lynn," I said. "Tell me your name."

She raised her head, and then an eyebrow. "It's Lynn. If you don't know that by now, then there isn't much hope for you."

"I mean, your real name."

"Also Lynn."

I hissed, frustrated. "Your birth name, then."

Lynn set down her empty bowl, placed her empty cup in it, rested her elbows on her knees and her chin in her hands, and said two words, slowly and distinctly. "Stop it."

"What?"

"I said, 'stop it,' and I said it very clearly. Hopefully, this is where you give in and back off. You never used to snoop. I liked it better that way."

"It's been more than a year. I've done my best, but I'm sick of hints and hypotheticals. Let's get it over with."

She waved an impatient hand. "Mistress—"

"Don't call me that when we're arguing."

"Dickhead, then. Why are you so obsessed with my past? Everybody has one, and mine is no more interesting than Corto's or Regon's. You know that Regon had a twin brother who died of five-day fever when they were nine?"

"Yes," I lied sullenly.

"Regon had the fever too. It went straight to his balls. He can get it up, with some planning and some effort, but he can't get a girl pregnant. Now *that's* a story. Much more interesting than anything you'll hear from me."

It was new information, and it distracted me for a second. So that was why women fought over Regon at every brothel. But I shook my head and refocused. "Stop changing the subject. I want to know who you are."

She sighed. "I'm *yours,* you dozy bint. Does anything else have to matter?"

"Yes, actually, it does. Because it matters to you. Don't try to deny it. And I can't help you to cope with whatever happened until I have the whole story. And helping you with it is my job. So you're going to tell me, Lynn. Right now."

Up until then, she had been annoyed, nothing more. At that point, her face shut down, like a door slamming shut.

"You don't tell me what to do," she said quietly.

"I just asked—"

"You didn't ask, you demanded. And you don't do that. You have no right."

"Excuse me?" I asked, getting ruffled. "You're the one who insists on dressing like a slave and acting like a concubine. I didn't ask you to call me 'Mistress' or brand my damn mark into your arm."

"Exactly. You didn't ask. *I* decided, Darren—*me*. And if I want you to tell me what to do, then I'll bloody well tell you what I want you to tell me to do."

I flung up my hands in despair. "Argh!"

"Oh, poor baby. Does it give you a rash when I think for myself?" She stalked over to the sea chest and pulled out a fistful of maps with shaking hands. "Get out of here already. It's past four bells, and I've got better things to do than listen to you sulk."

JESS'S FACE HAD a look of faint disbelief.

"Wait, hang on, let me get this straight," she said. "Lynn accused you of sulking . . ."

"Yes."

"And that made you mad . . ."

"Yes."

"So you decided to come up on deck and sulk some more?"

Grumpily, I tossed a few biscuit crumbs over the side. The water swirled as fish snapped them up. "I wouldn't put it that way."

"No, you *wouldn't,* would you?"

It was three hours since our spat, and Lynn still hadn't emerged from the cabin. I had spent the time lurking around the rest of the ship, inspecting things that didn't need inspecting and yelling at sailors that didn't need to be yelled at. At last, Regon told me in the nicest possible way that I was being a horse's ass and should take a time out. Which was why I was standing by the gunwale throwing biscuit crumbs to fish and letting my old girlfriend lecture me.

All things considered, I've had better afternoons.

"I think she's made it perfectly clear that she'll tell you about herself when she's ready. Why can't you just wait?"

"Because it's getting ridiculous. I already know everything that she's going to say, more or less. What's she waiting for? Why can't she just trust me? Haven't I earned that much by now?"

Jess rolled her eyes and hugged her cloak more tightly around herself. There was a chill in the wind. "Trust can be earned, Darren, but it can't be owed. You're just making things worse by demanding it."

I tossed the rest of the biscuit over the side, more violently than necessary. Why did everyone in my life treat me like a moron or a child? I wanted to stomp away from Jess, but there's only so much stomping away that you can do on the deck of a ship, and I would lose the few shreds of dignity I still possessed if Jess and I ended up chasing each other around and around the mast.

"I'm not asking for much here," I said through clenched teeth. "She doesn't have to tell me her life story. All she has to do is to admit that she's Ariadne of Bain."

"Has it occurred to you," she said slowly, "you inestimably stupid person, that maybe Lynn *isn't* Ariadne?"

"All the evidence supports it—"

"No, Darren." She freed a hand from her cloak so that she could tap my chest in emphasis. "You only *see* the evidence that supports it. Everything else, you ignore."

I caught the poking finger and pushed it away from me. "What do you mean, everything else?"

"Her *scars*, for one thing."

You can't live on board ship and be shy about your body. Everyone who sailed with me had seen the tracery of white marks on Lynn's skin, mainly on her back and thighs and belly. Nobody on board paid much attention to them, probably because just about all my sailors were patterned the same way.

I shrugged. "What about her scars? They're rope burns, old cuts, that kind of thing. I have them too. All sailors do."

"Ariadne of Bain is not a sailor. She's an only child, remember?"

This was true. Since Ariadne was her father's heir, she would have spent her youth at home, studying diplomacy and economics and fiscal procedure and law, sitting on a pile of cushions with a plate of sweet-meats at her elbow. Unlike me, she hadn't been shoved out to work on the merchant boats as soon as she turned fourteen. Lucky dog. "So she got the scars after she ran away. Gods know how long she was in that fishing town. She must have picked them up there, maybe from working on the skiffs. Or—aw hell, maybe it was her husband . . ."

At that, Jess was forced to take a couple of deep breaths. "Have you *looked* at those scars?"

"I've seen them, of course. I don't hold a candle up to them and ogle inquisitively. Why would I want to do that?"

"To *learn* something, you clot. The lines of those scars are broken up."

"So?"

"So? *So?* So she got them when she was still growing. Someone beat the holy hell out of her when she was a kid. How does that fit in with your precious theory?"

"Huh," I said, and then, "Well, there must be a way to explain that."

Jess threw up her hands. "Why? *Why* does there have to be a way to explain that? Because Darren of fucking Torasan likes the idea that her lover is royalty, so she won't bloody well let it go. Drop the theory and start from the facts. She's badly scarred. She's scrawny—probably didn't get enough to eat when she was little. She's a schemer and a survivor, and has nightmares, and she pushes you around unmercifully, because she's scared numb at the thought of someone else controlling her. Are you starting to get a picture here?"

Being told off makes me surly. I just grunted, though my stomach was beginning to sour.

"She's no pampered little princess, Darren. Someone messed with her. I don't know how or who or when or why, but *that* much is obvious. And she's just as much a commoner as I am. You think a noblewoman knows how to take a wine stain out of a shirt? You think a noblewoman would be happy to spend her life blacking your boots and gutting your fish? I'm sorry if all this offends your aristocratic tastes, but—"

"Now *that's* not fair," I snapped. "I never thought less of you because you were a peasant. I didn't give a damn!"

"You forgave me for it. I could see you making a physical effort to forgive me for it, every time I wiped my mouth on my sleeve or made garlic soup for supper. Now you've got a girl you like, you've convinced yourself that she's a blueblood like you, and your inner snob quivers ecstatically every time you look at her and think, *Ariadne.*"

"It has nothing to do with what I want," I floundered. "It's about what I know. Lynn didn't learn to read in the village where I found her, Jess. The other people who lived there had no idea that there was such a thing as writing. Or soap. Gods on high, I can still *smell* the place."

"Watch it, Darren," Jess warned me, "just watch it. Take a breath and pause before you say something that you'll regret later. I was chatting with Lynn last night . . ."

"Were you?" I asked grimly. "Sounds cosy."

"Stop it, you hopeless letch. We all know I'm not her type. The point is, I asked her whether she missed anything about home."

I was bristling. "I'm sure she does. That village was terribly scenic. The piles of rotting whitebait; the dung-filled hovels; the hordes of raiders, their armour glinting faintly in the summer sun . . ."

"If you don't shut up, I'm going to hurt you. Darren, she said that she misses her sister."

Usually, when someone gives me surprising news, I pretend that I already knew. But this particular revelation shocked me so much that I forgot to do any pretending. "But . . . Ariadne doesn't have any siblings."

"Finally sinking in, is it?"

It took a while. "Lynn has a sister."

"Yes, Darren."

A small black seabird skimmed the surface of the ocean nearby—a storm petrel, I registered absently. Its cry seemed very loud.

I ran my tongue along my teeth. "Her sister . . . her sister wasn't one of the kids that we picked up in her village, was it? None of them looked anything like her."

"I asked her about that. She said no, her sister was somewhere else, and then she clammed up. So I didn't push it."

I snorted. "Well, that was bloody inconsiderate of you, wasn't it? It's going to take me forever to dig the truth out of her now."

"She was crying when she told me," Jess said, in a frosty tone. "So I don't think this is really the time to dig."

"She never cries in front of me," I muttered, parenthetically, and then my train of thought veered off in a new direction. "Hang on. Did you imply back there that Lynn is *your* type?"

Jess's expression, at that second, suggested that she was about to attack me with her bare hands, but instead she just stalked away aft, making strangled noises. By the time she got back, she was more or less under control.

"Your brain," she informed me, "is composed entirely of soft unripened cheese. So it's in a spirit of charity that I tell you this. Every single person in Lynn's village got killed or abducted by armed thugs— every last one of them, except for Lynn and the handful you rescued along with her. And we both know what happens to young women who get taken by soldiers. If Lynn's sister was in that village, then she's probably a camp whore, *if* she's still alive."

I was going limp. "But if that's true, then why hasn't Lynn said anything to me? Maybe I can find her, maybe I can help. Besides, why is Lynn talking about this to you and not to me?

"Because you're so in love with your own stupid fantasy about who Lynn is and where she comes from. Do you think you're being subtle about that? It practically radiates out of you. Lynn knows damn well that you're not ready for the truth. You prefer your own answers."

My brain was sparking all over with frustration. "Well, if you're so in tune with Lynn's emotions, why don't you ask her? Just ask her flat out whether she's Ariadne of Bain."

Jess's grey eyes burned into mine. "I did."

Ten seconds of silence, then I found my voice. "And what did she say?"

Jess gave a tiny shrug. "She said, 'No.'"

LYNN DIDN'T COOK that night. The new casks of salt beef turned out to be maggot-ridden, so the men chewed cold biscuit and looked gloomy. To make it up to them, I had a barrel of ale hauled up to the deck. Before long, they were staggering about with drink-misted eyes, restored to grinning, back-slapping cheer. It wasn't particularly good for ship's discipline or for my mood, but I'll take drunken sailors over mutinous sailors most days. To keep casualties to a minimum, I had a lantern lit, and seated myself on a crate by the helm to keep a watchful eye on the festivities.

As I watched, I fretted. Should I tell Lynn that I knew about her sister? Offer to go looking for her? But if that was what Lynn wanted, surely she would have said something earlier. No, the best approach was probably for me to throw myself on Lynn's mercy and swear up and down that I wouldn't ask more questions for the next million years. Maybe I'd have to buy her some presents as well. I wondered if peasant girls liked getting flowers.

I was so deep in thought that I didn't see Lynn approaching until she plonked herself on my lap.

"Rejoice, O Mistress," she said, settling herself comfortably. "For I am over it. Come ye out of the doghouse, and bask in the sunshine of my smile."

I perked up at once. "You're not mad?"

"I needed to cool down, but it's fine, we're good. I'm still breaking you of a few bad habits. It's a work in progress."

She gave me a lopsided grin as she snaked an arm around my shoulders. With that touch, the tension all floated out of me in a big puffy cloud, and I smiled back.

"I'm sorry," I said. "I know I was being an ass. I won't try to pump you for information again. Not until you're ready."

"Yeah, she said that you wouldn't."

"She?"

"Jess put in a good word for you. She said that you take a while to learn things, but once you do, you don't forget them."

I raised my eyebrows. "Like a horse?"

"Like a parrot," she suggested.

"Like a pirate queen."

"Now you've got it."

LYNN REFUSED TO budge from my lap, and my legs were asleep before ten minutes had passed, but I still remember that as a perfect evening.

The largest cask of ale I had bought at the Freemarket turned out to taste a little better than goat piss, for a change, and we celebrated by drinking just about all of it. Somewhere halfway down the cask, people got to dancing, and if you haven't seen a drunken pirate do a staggering jig, then you've missed something in life. Jess didn't get into the action, but she sat near the mast, flickers of lantern light on her hair, and her eyes warm with amusement and interest. Sometimes Lynn talked, and sometimes she drank, and sometimes she sang, loudly and tunelessly. But whatever she was doing, she kept her right hand on me, rubbing her thumb back and forth against my shoulder, or drawing small circles on the skin of my back. It was like an unspoken promise that the next thing to happen would be even better than the last.

Times like that never last, do they?

CHAPTER SIX

THERE WAS NO warning. Lynn had been telling a fairly shocking limerick about a walrus in a brothel, with great gusto and accompanying hand gestures. All at once, she glanced up, and her body froze. If you think of a doe grazing, who suddenly snaps to high alert when a noise sounds nearby, then you'll have the right idea. I had seen her do this before, and had learned not to question her instincts. Motionless, I waited.

Her head tilted ever so slightly as she listened to something that only she could hear. Then she reached above her head, flicked open the door of the lantern, and pinched out the flame.

Twenty different conversations, bawdy jokes, and peals of laughter went out along with the light. Wind whispered, a board creaked underfoot. Lynn's voice sounded cool and calm in the darkness. "Weigh anchor, set the sails. *Quietly.* If anyone makes unnecessary noise, then my mistress will stuff your own feet down your throat."

I scowled around, to let the crew know that I would do just exactly that, but then realized that no one could see me in the moonless night. Anyway, there was no need. Regon and Latoya were swiftly prodding the sailors into place. We had been moored in the shallows off a coral atoll; now the crew prepared us to get back underway. Ropes rustled as men sprang up the rigging, and then came the rattle of anchor chain. Lynn, meanwhile, had peeled herself off my lap and hurried to the *Banshee*'s starboard side.

I joined her there. "What is it?" I hissed.

Instead of answering, she took my index finger and used it to trace a patch along the horizon. A dark patch, a ship-shaped shadow where the stars were blotted out. There was no way to see detail, but I could gauge the size roughly, and it was too big to be anything but a war galley. I swore under my breath. "How did you know it was there?"

She angled her head so she could speak in a whisper, directly into my ear. "There are gull's nests on the atoll. The ship frightened some of the birds into taking wing."

"Why the hell are they running without lights?"

"Because they like a challenge? Because their eyes are sensitive? Or because they want to sneak up on us and stick pointy things in our flesh."

"Bugger it. Well, at least we got some warning. All we can do now is wait to see if they follow us."

THEY FOLLOWED US.

It was the rattle of the anchor chain that gave us away. The clink of iron on iron spooked a flock of the gulls on the atoll, sending them shrieking and wailing into the night sky. The other ship was in motion before I had time to curse properly, and we settled down to a grim and silent race.

Night sailing is not a thing to be undertaken by the faint of heart. It feels a lot like riding blindfold on a galloping horse. I knew the area well and my mate Regon knew it better, but knowledge can only take you so far in the dark. Sheer dumb luck is more important, and sheer dumb luck is never something you can depend on.

Again and again, I lost sight of our pursuer and felt a great bound of hope—but each time Lynn shook her head. Shortly afterward, I would see the telltale silhouette against the starry sky, and every time, it was a little closer to us than it had been before.

Regon and I left Latoya in charge on deck while we made a hasty trip into the captain's cabin to consult a chart by a tiny candle flame.

"There," Regon said, his voice a hoarse whisper, jabbing at the map. "I'm fair-to-middling sure that if we bear west, we'll reach Jinak Isle before dawn. We'll thread the needle up the strait between Jinak and the barrier keys. Not one ship in a thousand knows that channel. If they manage to follow us through there, then I'll shake their helmsman's hand, I will."

"If you get us up that strait in the dark, then I won't bother with shaking your hand. I'll take you to the mainland, drop you off at Madame Lydia's, and put six bars of silver on deposit. You won't put on trousers for a week. Go take the helm and make magic happen."

If night sailing is like riding a galloping horse blindfolded, then threading through the Jinak channel at night is like getting a horse to balance tiptoe on the head of a pin. Still, I think my man Regon could have done it. Regon had been born shipside (his mother's pains began while she was hauling up a shrimp net) and he learned to sail before he learned to walk. When he did learn to walk, it was only so he could get more easily from one side of the boat to the other. To Regon, a ship was a living being, with nerves and a pulse and breath, and his senses reached out along the wood and canvas as if he could hear and see through them as well as with his own body. Yes, I think that Regon would have gotten us up the channel. I wish to every god in the deep that he'd gotten the chance to try.

Three hours before sunrise, and leagues away from Jirak, the wind began to die. We crowded on more sail, but I could feel the *Banshee* slowing, minute by minute and hour by hour, until she was all but crawling through the water.

Lynn was the one who ordered half the men below to sleep. I doubt I would have thought of it on my own. She herself refused to go down so of course, I couldn't either. When I was in my teens, it barely bothered me to stand an all-night watch, with a full day of work before and after, but these things change as you get older. By dawn, I was moving at a fraction of my normal speed and slurring my speech like a boozer after a week-long spree. Lynn still looked fairly fresh and whole, though, every so often, her right eyelid twitched.

By now, we could see the pursuing vessel. It was a war galley, fresh off the shipbuilder's stocks, planks still gold with varnish. The grappling hooks, with their freshly-sharpened barbs, hung like claws along the galley's sides, ready for use. The figurehead was—

"That's the *Silver Hind,*" I told Lynn, recognizing the deer's head. "I saw it at the Freemarket. Damn it, we never should have anchored. The bastards followed us."

"Not good," Lynn murmured. "Ten different kinds of not good."

At that moment, there was a *flap—flap—flap* above us, the tell-tale sign of a loose sail. The red canvas flopped against the mast in limp folds, heavy and empty.

The wind had died completely.

"Eleven," Lynn amended.

THE CAPTAIN'S CABIN, barely big enough for two, was cramped as a sack of rats when all of us had crowded inside. Spinner, Regon, and Jess sat side by side on the bunk. Latoya stood in the doorway, stooped because the ceiling wasn't high enough to let her stand erect. Her expression promised a dreadful fate to anyone who dared suggest that she sit on the floor. Lynn perched on the closed lid of my sea chest. All that left just enough room for me to pace two steps back and forth, up and down the cabin.

"All right," I said, to open the session. "Suggestions."

Regon spoke first, as always. "We sit tight and wait for the calm to end. Best we can do, captain, and you know it. The *Banshee*'ll run away from those bastards under a fair wind."

"We were running under a fair wind half the night," I said, pacing. "The *Hind* is a new ship. Smooth planks. We can't race her."

"Wait for help, then. The *Badger* and the *Sod Off* will be somewhere nearby, working their way north from the Freemarket. They could arrive here any time."

"Not in a calm. Besides, for all we know, the *Hind* is waiting for reinforcements too. They followed us, remember. They *wanted* to take on the pirate queen. If they've got enough sense to pour piss out of a boot, they came with some kind of plan for taking me down. Spinner, your turn."

He shrugged. "Spike and scuttle?"

By this, he meant a tricky, near-suicidal manoeuvre that works about once a decade. To pull a spike and scuttle, you pick out one or two of the most insane of your sailors. They swim or row to the enemy ship, armed with a saw and a drill, and try to bore holes in the keel. The idea is to start a slow leak which will eventually sink the ship. Almost always, the enemy sailors realize what's going on before long and smash the skulls of your volunteers by hurling down the anchor at them.

I shook my head impatiently. "They'll be on the watch for something like that. Not like they have anything else to do. Latoya."

My bosun cracked her knuckles. "Have to fight them sooner or later. Let's get it done. Lower the longboats, board them, and finish it."

"There's an appealing simplicity to that," I admitted. "But they've got more troops. The *Hind* could ship anywhere up to seventy men, and we're under strength from the fight with Tyco. How many do we have now? Fifty?"

"Forty-six, but you and I are two of them," Latoya pointed out. "I can handle fifteen of theirs. You can handle five."

I wasn't at all sure of that myself, and was relieved when Lynn's head snapped up.

"Absolutely not," she said. "We don't have a single advantage here. We know nothing about the enemy, we can't surprise them, and we can't manoeuvre. If we swarm onto the *Hind* and start hacking and slashing, half of us are going to die, whether or not we win. I won't accept odds like that."

Privately, I agreed, though I didn't know whether we had a choice. "Lynn, it'll make me very happy if you say you have a plan."

"Buy him off," she said simply. "That ship isn't flying colours, so whoever's in charge, it's probably another damn bounty hunter. He's being paid to go after the *Banshee,* so make him a counter offer. Give him a way to get paid without risking his hide."

"That makes us look weak," Latoya objected. "He'll just attack."

"Not if the offer's good enough. We can afford it. Anything else is too risky."

I mulled the idea over. It wasn't quite in keeping with the pirate queen's fearsome reputation. But there are times when staying alive just has to take priority.

Jess cleared her throat. "For what it's worth, I would agree."

Jess's opinion was, I decided, worth a lot. In spite of everything. So that clinched it. "Fine. Lynn, talk to Corto, find out what we have aboard, fill a chest with shiny stuff. Regon, the parley flag. And Latoya, don't sulk. Chances are good that you'll still get to kill something later on."

IT TOOK HALF an hour of shouting and flag flapping to get the captain of the *Silver Hind* to agree to a parley. It took the better part of four hours to decide where it would happen.

I tried to cut the discussion short by offering to go to the *Hind* myself. Lynn responded with a flat "no," which was obviously meant to cover any and all noble, self-sacrificing suggestions that I might make during the course of the day.

"We can't make it that easy for them," was how Lynn put it. Now, it's against all the laws of the sea to murder an envoy during a parley—and those laws may be unwritten and unspoken, but they're enforced viciously by the people who know them. Still, as Lynn patiently reminded me, I was an exile, a person outside the law's protection. Any Kilan had the right to kill me on sight if we met outside a truce zone. So it would not be altogether brilliant for me to swagger onto an enemy ship unarmed and alone. I couldn't fault Lynn's logic, but I could grumble and I did. She patted my cheek and told me not to be a brat.

Finally, after a long, sweaty time of waiting, a longboat began to inch over from the *Hind.*

During the wait, Corto had prepared the deck for visitors. He'd stacked biscuit boxes into a kind of lounge shape, dragged a bolt of crimson cloth up from the hold, and draped it over the boxes to form a makeshift throne. I eyed it askance. Sitting on the thing, I felt, would make me look like twenty kinds of twat, but what the hell. It wouldn't be the first time that I'd humiliated myself in order to feed the legend of the pirate queen. It wouldn't be the last.

Unless this thing went south and the men of the *Hind* cut us all to pieces, I thought morbidly. In that case, it would be the last.

Spinner bustled around the deck, setting goblets ready on an upturned barrel, but I roused myself from my funk when he produced a bottle of wine. "Not that stuff. That's the foul kind that tastes of pine juice. Go get some of the red. Where's Lynn?"

"She went below," he told me, as he dusted the goblets fussily with his sleeve. "Said she needed to change."

"Thank the gods," I muttered fervently. I was edgy about Lynn being around during the parley, but keeping her out of the way was not an option. I needed her to read faces and intentions. Still, I didn't want her noticed, and Lynn's usual taste in clothing—namely, not a lot of it—was noticeable, to say the least. It was reassuring to know that for this occasion, she would be in the same drab woollens as the rest of my crew, showing only a few square inches of skin.

But she hadn't resurfaced by the time that a longboat bumped against the side, and seven men from the *Hind* pulled themselves on deck.

The sight of them made my mouth go dry, if you want to know the truth. In the ancient game of intimidation, there's one thing that matters more than anything else, and that's confidence, self-assurance. It doesn't matter how strong you actually are. If you're going in, go in with a swagger and that may be enough to end the fight. Birds know this, with their colours and plumage; lizards and moths know it, and above all, Lynn did. Even I know it, and it's saved my life more times that I can count.

But I'm not immune to the trick just because I understand it. They looked *so* bloody confident.

The man in the middle was obviously in charge, three sailors flanking him on either side. Dressed simply, in black jerkin and high boots, he wore no obvious weapon. Yet he didn't bother to glance around the *Banshee's* deck, where my heavily-armed crew stood or sat in silent clumps. He strolled past them as if they were a bed of petunias. Without waiting to be asked, he seated himself on a box in front of my throne.

"Lady Darren, formerly of the House of Torasan," he said by way of greeting. "You *have* been busy."

I inclined my head briefly. "Your name?"

He smiled. "Timor," he said—and nothing else.

In Kila, when you're asked your name, you're expected to give your lineage or rank or allegiance as well. It's a soft kind of snub to do otherwise. It's also a way to deny your questioner any useful information. Timor's face and clothes gave no sign of what he was—noble or merchant, hired man or mercenary. I couldn't remember a lord named "Timor" but there are so many of us that it's hard to keep track.

I didn't rise to the insult. After all, Lynn had been insulting me that way for over a year. Instead, I leaned back in my ridiculous throne, folded my hands, and waited.

As I had hoped, Timor grew impatient after a few moments of silence. "Well? You were the one who suggested this. Don't you have something you want to discuss?"

"Since you ask so politely, I do," I said. "I want to discuss how we can stop this situation from erupting into stupidity."

He looked politely baffled. "I can't think what you mean, Lady Darren.

Oh. I beg your pardon, I should be saying 'Your Majesty.' You're a queen these days, I hear."

Slimy bastard. "If you know my name, you should also know that I don't like men who try to play games with me. If you want to talk, talk straight. Otherwise, get the hell off my ship, and later on, we'll meet in a less friendly setting."

He smiled wide, as if he were immensely pleased. "You can end this parley any moment you choose, my lady. But of course, we both realize that you would regret that decision more than I would."

It was tense, and growing tenser. With six of his crewmen towering around him, Timor looked calm and assured, utterly at his ease. I had attendants of my own—Regon stood at my right hand, Spinner at my left, and behind me loomed Latoya, her massive shadow leaving my whole body in the shade. Jess lurked amidships, her face grave and stony with concentration. But the person I chiefly needed was still nowhere to be seen. Where the buggering fuck was Lynn?

I desperately wanted to call a time out and go hunt for her. But I quashed the longing and pressed ahead. "Let's make this simple. Someone, I don't care who, hired you to hunt me down."

"More or less," Timor admitted, with another polite smile.

"Well, whoever it was, surely he gave you the catalogue." Ever so slightly, I adjusted my weight in the throne, letting sunlight glint along my cutlass blade. "Mara of Namor, Gorax the Savage, the hillmen of the eastern islands, the Tawran Beast, Tyco Gorgionson, to name a few. All people who underestimated me. All dead, or wishing very fervently that they were. Do you want to be added to that list?"

"Your concern for my safety is very touching," Timor said. "But I don't think you have much to worry about."

"I'm offering to make this easy. Five hundred crowns—"

He gave a startled laugh.

"Five hundred crowns, if you walk away," I finished. "Not what your employer is offering you, I'm sure—"

"Nowhere close," he said, amused. "I don't think that you know what you're worth on the open market, my lady. Even if your ship's hold was stuffed full of ivory and spices, you'd still be the most valuable thing aboard." He rose. "I've enjoyed our conversation, my lady, and I'll enjoy meeting you again later, I'm sure."

He turned to go, and his sailors turned with him. Spinner gave me a frantic, desperate look, and I stared stonily back until he got the message. Scoffing at an offer, feigning disinterest, is what bargaining is all about. Timor's amusement at the bribe could easily be an act, put on to drag a higher price from me. It's what I would have done in the same situation.

I waited until Timor had his hands on the rail, ready to pull himself over, and then I commented, "I might go as high as six hundred."

Timor looked over his shoulder; his grin was cheery. "You really don't understand how much I stand to earn here, do you?"

I gnawed the inside of my own cheek. Maybe I really didn't.

"WATCH YOURSELF, GIRL!"

Something had bumped against Timor just as he was about to swing onto the rope ladder. He caught himself before he fell, looked around wildly, and grabbed the culprit.

I rose halfway out of my throne. Timor was clutching Lynn's upper arm, so hard that she almost dropped the wine jug she was carrying. But that wasn't why my eyes were bugging out. Lynn had gone below to change her clothes. That was what Spinner had said, and that was true. She was now dressed—if you could call it that—in a piece of white linen barely bigger than a handkerchief. It was caught at her shoulders with two brass buttons, and belted with a girdle of white rope. A coppery pattern was stitched along the bottom hem, and a thin copper bracelet encircled each of her wrists.

That was all. But that was enough. The linen was thin as a sigh, almost sheer. The merest breath of wind set it floating. It whispered. It clung. It did other things which made it hard for me to breathe. Timor stared, and he just kept staring.

"Watch yourself," he repeated, more gently this time.

"Forgive me, lord," Lynn answered. "Will you take a cup of wine before you go?"

He hesitated no more than a second, and then he followed her. A part of me couldn't blame him. But that part of me was overpowered by the much greater part of me which now wanted to pound him into the deck until nothing was left but stains and bloody rags.

Lynn poured, deftly and silently, and handed Timor his cup of wine. Her arms were bare, like most of the rest of her, exposing her tattoo, the storm-petrel. Timor's eyes flicked to it, and for some reason, that made me seethe. I gripped the hilt of my cutlass so tightly that the ridges cut into my palm. It seemed a long time before Lynn was at my side, pouring my own drink.

"And what in hell do you think you're doing?" I said through gritted teeth.

"Not now," she whispered. "Trust me."

She bowed her head, ceremoniously, as she passed the wine to me, and I gave a little ceremonial wave in reply, hoping that would end it. Maybe,

I thought, she would head back to the cabin now and change her clothes again . . .

I should have known better. As soon as Lynn's hands were free, she turned in Timor's direction. Then, without the least trace of hesitation or shame, she knelt down at the foot of my throne.

It was pure shock, I think, that kept me from jumping up and yelping. That, and the fact that I was embroiled in a tremendously tense negotiation, and jumping up and yelping would have been about as appropriate as farting during an execution. But I had to fake a coughing fit to give myself a few spare seconds.

"I hope you're not ill, Lady Darren," Timor said, in his oily tone. "It can't have been the drink. It's very fine."

This with his eyes fixed somewhere between Lynn's collarbone and her belt. Every last drop of blood in my veins began to steam. I had to end this fast or I really would kill the man.

"Six hundred and fifty crowns," I said flatly. "In milled coins, full weight. I won't go higher. You can take it, or you can lose half your crew, and maybe your head, trying for more."

I gestured with my right hand as I said this. It was supposed to be a punchy, aggressive type of thing, but my fingers brushed against something soft. Lynn's hair. Had she put her head in the way? I was about to pull back my hand, embarrassed, but Timor's sharp eyes were there, all over us. I let my hand rest where it was, cupping the top of Lynn's blonde head.

"Six hundred and fifty," Timor repeated.

"Six hundred and fifty that you don't have to bleed for. Be sure to factor that part in." I took a furious gulp of wine with my free hand. "Has anyone ever told you what I do to the men I defeat? Because it's gripping. I intend to write a book."

Lynn's head dipped forwards, then tilted to the side. It made my hand slip down past her hair to her neck, as though I was—oh gods, it looked like I was stroking her. As if that wasn't bad enough, Lynn let out a little sigh as she pressed back against my hand. Exactly like an adoring pet. Red-faced, smouldering, I swigged more wine.

"Six . . . hundred . . . and . . . fifty," Timor said again, and it was clear that he was having trouble concentrating on the number. "It still seems a little inadequate, Lady Darren."

That was it. I was tired of this stupid dance. I uncrossed my heels, ready to surge to my feet and throw the man headlong from my ship, parley be damned . . .

"Mistress," Lynn said, her eyes still downcast. "May I speak?"

I hesitated for three full seconds. Her hand found its way back to my ankle and squeezed hard. *Trust me.*

"Very well, girl," I said gruffly. Oh, but I would make her pay for this later.

Lynn raised her head and sat up on her heels, looking Timor full in the face. "I will be delivering the gold on behalf of my mistress, lord. If you feel that the payment isn't enough, we can discuss it then." She paused delicately. "In depth. And I'm sure I can find a way to make up the shortage."

My heart clenched into a fist-sized ball of stone.

"Ahhhhh," Timor said, leaning back. "Ah."

His smile this time was less mocking, more knowing. I bit my lips to keep myself from lunging for his throat.

"I have to admit," he said gravely, "this gets more tempting by the minute."

No. *No.* Absolutely not. I rose, and Timor, startled, did likewise. Lynn stayed where she was, kneeling on the deck between us.

"You're a little too hasty," Timor warned me. "I haven't agreed yet."

And you won't get a chance to agree, you slimy son of a so-and-so. I opened my mouth to tell him exactly where he could go and exactly what he could do when he got there, but Lynn's hand touched my ankle again. It was almost apologetic, this time. *Trust me.*

The air hung heavy around me, waiting.

"Seven hundred," I whispered.

Timor nodded. "Done."

CHAPTER SEVEN

MY CREW WAS stone silent after Timor's longboat pulled away. Lynn rose to her feet and headed below without looking at anybody. I licked my dry lips and headed after her.

When I reached our cabin, she had the sea chest open and was rooting around inside. Maybe she was looking for something. Maybe she just didn't want to face me.

I bolted the door and rubbed my hands together. "All right. What's the plan?"

She glanced back briefly over her shoulder and returned her attention to the contents of the chest. "I'm going to go over there with the money."

"Then what?"

"Then I'll come back."

"And in between?" I prodded. "You had me worried for a second there—but you're not planning to sleep with that bastard. I know you better than that."

She turned around, slim and pale in her skimpy tunic and copper jewellery. "Do you?"

There was no answer to that, really. The silence in the cabin stretched and stretched.

"Why?" I managed to say at last. It came out a lot louder and harsher than I had intended. "Why would you do that? Do you think you're some kind of whore? Do you think that I think of you that way?"

Lynn reflexively pulled off her bracelets, then pulled them back on. "I know damn well I'm not, and I know damn well you don't."

"Then *why*? Why did you even start with the sex-kitten act? I had things under control."

"He was bored, and you were losing him," Lynn said flatly. "That's not control. We had to sweeten the deal."

"That doesn't mean *you* have to be the sweetener. Hell, we could have offered him Latoya!"

"Men don't really go for Latoya."

"Spinner, then!"

She stared, aghast. "You want Spinner to go through this?"

"Better him than you."

"How the fuck is that better? Darren, if this has to happen, why *shouldn't* it be me?"

"Because—" I began without thinking, then stopped myself.

"Because I'm yours," Lynn said, finishing the thought. "But that's not a good enough reason. Everyone on this ship is a person. Nobody deserves this."

My brain was spinning with that familiar reckless heat. "So let *me* do it."

Lynn sorted slowly through the contents of the sea-chest: linen shirts, kerchiefs, stockings. "You can't, Darren. Timor doesn't want you. And don't get ruffled—that's not your fault. I'm little and I look helpless and that's what he's interested in. It's pretty obvious. You saw the way he was staring."

To my horror, I realized that tears were pricking the corners of my eyes. "Lynn, you can't possibly want to do this."

She slammed the lid of the chest shut. "Of course I don't."

"Then don't. We'll find another way. We'll take our chances in a hack-and-slash. Anything's better than delivering you to that bastard *gift wrapped*."

"Anything's better?" she repeated in disbelief. "How do you figure? Every time we attack a ship, I know that you could come back missing a couple of limbs. You think I *like* sending you out to collect another set of scars? How is this different?"

"Because it's different. Getting wounded in battle is clean. It's nothing like having to lie there and take—*that*."

Lynn breathed out, carefully and evenly. "'That' has a name. It's sex. It's just sex. It's a weapon, just like a cutlass or a knife. Don't make too much of it."

"Do not you fucking tell me that I am fucking making too much of it. It matters, all right. It fucking matters!"

Lynn rested her head on her forearms. "*Nobles*," she muttered to herself, viciously. "My god, your priorities are twisted. Bloodlines. Descendants. *Family purity.* You sit up straight at the table and you observe codes of honour and you tremble at the thought of getting your hands dirty. Darren, this is how it works in the real world. Those of us who don't have pirate ships do what it takes to stay breathing. You think getting screwed by a bounty hunter is the worst thing that can happen to a person? You think I've never had to do something like this before?"

I gaped. "Oh, Lynn. Oh Lynn, I'm so sorry—"

She rubbed her eyes fiercely. "Stop. Just *stop.* I can't stand it when you get maudlin on me. I'm trying to tell you—*this* is life. If you want to survive, you do what it takes. Timor may be creepy and unclean, but you know what? I'd sleep with him every day of the week—and twice on Tuesdays—if that's what it took to keep you alive."

I slammed my hand down on the bunk. "What if I told you I'd rather die?"

Lynn rolled her eyes as she got to her feet. "Number one, that would be dumb. Number two, you're not the only one at stake. I'd fuck Timor to save Spinner's life. Or Latoya's, or Regon's . . . Hell, it may not be customary to admit it, but I would fuck him to save my own."

"Then fuck him to save your own life! Leave *me* out of it!"

We were facing each other now, our chests heaving. Then, with an effort I could almost see, Lynn gathered up her anger into a tight bundle and pushed it away.

"Fine," she said. "I'm going to go fuck Timor to save my own life. Hope you find something to do with your evening."

She brushed past me on her way to the steps. My anger had evaporated. I just felt cold.

But a thought was tugging at me. *Nobles,* Lynn had said, *you nobles . . .*

Lynn wasn't a noble. Lynn never had been a noble. Jess had been right after all.

And maybe, I thought dimly as I headed after her, maybe that's why we had such different reactions to this. Maybe she was too different from me, deep down where it counted, to understand where I was coming from.

NOTHING HAD BEEN done when we got to the deck. The longboat was still waiting in the hoists; the chest of gold hadn't been loaded. Most of the sailors were gaping at me with the same fixed, unbelieving expressions.

"Well?" I growled. "What are you sons of bitches waiting for? A sign from heaven?"

They moved then, unwillingly, lowering the longboat to the water. Lynn kicked the rope ladder over the side of the *Banshee* and climbed down, hand over hand. I stood staring at her as she took up the oars.

Regon looked from her to me, his mouth round with shock. "Captain."

If he hadn't spoken up, I'm ashamed to say, I would have let Lynn board the *Hind* alone. But Regon's words brought me partway back to my senses. "Latoya, go with her," I said, talking loud so my voice wouldn't crack. "Spinner, you too."

They nearly flung themselves over the side. Lynn didn't seem happy to see them. She let Latoya take the oars, then clambered forwards into the bow. Drawing her knees up, she hugged her legs with her bare arms.

Latoya rowed, step by steady stroke. Spinner's hand rested protectively on top of the chest of gold. The longboat cut a clean furrow in the water.

IT WAS QUIET as death over there.

The crew had wisely allowed me my space. I stood alone at the gunwales, shaving off slivers of wood with the edge of my dagger. I would have skewered any sailor who defaced the ship in this way, but it was my damn boat and I was angry and if anyone had a problem then I would cheerfully toss him overboard. *Me am boss.*

I felt a presence behind me, a sort of shadow, before Jess joined me at the rail. "Aren't you cold?"

I grunted, not interested in pleasantries. She was right, though. There was a chill breeze now that the sun was down.

A chill breeze. I glanced up at the sails—saw them flutter. The calm had ended.

Perfect. Just perfect. Regon had been right. We should have held the fuck on and waited for wind, instead of coming up with some daft-ass plan involving a crimson throne and a chest of gold. If Lynn was on board, then we could be running now, running straight downwind, the *Hind* leagues away. Lynn and I could be squashed together in our tiny bunk, pretending that the rest of the world didn't even exist. If only she hadn't done it . . .

"I know what you're thinking," Jess said.

I grunted again. "You always think you know what I'm thinking."

She ignored that. "Maybe you're right, maybe we could have escaped, but we can't be sure of that, can we? Maybe Timor would have attacked as soon as the wind rose, if you hadn't made the deal."

I rested my elbows on the gunwale, and my chin in my hands. There were lanterns moving about on the deck of the other ship, pools of orange light. Any minute Lynn would emerge from the captain's cabin, stepping into the lantern glow. Any minute, surely . . . it had been so long already.

"Do you know why it took Lynn so long to get back up to the deck?" Jess asked abruptly.

"She was getting dressed. Picking out the outfit most likely to seduce that revolting rat-bastard—"

"She was throwing up. Repeatedly. Or so Corto tells me."

I stared at my hands. "Are you blaming me for that?"

"Darren, no . . ."

"I didn't want her to do this." I felt the tears coming, and could only keep them at bay by speaking more savagely. "I didn't *ask* her to do this. I begged her not to. We could have come up with another way but hell, no, she'd made her decision. Why the hell wouldn't she listen to a word I said?"

Jess smiled sadly. "Because she loves you."

I carved off another chip of wood and tossed it over the side. "So what?"

"What do you mean, so what?"

"She did it because she loves me. I asked her not to do it because I love her. We're partners, for fuck's sake. Why is she the only one who gets a vote?"

"Darren." Now Jess was back in her schoolteacher mode. "It is her body. She decides how to use it. You can plead and argue and cajole, but if she doesn't change her mind, that's it. She made her choice."

My gorge was rising. "So she can do whatever she damn well pleases, and I get to sit and take it. Is that what you're saying?"

Jess's voice was filled with strain. "Of course you don't have to sit and take it, any more than she has to cope with *your* temper tantrums. You could leave each other. Any time. For any reason. But if you don't—let me finish, Darren. If you don't choose to leave her, then you're choosing to deal with what happens—I *said*, let me finish. I'm not saying that what Lynn is doing is right, necessarily, but she's doing it with courage and love, and she's doing it to protect all of us. You don't have to be grateful for that, but try to respect it."

"But she wouldn't listen—"

"Now you're just whining. The girl you adore is over on that ship, going through things that neither of us want to think about. And frankly, I don't know whether you're worried about her, or pissed because she left without your permission. When she gets back, what are you going to do? Deliver a stern lecture about how Your Word Is Law? Mope because someone else had a chance to play with your favourite toy?"

"That's not fair."

"None of this is fair. The point is that she'll need you. More than ever. I hope to heaven that you realize that."

I dug the tip of my dagger into the wood and wiggled it, making a deep hole. I knew that Jess probably had a point, but the bitterness in my stomach wouldn't go away. It felt like gall was eating away at the edges of a torn, jagged hole.

Suddenly Jess stiffened beside me. "Something's happening on the *Hind.*"

AN INSTANT AFTER she said it, a door banged over there. Whether it banged shut or banged open, I couldn't tell, because just at that minute, all their lanterns went out. I straightened up, every muscle in my body suddenly taut.

"Captain?" Regon called out. He was never very far away from me in times of trouble.

"Look alive," I told him. "Wake the watch below, get the men at their posts. If that ship so much as *twitches,* then we're coming down on Timor like the hammer of god."

It only took seconds. The men turned out silently, many of them still pulling on their trousers or fastening their belts as they hurried into position.

Jess's eyes were wide. "This is bad, isn't it?"

Twenty different sarcastic responses occurred to me at that moment. I pushed them all aside and went with, "Yes."

One minute passed, two minutes, three . . . no sounds from the other ship, no lamps, no nothing. I made my decision. "Regon, get the *Banshee* underway. Corto, prepare a boarding party. We're taking our people back."

I had barely finished talking when a door banged on the *Hind* again. This time, though, the noise was followed by the *clump clump clump* of hurrying feet. Though the deck of the other ship was almost invisible, I could just make out a cluster of men approaching their starboard side. Approaching it, and carrying something in their arms. It was a sort of long, cloth-wrapped bundle, the length of a person. It took me an instant to realize that the bundle was moving, struggling—

Then they bent, and heaved, and threw it over the side.

CHAPTER EIGHT

A SECOND OF no time, when everything seemed suspended—then the struggling body crashed into the water. The sailors of the *Hind* didn't even wait to see whether it hit. They were already springing to their posts. The *Hind* was moving, setting its sails, preparing to run.

"Move, move, *move!*" I screeched, dancing from one side of the deck to the other. "Get in the water! Get in the water, you useless dogs!"

Five men plunged overboard before I could finish talking. Jess, more composed, snatched up a coil of rope to throw. I pulled off one boot, getting ready to jump in the water myself, but then realized I couldn't do much in the way of commanding from that position. Instead, I waved the boot for emphasis as I screamed, "Lights! *Lights!*"

Someone rushed to the side with a lantern, casting a glow on the men in the water. Regon had been the first one overboard, and he had already reached the struggling swimmer. It was Spinner, half his face covered by a purple-black bruise. Regon held him steady on the surface, and I saw why Spinner was thrashing—his wrists were bound together. His ankles too, judging from the way he floundered.

Spinner was in the water. Lynn and Latoya were still on the *Hind*. The *Hind* had gathered speed, flying under full sail. My men wasted no time getting a line around Spinner and hoisting him up to the deck, but it still took too long, too goddamn long. I nearly howled in relief when the last of my sailors was finally aboard. Then I couldn't make any sound at all. I pointed furiously at the fleeing ship.

Regon, his dark hair slicked back with seawater, took up the call for me. "After them, you lazy scum!"

We crowded on every stitch of sail the *Banshee* could carry. She trembled, then surged forward, the waves churning around us. I stormed my way to the prow. With the breeze rushing past me on both sides, I could convince myself that we were going a little faster than we actually were. I would kill Timor, I promised myself. I would pop his eyes like chestnuts, shred his skin, knot his guts into ornamental baskets. If he had touched Lynn with one fat finger then I would do far, far worse . . .

It wasn't my imagination. We were gaining. The *Hind* was looming larger. I rocked back and forth, with eagerness and terror. Yes, yes, yes yes yes yes . . .

No. More movement on the deck of the *Hind*. *No.* Another body was being hauled out of the cabin. This one was far larger, and this one was motionless. I knew what was going to happen, and though I screamed my fury into the teeth of the wind, there was nothing, nothing, nothing I could do to prevent it. The sailors of the *Hind* didn't throw the second body. They rolled it over the side, and it crashed into the waves like a sack of wet sand.

Latoya. Dead? If she wasn't dead already, she had maybe two minutes. But if we stopped now to make the rescue . . . I pounded the rail in fury, not caring whether I broke the rail or my hand.

"Captain?"

Regon's cry was desperate. We had almost reached the spot where Latoya had fallen, and there was no sign of her. The water was bare, glassy, and black. She had already sunk.

I shut my eyes, gripped my cutlass hilt. "Oh gods . . ."

The obvious thought occurred to me.

I considered it. I'm not going to pretend that I didn't.

But the next second, I gave the order, Regon bayed it back in total relief, and the *Banshee* swung about. Again, the lanterns were trained on the surface; again, there were splashes as my sailors plunged over the side. This time they had to dive, and the sea was full of bobbing heads, gasping for breath before they plunged back beneath.

The *Hind* was gaining ground again, soaring rather than sailing. I tore out a literal chunk of my hair and hurled my boot down to the deck.

My instincts screamed for me to abandon the *Banshee*, leap over the side, and start swimming after Lynn. Instead, I stalked amidships to find Spinner. He was hunched over by the mast, curled in a puddle of bloody brine. The blood was coming from a sword slash in his side—not deep enough to pierce the guts, but ragged and ugly. His face, the half of it that wasn't crushed purple, was marble white. Jess knelt beside him, matter-of-factly folding rags into makeshift bandages,

But Spinner was talking, rasping out the words. "Latoya," he gasped. "Latoya—is she alive?"

"We don't know yet," I said tightly.

"They took a cosh to her," he said, his tone falling to a whisper. "Back of the head—soon as we went into the cabin. Then me. Then they just sat. Heard them talking. They were waiting for the wind. Getting ready to run. Captain, I think they played us."

Fan-bloody-tastic. That explained everything, except the thing I really needed explained, which was this: Fucking *why?* What the hell were they trying to accomplish? What did they want?

My stomach lurched. *Who* did they want?

The image of Timor's face swam up in front of me. *Someone hired you to hunt me down*, I had said. *More or less*, he had said.

He had been hired to hunt someone down.

But not me.

"Spinner," I said, "what did they do with Lynn?"

His eyes rolled until I could only see the whites. Jess stopped packing the rags into his wound long enough to hold a flask to his lips. He swallowed convulsively.

"Let him rest—" Jess tried to say, but Spinner's eyes fluttered open.

"He didn't touch her," Spinner managed to say. "Timor—he didn't—"

I grabbed his wrist; it was icy. "Spinner, *tell me* or I swear on your mother's grave I will kill you myself."

"He d-d-d-d-d-d-didn't hurt her," Spinner stammered, his whole body trembling. It was the cold, I guess, and the pain. "He said—he said—"

"Don't try to talk yet," Jess cut in. "Take a moment first."

"Gods' teeth, he'll talk or he'll bleed!" I roared.

Spinner's eyes rolled up to me. "Timor said, 'It's time for you to come home.' Lynn said . . . she said, 'Oh gods.' Then she tried to talk, but he . . . he . . ."

"He what?"

"He said . . . oh shit, I'm cold . . . Timor said, 'Save your strength. It's a long way to Bero.'"

I pulled him close by his gory shirt. "Bero! *Bero?* You're sure?"

Spinner nodded, head wobbling on his skinny neck. "Sure . . ."

I staggered to my feet. Bero, the northernmost island in Kila. Bero, the stronghold of the most powerful royal family in Kila. Bero, home of the House of Bain.

Ariadne's home.

Spinner's body was giving little lurches now. "He s-s-s-said—"

"Stop it," Jess put in quickly. "Darren, you have to let him rest."

But Spinner persisted. "He said, 'Lord Iason can't wait to have you back.'"

MY BRAIN CONVULSED, reeled, splintered. I wasn't all there for the next few minutes. Some part of me was watching as my sailors hauled Latoya back on board, twelve of them straining at the rope. Some part of me watched while Regon and Corto hurled themselves onto her chest and stomach, forcing out the water. I even felt vaguely relieved when she started to cough and choke. But it was all happening at an impossible distance.

The first thing I noticed, when I was ready to notice things properly again, was Jess. She was standing silent beside me, her hands stained red up past the wrists.

"I think Spinner will make it," she said softly. "As long as you let him rest a while before you do any more interrogations."

"You said that Lynn couldn't *possibly* be Ariadne." My voice grated painfully in my throat. "You said that was my inner snob, fantasizing."

Jess threw up her hands. "All right. All right. I may have been wrong. It hardly matters at this point, does it?"

"No," I agreed hollowly. "It doesn't really matter at all."

The last of Latoya's rescuers swung over the gunwale and squelched to the deck.

Regon snapped upright. "Ready, captain!"

The three seconds that followed seemed to stretch and stretch. Images from the past year flooded me—Lynn, chained to the mast of the *Badger* and dozing; Lynn's shoulder, bruised and bloody, the day that she was tattooed; Lynn sick as a dog during an eight-day storm the winter before; Lynn, just that afternoon, kneeling at my feet, head bowed.

I shut my eyes.

"Bring the ship about," I said hoarsely. "We're going south."

There was a chorus of smothered sound. Disbelief and confusion. The fury soared to my head, and I spoke in a snarl. "*Move,* you puking scuts. You heard me."

They scattered, most of them. Regon still stood in front of me, his hands clenching and unclenching. Jess's mouth was open and round.

"Turn about," I said again, just so there would be no mistake. "Let them go."

MAYBE, I THOUGHT, maybe giving up lovers was something that got easier the more often you did it.

By this time, I was safely down in our cabin—*my* cabin, I corrected myself, *my* cabin, mine mine mine. There was very little in there to remind me of Lynn, now she was gone. Once I'd closed the sea chest to hide her clothes, the cabin was as bare and dour as any cabin on any ship I'd ever commanded.

But I had a brandy flask. Half empty now. I took a long, rattling pull.

In the weeks and months after I left Jess, when I was wandering around the islands crazed with fear and guilt, I used to do this just about every night. Sit alone and drink and think about her and get disgusted with myself. As the months went on, the memory of that time seemed more and more rose-tinted, more and more dreamlike. I mean, honestly. The Lady Darren, formerly of the House of Torasan, master merchant, battle-tested warrior, learning to birth babies and tend beehives? My time with Jess was soul-renewing, in a way, and I would always be grateful for it. But our relationship had been doomed from the start.

My time with Lynn—*Ariadne*—had been just the same. A blip in her life as the all-privileged daughter of an all-powerful man. I wouldn't forget about her, certainly, but the wound would scab over and become an ordinary kind of scar. She had given me new energy, a new purpose, and that's what I would carry away. So it wouldn't really matter (my throat seemed to be dry; I swallowed hard) that Ariadne would come to her senses once she got back home.

They would ask her what she had been doing for the past couple of years.

"Oh, you know," she would say, scratching the back of her neck, "stuff."

And then she'd quickly change the subject to horses or jewellery.

I downed the last of the brandy and realized that I hadn't drunk nearly enough to render me unconscious.

I could always beat my head against the wall, I supposed.

AND THEN THERE was a knock at the door.

"Go 'way," I said dully.

There seemed to be a whispered consultation going on out there.

I pulled off my last remaining boot and hurled it at the planks. "Go 'way, I sss-ss-aid. Geddout of it, or, by crumbs, I'll have your heads!"

The whispers grew a little softer.

Then there was a great splintering *wham,* and the door flew inwards in two separate pieces. Latoya shook out her hand and stepped inside. She was still unsteady on her feet, but she was moving on her own power. Spinner, who came in next, had to lean heavily on Regon's shoulder. Last of all came Jess.

I glared murderously at each of them in turn. "And whaddid I tell you?"

"Begging your pardon, captain," Regon said gently. "But you never told us not to smash in your door."

"Goddamned technicalities," I muttered, and took another pull at the brandy bottle, forgetting that it was empty.

They were all glancing at one another, as if trying to appoint a spokesman. After a few seconds of this, Latoya lost patience and shoved Jess forwards.

To Latoya, Jess said, "Thank you." To me, Jess said, "You total moron, what in hell do you think you're doing?"

I blinked at her owlishly. The brandy had gone to my head faster than expected. "Iss perfectly simple. Me am boss."

"You am—*what?*"

Latoya had to catch Jess's arm and drag her back to stop her from leaping at me. "What the hell do you mean, Darren?" she yelled. "What is the matter with you? Did you think for two consecutive seconds before you decided to abandon Lynn to a bounty hunter? Did you even have a reason?"

"I did so. Four reasons." I counted them off on my fingers. "Four reasons why. One, iss better for her. Two, iss better for me. Three, iss better for the ship. Four . . ." Well, I couldn't remember reason four, so I just waved the fourth finger around emphatically. "So there."

Jess's mouth was opening and closing, but the noises coming out were totally incoherent.

Regon took hold of her, gently, and moved her to the door. "Right. I don't think we're going to get any farther until we take some drastic measures."

Latoya nodded agreement. "Bath time."

"Wait," I said, feeling much more sober all of a sudden. "I don't think that's necessary—no, I really don't—oh, you bastards. You bastards!"

Latoya caught me around the middle and hauled me dispassionately up to the deck, ignoring my flailing and pounding as I tried to loosen her grip. Once I was out in the open, all my crewmen busily whistled and looked the other way while Regon tied a rope around my waist. Then, for the third time that night, a body went crashing into the cold water.

They let me thrash around for a few minutes, swearing and yelling, until the last of the brandy had oozed from my pores. Then they hauled me up, gasping, freezing, soaking, and horribly clear-headed.

Jess had a blanket ready, I'll say that much for her, but her eyes hadn't softened any. As soon as I had coughed up my lungful of water, she went on as if nothing had happened. "You were saying?"

"Jess," I said through chattering teeth, "you bleeding she-demon—"

"Takes one to know one. Continue."

"I didn't abandon Lynn to a bounty hunter. She's going back to her father, and that's probably best for both of us."

"I've heard this before," Regon murmured.

"So have I." Jess glared at me. "When are you going to stop leaving people for their own good, Darren?"

I clutched the blanket more tightly around me, trying to assemble my thoughts. Though I was less bleary after the saltwater dunking, I was soaking wet and freezing cold, which did not put me at the top of my game so far as arguing was concerned. "Hell, Jess, I was right to leave you. You know it, I know it, everyone knows it. You needed something I couldn't give you, and *I* needed to go and do my work."

Jess's voice sawed up through the octaves, growing high and shrill. "You . . . were . . . *afraid*, Darren! Don't try and make it sound noble, don't try to defend it. You were swaggering around making out you were macho, and all the time, you were this terrified girl-child who didn't believe she was good enough to be loved. You left me because you decided you would rather be alone than be with someone who *might, possibly, someday,* leave you. That's what happened, so don't delude yourself."

"That's a fucking lie. And anyway, what the hell does that have to do with Lynn?"

She made an incoherent sound of rage. "Don't you see? You're doing the *same damn thing.* You can't even pretend that it's about your damn work this time. Because Lynn accepts your work, she's part of your work, you couldn't do a *fraction* of what you do without her."

"I know that, Jess!" I howled at the moon. "It's time that I stopped fucking *taking* from her."

"Taking? *Taking?* "

"You heard me. That man Timor, he was sent by Lynn's father. Sent by Lynn's father to bring her back to the *castle* where she *lives.* And what did he find when he got to us?" I didn't have anything to throw or kick, so I smacked my thigh. "He found Ariadne kneeling beside me like a goddamn terrier! He found me whoring that girl out to save my own skin!"

"Captain," Regon put in. "Captain . . ."

"Don't you 'captain' me. It's sick, you hear me? It's sick and I won't be that person!"

"Captain," Regon said stubbornly. "She left that castle. Doesn't that mean anything to you?"

"She ran from her husband, and he's feeding worms. It doesn't matter anymore. Besides, even if she does need help, who the fuck am I to give it to her? I've been groping around in the dark, because she won't tell me anything. The only things that she *does* say are riddles or lies. I don't know how to fix anything. I'm only making it worse!"

The crew had stopped pretending to ignore me. There was a ghostly circle of faces all around. I pressed a hand to my heaving chest.

"Ariadne's being taken home to Bero," I said dully. "We couldn't reach her there if we tried, and anyway, there's no need. She'll be with her family. They have every reason on earth to treat her well."

Spinner, of all people, spoke up. "So why was she so afraid?"

I paused at that, not having a ready answer. There was such total silence from my crew, I could hear the drops of water as they slid from my clothes and hit the deck.

"She was terrified, captain," Spinner went on. "Totally green. Close to puking. And it happened as soon as that man Timor mentioned the word 'home.' Of course, I only saw her face for a few seconds before they put the hood over her head."

"Before they put the *what* over her *what*?"

"Hood. Head. A thick cloth bag. And they tied her hands. That's all I saw before they dragged her away."

Silence.

Drops of water on the planks.

"You couldn't have told me this before?" I floundered.

"Would you have listened?" Jess countered. "You're not one to let reality get in the way of a good rant. It's always the same, Darren. You hear what you want to hear. Why are you so ready to believe that Lynn is better off without you?"

I looked off at the dim horizon. The *Silver Hind* was nowhere in sight.

"Captain," Regon said, "you'll forgive us for going so far. We wouldn't, if you were the only one at stake. But you're not, you see."

Spinner took up the thread. "We don't know everything about Lynn. But all of us know what she wants."

Jess nodded. "I'm not going to pretend I understand the situation. Maybe she's Ariadne and maybe she isn't. But the point is—"

"Would you all, *please*, just shut up for *one* moment?" I asked, my eyes tightly closed.

Deep in my mind, rusty gears were finally starting to turn.

"You can ask for anything you want," Lynn used to assure me. But what had she ever asked me for?

Nothing, directly. But what if, in her way, she was just as bad as I was at asking for what she needed? What if she had to use hints, sideways nudges?

Why did she make me tie her to the mast the first day we met? Why did she insist for so long that I had to keep her chained? Why had she tattooed my signature on her shoulder? What had she been saying? The answer was obvious. *You have to keep me with you.*

And what about the things she had done to me? Why did she prod me towards building a fleet? Why did she help me assemble an army? Why did she turn me into a pirate queen? Because she believed in my mission to help Kila? That was part of it, I was sure. But Lynn had always said that she wasn't a selfless person. Was there something in it for her as well?

I'd seen Lynn hold her own against bounty hunters and raiders, light-ning storms and ocelots, but if Jess was right, there was something in the world that she couldn't face. What if—*what if*—she had been slowly, determinedly turning me into a person who was strong enough to protect her?

If that was true, my first instinct was to quit the job. I was not doing well. I hadn't even managed to figure out what I was supposed to be protecting her from. I'd let her row off to the *Silver Hind,* when I should have knocked her down and sat on her to keep her where it was safe. Then, when the *Hind* started to run, I just let it go.

I felt the familiar black wave of guilt rising, but for once I wrestled with it, and managed to crush it down. My guilt had never done anything for anyone. It was just another thing that Lynn had to carry for both of us.

Lynn had always done the believing in our relationship. And now it was my turn to take a leap of faith.

I opened my eyes.

The stars on the horizon were tiny points of ice. My chest felt tight and hard.

"We're going to tear that girl from the bosom of her family," I rasped. "And we're going to drag her back into slavery, where she belongs."

Jess nodded. "That's more like it."

PART THREE

WHIPPED

Narrated by Darren,
formerly of the House of Torasan (Pirate Queen)
and by Lynn

CHAPTER ONE
Lynn
Afternoon, Day III

I GUESS I should have seen it coming. I guess, in a way, I did. When the *Silver Hind* hoved into view, my first instinct was to run, in no particular direction, and without stopping so long as I had feet left to run with. But when you've been a runaway for a while, you stop trusting that inner voice that tells you when it's time to panic. You stop trusting it because there's always some reason to panic, and you can't spend every minute of every day retching and cowering.

My emotional waters grew still muddier after I offered to go to Timor. As you can imagine, the prospect didn't exactly thrill me. You'd be able to imagine it even better if you'd seen the bastard up close. He had the over-smooth, over-starched look of a man who keeps his fantasies bottled—and that kind of man tends to go too far when he suddenly gets a chance to do whatever he wants.

When Darren was yelling at me in our cabin, I was more than a little distracted by the thought of what I was about to do. I have a pretty vivid imagination and the scene wasn't hard to picture—the weight of Timor on top of me, the rasp of his bristly face, his smell. (I'd caught a whiff of him earlier, and he wasn't the sort of man who kept a pomander in his pocket, if you know what I mean.) I'd done worse things to stay alive—hell, I'd done worse *men* to stay alive—but it had been a while, and I was out of practice. That's the problem with being with a person who loves you more than her own soul. It kind of ruins you for anything else.

So, while Darren was ranting at me, I could only give her half of my attention. I was mostly concentrating on not throwing up, for the sixth time that day. My instincts were screeching at me in seven part harmony, *Don't do it. Don't. Don't. Don't.* And maybe if Darren hadn't been so priggish, so self-righteous, so goddamn *noble*, I would have listened both to her and to my own gut, and let her talk me out of it. But she was. So I didn't.

Whatever. I didn't see it coming. As Latoya rowed us over to the *Silver Hind*, my insides were crawling, but my mind was made up—I was going to go through with it. I would give Timor whatever he asked for, do things that he hadn't even believed to be biologically possible, if that was what it took. I was going to finish it as fast as I damn well could and I'd go back home to the *Banshee*. Maybe Darren would be over it by then. Maybe she'd still be sulky and I'd have to let her mope for a few days before she came to her senses. I could cope with that. A moping Darren is a *living* Darren and, in my book, that counts for something. When I swung onto the *Hind's* ladder and started to pull myself on board, I was tired, I was nauseous, I was pissed as all hell— but I wasn't really afraid.

Not yet.

THIS IS NOT my favourite memory, so I'm going to make things easy on myself and keep this short. Besides, the memory itself is kind of blurry. You have to understand, it happened so fast.

Latoya went through the cabin door first, so she was the first to get dropped. There was next to no warning—just a faintest whirring sound as the cosh whipped round to take her on the back of the skull. She turned slightly as she fell. I remember her eyes, round and almost thoughtful, before they rolled into the back of her head. They grabbed me just as they hit Spinner. I didn't see him go down.

At some point, I might have yelled for help, I'm really not sure. There wouldn't have been much time. I was hooded and bound within a few seconds. But those few seconds were enough for Timor to tell me what was going on. He knew who I was, and he knew who wanted me back.

That moment—*that* moment—was the thing I had been dreading since the day I escaped. I had pictured it happening in so many ways, in so many times and places. I'd woken so often in the middle of the night, sweating, close to screaming, and thinking that it had happened for real. It overpowered my imagination whenever I let myself brood. It was the single thing that had the power to scare me speechless.

So I should have seen it coming.

I just didn't, that's all.

THE *SILVER HIND* didn't have a brig. They kept me in a storeroom. Timor was the only one who ever opened the door. When he came, he took the hood off briefly, so I could eat, but he wasn't a great conversationalist.

"They're alive, so far as I know," he told me, the millionth time I asked about Latoya and Spinner. "Which is more than they'll be if they try to follow you to Bero. So you'd better hope they're smart."

"Let's talk about smart," I said. With my hands still tied in front of me, I was rapping a biscuit against the wall, trying to scare the maggots out. Ship's maggots are plucky little things that don't scare easy, so it was taking a while. "Do you really think that the word 'smart' applies to what you're doing? It's safer to swim naked in boiling tar than it is to discover one of Lord Iason's secrets. Now that you've seen me, do you really think he'll just hand you a bag of cash and send you on your merry way?"

"Shut your mouth."

"Timor, would you listen? I don't know whether he told you the truth or whether you guessed it, but either way, he can't afford to let you live. Don't you see that? What do you think is going to happen?"

"You know what I think?" Timor said. "I think you're done eating."

He grabbed the biscuit away and tied the hood over my head again. After that, he gave me a sharp cuff on the ear every time I tried to talk.

On the third day (my guess—it was flat dark down there), he led me upstairs, and let me put my tied hands on the rail, and then pulled the hood away.

When my eyes stopped burning from the glare, I saw it all at once. The great cliff of white limestone. The white limestone castle that roosted at the top, like a pale gargoyle, its crenulations spiking up like teeth and claws. And surrounding us on every side were white-bannered war ships, gliding through the calm waters of the bay. It was the exact same view that I had stared at for over ten years, from one of the towers somewhere up on that cliff. Back then, though, I saw it in reverse—first the battlements of the castle, then the harbour and warships, and beyond that, free and wild and wonderful, the ocean.

Of course, I had known from the start where Timor was taking me, but I'd kept the panic at bay by telling myself that we would never reach Bero. Something would get in the way. A freak waterspout, maybe. An attack by a giant sea serpent. Failing that, I'd escape. I'd done it three-and-a-half years ago, and since then I'd learned some useful new skills, like how to strangle a man with his own tongue. I could have done some damage to Timor when he was down in the storeroom delivering my meals. I didn't need to see him to aim a blow—his boots clicked in the dark—and though he was twice my size, I was big enough to reach his groin, which was all I really needed.

But I'd forced myself to bide my time. There was no point in rocking the boat (so to speak) until the *Silver Hind* reached some place that was better suited to an escape attempt. Like oh, say, some place with land. The best plan was to act meek and innocent, in the hope that Timor and his men would have lowered their guard by the time my chance came.

A wise plan. But my chance hadn't surfaced. In no more than two hours, I would be back on Bero. Back with *her.* And as soon as I saw the fortress on the cliff, my brain leapt straight out of my skull and started to shriek. Screw what was sensible, I was *leaving*!

I didn't give myself any time to think about it. I pivoted, braced my back against the rail, and drove my heel into Timor's knee. The blow wasn't dead centre so I didn't break the cap, but still he folded, howling, and that gave me the time to deal out two more kicks, one to his other knee and one to the crotch. He howled good and proper that time, but I barely heard him. I was trying to use the momentum to hurl myself backwards over the ship's side, into the bay waters.

On an ordinary day, I could have managed it. But my muscles were rubbery, my vision blurry, my stomach shrivelled—they hadn't been feeding me much. I couldn't get the height. My spine rammed into the rail, and all the breath *whooshed* out of me, the pain so piercing that I saw red sparks. Then there were hands on me, sailors' hands, callused and rough, pulling me back onto the deck. They lowered me with a kind of gentleness, but at Timor's snarl, they let me drop.

Gasping, I sprawled on the sun-hot boards. Timor's face loomed above me, a shadow in the burning white sky.

"What?" I panted. "You thought I was going to make this easy?"

His eyes narrowed; that was all the warning I got, but at least I had the chance to tense. His boot crashed into my stomach. I rolled to soften the impact, but he kicked again, this time at my back. The red sparks in my vision exploded into blood-red blooms of fire.

I screamed. Not much else to do in that situation.

Timor stood above me, his fists flexing as he got himself under control. Then with a quick lunge, he grabbed the front of my tunic and lifted me from the deck. "You are damn lucky that your father wants you alive."

"Yeah," I managed to wheeze. "Lucky me."

Timor let go, and I slumped. He shook his fingers, as if cleansing them of something filthy, then snapped them. The hood dropped over my head again.

"Take her below," I heard him say. "Make sure she can't go anywhere."

DOWN IN THE dark mugginess of the storeroom, I tried to cudgel my brain into coming up with a decent plan. That did not work. My thoughts went around and around in a tight, unhappy spiral—the pain in my back, the saltiness of my bleeding lip, the tightness of the hood's drawstring around my throat, the shackles rasping on wrists and ankles. The hood kept in the air, so my lungs were taking in nothing but my own stale, warm breath. But somehow, the cloth still let in all of the smells—musty wood, rotten meat.

None of that really mattered, though. What mattered was that, with every minute that passed, I was getting carried ever more swiftly back to *her.*

Escape, I reminded myself. Escape. I'd done it before. My chances had to be better this time around. This time—who knew?—I might even have some help from outside.

Just as soon as the thought occurred, I dismissed it. Darren had come a long way, but there was only one person who had a chance of taking on mighty Bero and surviving the experiment.

The pirate queen. I couldn't help it; I let out a weary sort of laugh. The pirate queen, whose fleets spanned entire seas, who commanded the love and the fear of noble and commoner alike. The pirate queen, who would rip whole cities apart to reclaim a woman who bore her mark. (I let my fingers explore the storm-petrel tattoo on my shoulder.) Problem was, that wasn't Darren. Not yet. Not quite. I hadn't had enough time.

Damn it, but I'd come so close. I'd already molded Darren into roughly the right shape; all she needed was some polish. A couple of years would have done it. Just two little years, and I would have made her a legend. Even the white warships of Bero would have hurried in another direction as soon as they saw her flag, pretending that they'd just remembered something very important which they had to do immediately on the other side of the world.

If I had only had a little more time . . .

It was no use thinking about it. Darren might try to come after me and she might not, but either way, I couldn't afford to wait and hope. I knew what was in store for me on Bero, and once it happened, I wasn't going to be running anywhere fast.

So, no waiting around for the pirate queen. That was fine. I had escaped before without any piratical intervention. And it had only taken me ten years.

Oh gods . . .

An invisible hand hoisted me to my feet.

"TIMOR," I SAID. "Timor, Timor, *Timor*, listen."

The hood was still tightly in place as he dragged me through the streets. The chain had been left on my legs so that I could only hobble, and I stumbled every other step. Before we left the ship, he had made me pull on a long, respectable woollen tunic over the shredded remains of my linen one. The weight and the length were both awkward and confining.

From the sounds and smells, I guessed that we were in the lower city, the part sloping down to the harbour. It was a long, uphill trip to the fortress. It couldn't be long enough for me. This was my last chance to make the man see sense.

"Timor . . ." I began again, through the thick cloth, but he caught me by the scruff of the neck and gave me a quick shake.

"Just keep your mouth shut, girl. You're not going to be my problem for much longer."

A fold of cloth was wedged between my teeth. I pushed it loose with my tongue. "*Nothing's* going to be your problem for much longer. Do you think I'm joking about that? You think you know Iason better than I do?"

There was no answer. Maybe he couldn't even hear me through the hood. Maybe that was why he'd put it on me in the first place.

"Timor," I tried once more, but then my toe drove into a cobblestone and I tripped headlong. Timor grabbed me by the neck again and hauled me along a few paces until I could get my feet back under me.

We came to a halt in a place that smelled of straw, dung, and cattle. Timor grabbed me around the waist and, with a grunt, boosted me up onto something. The bed of a wagon, I guessed, because I felt grain sacks underneath me. My wrist fetters clinked, and then there was tension, pulling my arms taut in front of me. He'd tied me to the wagon rail.

Wooden wheels groaned. The wagon was moving, and the bed beneath me tilted, as we started to go uphill.

My throat closed up, and I stopped even trying to talk.

HIGHER AND HIGHER and higher. It took hours. The fortress at Bero had six concentric walls, and to get past each, you needed a fistful of pass tokens and a headful of passwords and countersigns. Timor nearly went hoarse, answering the questions of all the guards. Interestingly, nobody asked why Timor had a bound-and-hooded woman on his ox-cart. Which made sense, when I thought about it. My father was always arresting people, so bound-and-hooded people had to be a fairly common sight around these parts.

Higher and higher and higher, and still I kept quiet, but my heart jolted painfully each time another gate slammed shut behind us.

When we were through the inner wall of the castle, Timor pulled me down from the ox-cart, and we went the last hundred yards on foot, trudging up to the door at the base of the keep. There, he finally unlocked the shackles and pulled the hood off my head.

He squinted at my sweat-soaked hair and bloodied lip. "You're not much to look at. But it's not your face that they care about, is it?"

I swallowed bile.

"Up," he said, his voice going ugly. "Now."

This was it, and my head was swimming. This was the last leg of the trip. We headed up the spiral staircase, around and around and around.

Wild thoughts swarmed around my brain—I would hurl Timor down the steps, I would bite through the walls, I would throw myself out a window screaming—but something inside me had gone very cold and weak. Another step. Another step.

Then there was a door on our right, the sight of it familiar as my own skin. Stained cherry-wood, with a gilt knocker in the shape of a ram's head.

Timor knocked with his right hand, gripped my arm with his left.

"Enter," came the voice from inside. And that voice was familiar, too.

The room beyond, I didn't know as well. I wasn't invited into the map room very often while I was growing up. I did know it well enough to see that it had changed since the war began. The walls were papered from floor to ceiling with charts, figures, and diagrams—army rosters, fortifications, pay schedules. The great sand-table, with its model of the islands, was dotted with little brass boats and figures of men, used for plotting troop movements. Almost fifty ships marked with white paper flags were clustered around Bero. I winced. He'd always been paranoid about the castle's defences, but it looked like he was getting worse.

And there he was—Iason of Bain, lord of Bero, standing by the sand table, slowly revolving a tiny brass ship between his fingers as if he found it fascinating. He wore a dressing gown of violet silk, and his hair stood up in pale unruly tufts. Apparently, he wouldn't be holding court today. *She* wasn't there, so the pressure in my chest eased the smallest degree, but there was someone else waiting with Iason.

A young woman. Slightly older than me, slightly taller. Her face, I knew, looked something like mine when it was bare, but today, as usual, it was caked with powder and rouge, and her blonde hair was teased into a mass of ringlets. With all the frills and flounces on her gown, she reminded me of a giant meringue sitting in a puddle of cream. She was slouched at Iason's desk, and her drumming fingers made his quill pens bounce in their cherry-wood cup.

Timor bowed; I didn't. "I brought her, my lord," he said unnecessarily.

Iason's milky blue eyes came up to me. His expression, as always, was part fond, part wounded, part disappointed. It irritated me, and irritation, for the moment, overcame fear. I spoke as if I was calm as a glacier.

"Hello, father," I told him. Then I glanced at the girl. "Hello, Ariadne."

CHAPTER TWO
Darren, formerly of the House of Torasan (Pirate Queen)
Afternoon, Day III

Pirates may not be what you would call masterminds, but they ain't exactly stupid. And the crew of the *Banshee* knew me well. So after Timor disappeared over the horizon with *my* woman, it didn't take them long to figure out that the mere mention of his name was enough to provoke me into a howling, stamping fury. Some of them, I think, thought about repeating the name as often as possible just to see how far I'd go, but cooler heads prevailed. So it became routine to refer to Timor as "That Goat-Testicled, Slave-Stealing Sack of Shit." "Goat-boy" for short.

It was three days after Goat-boy's escape that we met up with the *Badger*. This is what they tell me. I wasn't in a state to notice details. I hadn't slept since the night before Lynn was kidnapped, and a ninety-six-hour stretch of sleep deprivation, coupled with wracking, ball-shattering worry, doesn't leave you at your most alert.

By the end of it, I couldn't do much but twitch and curse. Regon humanely propped me up against the mast so I could snarl at crewmen who weren't moving fast enough, but that was about the limit of my powers.

So I was leaning on the mast, snarling and cursing and doing my best not to fall over, when he all of a sudden swung over the rail and onto the deck. Grizzled and grey and stern-faced and ugly, half of his right ear missing and a scar crossing his face from chin to brow . . . it was my old helmsman, now captain of the *Badger*. Teek.

The sight of him made thirty pounds of lead roll off my shoulders. I commanded my first merchant boat when I was fourteen, so green that I didn't know the difference between my own ass and a marlinespike. It was Teek who saved me from disaster on that voyage, Teek who quietly ignored my shrill commands as I tried to ram us into every rock in the southern sea. He was the first person I knew who took my problems onto his own back, guided me from triumph to triumph, and then pretended that I'd done everything myself. Lynn was the second.

"You old bastard," I said, blinking at him through a fog of exhaustion. "Where were *you* a few days back?"

He shrugged. "I'd have been here if I'd known, captain."

"You don't call me captain, *you're* a captain now. And we'll see how you like it. Did Regon bring you up to speed?"

"Got the gist of it. You need to get your girl out of trouble. *As* usual."

Which was bullshit and he knew it (it was normally the other way around) but my pride appreciated the little white lie.

"And you're heading straight for Bero," he continued. "Best defended island in Kila, circled by ships that could take on a kraken, and you're charging straight at it, banners flying. Ambitious of you, captain, but that was always your style."

"I'm not charging straight at it," I said defensively. "I'm heading for it rapidly, that's all. Obviously, we can't just waltz into their harbour. We'll need another plan."

"We'll need another plan *soon*, captain," he said, gentle but insistent. "The white ships keep a wide patrol around the island. We're almost at their waters. Lucky as I met up with you first. Won't do your girl any good if you end up ten fathoms deep."

"Mmph," I grunted.

"Teek's right," Regon said, stepping forward. "We can't put it off any longer."

I glared. "If it's so goddamn urgent, why haven't you brought this up before?"

"I did, captain," he said tactfully. "You threw a chunk of cheese at me, turned your pockets inside out, and then lay down on the deck and gurgled. You've been a bit funny the past day or so."

"I am having," I said, with an effort at dignity, "a *very* bad week."

With a sigh, I looked off the starboard bow. The *Badger* was pulled up alongside us, balky and battered as ever. A lot like Teek himself, in fact. It made me think of old times, of Teek's sure hand on the helm as he piloted us through the ship's graveyard to the secret harbour. That thought sparked another, and another, and another. My fingers began to drum along my arm.

"Only real option is to turn the ships around," Teek was saying. "Go to the harbour, like, or to Freemarket, and think it out. Men been trying for years to break Bero without any luck. Can't expect the captain to come up with a plan in five minutes."

"And that, Teek," I said, rousing myself, "that is where you are wrong."

I peeled myself off of the mast, staggered to the nearest fresh-water barrel, stuck my whole head in, burbled for a minute or two, and pulled out, gasping and revived. "Get Jess and Latoya and Spinner, meet in my cabin. Broach a new cask of ale and pour me a tankard big enough to fell a buffalo. I know *exactly* what we're going to do."

CHAPTER THREE
Lynn
Late Afternoon, Day III

"Hello, father. Hello, Ariadne."

There was silence for a few seconds, broken only by the tap-tap-tapping of Ariadne's nails.

Lord Iason pinched the bridge of his nose and leaned forward. As though he had a nosebleed, or a terrible headache. All he said was, "Gwyneth . . ."

What he meant was that it just wasn't *done* for a bastard child to address her father as "Father." But saying that out loud would kind of defeat the point.

He waved his fingers at Timor without looking at him. "You, man. Report to my steward; he'll give you what you're owed."

Timor bowed hastily and went out with quick, impatient steps. I watched him go, knowing that I'd never see him again. There are many entrances to the dungeons on Bero, but the only exits are below the tide line. Now and then, the bodies wash up on shore, the corners of their burlap shrouds flapping. What can I say? I tried to warn him.

I had been doing my utmost not to think about her, but all at once the image flashed before me: Darren sewn into one of those burlap bags, a long lanky bundle among the other corpses. The horror of the picture hit my brain like a flood of ice water, washed it clear and clean. Whatever happened, *whatever* happened, I had to keep Darren out of this.

We all listened to the clump of Timor's boots as they descended the stairway. Then, with a great effort, my father put on his oily smile. "It's good to see that you're all right, child."

I snorted. "Is it?"

He sighed. "Things have been rocky between the two of us sometimes, Gwyn. But you need to know that I care what happens to you."

My father's helpless-nice-bloke act was harder to take than his rages. I trained my gaze through the map room's narrow window. We were about halfway up the tower, high enough to make out a patch of ocean. It was glassy green that day.

"Tell me what happened," he said.

"What happened when?" I asked wearily.

"What happened three years ago. When you left us."

Left us—that was one way to put it, I supposed. I should have tried to placate him, but my maverick side bobbed to the surface without any warning. "What's there to tell? I thumped Ariadne on the head, tied her up with her own petticoats, dressed in her clothes, and walked out of the castle. Stole her horse, sold it, used the money to pay for passage off the island. Since then, I've mostly been fishing. How the hell have *you* been?"

"You see?" Ariadne said, breaking into the conversation for the first time. "This is exactly what I've been telling you, Father. That little peon laid hands on me, she *assaulted* me. She just admitted it."

"Yes, Ariadne, I know." Helpless-nice-bloke was giving way to highly-important-and-overstressed-man. "It won't happen again. Your mother will make sure of that."

I had been braced for it, but there are some impulses that I can't control. The mention of Melitta made my heart pummel the walls of my chest so hard that I thought it would burst through. Automatically, just as I used to, I pinched the soft skin inside my elbow as hard as I could. The pain helped ground me.

"My mother will do nothing of the kind," Ariadne was saying. "She obviously can't control the girl. If you insist on keeping her here at all, then you'd better let me deal with her. It doesn't seem like anyone else is able to cope."

"Gwyneth was your mother's handmaid for something like ten years." Now he was using his pained-patience voice. "I assure you, Melitta can cope."

I found my tongue. "Father—"

"Gwyneth, *please.*"

"My lord," I corrected myself grimly. "If you're going to keep me here, then, for the love of all the gods, stick me in the dungeon or something. Or the stables. Or the pigeon cote. Really, I'm not fussy. But if you send me back to Melitta . . ."

He waved a weary hand. "No hysterics, please. Melitta's strict, that I'll grant, but she's fond of you, in her way."

"She hates my guts and you know it." There was a tight knot in my throat. "You have *always* bloody known it."

His glance was tired, nothing more. "Don't swear."

Ariadne jumped in again. "The problem is that Mother spends too much time hating and too little laying down the law. Now, if you let me handle Gwyneth—"

"Darling," my father interrupted. "I appreciate the input, but this is outside your area of expertise."

"But I . . ."

"Darling," he repeated, "go to your room."

Ariadne looked ready to launch an all-out tantrum, but Iason's eyes were hooded and she knew, as well as I did, that it was no use trying to cross him for the present. She flounced to her feet and headed out, her skirts bouncing around her.

"I'll see you soon," she said in warning as she passed me. "*Very* soon."

"Can't wait," I muttered.

The door shut behind her with a bang. My father stared at his sand table. The parts that represented water were bare blue plaster. I looked at them and thought of waves, and typhoons, and sea spray, the clean cool world of the ocean. A week earlier, that whole world belonged to me.

"My lord, please," I said. "If you're not going to let me go, *please*. Just don't send me back to her."

I rarely asked my father for anything. There were two reasons for that— first, it made me sound pathetic, and second, it didn't work. On this occasion, he gave a pained grimace, as if it embarrassed him even to hear me asking. "You might try provoking her less often."

"I can't. I've tried." I could have howled. Nearly four years of running, of fighting and scheming, only to end up back *here*. "You know that. You know damn well why I ran."

"And you," he said, with rare honesty, "you know damn well why I can't let you leave." He spread his dainty hands, palms up. A nobleman's version of a shrug. "So we're at an impasse, aren't we? Except that one of us is lord of the house of Bain, and one of us is a runaway servant. So one of us is slightly more likely to get his way." He flicked over one of the brass soldiers on his sand table, watched it wobble and fall. "I believe that we're done here. You may go on up to Melitta's room."

I wouldn't, I told myself. I would run, fight, break apart, fly—

"She's waiting for you," he said more quietly. "And I don't think she'll be happy if she has to collect you herself."

SOMEHOW, I MADE it back to the stairway. My feet seemed to have acquired a mind of their own. I certainly wasn't the one telling them to head up, step by step, around and around the central pillar.

Two turns up the flight of stairs, there was another door, this one of rosewood—the entrance to Ariadne's bower. Two more turns, another door—Iason's bedchamber. He and Melitta had slept in different rooms for years, further back than I could remember. Maybe Melitta moved out when she learned about my father's fling with a palace servant, the one that resulted in my birth. But maybe it happened even earlier. The two of them couldn't stand each other. Were it not for one very vital detail, Iason would have cast her out years ago. As things were, all they could do was stay out of each other's way as much as possible.

Two more turns. The topmost floor of the tower. Another door. The bronze handle was shaped like a wolf's head. To the right of the door, a narrow alcove. I was determined not to look at it, but of course I did and my jaw locked tight. Lying there on the alcove floor, as always, was a narrow pallet of straw and a wadded blanket. Had someone else been sleeping there while I was gone? Or had Melitta kept it exactly as it was, waiting for me?

The door was open. I could see motion—an arm in a green sleeve moving rhythmically up and down, up and down, as Melitta brushed her hair.

My brain said, run. But somehow my feet took me forwards instead.

I didn't bother to knock. She knew I was coming. Her back was to me, her face to the mirror. She didn't turn around, but I could see her eyes flicking over my reflection, taking me in.

Her hair was more speckled with grey than it had been when I escaped. Salt and pepper.

She set her brush down gently on her vanity table, but she didn't bother to turn before she spoke to me. "So. You're back."

CHAPTER FOUR
Darren, formerly of the House of Torasan (Pirate Queen)
Late Afternoon, Day III

ONCE AGAIN, WE crowded into the cabin for a council of war. But this time, no one tried to sit on the lid of the sea chest, or even rest a mug of ale on top of it. I think they all knew that I would slap their heads off their necks if they tried. That was Lynn's spot, and gods help me, I was going to bring her back there.

Little Spinner, his face still badged blue and purple from the hits he had taken on the *Hind,* poured out the ale. Mine had a sharp, funny aftertaste, but I put that down to exhaustion.

"All right," I said, sticking my thumbs in my pockets. "The Goat-Testicled, Slave-Stealing Sack of Shit took Lynn. We all have a problem with that, yes? So we need to go after her."

I unfurled the map, and they all leaned around me to see it. "We are here. About a day from Bero, as the gull flies. But there's a whole damn navy between us and the harbour. So that's a thing. Also, we know that Goat-Boy is taking Lynn to Iason. That means she'll be in the fortress on the cliff, here. Even if we can get to the lower city, we'll have to get past five or six enormous walls, manned by enormous numbers of archers, and enough swordsmen to choke the gates of hell. This is going to be just a little bit tricky, is what I'm trying to get at."

Regon scratched his chin. "I don't know, captain. Maybe we need to assemble the fleet. All twelve ships together, we could make a good stand of it—"

"Before we all died," Jess said flatly. "All your ships and men put together couldn't make a dent in the forces of Bero."

"Exactly." I took another gulp of ale. "We can't bash our way through the defences, so we're going to have to sneak. Land a shore party—a small one—and pussyfoot up to the fortress."

Jess looked deeply dubious. "And how are you going to get back off the island?"

"That?" I said. "I do not know. I cannot tell. But if we can reach Lynn, then she ought to be able to think of something. She knows Bero, after all. If we can't reach Lynn . . . well, then, I'm not leaving. Sorry, and all that, but I won't."

They digested this.

"How many? And who?" Latoya asked.

"In the shore party? I'm thinking three. Any more than that and we'll be too conspicuous. Me and two volunteers. I won't take anyone who's unwilling to go. But you, Regon, and you, Latoya, you're the ones I want." I glanced at the bruise that wrapped halfway around Latoya's sinewy neck. "As long as you're up for it. I'll understand if you're feeling a bit below par."

"How about if I break your face?" she offered. "Then who'll be below par?"

"A convincing argument. Regon? You in?"

"Oh, sure," he said, from behind his ale mug. "Land on an island crawling with soldiers, with no idea how to get off again. Who would want to miss that experience?"

"Glad to hear it. Any questions?"

"Aye." Teek poked a stubby finger at the map. "You still haven't explained how you'll get *on* the damned island."

"Ah. Right. That. That's where you come in, Teek. Obviously, we can't charge straight for the coast, flags a-waving and swords a-bristling. So instead, we'll do this. East of Bero, there are reefs."

That was an understatement. There are reefs, and then there are *reefs*, and the rocks east of Bero fall into the latter camp. They're the gouging, jagged, ship-killing kind that can rip the bottom off a boat like the peel from an orange.

Teek knew all this, of course, and his face changed. "You're not serious, captain."

"I'm dead serious, captain. We're going through the reefs. It's the only part of the waters near Bero that they can't patrol. We won't be taking the *Banshee,* of course. It'll be the four of us—me, Latoya, Regon, and you—in the *Badger.* She's small enough to make it, as long as she has a master helmsman steering her." I traced a path on the map with my finger. "That'll get us within a few miles of the shore."

"But they'll have seen us from the watchtowers. What then?"

I told them.

There was silence for a few minutes afterwards.

"Did someone drop you on your head a bunch of times when you were a child?" Jess asked quite seriously. "I really don't think I can imagine a plan in which so many things could go wrong. What plans did you reject because they were inferior to that one?"

"It's all I can think of," I said. "And doing nothing is not an option. I have to get her back. You know I do."

Or at least, that's what I tried to say. It came out as a sort of burble.

Strange. My tongue felt kind of thick, and my mouth dry. I shook my head, trying to clear it.

Spinner measured me with a narrowed eye. "Looks like the stuff finally kicked in."

"About damn time," Regon said.

Now blackish pools were swirling in the centre of my vision. Bollocks. Just *bollocks*. I ran my finger along the side of my ale cup, and felt a damp, gritty residue. Dried herbs.

"Oh, you rotters," I managed, as I dropped. Dimly, I felt Latoya catch me before I could hit the floor.

"You need your sleep, captain," I heard Regon saying, as someone pulled off my boots. "Got to be well-rested if you're going to do the impossible." And then, crisply, to the rest of them, "We've got our orders. Look alive."

CHAPTER FIVE
Lynn
Evening, Day III

MY PALLET SMELLED the same as always—stale straw, must, and mould. Different blanket though. Brown, not grey.

The stone floor was cold (there are always drafts in castles) and my lady Melitta was down at dinner. So, just like I always used to on cold nights, I crept inside her room and sat by the hearth, huddled in my blanket. The warmth lulled me to a doze. I hadn't realized until then how tired I was. The frightening thing was that in my drowsy state, it was all too easy to believe that the past four years had been a dream, and I had never really been gone.

My name is Lynn now, I kept telling myself. *I have a life, I have a pirate; I can sail a ship and throw the long knife and throttle a man three times my weight. Sailors hop to attention when I clear my throat. I left this place; it's not who I am anymore.*

But it was hard to hang on to all that. Everything here was the same. The smell of the pine logs as they crackled in the coals; the reddish spot on the largest hearthstone; the way that violet curtains of Melitta's bed swayed in the draft through the door. And the sour dread, deep in my stomach, that Melitta would come back all of a sudden, and find me stealing her fire. I pinched the inside of my arm every few minutes so I wouldn't fall all the way into sleep.

But the next sound I heard roused me completely.

Footsteps, soft slippered footsteps, were heading up the spiral staircase. That was familiar too. Those footsteps had headed here once or twice weekly from the time I was eight. A giant lump rose to my throat.

The footsteps grew faster as they came closer—a dark shape ghosted through the door—and then, all at once, she flung herself down by the hearth and her hands were on me. "Gwyneth!"

"It's all right, Ariadne," I said, gripping her forearms. "I'm all right."

"Like hell you're all right." She was already inspecting me, tilting my head gently towards the fire to check for bruises. "What did that bitch do to you this time?"

"Shhhh. Nothing. She gave me a fishy stare for a while, then told me to fill her washbasin, then she just sent me to bed . . . How long do we have?"

"The banquet will go on for at least another hour, and both of them are dead drunk, so you can relax for a while. Let me see your lip. Who bust it?"

I touched it gingerly. For some reason, it wasn't scabbing over. "Timor. We had some differences of opinion on the way back here."

"Timor," Ariadne growled, as she shook rags and vials out of her reticule. "That slimy, arrogant son of a bitch. Of all the people Father hired to go after you, he's one of the worst. And that's saying something. Here, take this."

I pressed the damp cloth against my lip. It smelled acid and strong, and stung where it touched raw flesh. "How many did he hire?"

She was still sorting out her vials, and didn't answer for a few seconds. At some point since we met in the map room, she had washed off the powder and rouge. With her face bare, and her hair simply braided, she looked older, infinitely shrewder. This was her real face, the one that she never let her parents see.

"At least twenty," she said at last. "It's been bad since you escaped. I mean, we knew it would be, but . . . Every time they spoke about you, their eyes would *glitter*. As if they were rabid. Or mad." She stared blankly at a tiny bottle of lavender oil. "I'm so sorry, Gwyn, I'm so, so sorry. I did everything I could think of to put them off the scent."

"I know you did your best, Ariadne," I said weakly. "Please don't." It was selfish, I guess, but I couldn't deal with one of her fits of guilt. Not right that minute.

There was silence for a few seconds, as she daubed at one of my bruises with a rag dipped in some kind of sharp-smelling infusion. Arnica, probably. Then she went on, more quietly. "The way they looked when they heard that Timor was bringing you up . . . Mother's eyes went all hard, and Father paced around and around the room, with this *smirk* . . . Gods, I hate them. I swear I'm going to strangle them one day."

"Could you strangle them today? Does today work?"

To my relief, she laughed, the soft snuffling laugh that meant she was crying at the same time. "I've missed you so much. It's so strange. I hoped they'd never find you, but it's so good to see you again."

"Me, too. I mean, you." I propped myself up (which hurt) so I could look at her face. "You've mastered the stone-cold-bitch act since I left. For a moment down in the map room, you almost had me worried."

She laugh-hiccupped. "You like it?"

"What's not to like?" A thought struck me, and I sat up straighter. "Hell . . . you got married, didn't you? I can't believe I forgot. What was it like? What happened to Gerard?"

She waved that off. "Nothing much to tell. It was fine, I guess. Gerard was clean, at least, even if he had fewer brains than the average pudding. But he took a header from his horse a couple of years ago and broke his neck. So I'm back on the market. Father's still trying to negotiate a marriage deal with someone who has an equally good pedigree."

"I'm sorry. That must have been rough, when he died."

"Not really. I only saw him on Monday evenings, and all he did then was grunt for a while above me and then pass out."

My next question stuck on my lips for a second. It was an awkward thing to ask, but I had to know. "You didn't get pregnant, did you?"

She grinned, without any humour. "You know I didn't. If I had, would you be here?"

Yes, I had known that, but I guess some part of me had hoped . . . I stared into the orange coals, and then stiffened. "Damn it. I am *really* out of practice as a handmaid."

"Why? What is it?"

"Wood. I forgot to get more wood, and the fire's dying." The copper woodbin next to the fireplace held only a couple of logs, and a scattering of bark dust. "I have to take care of that before Melitta gets back, or—"

I didn't elaborate on the "or"; I didn't have to. Not to Ariadne. She had patched me up countless times after the "or" happened.

"Well, there's no need for *you* to get up. You look like you've been run over by a herd of mules." Acres of silk flounced around her as she got to her feet. "Sit still and keep warm. I'll be back."

Her skirts swished out of the room, and I leaned against the cooling side of the grate. I wasn't worried that she would get caught. Everything that I know about being sneaky, I learned from my big sister.

Since the two of us were tiny, Ariadne had been my best friend, my partner-in-crime, my secret sharer. When my mother was still alive, I lived with her down in the kitchens, territory completely off limits to a pint-sized princess. But Ariadne always found a way in. Our games took us all around the servants' quarters, from the roofs of the stables to the beer cellars. Together, we investigated manure heaps, chased stray pigeons, and got hideously sick sampling the leavings of the brandy. After we were finished playing, she would brush herself off, adopt a princessly scowl, and flounce off to dinner, no one the wiser.

After I became Melitta's handmaid and got moved upstairs, the differences between us became far plainer. Though we lived on the same few floors of the same tower, we might as well have been on different planets. She spent her days with her nurse, and, later on, with her tutors. I spent mine at Melitta's beck and call, learning afresh every day exactly how much she hated me, long before I understood why. Officially, I wasn't allowed to speak with anyone except Melitta and, now and then, my father, and there were days when the loneliness seemed worse than anything else they could have done.

But my sister fought back. During that entire miserable ten-year stretch, she visited me as often as she could. Usually two or three times a week; always late at night. Those hours were somehow all the sweeter for being stolen. Sometimes we talked and sometimes we played, but more often, she taught me all the things that I wasn't supposed to know. It was from her that I learned to read and write, to do simple arithmetic and geometry. She would bring a lump of chalk, and use the flagstones under my pallet as a slate for words and figures.

I learned less serious things as well. Ariadne liked games, and she taught me any number of them, from koro to knucklebones. Besides that, there were practical lessons, like how to accidentally-on-purpose trip an annoying man into the fireplace and look innocent afterwards. She also passed on a number of the foulest curses you can imagine. She learned them from the soldiers who guarded her and used them to describe her parents every time she had to tend my cuts and bruises.

But Iason and Melitta never knew. Except for her late-night visits, Ariadne was all royal sneers and haughtiness towards me. She didn't even glance at me if we passed each other in the corridor. Even at the age of eight, she had understood what the consequences would be if someone realized what was going on.

IT WAS A long way, as I well knew, to the woodpile at the bottom of the tower, but Ariadne moved fast. In a very few minutes, she was back, wobbling under an armload of ready-cut logs. She stacked them neatly in the woodbin, and then brushed sawdust and beads of resin from her sleeves. "Ruined another dress. Oh, well. I'll have to have a tantrum and blame it on the laundry."

She set a fresh log on the fire and poked it until the bark caught flame. The pearls around her throat seemed to burn orange as they caught the glow. "All right," she announced, her tone all business. "We've got to get you out of here."

It sounded so easy, just said like that. "They'll be expecting me to pose as you again. That trick won't work twice."

"No," she agreed. "We'll have to come up with something new this time. And it'll have to be good. The castle guard has tripled since the war began. Even *I* have a hard time getting out. And they'll be watching you closely."

My face was turned to the heat. It was something about the warmth, and Ariadne's closeness, but I felt something in me start to crack, and

I bit my lip. "You know, honestly, I think they might just kill me this time."

"You know better than that," she said grimly. "They can't, no matter how much they might want to. They need you too much."

This was true, though not very reassuring.

The fire was flickering well, now. Ariadne flopped down on the pallet beside me, and her arms came around my shoulders.

"I like the haircut," she said. "By the way, is it true about you and the pirate?"

"Oh gods. Does our father know about her?"

"At this stage, it's all hearsay and rumour. Is it true?"

I smiled painfully. It was still too hard to think about Darren. "It *was* true. Don't know whether it's still true. I think I managed to really piss her off, right before I got grabbed."

"Why, what did you do?"

I sighed. It seemed so long ago. "I tried to seduce Timor."

"Hmm." I could see that she was trying to picture it. "I have to say, Gwyneth, that doesn't sound like your all-time-best-ever idea."

I leaned back into her. Her dress smelt reassuringly of bark and pitch from the firewood. "That's the other thing. I go by 'Lynn' now. Would you mind?"

"Lynn," she repeated. "That suits you, doesn't it? 'Gwyneth' always seemed like a lace-and-ribbons kind of name to me. Lynn is more—"

"Tough?" I asked ruefully. My head was beginning to throb again.

"Tough," she agreed, as she stroked my hair. "Definitely, tough."

CHAPTER SIX
Darren, formerly of the House of Torasan (Pirate Queen)
Morning, Day IV

THE HERBS PLUNGED me into a deep void. It was forever, or so it seemed, before I surfaced enough to dream.

With Lynn sick, everything around the Banshee *ground to a halt. Meals didn't get out at the right time, the men on the dog watches were sullen, and none of us knew exactly what we were supposed to be doing. I wasn't the only one who noticed. Every time I came up the gangway stairs to the deck, a bunch of expectant eyes turned to me hopefully, and then fell away when they realized that I wasn't her.*

I spent as much time as I could in our cabin, but I wasn't much of a nurse. My hands seemed too big, too clumsy. Lynn had to remind me, in her painful rattling voice, to wipe the sweat off her forehead, air out the damp blankets. But after a few days, I made up my mind to take some initiative, and I set my shoulders and gritted my teeth and marched into the galley.

It took a lot of effort and my eyebrows got burned off in the process, but I managed to make something that I intended to call "soup." I was kind of proud of it, though I didn't know why it moved so gloopily in the pot, or where all the little gritty bits at the bottom had come from. Never mind. It was hot and I was reasonably sure it wouldn't kill her, so I scooped out a cup of it and headed for the cabin.

I dropped it as soon as I got there. Lynn had been better when I left her that morning. At least, her eyes could focus on something for more than five seconds at a time, and she could raise her head to gingerly sip a little water. But now she was sprawled across the bunk, motionless as a dead girl, pale lips parted.

I leapt across the cabin and grabbed the bits of her that came most easily to hand. "Lynn Lynn Lynn Lynn Lynn! *Talk to me. Are you all right?"*

One eye fluttered open. "I am definitely not all right."

"I have some soup for you—" I began to say, looking around for it blankly, before I realized that it was now in a gloopy puddle by the door. I wondered if I could get it back into the cup without her noticing.

"Soup cannot help me now," she said gravely. "Too great is my

affliction. Pirate queen, mistress of my heart, I am so horribly, deathly bored that my brain is decaying into gruel. Have mercy on your powerless chattel, and entertain me."

"Huh," I said, as I checked her forehead. It was definitely cooler. "Well, I'd love to help out, but I'm not much of a singer, and I haven't juggled in years."

"And here I was desperate for some juggling," Lynn complained. "I guess I'll just have to come up with another idea."

Gods on high, that girl could move fast. One minute she was stretched on the bunk, the next she had bounced up and onto me, clinging to my torso like a koala bear.

I staggered back, trying not to overbalance. "How the hell is this entertaining?"

"Well, I'm *having fun*."

I twisted, bucked. It was no good; she still clung. "All right, you're not sick anymore if you can hang on like that."

"Victory is mine," she said into my chest. "I have defeated the mighty Darren. I have freed the world from the scourge of her godawful cooking."

"Just for that? You're not getting any of my wonderful soup. I'm going to go find a new slave and feed it to her." I tried bouncing on my heels, then spinning. She just clung tighter.

"If that's what you plan to feed your slaves, you're going to see a big increase in escape attempts."

"I need less picky slaves. Or maybe I should just buy a cat. Lynn, ow. You're hurting my back."

She hopped off immediately, guilt in her eyes. "Oops. Sorry, I didn't mean—"

I pounced, grabbing her arms and shoving her backwards onto the bunk. In one hop, I was on top of her, straddling her chest. It took just one of my hands to encircle both of her thin wrists, holding her hands immobile above her head.

"You're far too trusting, girl," I snarled.

Lynn wriggled. I knew from experience that she wasn't trying to get loose. She was just arranging herself in a more comfortable position. "Far too trusting," she agreed.

I put two fingers beneath her chin, forcing her to raise it. "You're uppity, too."

"That's what happens when you leave me unattended." She didn't bother to hide her smirk. "So, Mistress, if you're not going to feed me horrible soup, what are you going to do with me?"

I WOKE WITH a jump, as you do when your nerves are shot. Regon was squatting beside me, one hand on my shoulder, while the other carried a cup that steamed.

"Storm's brewing in the east, captain, and we'll need you on deck." He cleared his throat. "I hated to wake you, though. You were smiling."

CHAPTER SEVEN
Lynn
Morning, Day IV

TING . . . TING . . . TING . . .

I was awake by the second *ting*, and started to move without even opening my eyes. Rolled over, yawned, scratched the back of my neck, reached under the pallet for my spare shirt . . .

It wasn't there and that's when I remembered. My chest clamped and I curled up tightly.

Ting . . . ting . . . ting . . . that fucking bell. For ten years, I'd woken up to that bell every single morning. It was how my lady Melitta let me know that she was ready for me to come in and start my chores. After I escaped, it was hard to get used to waking up without it, and if that sounds like a complaint, it isn't. That first morning, when I drowsed until noon and only woke when the sun was beating hard through branches above me, I opened my eyes with such a sense of delight that I felt friendly to the entire world. When I realized the bell was gone, that's when I really knew that I had made it out.

When I heard it again, that's when I really knew that I was back.

Ting . . . ting . . . ting . . .

Now what? I sat up, hugging my knees, thinking. It was the old, familiar choice. Jump when Melitta whistled, or hold my ground and make her fight for everything she got? It was easier to hold onto my self-respect when I was resisting, but before long, she'd turn the tables by making things painful or hard enough that I'd break completely. Then, for a time, I would barely be able to speak without her say-so. My petty little rebellions were always doomed, and more than that, I suspected that Melitta enjoyed them. Sometimes, on days when I wasn't even trying to disobey, I would catch her looking at me with a kind of longing. *Give me a reason*, she seemed to be saying. *I want you to give me a reason.*

Ting ting ting ting . . . she was getting impatient.

My heart was pounding now. I slapped my cheeks sharply. This was insane. I wasn't a child anymore. I had escaped from the castle, caught a ship away from Bero, travelled across three islands, done whatever and *whomever* I had to do to keep breathing, talked my way into a fishing village, learned to empty lobster pots and set drag nets, faced down marauders, seduced a pirate, built a navy . . . after all of that, was I going to trot to Melitta's side as soon as she snapped a finger? Did they really think that I would just fall in line?

They're counting on it, I could imagine Ariadne saying. *They think that if they act like nothing's changed, they can make you forget . . .*

Tingtingtingtingting . . . I had to make the choice now or it would be made for me. Melitta would not be happy if she had to come and collect me herself. What would Ariadne tell me to do? Hell (and my stomach plummeted) what would *Darren* tell me to do? Ariadne would never think less of me for giving in. In fact, she often begged me to. ("What are you trying to prove?" she had hissed at me more than once, in the dead of night, as she wrapped a bad cut or splinted a broken toe.) But *Darren*? Darren had never known me to back down, not from anything. And I believed . . . I had to believe . . . that she liked it that way.

But Darren wasn't there. What happened next wouldn't make a difference to anyone except me. And I had to husband my strength. I would need all of it.

From behind the door, there came the sound of an exasperated snort, and then the swish of the heavy bedclothes being swept aside, and her feet hitting the floor. Although I had decided, more or less, what I was going to do, my reaction to that sound was instinctive rather than reasoned. I shot off the pallet and scrambled onto my feet. I smoothed my tunic with one hand, my hair with the other, and pulled the door open just as Melitta was rising from her bed. Hastily, I bowed my head so I wouldn't have to look at her.

"I'm sorry, my lady," I said.

No explanations; they never helped. I waited, not moving, and after a long stony pause, the bedclothes rustled as she lay down again.

"Get started," she said. "You know the routine."

"Yes, my lady."

I headed for the mahogany nightstand that held her slop pail. As I walked, I dared a quick glance at her face. The smugness that I had expected was there, in the lines of her lazy smile. I stared fixedly at my hands, trying to get myself under control, as I pulled out the pot. Full today. I could smell it.

"Don't take too long," she said.

"No, my lady."

Out of the corner of my eye, I saw her smile again, and acid trickled through my guts. This was my brilliant plan? Doing exactly what the bitch wanted me to do? How could that be the answer?

But there was no answer. There had never been an answer. That was the whole point.

MELITTA'S SLOP PAIL hardly deserved the name. Its rim was edged in gold and there were climbing roses painted all over the lid. Typical of nobles, to want something beautiful to piss in.

Out of sheer force of habit, I studied the twining roses as I tromped down the stairs towards the middens. For ten years, I had carried that pail downstairs first thing each morning, and I knew each flower, each leaf, each godsbedamned artistic frond. I was strongly tempted to smash the stupid thing down on the stone steps; about the only reason I didn't was that I didn't want to foul my bare feet.

The old refrain was ticking away in my head. *I hate my life . . . I hate my home . . . I hate my life . . . I hate my home . . .*

Down in the stable yard, I emptied the pail, letting the stuff plash into a pile of stale hay and manure. Dipping water from the rain barrel, I rinsed it. Hostlers and stable boys tromped by incuriously, not even seeing me. *IhatemylifeIhatemyhomeIhatemy—Goddammit!* I took a deep, shuddering breath, as heat prickled behind my eyelids. *Damned* if I was going to cry. I pressed my forehead against the cool stone of the fortress wall, reorienting myself, and took a couple of breaths.

What next?

You remember the routine, Melitta had said. Well, the slop pail was done. Next, I would need to carry up wood, carry up water, heat water for Melitta's washing, empty the washbasin, clean it, take down the empty supper tray, bring up the breakfast tray, brush yesterday's clothes, clean yesterday's shoes. Then the dusting, then the sweeping, then the scrubbing, then more wood, then more water . . . It took no effort at all to remember the litany. There was an alternative, of course: carry up wood, carry up water, go stark raving mad, charge out of Melitta's rooms, hide in the pigeon coop or the laundry, get hungry, sneak out to filch food, get caught, get dragged up to my father, endure a doleful lecture, get turned over to Melitta, get thrashed, inspect bruises, sleep fitfully, have double chores tomorrow. That routine was almost as familiar. But not today . . . not today. Saving my strength and waiting for an opportunity wasn't much of a plan, but it was all I had at the moment.

In my head, an imaginary Darren dropped her jaw in disbelief. I closed my eyes hard, banishing the thought.

Then I headed for the woodpile.

CHAPTER EIGHT
Darren, formerly of the House of Torasan (Pirate Queen)
Noon, Day IX

IT WAS TAKING too bloody goddamn long. So long that I began to wonder whether all the gods in creation had decided to get their jollies that month by trying to slow me down. First there was the storm—even with all our sails reefed to the size of pillowcases, it blew us nearly a day off course. Then the wind dropped again, not to a dead calm, but to a miserable little puff of a breeze that barely made the sails flutter. Most of the way back to Bero, we could only move at a torturously slow creep, sometimes progressing only a few yards in an hour. It seemed like the *Banshee* was pinned in place on the ocean, which was not a comfortable feeling, when we knew white warships could appear on the horizon any second. More than once, I stormed into my cabin, buried my face in the bunk, and screamed in sheer frustration.

Every single minute that ground by, I imagined some different dreadful thing happening to Lynn. One minute she was murdered by an evil vizier; the next, she was married off to a curly-haired prince with a soppy smile and enormous trousers. The next, she was poisoned at a state dinner; the next, someone noticed my slave mark on her shoulder and had it burned off her skin. Every second, she could be hurting, could be breaking, could be dying, and there was absolutely nothing I could do about it.

At long, long last, when my throat was scratched from screaming and my nails had dug eight crescent-shaped scars into my palms, we reached a point just east of the reef. Only a few rocks showed above the surface, saw-toothed like broken fangs. If I squinted, though, I could make out more of them below the water, gleaming golden-green with their slick coating of algae. Beyond the reef were the cliffs of Bero, forested with sentry towers.

If you ever see a captain or noble or soldier looking stone-faced and silent before a battle, you may think that they're being stoic, too-tough-for-all-that. Take it from me. They're just keeping their mouths shut because they know that they'll vomit, or gibber madly, if they don't.

I myself tend to do both. So I was particularly stone-faced and silent as I watched the horizon. Watching the horizon is another good trick when you're scared to death; it means that you don't have to look at anyone, and it helps control the nausea. It also makes it seem like you're deep in thought, which is a side benefit.

I didn't see Regon approaching, but I heard him clear his throat. "Report," I ordered.

"We're on," he said. "Anchored by the end of the reef, standing out like a couple of great yellow boils on a great red arse. And in plain view of those towers, by the way. In another few hours, they'll send half a fleet by to see what's what."

And they would know that the ships belonged to the pirate queen as soon as they saw the red sails. Red sails are good for getting people's attention, not so good when it comes to sneaking into enemy territory unannounced. Fortunately, my just-this-side-of-insane plan took that into account. I wanted us to be noticed.

Still, we couldn't sit around here twiddling our thumbs for very long. So it was time for the *Banshee* to be on its way. I took a few deep breaths. "Regon, get the men up on deck."

Some first mates like to pipe the men to assembly with a stupid little whistle. Regon preferred to bawl the order at the top of his lungs and break a few noses if he really needed to. It worked just as well. Within a minute, fifty-eight pirates were more or less lined up on the deck, in ragged rows. I let my eyes travel over them. Mismatched clothes, scarred leather jerkins, red silk kerchiefs, bare brown feet. Stubble-faced men, smooth-cheeked boys, a woman here and there. I'd known some of them since I was a child, and some had clambered on board a month before, barely knowing where to look to find the crow's nest.

All the faces in front of me had a kind of fixed, frightening intensity. You'll know that look if you ever see it. It means that, if you want, you can ask your men to follow you through ice and fire.

But I didn't want that. They had more important things to do.

Jess was by the mast, hands in the pockets of her landsman's tunic. When I glanced at her, she gave me an encouraging nod.

"Right," I said grimly, to everyone and no one. "Right."

I slid off my good blue coat, the one Lynn always had me wear when I needed to look imposing. I folded it lengthwise and tossed it onto a crate. Then I loosened my belt buckle and slid off the clip that held my cutlass scabbard.

"Teek, Jess, front and centre," I ordered. "Come on, let's be having you."

My grizzled helmsman pushed his way to the front instantly and stood soldier-straight in the front of the ranks. Jess drifted forward more warily, with a question in her eyes.

They had met already, but I did a brief introduction anyway, using the tip of my sheathed blade to point. "Teek, you remember Jess. She's my old girlfriend and she scares me to death, but she's very good with people. Jess, Teek. He's the best sailor I've ever known." I stepped back from them and raised my voice. "I'm leaving these two in charge. If I don't come back, they'll handle things."

"What things?" Jess asked, looking suspicious. "You mean, your fleet? Your ships? The hundreds of people who have sworn loyalty to you, personally?"

"Yup," I confirmed. "Those things."

She raised a forefinger. "You never mentioned this part of the plan."

"Jess, you said it yourself—you and Holly are part of this movement now, no matter what any of us want. And they're going to need you."

"Need me for what? I don't know anything about warfare."

"You're a midwife. You're used to blood and screaming. It's not as different as you think. Seriously, though . . . they're going to need you when I'm gone. You'll be the voice of reason, or the adult supervision, or whatever."

She huffed. "If you think you've been providing adult supervision, then your capacity for self-delusion is truly massive."

"Captain, think this through," Teek interrupted. The worry lines in his face were as deep as razor cuts. "You can't ask us to keep this up without you."

This discussion was taking too long, I decided. Time for a shortcut. I reached deep, summoned everything that Lynn had ever taught me, and sneered a full-out pirate sneer. It actually made the burly helmsman step back. "I believe I just did. You mangy dogs can save Kila just fine without my help. You can sail as well as me, fight as well as me, lead as well as me. So don't you dare try and keep me from where I'm needed. Lynn put herself in my keeping, and she comes first."

"Captain, people won't follow us," Teek said doggedly. "Not the way they follow you."

"Why not? Because blood is rank, blood is right, blood alone is leadership? Bullshit. It's all about the story, and I'm not the only one who can become a living myth. All you need is someone who can sneer, swagger, talk a good game, and look pretty on the quarterdeck. Catch, Spinner."

I tossed Spinner my cutlass, and he caught it by reflex. He looked from the cutlass to me and from me to the cutlass, and his eyes widened. "Oh, you are fucking kidding me."

"I don't kid when I'm in a hurry." I kicked the rope ladder over the side. "You keep my blade for me until I get back. And if I never get back, then enjoy my cabin and get used to barking orders. Three cheers for the pirate king, everyone."

I waited a second, then raised my voice in the dead quiet. "Well? Cheer, you whoresons, *cheer*!"

They cheered, startled but loud, which was good enough for a start. They kept cheering while Regon, Latoya, Teek, and I climbed down into the waiting longboat. As Latoya took the oars, Spinner's head appeared over the rail. His bruises had begun to heal by then, so his skin was a blotchy map of dark blue, yellow, and green. Even with his face pulped that way, he managed to look dangerous in that moment. I think it was the wild desperation in his eyes.

"Darren, you bastard!" he yelled. "I can't fucking do this!"

"Neither could I," I yelled back. "Turns out, nobody could tell."

"But *captain* . . ."

The rising wind whipped away the rest of his words. I leaned back on the benches, rested my head on my hands, and let the breeze ruffle my hair as Latoya took us through the water.

None of us spoke until the longboat drew level with the *Badger*. I sighed, looking over my old ship. She still had that list to port—I'd never managed to get rid of that, shift the ballast as I might—and the sails were patched and torn. Compared to the sleek *Banshee*, she had all the grace and elegance of a tin washtub. Yet it somehow seemed right that I would be riding the *Badger* into this particular battle. We understood each other, the *Badger* and I. Neither of us specialized in style, but we got the job done.

"All right, I'll bite," Regon announced abruptly, breaking into my thoughts. "Why give Spinner the big job?"

I shrugged. "He listens."

"That so?" Teek asked. "I thought it was because he'd look sweet in velvet."

"Well, that too, obviously."

The *Banshee* was already underway. We watched her tack west through the darkening water, and I felt a sudden lightness. My flagship, my fleet, the future of Kila, all the things I'd fought for . . . they were all out of my hands now, and I found that I didn't really care. Spinner couldn't be exactly the same kind of leader I had been, but with Teek and Corto to keep him alive, and Jess and Holly to keep him honest, he'd figure out a way to live a legend of his own. I would leave him to it.

The four of us climbed up to the *Badger's* deck. Even the planks felt familiar underfoot.

For the next two hours, there was no conversation, no idle words that might distract Teek. He steered superbly, of course, guiding the *Badger* between the murderous rocks like a shuttle through warp and weft. There was one bad moment when a strong gust hit us unexpectedly, almost spinning us into a boulder, but we managed to quant off of it, just in time. It was almost an anticlimax when we slipped into calm water on the far side of the reef.

There was no wasted time when it was over, no long goodbyes. Teek clasped all of our hands one by one. Then he clambered down into the *Badger's* longboat. We'd rigged an improvised sail, but Teek couldn't spare a minute if he was going to get back to the *Banshee* before the white warships arrived. I didn't even watch him as he started to tack his way east through the rocks.

Regon tapped my shoulder. "Ready to be a hero?"

I sighed. "No. Well, I mean, yes . . . but really, no. Because there's a good solid chance that we're about to die horrible deaths, and it's hard to be ready for a thing like that."

Regon shook his head. "If we survive this, you're going to work on your pep talks."

"And you're going to learn to wash regularly. Enough chit chat. Workies."

CHAPTER NINE
Lynn
Evening, Day IX

"THAT'S IT, I guess," I finished.

All the time I was talking, Ariadne had been perched beside me on the hearthstone, listening with total, furrow-browed attention. Not that I had been talking all that long. It was strange, and worrying, that the entire story of my life with Darren could be told in half an hour. Fifteen minutes, if you cut out all the spicy bits.

Ariadne didn't comment, not right away, so I got up and put another log in the fireplace. The easiest way to measure time in the tower was to track the number of logs that had crumbled to embers. We had about an hour before Melitta returned from dinner.

As I settled back down, Ariadne spoke at last. "Darren's going to come for you."

"Why so sure?"

Her voice climbed with princessly outrage. "Because if she doesn't I'm going to find her and I'm going to beat her silly head in, that's why so sure."

"That's very sweet," I said, poking the new log until its crumbling bark began to smoulder. "Now will you keep it down?"

She waved that off. "We're ten floors up from anyone who might be listening."

"You don't *know* that. Keep quiet."

"You're just on edge. I promise you, no one's going to hear. Will you please eat some more?"

I glanced at the greasy bundle she had brought and swallowed carefully. "No, really, I've had enough."

"*She* doesn't let you eat anywhere close to enough, she never has. And I don't know when I'll be able to get up here again, so no arguments. Have the pigeon pie. If you can get through that, it'll keep you going for a week."

I picked off a small bit of meat and pastry and went through the motions of chewing, hoping that would satisfy her. As always, Ariadne had only the best intentions, but she had never been really hungry herself, so she never *could* remember that rich food doesn't sit well on the stomach after days of dry bread and broth. There were uncomfortable gurgles going on down there already, the first stabs of cramps. I just hoped that I could keep myself from throwing up until Ariadne went away. She didn't need another thing to worry about.

While I dissected the pie, trying to make it look like I'd eaten more than I actually had, Ariadne played with the lacy sleeves of her gown. It was lilac that night.

After several minutes, she asked, "Melitta hasn't done anything . . . big . . . yet, has she?"

I crumbled some flakes of lard pastry between my fingers. "No. She's barely said two words to me, as a matter of fact. I've been doing my work and that's about it. Maybe Iason told her to back off?"

"Maybe," Ariadne agreed. "Or she might be waiting for you to slip."

"Or that," I admitted. The smell of the pie was making my stomach clench, so I stood up, casually, as if I just needed to stretch my legs, and paced around the room. "If that's her game, then she'll get what she's after. I've played the trotting lapdog for the past six days. I can't keep it up much longer."

Ariadne snapped straight. "You have to, Gwyn—I mean Lynn. No, listen. If I know anything about my mother, she's set to deliver something brutal the second you step out of line."

"You think I don't know that?"

"So please, please, *please,* I'm begging you, just keep your head down until I can figure out a way to get you out of here. It may take a while, but I *promise* that I'll think of something—does your arm still hurt in the damp?"

I had been rubbing my right forearm without thinking about it. Now I took my hand away. "It's nothing."

"Like hell it's nothing. That arm still hurts when the weather turns, doesn't it?"

Both of my arms were aching, but as usual the right one was worse. The pain in my left arm felt like tiny red threads criss-crossing the muscles; in my right, the pain was fat red ropes that throbbed. I shrugged.

"Doesn't it?"

A shrug or glare was usually enough to stop Darren from asking questions. I'd almost forgotten how pushy my sister could be. "Yes, it hurts; yes, there's a storm coming; no, it's nothing new; no, there's nothing you can do about it and will you *stop shouting?*"

Ariadne slapped her hand against the hearthstone, almost triumphantly. "This is exactly what I was talking about."

"When?"

"Just now. Lynn, you know perfectly well that my mother is insane. Do you remember the day when she broke your arm?"

My right arm and my left arm got broken in two different incidents, on two different days, but we both knew the one that she was talking about. I was sixteen at the time, getting harder for Melitta to handle, so she put extra effort into it. When the bone in my forearm cracked, the noise was enough to bring my father storming up from his room below. Ariadne came up behind him, and the sight of her chalk-white face would have given away her feelings if either of her parents had been paying the least little bit of attention.

That time, they had no choice but to call for a healer. Some hours later, I lay on my pallet, still half-doped with the wine and opium I was given before the bone was set, and listened to Iason and Melitta arguing in the next room. In my foggy state, I couldn't make out any words, but I did hear it when the door banged open and Iason strode out. He went down the stairs very quickly, without looking back at me once. At that moment, even though I was drugged to a stupor, I knew that Melitta had won some kind of victory. She didn't do much to me while the bone was healing, but after that things got messy.

"What's your point?" I asked, interrupting Ariadne before she could launch into a blow-by-blow account of the incident. That day was not one that I needed to relive.

"What did you do right beforehand? Right before she broke your arm?"

"I called her a heartless bitch. You know that."

Ariadne slapped the hearthstone again, and I winced, imagining twenty palace guards galloping up the stairs inquisitively to find out what was going on. "Please stop it. Just cut it out . . ."

"You cut it out. You. Lynn, you *cannot* give her an excuse. None of it is your fault, none of it has ever been your fault, but if there's something you can do to keep her from hurting you, then put your pride in your pocket and bloody *do it*. Do what she tells you, just behave. Because I am not going to see you with bone splinters coming out of your arm again."

"Ariadne—"

"Bones belong inside the skin. Not outside of it! Inside!"

"Shhh. Ariadne, just hush." I sat back down beside her. "I always do what I need to do to survive. I always, always have. Sometimes, to survive, you have to let yourself get hurt. Sometimes that's the only way to protect something bigger, more vital."

Ariadne whipped a hanky of lilac lace from her sleeve and pressed it against her eyes as if she could push the tears back in.

I put a hand on her shoulder. "Hey."

The hanky went down, exposing my sister's face, flushed and grim.

"One day, she's going to push you too far and you're going to jump out the tower window. I *know* it."

"I'm not going to jump out the stupid tower window. If I was going to do that, I would have done it years ago. Calm down. Nothing's happened yet. My bones are all inside my skin. Why are you having fits?"

That just set her off again. "Because you're my sister, dammit! You're my baby sister!"

"I'm only four months younger than you, you drama queen."

"Still counts. You're still the baby. Deal with it." She drew a deep breath and scrubbed her face with the hanky, leaving it even more flushed than before. "I should get going. I'm leaving the food—eat as much as you can before she gets back. That's an order. From your older and far wiser sister."

"Wiser?"

"Infinitely so. And better looking. Don't you forget it."

As soon as her slippered footsteps had whispered down the stair, I gathered the rest of the food into a squashy bundle, pried the window open a crack, and lobbed it out. When I pulled my hands back inside, they were slick with raindrops. The ache in my right arm had turned into a steady, pounding throb. It was going to be a hell of a storm.

CHAPTER TEN
Darren, formerly of the House of Torasan (Pirate Queen)
Evening, Day IX

THE RAIN BEGAN suddenly. One minute it was fat, deliberate drops, and the next a heavy drenching downpour that made the horizon dissolve in a wash of grey. Here and there were glowing orange dots in the gloom—flames at the top of sentry towers, along the cliff of Bero.

Latoya deftly rigged a sail into a tent, and, hunched beneath it, we had a quick makeshift meal of dried meat and groats. We weren't hungry, but we weren't sure when we would next get a chance to eat. Besides, it would help to keep us warm.

Beside us were three separate jumbles of wood and rope—sections of planking cut from the *Badger's* deck, lashed to sealed and empty casks. We were already carrying the rest of the gear. We each had a knife—two in my case—bound at the back of our belts, the blades wrapped in cloth smeared with pig fat, to protect the metal. Our boots would be tied to our waists. We couldn't take much more than that. We had to travel light where we were going.

Regon and I sat on the wet deck to eat, but Latoya stayed on foot, her eyes roaming, restless.

"We should go," she reminded us. "No sense in waiting."

"We're probably all about to die," Regon said thickly, chewing his fifth biscuit. "Putting that off makes sense to me."

She dismissed him with a flick of her eyes and looked to me instead. "The navy will have seen us, sent scouts. We should go."

Reluctantly, I got to my feet. "Yarr," I mumbled, trying to get myself into a swashbuckling mood.

"What?"

"Nothing, Regon. Get your lazy arse to the tiller. Make your course west by northwest."

He crammed in the last of the biscuit, and licked his fingers. "West by northwest it is, captain. But couldn't you just say, 'Head for the damn big rock over there?'"

"You just *had* to mention the rock. I was trying not to think about the rock. Latoya, set the sails."

I watched her sidelong as we worked. Regon and I had been laughing too loud and making unfunny jokes all through the evening. Latoya had been calm as a closed oyster.

"Aren't you scared?" I asked abruptly.

"No point," she said, making a knot fast with a jerk. "If we die, we die."

There wasn't much arguing with that statement, but it annoyed me anyway. "Don't you try that with *me*, sailor."

"Try what?"

"The 'too tough for my shorts' act. I *invented* the 'too tough for my shorts' act. Hell, I *am* the stinking shorts."

That was enough to make her glance up, eyebrow raised.

"That might not have been the best phrasing," I admitted.

"You spout crap when you're nervous," Latoya said with interest. "Maybe you ought to gag yourself or something."

"No, no . . . it's probably good that I'm getting it out of my system before I see Lynn again."

I looked up, raindrops drumming on my face. The sails were billowing out now. The *Badger* was underway, for the last time.

"Heading for the big damn rock, captain!" Regon yelled from his spot by the tiller.

I could just make it out, a black humpbacked shape in the gloom. "You'd better get over here."

He didn't bother to respond, but I heard rustling back there and I knew what he was doing: lashing the tiller in place, then hurrying to join us amidships. Latoya and I were already waiting by the gunwales by the pile of planks and barrels. The three of us stood together, watching almost reverently as the rock loomed larger and larger in the choppy sea. Beneath us, the planks of the *Badger* groaned and creaked.

"Will she keep together until we get there?" Regon said, mostly to break the silence.

"She'll do," I murmured, giving a fond stroke to the gunwale. "All right, time to be stupid."

We picked up one knotted mass of planks and barrels and heaved it over the side. It hit the water with a loud wet smack, but, I was relieved to see, floated immediately. Regon spat, rubbed his hands, and vaulted over the side himself. In two strokes, he caught up with the floating planks, pulled himself on top of them, and got a good grip on the ropes with fingers and toes.

Latoya and I tossed in the other two makeshift rafts, and then Latoya herself crashed down into the sea. I stood at the gunwale, waiting to make my own jump, and thought the thoughts that one thinks when one is about to leap into ice-cold water in the middle of a raging storm. Which can all pretty much be summed up as *Oh, shit.*

The rock was looming very large now.

I've never been religious, exactly, but an old sailor's prayer swam into my head as I looked at the shuddering waves. *Lords of the deep, see our weakness; lords of the deep, allow us passage. Lords of the deep, know our need; lords of the deep, allow us passage.*

Lords of the deep, let me find Lynn, I finished off, adapting the end of the prayer for the occasion. *Lords of the deep, don't let her be too pissed at me . . .*

I leapt.

IN THE FIRST ten seconds after I hit the water, the *Badger* hit the rock. The planks of the bow splintered with a noise like chicken bones breaking, and the little ship began to list to starboard as water poured in. Latoya had done some hard work down in the hold with a hatchet, weakening supports and opening gaps, to make sure it all happened quickly. The *Badger* would break apart or go to the bottom, and when Iason's ships reached the rocks, they would find the shattered wreck. With any luck, they'd reach the obvious conclusion, that the pirate queen had tried and failed to make it to Bero through the reefs.

It was a good plan, sacrificing the *Badger* to put Iason's navy off the scent. Probably the best part of what was otherwise a very sketchy plan indeed. Still, my throat almost closed as I watched the little ship flounder.

Pirates have their sentimental side. I'm no exception. Deal with it.

But I didn't have long to think sentimental thoughts, or rational thoughts, or plan-related thoughts, or indeed anything that you could call thoughts.

As I clung to the raft, what was running through my head, at any given moment, was this: "Bad idea bad idea shit cold very cold shit dammit dying now bad idea bad idea ow was that a shark? shit cold stupid Darren bad bad bad bad *bad*!"

For the million years that I was in the water, I did my best to focus on breathing. The trapped air in the casks kept me and the raft at the surface, more or less. But with whitecaps breaking over my head every few seconds, and solid sheets of rain bucketing down at the same time, that didn't seem to make much of a difference. With my mouth always open and gasping, I drank pints of seawater within a few minutes, and before long my throat was on fire, my stomach cramping, and my tongue swollen to a fat slug.

It was a toss-up which was worse, the thirst or the cold. Every now and then, I would upturn my face to the rainy sky, trying to get a mouthful of fresh water. The drops smacked every part of my face, it seemed, except my salty tongue, and the rainwater was so much colder than the surrounding sea that, within a few seconds, I had to dunk my head under the surface to get rid of the freezing slick.

Again and again, I raised my head and squinted desperately around, trying to make out the orange flames of the sentry-towers somewhere in the murk. Sometimes I thought I saw them in the distance, and sometimes up close, and sometimes I didn't know whether I was seeing towers, or the reflection of stars on the water, or fireflies, or death, or dreams. It was no good trying to swim properly, to make headway, and the three of us had made up our minds not to try. With an immense amount of luck, the tide would wash us up on shore. Without an immense amount of luck, we were dead anyway. But as the night wore on and I got more tired, the animal part of me came to the forefront. I found myself struggling madly, kicking and thrashing and yelling myself hoarse, for whole minutes at a time, before I could force myself to go limp again.

The whole universe had shrunk to a dark pit filled with cold water, and I seemed to be all alone there. It was hard to cling to the knowledge that two of my sailors were somewhere nearby. Once, just once, a wave sent me crashing headlong against Latoya's raft. She looked like damp seaweed draped over a piece of flotsam until lightning flashed on her face, showed it calm and thoughtful.

"Ow," she commented darkly.

And then the waves tore us apart again.

A few eternities later, when nothing was real to me but the salt and the cold and each gasp of air, some part of me became dimly aware that my shoulder was scraping against barnacled planks. I looked up. My raft was floating alongside a tall white warship. There were lights moving on deck. I flattened myself against the raft, waiting for the whistles and shouts, the roar from the sailors on board, but there was nothing. The tiny craft drifted harmlessly past.

That was the first of many encounters in that long stormy night. Again and again, the raft slipped between the ships of the mighty navy of Bero, invisible in the downpour. I couldn't see Regon and Latoya any more, and could only hope that they were having the same luck, in the rare moments that I had the energy to hope.

Then the storm was fading, and a grey glow lit the horizon . . .

And then, without warning, my knuckles were scraping rock.

I was so bleary after the bashing I had taken that it took me a good few minutes to realize where I was. The raft had washed up under a wooden pier, and I was draped across the rocks that steadied the dock pilings. Groggy as I was, I knew that I couldn't waste a minute getting undercover. I couldn't see anyone watching, but I couldn't see anything anyway, with my salt-scarred eyes. After a few tries, I managed to free my knife with a trembling hand, and cut the ropes that held the raft together. The planks and casks, I floated underneath the dock. With luck, they wouldn't attract any notice. Then I slipped into the water and half-swum, half-staggered to the beach. The nearest shelter was a boat overturned for scraping, and I slipped underneath it.

Plan, I thought, *need a plan, need a plan . . .*

That was as far as I got before I passed out.

"CAPTAIN, WAKE UP. Captain . . ."

Not very patient, that voice. With great reluctance, I opened my eyes.

Latoya and Regon were crouched beneath the overturned boat with me. Both of them looked like they'd been stoned by a hostile crowd, and then drowned for good measure.

Latoya summed up the situation in her usual accurate way. "That sucked."

There didn't seem to be much more to say about it. Latoya had a skin of fresh water with her; she'd lashed it to the underside of her raft before we set out. We passed it round, swilling our mouths and spitting out the brine.

"All right," I said when that was done. "Everybody functional?"

Regon winced and Latoya rolled her eyes. I wondered why I'd even asked the question. We all felt like living, breathing crap. But we had four limbs apiece. It would have to do.

"So now we sneak into the fortress, yeah?" Regon asked, sounding exhausted. "Remind me, was there a plan about how we were going to do that?"

"I think we were going to, um, assess the situation on the ground."

"Assess the situation on the ground," Latoya growled. "You mean you're going to make it up as you go along."

"Hey, a little less of the skeptical tone, sailor. Did I get us to Bero? Yes, I fucking got us to Bero. So far, my plans are coming up aces. I—Regon? Pay attention to the fascinating things that I'm saying."

He was peering under the bottom edge of the boat. "I don't think we need to get up to the fortress."

"What? Of course we do."

He jerked his head. "Look there."

I looked there, bending so I could peek through the gap between the boat and the sand. My heart stopped beating for a full five seconds, and then began to pound out a loud and triumphant tattoo. *Lynn*. It was bloody *Lynn*, blonde hair almost white in the pre-dawn glow as she hurried across the beach. Her progress was halting. Every other minute, she stopped to glance behind a beached ship or a boathouse, obviously looking for something. *Someone*. Granted, she was in a dress that made her look totally unlike herself (mounds upon mounds of pale apricot silk) and there was something different about her hair, but that wasn't the point. She was there and I didn't think, not for a second.

I lurched out from beneath the boat and threw myself at her. My legs almost buckled beneath me, but I got my balance back when I grabbed her. One hand on her head, the other at the small of her back, I pulled her in and kissed her with all my might. She froze a second, startled, but then relaxed into it.

It was only after the first ten seconds of mind-melting relief that I began to notice things.

I wasn't bending over as much as I usually had to when I kissed Lynn. The shoulder I could see looked fleshy rather than bony. And she didn't taste quite right.

That was also when I became aware that the woman in my arms was gently, ever-so-gently, pulling away.

I released her and took a step back, baffled.

"Thank you," the woman said politely. "That was very nice. But I think you meant to give it to my sister."

CHAPTER ELEVEN
Lynn
Morning, Day X

SOMETHING WAS DEFINITELY up.

When I came up the stairs with Melitta's breakfast tray, there was a green handkerchief wedged in the crack of Ariadne's bedroom door. This was a message in our old code, and meant simply, "We need to talk. I'll find you later."

My father spent an hour in the map room with his advisors, and when he left, he was wiping his forehead on his sleeve. He looked tired, but pleased, so I figured that something must have gone right for him that morning.

But when I got back from dumping the wash water, he and Melitta were at it again, behind the closed door of her bedroom. I went partway down the stairs so that I could listen without being seen.

"It solves one problem," Iason was saying. "But that's hardly the real issue here. What I really want to know is how you're going to deal with *her*."

Melitta's response was quieter. I could hear the venom in it, but couldn't make out any words until the very end, when her tone suddenly soared: ". . . that defiant, sullen little *slut!*"

You never hear anything good about yourself when you eavesdrop. Have you ever noticed that?

Iason's voice was half highly-important-and-overstressed-man, half helpless-nice-bloke this time around. "Woman, listen to yourself. You don't *need* to go that far."

"You have always said, you have *always* said that it was my decision how far to go."

"It was, it is, but Melitta, listen. If you lose control, she could end up dead. And you know as well as I do what will happen if that girl dies."

I pinched my inner elbow, hard.

Their voices sunk to murmurs. I considered going closer, but that would leave me in plain view if one of them suddenly yanked the door open.

At last, Iason spoke hard and businesslike. "It seems like you have it all figured out. So why bother to ask me?"

"I want you to say it, Iason." Melitta's voice had grown even sharper, now that she had almost won. "Look me in the eye, and tell me that I can do whatever I think is necessary."

The voices went quiet again. I strained my ears until my jaw hurt, but the next thing I heard was the door opening. It swung, it didn't bang, which meant that they had reached some kind of agreement.

Not good. Not good at all.

My father, Lord Iason, clumped down the stairway at a methodical pace, left-right-left-right. A tired man, a busy man, a man who wished that people wouldn't bother him with unnecessary drama. He gave me the merest glance as he passed.

"She wants you," he said. "Go on now."

CHAPTER TWELVE
Darren, formerly of the House of Torasan (Pirate Queen)
Morning, Day X

"*YOU'RE* ARIADNE?" I repeated for the fourth time.

"Yes, yes," the noblewoman said impatiently. She was leading us through a labyrinth of narrow alleyways at high speed. The three of us almost had to jog to stay level with her.

"You're Ariadne," I repeated again, for a total of five, "and Lynn is your *sister*? But Iason only has one child—everybody knows that."

"Everybody knows it, do they?" The scorn in her voice was stinging. "Well, you're out of your mind if you think that the public knows everything about my father. He has any number of guilty little secrets, and a few guilty big ones. The guiltiest and biggest is Gwyneth."

"Gwyneth?"

"Lynn, I mean. Sorry, Lynn. I keep forgetting. Here we are."

She ground to a halt by a low-slung plank building. It had a heavy, iron-clamped door with a bastard of a padlock, but the princess produced a key from somewhere in the billowing folds of her dress, and clicked it open. The door didn't budge when Ariadne tugged on the handle, but Latoya quickly joined her and wrenched it ajar with one hand. Beyond was the smell of musty straw and leather. A disused stable, it looked like.

"This used to belong to my husband," she said breathlessly. "It was his hunting stable, and he's spectacularly dead now, so I suppose it belongs to me. Anyway, no one will wander in here. You two—yes, you, the short man, and the other one that looks like a bear in trousers—you'll have to wait here. Darren . . . you are Darren, aren't you? Pirate queen, right? Darren will be back in an hour or so."

Regon gave me a quick sidelong glance, and I nodded my approval. The two of them slipped inside, and I heard the grunt as Latoya hauled the door back in place.

Ariadne tapped her foot. "Quick, we have to hurry."

I didn't know how much hurrying she could manage, considering the yards of apricot-coloured silk that were draped around her, but she bundled her skirts up under one arm and trotted along gamely. Within a very few seconds, we had emerged onto a busy, rain-washed street. This was the lower city, where the ordinary folk of Bero lived, and the people tramping by were peasants—fishermen, fruit vendors, masons. I straightened my salt-streaked clothing and tried to act natural.

"I haven't got long," Ariadne said over her shoulder as she picked her way through the puddles. "They know that one of your ships crashed on the reef last night. I heard my father talking about it this morning."

"How did you know that I made it to shore?"

"I didn't. Just hoped. And I knew that if you did make it this far, you'd need my help to get any farther. I had to throw a really terrible tantrum to get out of the castle—said I wanted to go riding—slipped all six of my bodyguards and lord knows where they're looking for me. I've only just enough time to show you the way."

"Where are we going?" I panted, trailing after her. "Where's Lynn? How is she? Can you get me to her?"

"Halfway up to the wall. In the high turret. Pretty awful. And no. The fortress is heavily guarded even at the best of times, but my father tripled the soldiers on tower watch once Timor got back here with Lynn. This is going to be a tough nut to crack."

"Well, they have to open the gates sometime, don't they? I mean, supplies don't levitate into the fortress."

"Every shipment that goes through the gates is searched, no matter whether it's going in or out. Every bag of apples, every wagonload of hay, every empty barrel. Trust me on this. Lynn and I spent years trying to figure out a way to beat the system . . ."

A brilliant thought occurred to me. "Wait—*you* can get outside, right? What if Lynn pretends to be *you,* and—"

She gave a snort of the utmost impatience. "Did you honestly think we never thought of that? That's how we got her out four years ago, of course. But they're watching for it now."

"Well . . . for fuck's sake, you're a princess. Can't you grab a few guardsmen and order them to escort Lynn down to the harbour?"

"I don't have that kind of authority."

"Then scream until they *think* you have that kind of authority."

"You're underestimating my father's paranoia. He's obsessed with the idea of assassins. Nobody but my father or the captain of the guard can approve an unscheduled entrance or exit, and I can't change that no matter how loudly I scream. Besides, we're not talking about getting just anyone out of the castle. We're talking about Lynn, and she's on a very tight leash at the moment, and it's only going to get worse. If he has to, my father will spend his entire fortune to make sure she stays put."

I let out a frustrated pant. "But . . . *why?*"

She raised an eyebrow, surprised. "You mean, you don't know?"

THERE WAS SILENCE then, as she led me through a dizzying series of back-alleys and narrow streets, up stairways and down other ones. I gave up interrogating Ariadne, and just tried to keep up. I'm not much of a runner. I mean, I'm in shape and everything, but you don't get much practice jogging when you live on a ship.

"Ariadne," I said at last, puffing along behind her. "I'm sorry about this, but if you don't explain to me exactly what's going on, then I'm afraid I'm going to scream. I'm sorry but I shall."

"Lynn said you were smart," she called, again over her shoulder.

"She's over generous. Use small words."

"Oh, fine." She waited for me to catch up. "It's not complicated, really. It's the simplest of stories. The oldest of stories. My father is lord of the house of Bain and I am his firstborn, his heir. My father is also a selfish pig and while my mother was pregnant and he couldn't sleep with her, he used her handmaid instead. Elain, her name was. Nice lady. Liked cats. Before long, she was pregnant too. My mother Melitta—who is likewise a selfish pig, but nobody's fool—figured it out very quickly. She flew into a rage, dragged Elain twice around the castle by her hair, then threw her out. Elaine went down to live in the lower city—here, in other words. Fortunately for her, she had an uncle who was willing to take her in. And a few months later she had her baby . . ."

"Lynn," I finished. "So Lynn is Iason's bastard. But why was he so hell-bent on finding her?"

Nobles aren't famous for restraining their sexual urges, so most lords have at least a few half-blood children scampering around the servant quarters. But bastards can never take the throne, or marry into a good family, or, indeed, wield any real power at all. For all practical purposes, they're irrelevant. So their fathers either ignore them or get rid of them before they can cause trouble—tossing them into the army is a common trick. I'd never heard of anyone going to such lengths to drag a half-blood home.

Ariadne knew all of this. She raised an expressive eyebrow. "Five-day fever."

"What—" I began, and then, slowly, "Ohhhh."

"My father caught it off of a Tyranese ambassador, and my mother from him and I from her. The disease didn't spread any farther, but the damage was done. Both my parents had serious cases. Running scabs over half their bodies, so I'm told."

"Oh lord," I breathed. I had to slow to a halt, leaning on a nearby wall for support, as everything suddenly snapped into place. Five-day fever is about as ugly an illness as you can imagine, but it has one lasting effect that, to a noble, would matter more than any other. "It left them both sterile."

"Sterile as hot glass. I haven't seen for myself, of course, but apparently my father's balls actually *withered*. So you see. We need to go up here."

I barely saw the stairs beneath my feet as I followed Ariadne. I can try to explain how a Kilan noble would feel about losing the ability to bear children, but unless you're a Kilan noble yourself, I doubt that you can even come close to understanding. *Nothing* meant more to nobles than the survival of their bloodline. Children meant richness, fame, immortality. Childlessness meant failure, dissolution, annihilation; it meant a once-great house would crumble, be eaten from within by rebellion and rivalries, and would finally die and rot.

It had always been suspicious that Iason had only one daughter, and of course there had been rumours. But there are rumours about every lord in the islands, myths that breed the catcalls and insults that sailors swap in taverns. I had never for a moment thought that one of them could be true, that Iason of Bain really couldn't father a child. Just as I never thought that Nimian of Jiras *actually* slept with turtles.

This changed everything.

While I was still deep in thought, we emerged onto a stone porch that jutted from some high building—a temple, maybe—far above the streets. The lower city was spread out beneath us like a map, and we had a good view of the castle up the cliff to the west. But I couldn't concentrate on that, not when things were finally beginning to make sense. "So if anything happened to you, the house of Bain would be completely wiped out."

"It's worse than that," Ariadne said grimly, resting her arms on the balustrade. "I had the fever as well, remember."

"You mean, you're . . . well . . . ." I couldn't quite bring myself to say it, but I gestured vaguely in the direction of her stomach, and she grinned.

"You're shy for a pirate. I don't know whether I'm barren. Not for certain. None of us do. I had a much lighter case of the fever than either of my parents. No scarring, and I was only in bed for a week. But my physicians at the time said that there was a fifty-fifty chance."

I was willing to bet that the physicians who made that assessment didn't live long afterwards. "Is it true that you were married?"

"For a full two years," she confirmed, "and for all that time, I was being rutted as regularly as a prize mare. And nothing came of it but some medium-bad chafing. Now, that's not proof. Maybe Gerard was the one shooting blanks. But I wouldn't place any large bets on it."

My jaw locked. "And that means . . . ."

"That means that my mother and father can never have another child.

And I probably can't have one at all. And you know that I won't be able to hold the throne if I'm childless. If the house of Bain, my father's line, is going to survive, then he needs grandchildren and there's only one place he can get them. There's only one person who has both my father's blood and a working womb. And that's—"

CHAPTER THIRTEEN
Lynn
Noon, Day X

"GWYNETH." MELITTA ACTUALLY looked up at me when I entered the room, for a change. "Sit down."

She was at the small tea-table. I sat in the chair across from her, warily. Something was definitely up.

The table held a tray of cakes and hot spiced wine steaming in two silver tumblers.

"Please," Melitta said, waving an airy hand towards the food. "Eat something. Wherever you've been, you can't have been fed well. You're a skeleton."

The sheer hypocrisy of it made my bones itch, but since I'd been sick three times the night before and hadn't been given breakfast that morning, I was more interested in eating than arguing. The cakes were probably richer than was good for me, but I was hungry enough not to care. I took a cake and cracked it in half. It was filled with sweet almond paste, and that broke down the last of my resistance. I moved the tray closer to me and set to work. Within five minutes, half of the cakes were gone. The wine was strong and scalding. After a few mouthfuls, there was a comfortable burn all the way through my torso.

Melitta watched me indulgently as I ate. "Good, aren't they? When Iason conquered Gantra last month, he brought me back a new pastry cook. I've told him that he needs to conquer Retlio and bring back a new seamstress."

I wiped my mouth on my sleeve. The wine had made me light-headed. "I'm not a pet, you know. You can't buy my love with food. Iason never really understood that, but I thought *you* were smarter."

"It would be stupid to try to win you over that way, wouldn't it?" Melitta agreed. "Considering the history of our relationship. And we do have a lot of history, don't we? Go on and think about it."

I didn't want to. "What's your point?" I asked, as I reached for my cup of wine again.

Melitta's hand darted forwards. I flinched back, but her target was my wine-cup. She hit it backhand; the wine splashed over the table and floor in a long bloody stream, staining the rug. The next second, she grabbed the tray of cakes and flung it against the wall. The tray clashed horribly; the cakes pattered down onto the stones with soft little *thumps*.

It didn't startle me, exactly. I was surprised that she hadn't done it earlier, and was glad that I'd eaten as fast as I had. But it was a sign that we were moving into a less pleasant stage of our conversation. Under the table, I rubbed my sweaty palms against my tunic.

"Gwyneth, I couldn't care less whether you love me," Melitta began. "I care about one thing. Just one. Exactly one. I care about whether you do what you are told to do, *when* you are told to do it, instantly, perfectly, and respectfully. Because you haven't done that in the past, have you, Gwyneth? You're rude, or you're sullen, or you're slow, or you're lazy, or you talk back, or you go off and whimper to my husband. I don't think you know how much trouble you've given me, over the years. Do you think I *enjoy* having to straighten you out?"

"I'm sorry," I said, because it was obviously expected.

The apology seemed to excite her, somehow. "There, you see? That's it. That's the insolence. No matter what you're saying, there's never a grain of *real* respect, real . . . submission. You still fancy yourself a sort of princess, don't you? You still think that your attachment to Iason makes you *special* in some way. And that, my girl, makes you believe that you're too good to do what I ask of you. Too good to be a servant, too good to do chores for your keep, too good to run errands for Iason's wife, too good to bow your head to the lady of Bero . . ."

Her voice got higher as it got more spiteful. As if as an afterthought, she picked up her own glass of wine and took a long swallow. That seemed to calm her, and she gave a long, reflective sigh.

"Isn't that what you think?" she said, now smiling pleasantly. "That you're different?"

I knew I was making a mistake but couldn't help it; wine makes me blurt things out. "I *am* different, or none of this would be happening. I wouldn't even be here if Iason wasn't my father—"

I literally slapped a hand over my own mouth, but it was too late. Melitta's face turned ugly, as if a flat stone had been flipped over to reveal the crawling things beneath. I stumbled backwards, knocking over my chair, and started to scramble away, but she caught up with me in three long strides. This was the moment, back in the day, when she would have grabbed me by my hair, and sure enough she tried, but the short locks slipped out of her fist. Even in my panic, I felt a moment of triumph, but that was cut short when she snatched my right ear instead. Her thumbnail and the nail of her forefinger almost met as her pinch pierced the skin.

Some faint cool voice was in my head, telling me that I knew how to deal with this. Little disconnected thoughts swarmed all over my brain, words like *knee strike, joint lock, choke hold,* but I barely remembered what any of them meant, let alone how to make them happen. The only thing I knew was that I was deep, deep, deep in trouble. As the blows began to hammer down on my face and head, I launched a half-hearted kick at Melitta's shin, but that just made the force of the hits redouble. I shielded my head with my forearms as best I could and let the rest of me go limp. Sounds from somewhere far away buzzed in my ears.

Some time later, Melitta tossed me down. She was breathing through her nose, in short snorts, and she settled herself back into her chair gingerly, as though she was the one in pain. Tears stood out in her eyes, and her chin trembled. She was always like this afterwards. While she was composing herself, I picked myself up, very, very carefully, and stood my chair upright again. As I waited, I tasted the blood on my teeth.

A few minutes later, she smiled again, and waved a hand at my chair. "Please. Sit."

I sunk down, my heart ticking painfully on my ribs.

"Iason's not your father," she said, still smiling. "Because that would make me your stepmother. Which I'm not. I'm just your keeper. Iason gave you to me long ago, did you realize that? I have his blessing to do whatever I like with you, and if it wasn't for one thing, I would have had you whipped to shreds by now."

She sighed, tracing the pattern on her wine goblet. "Blood. That unfortunate matter of blood. Something very precious, Iason's blood, is trapped inside you. It's as if you stole a priceless diamond from him and swallowed it. You're holding all his descendants prisoner."

If you want my blood, I thought for the thousandth time, *cut me open and take it out, I don't care, I don't want it.* The tightness of her smile told me that she knew what I was thinking, and, more than that, she had considered it.

"So what does all of this have to do with almond cakes?" she said conversationally. "Well, Gwyneth, this is how it is. I'm sick of your defiance, so I've decided that it's never going to happen again. From now on, every moment that you are awake, you will be obedient, and docile, and attentive. You will do what I tell you to do, and only that. You will live how and where I decide. You will do this because every moment of pleasure or comfort in your life, every moment that you spend without broken bones and lash marks, will be a gift to you from me. And you will get those gifts only when I am satisfied. Iason is not going to intervene. No one will. So you'd better start improving."

"I'm not a child anymore," I said. I had meant for it to be louder, a ringingly defiant proclamation. But it came out as a whisper instead, and there was a hint of pleading in it.

"You're right," she agreed. "You're not a child anymore. It's a great relief, have I told you that? You're not a little blonde imp for whom Iason has a bit of a soft spot. You're a common, cheap sort of woman who doesn't understand her place in the world. And I'm here to teach it to you. It's as simple as that. It doesn't particularly matter what I have to do in order to bring the message home."

My chest was getting tighter and tighter. "You need me. You need me to—"

"We may need you to whelp a couple of times, yes," Melitta agreed. "Do you need both of your hands to bear children? Do you need both your feet? Do you need your hamstrings unsevered, do you need your ears attached? Look at me and tell me that I wouldn't do it."

I didn't even try.

"So understand this clearly," she said, as her fingers curled again around her goblet. "You obey me. That is all you do. Whether I order you to pour a glass of wine, or bow, or kneel, or knock your own head against the wall, or bed the stable boy, you don't hesitate. Your purpose in this life is to do as you are told. So remember. The next time you disobey me, I will beat you with the fireplace poker. And if you leave this tower without permission, then I will blind you with it."

She broke off to take a swallow, then set the cup down with a click. "I prefer you with long hair. That's one of the things we'll have to fix."

CHAPTER FOURTEEN
Darren, formerly of the House of Torasan (Pirate Queen)
Noon, Day X

FAR BENEATH THE stone porch where Ariadne and I were standing, sailors and soldiers trooped past, unaware. I barely saw them.

"So you had the fever when you were little," I said to Ariadne. "And Iason knew that it might have made you barren. All those years ago, he knew that you might never be able to give him an heir. So what did he do?"

"What do you think he did? He came up with a contingency plan. And by that I mean, he went and found Gwyneth—Lynn, I mean—and he had her brought up to the castle. She was two."

"And her mother? Elain?"

"Oh, he brought Elain to the castle as well. She became a scullion—rotten job, but at least it got her away from my mother. She lived in the kitchens with Lynn for about seven years."

"What happened then?"

"Elain died."

"How?"

"She fell down some stairs. That's what I remember being told."

I knew this story. "And it was very sudden, am I right? And nobody saw her fall and they buried her very very quickly?"

"Yeeesss . . ." she said, confused now. "Why?"

"Oh, come on," I said. "When somebody's existence is an embarrassment to a powerful man, and that somebody dies very suddenly, then chances are, it wasn't an accident. You *must* have thought of that before."

I watched her eyes grow stricken.

"Apparently not," I murmured.

"Are you saying," she asked very slowly, "are you saying that my parents murdered Elain?"

"Can't be sure. It's not like I was peeking around the corner and taking notes at the time. But it seems the likely thing. It's what *my* father would have done. He would have killed Jess if we hadn't escaped in a blistering hurry, and . . . and that reference will make no sense to you." I coughed. "Anyway."

Ariadne was sporting an odd look by then. It seemed that she was turning over this new information, weighing it, and then accepting it, and mentally scribing it on the thousandth page of a book entitled *Why I Hate My Parents.*

"She was always kind to me," she said at last. She bowed her head, and long blonde curls fell around it, shutting out her face from view.

I gave her, oh, two-and-a-half seconds to mourn. We were in mid-crisis, after all. "What happened then?"

Ariadne brushed her hair back, sighed deeply, and refocused on the story. "After Elain died—after she was murdered—that's when my mother started taking an active role in things. She brought Lynn upstairs, out of the kitchens, and took her as a handmaid."

"But Lynn must have been . . . what, nine years old?"

"Eight."

"That's ridiculous-" I began, and then I stopped myself. It wasn't ridiculous. I had servants that young myself, once upon a time. With a pang, I remembered a fawn-eyed girl who used to bring the wash water to me and my siblings in the early morning. The jug was too big for her and she walked very slowly with it, swaying from one side to the other. If the water had cooled by the time she got to us, it was considered the done thing to give her a clump on the head. I usually didn't participate in the clumping, preferring to wash before the water grew even colder. But now it appalled me to remember how I used to turn my back on the whole scene, blocking out the girl's yelps and squeals as I got dressed.

I'd spent so many nights in my life sitting paralyzed in a drunken, guilty stupor. Funny how I'd never remembered the wash water girl on any of those occasions. I'd spent my entire adult life apologizing for the wrong things.

"Melitta used to beat the hell out of Lynn," I said, stating it rather than asking.

Ariadne's fingers drummed on the balustrade. She nodded.

"Anything else?" I asked savagely.

"Yes. Of course. My mother is an innovative person. Over the years, she made up endless ways to punish Lynn for being born. She humiliated her, she piled work on her, she wouldn't let her eat enough, wouldn't let her sleep. There's a closet in my mother's room where she used to put her . . . Honestly, Darren, I can't talk about this. I may be sick."

"But *why*? *Why*? None of this is Lynn's fault. Why would your mother blame her?"

"Oh, please don't ask me to explain the perverted mystery that is my mother's brain. She resents Lynn, I guess. Resents Lynn for being a bastard brat, the living proof of my father's indiscretions, who nonethe-less means more to my father than anyone else in the world, because she can give him something that no one else on earth can provide. No, scratch all of that. That makes it sound far too rational. Let's stick with, 'My mother's an evil bitch.'"

"But what about your father? Doesn't he care? Doesn't he try to protect her?"

"Not he," Ariadne said, scornfully. "Sometimes he plays the sorrowful-eyed innocent, but don't let that fool you. It suits him fine, the way my mother treats her. It would be a horrible loss of face for him if people knew about his . . . you know . . ."

"His withered balls," I contributed.

"Yes. Those. So he can never let anyone find out who Lynn is and why he needs her. That means that he has to keep her close, but under control. Dependent and unambitious. Every now and then, when she was small, he used to spoil her a bit, just to keep her off balance. You know, he would give her sweets and fruit and let her play with my toys, that kind of thing. But she never bought the act. Not ever. One of the best moments of my entire childhood was when she took an apple from him and then used it to sock him in the side of the head."

There was so much pride in her tone, I had to smile ruefully. The funny thing was that I had seen Lynn pull off the same manoeuvre myself. Except, that time, her opponent was a marauder the size of a gorilla and instead of an apple, she used a coconut.

"All right," I said. "But say you are barren. Say that your father needs Lynn to breed the next generation. What happens then? Would he acknowledge her as his child? As the mother of his grandchildren?"

"We've wondered about that," Ariadne said absently. "There are a number of possibilities, of course. The most likely, I think, is that he would keep her hidden during her pregnancies, have me fake a big belly and morning sickness, and then smuggle the babies to me as soon as they were born. She would have to be kept well hidden for that to work. Maybe locked up. Or he could try to pass her off as a relative of his—cousin or niece or something—marry her to some minor nobleman and adopt her children when they were born. Or, if he's *really* desperate, he could get rid of me and have Lynn take my place. I don't think that last one is very likely, but it's possible."

"My god, Ariadne . . ."

She threw up her hands. "My parents are horrible people. This is what I've been trying to explain."

"He expects Lynn to just go along with any of those plans?" I couldn't picture it for a second. The Lynn I knew, if she was locked in a cell, would chew her way through the door.

"He'll have a hard time keeping her in line whatever he decides,"

Ariadne agreed. "So he must be counting on my mother to have her squashed good and proper by the time he's ready to start. Unless I miss my guess, my mother's been told to pummel Lynn until she doesn't know which way is up. So you see, we don't have much time."

I stared at her, not sure why she was so calm. Lynn, impregnated by force, locked away, or beaten into silence . . . There were tremors of electricity up and down my spine. After a minute I recognized what they were: sheer, pulsing fury.

"I really need to get back," Ariadne said suddenly. "Let's get to work."

ARIADNE SPOKE IN rapid, clipped sentences, pointing out the important features of the lower city—guardhouses, armourers, sentry towers. Then she moved on to describing the castle, the parts of it that weren't visible from our perch. I was listening carefully, of course, but at the same time I couldn't tear my eyes from her face.

She didn't really look *that* much like Lynn, not now that I was paying attention. The eyes and the hair colour were the same, the faces were a similar shape. And they both had the same breathless way of speaking, the same (I searched for a word) strong-mindedness. But Ariadne was at least three inches taller, curvy at the waist and hips where Lynn was scrawny; her hair was fuller and thicker, and her skin was unmarked by scars or calluses.

They would have been near identical, I realized, if Lynn had been decently fed and treated when she was a child. And now it seemed all too obvious—Lynn's waifishness was the pinched look of somebody used to the thin end of the stick. Jess was right. I had ignored the signs, because I wanted to believe that Lynn was a noble like me. I wanted to believe that she came from the same place I did, that she was . . . as *good* as me?

I'm a moron, I thought, dazed. *Lynn's in love with a moron.*

" . . . and that's about it," Ariadne finished. "Have you got all that? Now, about getting you into the castle. Is there some clever pirate trick you can use?"

"Um," I said, trying to think clever thoughts. "We could try going over the walls, I guess."

She clucked impatiently. "That's always the first thing people try. We have a collection of skulls in the atrium, reaped from the corpses of raiders who made that mistake. Well, here's *my* idea. I think you should adopt a disguise."

"What kind of disguise? You want me to dress up as a sea gull?"

"I'm serious, Darren."

"Well, so am I. You just told me that every person who tries to enter the castle gets searched by humourless men with very cold and pokey fingers. What kind of disguise will keep me from being noticed? Should I pretend to be a stable hand? A laundry woman? A rock?"

"You're going at this from the wrong end. You're going to stand out, no matter what we do. We can't change that, so we have to use it. Don't pretend that you're somebody too small to be important. Pretend to be someone too important to challenge."

"Someone important . . . like who?"

"Someone like the very special guest who'll be arriving at the castle soon. My father's never seen him face to face, so with a bit of luck and a lot of violence you can sneak in on his coattails. What do you think?"

"I like all of it except the word 'soon.' When is this guest coming?"

"The day after tomorrow. I know. I know. But Lynn's been sort of all right for almost a week now—"

"You said she was awful."

"*Pretty* awful, I said. Look, here's what we'll do. See that tower?"

"The big bastard? Topmost bit of the cliff?"

"That's the one. The third window from the top? That's mine. At dawn tomorrow, and again the day after that, I'll fly a flag out the window. If it's blue, then things are going as well as can be expected and you should wait to sneak in with the guest. If it's red, then there's an emergency and you need to get your bony pirate rear into the castle. Immediately if not sooner."

"Yes . . . but *how*?"

Ariadne stomped her foot. "I cannot think of *everything*, Darren."

She seemed on the verge of having a regular royal hissy fit, and I had seen those before, so I raised my hands, surrendering. "You'll need to tell me more about this guest."

Exasperated, she glanced at the sun, checking the time. "I suppose so. I *really* need to get back. I don't suppose you can find your way back to the stable on your own? Fine. Fine. We can talk as we walk."

"FINALLY," ARIADNE GASPED, when we reached the stable door. "My god, it's been hours. I'll have to lie myself blue in the face to explain this one to my bodyguards. Look, I'm going to talk to Lynn tonight, let her know that you're on your way. Should I tell her something else from you?"

"Tell her . . ."

My mind went blank. *Tell her I love her? Tell her I'm not mad about Timor anymore? Tell her that I'm sorry, as usual, for being a stupid chump, as usual?*

"Tell her that I'm coming as fast as I can," I said at last. "And give her this."

I dug in my pocket for the coil of leather, pressed it into Ariadne's hand, and closed her fingers over it. She inspected the thing, and then her eyes came up to meet mine.

"This is a weapon, right? A . . . a garrote, you call it? Does Lynn know how to use it?"

"Lynn's an *artist* with it. I'd feel a hell of a lot better if I knew she had it in reach."

She winced. "If my mother finds it, things are going to get worse in a very big hurry."

"It's a strip of sinew, not a battle axe. Lynn'll be able to hide it. Please, Ariadne."

She still looked reluctant, but she tucked it somewhere into the piles of apricot silk she was wearing.

"And now I really *have* to go," she concluded. "Remember to watch for the flag. Oh, and Darren?"

"Yes?"

She grabbed a fistful of my shirt and yanked me down to her. "You *do* plan to marry her, don't you?"

"Urk," was my first, not very intelligent, response, but it didn't take a genius to figure out that there was only one safe answer. "Yes?"

Ariadne jerked me down even harder.

"Of course," I added. And then, when that didn't seem to be working, "Very soon." And then, "Next week?"

She released my shirt and dusted her hands off like someone who had just performed an unpleasant but necessary task. Then she solemnly shook my hand.

"So glad to have met you," she said. And then she was off, her blonde curly head bobbing through the crowds.

My gods, I realized, *there are two of them.*

Maybe we did have a chance of winning.

CHAPTER FIFTEEN
Lynn
Evening, Day X

"COME ON, ARIADNE," I muttered to myself, pacing up and down Melitta's room. "Come on, come on, come on . . ."

It was late in the evening, and, for the first time in almost ten hours, I was alone. Melitta had kept me at her side all through the day. During the morning, I trailed behind her as she made a tour of inspection around the castle (and you can be sure that the servants all snapped to attention when they heard *her* coming). Then I stood behind her chair when she and Iason ate lunch in their private dining room. Afterwards, we returned to her chamber, and she handed me a heavy piece of embroidery to unpick while she sewed. In all that time, she didn't say a word to me. She would beckon to show where she wanted me, frown when I made a misstep.

She didn't even make me go down the stairs for wood and water that day. A footman did that, slinging the buckets around with casual ease. It should have been a relief (toting an armload of logs up a hundred–and–twenty stairs is no joke), but it wasn't. I would have carried wood or cleaned out stables or castrated cattle or done *any* job, just to get a few minutes alone, safe from Melitta's piercing eyes.

The only thing that kept me sane was the prospect of seeing Ariadne that evening. We might be able to figure out some way to deal with the crackdown, the two of us together. Just as the two of us together had been able to engineer my escape.

We had talked about running away, on and off, ever since my mother died and Melitta brought me upstairs. But it was Ariadne's looming marriage that finally pushed us into action. Once married, she would either have children or she wouldn't. If Ariadne had children of her own, then I wouldn't be needed, and Melitta would make sure that I ended up in a burlap bag below the tideline. If Ariadne turned out to be barren, then I *would* be needed, and Melitta would make sure that what happened next was nowhere close to fun.

We knew it wouldn't be easy. We knew that they would come after me. But if I could manage to stay clear until Ariadne got pregnant, then they would stop looking for me. Surely. Even *Melitta* wouldn't track me across the known world, just for the pleasure of throwing me out of a tower window.

"Don't take this the wrong way," I told my sister, the day of the escape, as I was tying her into a chair with strips of cloth torn from her petticoat. "But I hope that you get pregnant very, very fast. Tomorrow, even. Does that make me an awful person?"

"Of course not. I'm hoping the same thing."

"That's sweet."

"Not really. I—I *want* them, you know."

"You want what?"

I must have been looking at her funny. Ariadne fidgeted in the chair, as best she could, considering that she was bound hand and foot with all of the best knots that I knew. "I want . . . children. Not for the greater glory of the house of Bain, I mean. I just want—you know— children. I want to be a mother. And maybe I never can be."

That brought me up short. I had come to think of babies as things that you only had because someone else forced you to have them. If someone had offered to cut my womb out, I'd have thanked them with tears in my eyes. But what the hell. Tastes differ.

"If you want children, you'll get them somehow, whether you're barren or not," I told her. "Remember the Clever Lass. Remember the fishing net and the goat. There's always another way, right?"

"That's what we're hoping," she agreed. "Now gag me before I start to snicker. You look truly ridiculous in that dress, have I mentioned that? Remind me again why we chose the pink one?"

There's always another way, I reminded myself as I paced up and down the tower room. I knew that it was true; I just hoped that we could figure it out in time.

"ABOUT TIME YOU got up here," I snapped when I heard the door open. "Now tell me what was so important—"

I turned, and my voice, quite simply, died.

It was *her*, it was *her*, it was Melitta; the candle she was holding made a demon-light leap in the pupils of her eyes. "I can't say that I'm disappointed," she said slowly. "Because I expected this, of course. But oh Gwyneth, little Gwyneth, this is something you should not have done."

All the blood in my body surged down towards my feet. "I didn't . . . I haven't . . ."

"Hush, Gwyneth, hush," she said, as though she wanted to soothe me. She set the candle on her nightstand, where it lit the stone walls brassy red. "I know perfectly well what's going on, so don't dig yourself in any deeper. Sit down."

My legs folded beneath me, and I started to sit on the floor. Melitta snapped her fingers impatiently. "Beside me, on the bench. *That's* right. And now we can wait together, can't we, my Gwyneth? We can see who it is that you're so anxious to meet."

Her long fingers reached out and snuffed the flame of the candle. We were left in the flickering firelight. Her hand found mine and clutched it tightly, her nails digging into my palm.

"You'll need to be quiet now, Gwyneth," she said, and her voice was still light, dreamy. "Quiet as a mouse . . ."

The fire snapped in the hearth. Melitta's breathing was quick and eager beside me. On the stairs below, dead silence. I felt my hand, the one in Melitta's grip, growing clammier and colder.

Ariadne would burst in any minute.

It would be fine, I told myself fiercely. Ariadne would come up with some kind of excuse; she'd lie, or bluster, or cry, if absolutely necessary. Or even if she couldn't, what would it matter? Ariadne *never* got punished. She would be sent to her room, maybe. *Maybe.* And only if Melitta was in an especially bad mood.

Footsteps. Soft, slippered footsteps as someone took the stairs two at a time. Melitta's grip on my hand grew even tighter, crushing my fingers together. Her breathing rasped louder. She was excited; the energy of it was *pulsing* from her. And I knew—

I knew Ariadne wouldn't be punished, and I knew that didn't matter. I had just given Melitta the opening that she had been waiting for, aching for. If she found out about my friendship with her daughter, then it didn't matter whose fault it was. I would be the one to bleed for it . . .

The footsteps began to head up the last landing.

"She's here!" I yelled—the words just tore themselves out of me. "She's here, she knows, go, run*! Run!*"

Melitta was on her feet and so was I; she stalked for the door and I threw myself in the way; she brushed me aside, wrenched the thing open and took a cursory look around—but she already knew what I knew. Those few seconds had been enough of a delay; the person mounting the tower stairs had heard me, the footsteps had fled back down. Ariadne was gone, the blood sang in my ears, and Melitta's face was a plaster mask as she closed the door again.

"That was pointless," she commented, moving towards the fire. "I'll find out who it was soon enough."

"He'll never be back here," I said wildly. As a bluff, it was probably too little and too late, but anything to muddy the trail. "He's not stupid—"

"Then he's got a damn sight more brains than you have." Melitta was holding the fireplace poker now, and with its tip, she carefully raked over the logs. They hissed, steamed.

"I'm leaving this room now," I said, as if by saying it I could make it happen. "I'm going to go to bed."

"No," she said, giving the logs another thoughtful poke. "No, I don't think so. I don't think that you're leaving this room. You've been getting up to all kinds of things in the dark hours—*that* much is clear. It seems that I've been giving you entirely too much freedom. Especially at night. That will have to change. You've been running wild, my girl, and the only thing to do about it is to shorten your leash."

Just those few quiet words, and I felt myself slipping. I knew that she meant it. She wouldn't leave me alone in the tower anymore, wouldn't leave me *alone*, wouldn't give Ariadne any chance to reach me. And just like that, the one thing that made life bearable in the castle would be gone. Just like my mother—whom I could barely remember—just like *Darren*—

"I won't let you do this," I said, to her and myself. "I won't."

She turned, still holding the poker. "Gwyneth, Gwyneth. We've discussed this, don't you remember? You have that tendency, that *unfortunate* habit, of thinking that you're special. But you're not special, Gwyneth, are you? You're my servant; you belong to me just as my horse and hound and falcon do, except that you weren't nearly as expensive. You tame a horse by working it to exhaustion, and you tame a hound with whippings and a falcon with darkness and hunger. I'm not sure what will work best on you, but I'm prepared to try them all. For as long as it takes, Gwyneth. Until you sit or kneel or run or hunt on command. Until you are able to remember your place in the world. I wonder what would help to jog your memory? Perhaps if you sleep at the foot of your mistress's bed—"

"You are *not* my *mistress!"*

I screamed it, louder than anything I've screamed before or since, and her eyes seemed to go wide for a second, but perhaps that was just a trick of the light. An instant later, certainly, her face was the same as ever—pale, faintly amused, faintly scornful.

"Get on your knees," she said, and the tip of the poker twitched. "Go on now . . ."

I launched myself at her. It was pure fury, no trace of method, but I think I meant to go for her eyes. She stepped out of the way nimbly, the tip of the poker weaving patterns in the air.

"Every second, you're making it worse," she said. "Every second that you disobey me, you're getting in deeper. You've been here before, Gwyneth, you know how it ends. This is pointless; you know how it ends . . ."

There was a fierce pain tearing at my chest, and I knew I was close to breaking down. I went after her again, but this time there was no real strength in my fists. I pounded her chest harmlessly, three times, four times . . . the blows wouldn't have dented a pound of butter. Then, without any effort, it seemed, Melitta caught me by the back of the neck and tossed me down on the floor. The poker glinted in the firelight as she raised it over her head.

It came down, it came down, it came down, it came down, and in the next minute, I lived sixty different violent lives and died sixty ugly deaths. The pain was crimson wells, it was dragons' teeth, it was singing birds and it was tines of lightning. I screamed, I went numb, I thrashed, I couldn't move, I begged her to kill me, I begged her not to; I blacked out and woke up and screamed again through tears, my face was a mask of mucus.

At last the blows stopped; I curled, waiting, and flinched when there was a gentle touch on my face—Melitta wiping it clean with her own handkerchief.

"This can happen for as long as it needs to," she said softly. "This will just keep happening until you learn. Now *get up*."

I didn't think that my legs could possibly carry me, but the poker twitched in her hand and I somehow lurched upwards.

"You are not going anywhere," she said. "*Say it*."

There was no conscious thought involved. I blurted, "I'm not going anywhere."

"You belong here."

Another twitch. Gleam of fire along the metal. "I belong here."

"You belong to me."

"I belong to . . ."

The words stuck in my mouth for a moment, no more, but that was too long. The poker swung, and pain exploded on my elbow. I don't even know how hard she struck me that time, but the blow seemed to crush nerves that scorched all the way up my arm. The scream that came out of me didn't even sound human.

I staggered, nearly fell . . . but Melitta pointed the tip of the poker at my chest, as if it was a sword. "Get . . . up!"

I straightened, gasping for air.

"Step back. Twice."

She must have opened the closet door when I was unconscious. Two hobbling backwards steps took me into it. The walls closed in on either side.

Melitta was a dark shadow, framed by the door. "You belong to me. And you are not going anywhere. Get used to it."

The door crashed shut.

And it felt like another one crashed shut in my own mind.

CHAPTER SIXTEEN
Darren, formerly of the House of Torasan (Pirate Queen)
Morning, Day XI

"I DON'T CARE if it's traditional, I'm not *gonna say it!"*
Lynn's eyes danced. "You've forgotten about my superhuman powers of persuasion, have you?"
"Oh-ho-ho, no." I clawed my way out of the bunk, snatched up the blanket and wrapped it around me. "No more persuading. You've been persuading me for hours now. I love being persuaded and all, but I think I pulled a muscle in a very *important place. Besides, it's my turn; I still haven't done you."*
Lynn propped herself up on one arm, lounging across the narrow wooden shelf. She was completely bare—I'd taken the only blanket—but that never bothered her. "Mistress, the sky is not going to fall if I take two turns in a row. And I'm enjoying myself."
"I hate being a taker."
"You have to take things sometimes. You took me, *right? Where would you be if that hadn't happened?"*
That was easy. "Dead."
"Exactly. But if you're really feeling guilty, then why don't you get off your piratical high horse and say *it* already?*"*
There was just no way I was going to win this one. I let out a feeble sigh and kicked the deck boards with my toes.
"Shiver my timbers," I muttered, and then hurried on. "Lynn, it just sounds ridiculous. What is that even supposed to mean?"
"Well, your timbers are your legs," she said, slipping off the bunk. "As for the 'shiver' part—"
"Captain—captain—captain—"
"What, what, what?" I snapped, rubbing my eyes. "Dammit, Regon, there ought to be a rule against waking your commander in the middle of a very good dream."

Heavy shutters fit over the stable windows, so the light was dim, but I could make out the grim lines on my first mate's face. "The flag is up at the tower. And captain—"

I didn't need him to finish. Hurriedly, I pulled myself out of the pile of stale straw where I'd been sleeping. We had figured out the day before that you could get to the stable roof quite easily by pulling yourself up on a railing and using the lintel as a step. I did that now, kicking away a couple of offended chickens who were nesting in the thatch.

Latoya was already up there, and she gave me a curt nod without moving her eyes from the tower. Ariadne's flag was there, almost too tiny to make out, a bright speck against the white stone. Red.

"Oh, for the love of—"

My vocabulary got a workout then. I used every curse that I knew, in every language that I knew, some of them backwards and all of them loudly. The thatch of the roof shuddered around me as I went at it. Latoya waited patiently until the torrent slowed.

"Better?" she asked.

" . . . on a *stick!*" I said desperately, finishing. "I knew this would happen. She could be *dead*, Latoya, she could be dying, she could be—"

"Anything," Latoya agreed. "So we need to get to her. How?"

That was the question I had dreaded, and just hearing it exhausted me. I sat down on the soggy mildew-smelling thatch and ran a finger over the calluses on my sword hand.

"We can't," I admitted at last.

Latoya's eyebrows went way, way up.

"We spent all of yesterday trying to hash this out. And we don't have a clue how to get into the castle, unless we use Ariadne's plan. We can't climb, we can't dig, we can't stow away, we can't fly. We could poke around the city and see whether an opportunity falls in our lap, but if we keep tramping around the streets, then sooner or later, someone will realize that we don't belong here. We could run at the walls howling and hope for a miracle, but we can't just throw our lives away. We're all that there is, Latoya. Lynn has no one else to come after her. We are *it*. She loses her only chance if we charge in blindly. We need to wait and take our best shot."

It was all true, and yet, and yet . . . I fixed my eyes on that tiny speck of red in the distance.

Latoya heaved a sigh. "Which of us are you trying to convince?"

"Me," I said miserably. "I'll go down and tell Regon. We need to do something useful while we're waiting."

WE DID NOT do something useful while we were waiting. Our clothes were still salty and battered from our raft ride, so we attracted strange looks whenever we went out the door. We couldn't afford to be questioned by watchmen, so we huddled in the stable, not talking much. Around noon, it began to rain again, and a puddle collected below a leak in the roof. Every few seconds, a drop of rainwater smacked into its centre, and the reflections on the water rippled, as if forming a different horrible picture. *Drip*—and Lynn was writhing in Melitta's grip, her left arm broken. *Drip*—and she was thrown into an oubliette under the walls. *Drip*—and she was raped by a grinning soldier. *Drip*—

As the minutes crawled, I flogged my brain, trying to think of some way, *any* way, to get up the castle that day. The massive white walls loomed in my imagination, stark and blank.

When the rain started to come down harder, Latoya and Regon left me to my mood, slipping out into the grey streets. They came back with armloads of plunder—a few loaves of bread, melons, oranges, a wedge of sheep's milk cheese. Dinner the night before had been a few handfuls of wizened hazelnuts that we'd found at the bottom of an abandoned saddlebag, so I did my best to get through my share. Every bite tasted like ashes.

I SLEPT VERY little that night and woke with a pounding headache. As I staggered towards the stable door, I stumbled over Regon's prone body, and he gurgled in protest.

Once again, Latoya was already on the roof. This time, she was sitting cross-legged in the damp thatch, studying the distant flag.

"Red again," she observed.

"Right," I said, and bit my hand in frustration.

"Bigger today," she went on.

That was true. The red speck in the distance had become a long red tail billowing from the window. Ariadne must have tied together every red piece of cloth that she owned, letting it all float free in one big banner.

"Things are bad," I said, translating the obvious message. "Things are very bad—*buggering fuck*. I don't know what to do. I'm empty here. Completely dry. I don't do the plans, Lynn does the plans, I just yell at people. And sometimes I snarl. If you can think of anything, Latoya, anything at all, then hell on a biscuit would it *ever* be a good time to say so."

Latoya's brow furrowed and her eyes turned to slits. The signs of deep, deep thought. I waited, chewing my lip.

At last, she said, "What's that on the end?"

"What's what on the end of what?"

"The end of the flag. Look."

I glanced up, hassled. The tip of the red banner was divided in two, like a snake's tongue. "That's a pair of bloomers. Silk ones."

"A pair of *what*?"

"Underwear. Fancy underwear."

"That . . . *that* . . . is underwear?" I could see Latoya mentally measuring the size of the billowing knickers. Her head was cocked to the side in fascination.

"Underwear for a noblewoman. The richer you are, the more important, the more layers they make you put on."

"But *why*?"

"Probably because it's harder to get 'em naked that way. Extracting a noblewoman from her clothes is a little like getting at the meat of a crab. You can *do* it, but you need a lot of patience, sometimes some special equipment . . ." I shook away old memories. "Does this help us? Like, at all?"

"No," she admitted. "I've just never seen anything like that before."

"Fine," I announced to an uncaring sky. "Fine. Wonderful. Lovely. So we have no plan. I'll go see whether Regon can pull a rabbit out of his ass—"

"Captain?"

"It's a figure of speech, Latoya."

"How do you get a girl?"

I had never heard Latoya, with her barrel of a chest, speak so softly, and despite my panic and misery, that stopped me short. "How do you get a girl—you mean, how do you get a girl to . . . um . . . be with you?"

Latoya gave a small, embarrassed shrug.

It was the first time in my life that anyone had ever asked me for advice about women, and I had never in my life felt less qualified to give any. But Latoya had followed me to virtually-certain death, so it wouldn't have been fair for me to respond with a snarl and a well-aimed boot. I rubbed the back of my head and tried to think.

"Well, in my experience . . . you wander the seas rescuing peasants and fishermen until a girl storms out of nowhere and challenges you to a duel. Then you haul her on board your ship, tie her to your mast, and within a few days she's running the place. Is that helpful?"

Latoya gave me an exasperated glare.

No, not helpful. I rummaged around in the dark cobwebby corners of my mind where I stored information about romance. "I guess . . . I guess . . . you try to recognize opportunity when it comes along. Opportunity is terrifying, by the way. That's how I always recognize it. When the right girl comes, you take your chance, and damn the consequences. And if you don't let her get kidnapped by a goat-testicled slave-stealing sack of shit, then you're doing better than me." I poked Latoya in her shoulder—it felt like I was poking a solid slab of beef. "Come on, let's get inside."

MORE WAITING.

Latoya confiscated all our knives and put a fine edge on each of them. The slow, measured sound of the honing rasped on my second-last nerve. Regon whistled tunelessly, and that rasped on my last one.

After an epoch of waiting, I pulled a shutter ajar for the thousandth time and saw that the sun was finally down.

"Let's move out," I ordered, with vast relief, and tickled my palm with a fresh-honed knife point.

ALL THE STREETS in the lower city were narrow; space is at a premium when you live in a fortress town. The three of us were crouched in alleyways that connected with the main road. From my post, I could have reached out and touched the leg of any passing horse.

Ariadne's planning was perfect. It was an hour after sundown, just as she had calculated, when the carriage came rattling up the narrow street. The moonlight glistened on its gilt trim and on the silver buttons of the coachman. The coachman, two footmen . . . they were all the attendants that I could see. I glanced to the other side of the street, where Latoya and Regon were waiting, for confirmation. Latoya nodded, holding up three fingers.

Three men was a ridiculously small escort for a lord as important as the one riding inside the coach. But, as Ariadne had told me, Iason was so afraid of assassination attempts that he didn't allow even his most important visitors to bring their own troops and bodyguards into the city. For once, his paranoia would work in our favour. I cracked my knuckles and waited.

When the carriage came abreast of us, we all struck at once. Regon bounded up onto the shafts, his knife a silver flash as he cut the traces. The horses, spooked, bolted free; Regon thrust the knife between his teeth and raced after them. The carriage box skidded to a halt. The gaping coachman sat frozen, holding the ends of the useless reins. He was still gaping when I put him out with a chop on the neck. From behind the carriage, I could hear the muffled thuds as Latoya took care of the footmen. Pounding each of their heads against the cobblestones, so far as I could tell.

While all of this was going on, a piping, peevish voice within the carriage was shrieking its objections. As soon as I got the carriage door open, I found the face that fit the voice—a young man whose downy face was cranky, whose hands dripped with gold rings, and whose plum velvet suit must have cost as much as the average warship.

"Lord Jubal?" I asked him. "Jubal of Oropat?"

"What?" he said, surprised. "Yes."

"Good," I answered, and swung my homemade cosh. It was a rock tied into the end of a rag, nothing more than that. Very simple, but very effective. One quick blow sent him snoring.

After that there was no need to discuss anything. Latoya stuffed the three prone bodies into the box of the carriage, Regon brought back the horses and repaired the traces with a few expertly tied knots. We ghosted back to the stable through the quiet streets, hauled the bodies out onto the stable floor, stripped them, and tied them up with old pieces of harness.

For once, it had all gone right. I just hoped that we hadn't used up our entire store of luck.

AN HOUR LATER, I sat in the gently rocking carriage as it rolled through the last of the castle gates. I was about as uncomfortable as a person can possibly be when sitting on a velvet bench. My breasts were tightly bound so that I could fit into Jubal's fine shirt and doublet, and I was encased from the waist down in his foppish purple hose. Grey gloves, mink-lined cape, and a cascade of lace cravat completed the ensemble. Breathless, overheated, and sweaty, I was almost miserable enough to forget about being terrified.

So far, no problems. Ariadne had been right again. The guards at each gate had gone through the motions of asking for pass tokens and passwords, but when I flew into a temper and threatened to have them all impaled, they backed off pretty quick. Nobody wanted to be the one to throw Lord Iason's very special guest out the front door.

We were in. Now came the hard part. The part where I had to introduce myself to Lynn's father.

Regon was smirking wide as the moon when he opened the carriage door. The coachman's uniform fit him well enough, though we'd had to cut off the ends of the trousers. "Captain, you look good enough to eat with a silver spoon."

"Thanks for that," I muttered to him, stepping down into the courtyard. "I still think you should be playing Lord Jubal."

"I couldn't hack it, captain. No one would be convinced."

"How am I going to be more convincing than you? I'm not even a man." A palace steward was bustling over to us across the courtyard. I directed a patronizing little nod in his direction.

"You're a noble. Or you were, once. That's all that they'll see."

True enough. I hadn't been to court in years. I'd believed that part of my life was over for good. But now, just the feel of the velvet and gold against my skin was causing old instincts and feelings and understandings to flock back. I was remembering the thousand habits and mannerisms that nobles absorb as a matter of course during their upbringing.

So when the steward came panting up and bowed so low that his forehead nearly touched his pointy shoes, I didn't even acknowledge him. Instead, I sneered around at the castle courtyard as if it wasn't nearly as big as I had expected.

"Lord Jubal," the steward said reverently, and bowed even further, almost tipping over. "We are most honoured that you have chosen to favour the Lady Ariadne with your courtship."

"Naturally," I said, with a sniff. "That being the case, why is it that I'm being welcomed by Iason's butler rather than the man himself?"

The steward coloured. He had obviously been afraid of this question. "My apologies, my lord—my *deepest* apologies—but my Lord Iason receives guests only in his own chambers. He will make no exceptions. If you will follow me, I will take you to his private dining room for refreshment."

I sniffed again and stalked past him, so the tubby man had to scamper to take up a position in front of me. Lord Jubal wouldn't have looked back at his servants, so I didn't look at Regon and Latoya. I just hoped they'd find a way to stay close, so they would be with me for the disaster towards which we were no doubt lurching closer and closer with each passing second.

And gods help me, I was wearing tights.

A PRIVATE DINING room. What a stupid way of showing off.

The stupidity was compounded, in fact, because it was on the fourth floor. I couldn't think of any reason that anyone would want a dining room on the fourth floor, unless they got a kick out of forcing their servants to run up four flights of stairs with platters of meat and cauldrons of hot soup, and down again with the stacks of empty dishes.

The steward prattled on as he trotted in front of me. Back where I came from, I mused idly, a servant who talked so much would be given a good whipping—then I caught myself. Where the hell did that thought come from?

"And *here* we are, my lord," the steward said at last, bowing me through an open door. "May I humbly wish you the best of luck in your wooing."

The thought of me wooing Ariadne was so very wrong on so very many wrong levels, but there was no other way. It was no accident that Jubal had been summoned so suddenly to the castle, right after Goat-Boy dragged Lynn back there. Lord Iason, who had been putting off his daughter's marriage for years with various excuses, now needed to make it happen as quickly as he could. Once Ariadne was safely married, Lynn would be expected to fulfil her function—to give her father grandsons who would inherit his throne and his name.

It occurred to me suddenly that Iason might well be planning for Jubal to be the father of his grandchildren. If so, he intended Jubal to do things to Lynn that I couldn't even contemplate without panic. Silently, I cursed myself for a fool. Back in the stable, when I was removing Jubal's tights, I should have taken the opportunity to remove a few other things from him as well. It wouldn't have taken more than a minute with a string and a razor. Too late now.

I gave the steward one last sniff and stalked through the doorway.

The room beyond *glistened*, there's no other way of putting it, with silver plate and candles, with gold-edged doublets and jewelled brooches. It took a few seconds of blinking before I could even make out the people. There was Lord Iason, ensconced at the head of the table, so splendid in his crown and brocade that you didn't notice all at once how short he was. There was Ariadne to his left, primped and powdered into a kind of doll, though the eyes that glared out from under the curly bangs were keenly sharp. Further down the table was a clutch of other men—generals, perhaps, or minor lords. And at Iason's right . . .

The only thing I could think of, looking at the Lady Melitta, was . . . ordinary, ordinary, ordinary. Dark hair, a pleasant-enough face, lined around the eyes and cheeks. Her green gown was sleeveless, in the new, fashionable style, and the flesh of her arms was soft, drooping a bit with middle age. *This* was the demon of Lynn's childhood? The youngest of my sailors could have knocked her to the ground and rolled her around for an hour without breaking a sweat. Lynn had fought experienced soldiers before, had fought them barefoot, with no weapon except a coiled garrote and a small sharp blade. She had pressed her every advantage, pounced on their every weakness, *forced* her enemies to respect her. How could this fleshy old broad give her any trouble?

I knew that Lynn wouldn't be in the dining room. Handmaids don't serve at supper. Nevertheless I cast a quick glance along the row of servants who stood motionless against the wall, waiting for orders. An older woman whose knees trembled as she waited, a tall attentive man whose muscles stood out in lumps—he would be Iason's body servant— a sallow dark-haired girl, a plump little boy . . . sure enough, no Lynn. I resigned myself to an evening of awful and awkward conversation, and made my bow.

Lord Iason had remained seated when I entered. The house of Bain ranked above the house of Oropat in the hierarchy of the islands, and the niceties had to be observed. But now he did rise and come towards me, and Ariadne came with him.

I'll spare you an account of the back-and-forth that nobles exchange when they meet on a formal occasion. Life's too short to spend repeating that drivel. But after we had called down blessings from all the appropriate gods, and smarmily praised each other's houses and our own, Iason finally nudged Ariadne forwards. "And now, allow me to present the greatest treasure of the house of Bain—my daughter."

Children are treasure is an old Kilan saying, but that's a double-edged sentiment. What do you do with treasure? Lock it away. Put it on display to impress your friends. Trade it for something else that you'd rather own.

"My lady," I murmured to Ariadne, and bent to kiss her hand. While I was down there, her fingers found my nose and gave it a vicious pinch and a twist. It took all my self-control not to yelp. Instead, I straightened up and handed her a dirty look.

"My lord," she tittered, toying with a blonde ringlet. "I'm delighted to meet you. Positively delighted that you're here. I've been so *eagerly* anticipating your arrival. In fact, I had hoped that you would *get here earlier?*"

Her voice turned hard at the end. I hoped that Iason wasn't watching too closely.

"A thousand apologies," I said. "I came as fast as I could."

Iason laughed the kind of breezy, meaningless laugh that I've always hated. "My daughter has suffered through every second of this long betrothal. But it's allowed the two of you the pleasure of anticipation, hasn't it? And now, Lord Jubal, will you sit?"

He gestured to a seat beside Ariadne's. I bowed again, took her arm, and led her around the far side of the table.

"Seriously," I muttered, hoping we were out of earshot. "I came as fast as I could."

"Tell that to Lynn," she hissed.

We reached our chairs. As I pulled Ariadne's out, ready to seat her, I leaned close and whispered, "Where?"

For a second it seemed that she hadn't heard me, or that she had chosen not to respond. Then, as if casually, she tossed a glance towards the back wall where the servants waited. I looked myself, saw nothing, was about to tell Ariadne so when one of the servants—the sallow girl—lifted her head.

I almost fell out of my seat. It was Lynn. They had dyed her pale hair, and not very well; it was now a piebald kind of brown that made me think of liver-spots and mange. She wore a long grey tunic that covered her arms down to the wrists, concealing both her sailor's tan and the storm-petrel tattoo, the slave mark. When I first looked over the servants, I had noticed the bruises on her, but now I saw them again with mounting horror—small dark pebbles like fingertips on her neck, a mahogany stain over her cheekbone, a black eye.

But those were details. The real difference was in her bearing. This wasn't the girl who had throttled Tyco Gorgionson, the girl who had out bluffed Mara of Namor and drowned her minutes later. This wasn't the girl who mapped out the strategy of an entire fleet of ships and whispered unrepeatable things to me late at night. This wasn't the girl who—

"Gwyneth." Lady Melitta didn't have a loud voice, but it carried. "Eyes."

This must have been a command of some sort, because, without any hesitation, Lynn bowed her head again. Yet she *must* have seen me. I studied her in my peripheral vision and saw her tongue come out to wet her lips, saw her fists flex. She had seen me, all right. She knew who I was.

But I hadn't known her, not in her cowed state. She looked like a servant and I had looked right through her. I felt like snatching up a silver platter from the table and beating my head against it. But it wasn't quite the moment for that.

Iason clapped his hands, and dinner began.

I TRIED TO catch Lynn's eye while the servants were passing around finger bowls and pouring wine, but she either didn't realize, or she was ignoring me. When she wasn't making rounds of the tables, she waited at the back wall, silent as a post. Melitta didn't have to warn her again to keep her head down. Could she actually be frightened? Or was she just that pissed off?

It stunned me so much that I could barely keep my mind on what was passing for conversation around the table. I should have been grinning away foolishly at Ariadne, pretending to be a lovesick, or at least sex-starved, young man. But I couldn't do it. Never, not once, had it occurred to me that I might have to figure out a way to escape from the castle without Lynn's help. Now, there was a big glowing blank in my brain where there should have been an exit strategy. There was Lynn, and here I was, so how was I going to get the two of us out of here? Should I keep up my disguise as Lord Jubal for weeks or months, waiting until I found an opening? Should I lunge forward, grab Lynn around the waist, and run out screaming?

Again and again, I lapsed into a dark daze at the table, and there were awkward pauses that even Ariadne, labouring mightily, couldn't fill. At

last, Iason appeared to make a determined effort. He leaned across the
table towards me. "Lord Jubal, tell us about your younger brother. How
is Haddrian getting on?"

"Haddrian," I repeated carefully. "Well, Haddrian is . . . fine. Really
fine, absolutely fine. Very very fine, actually."

Ariadne hissed beneath her breath, and I couldn't blame her. I wasn't
exactly carrying off the impersonation with aplomb. But Iason seemed
satisfied. He leaned forward even further, and asked, "So he's no longer
planning to give up his title and go off to become a travelling musician?"

"No," I said, "that turned out to be a passing phase."

"He doesn't keep you up until all hours of the night, playing
improvisational drum solos?"

"No, he's over that now."

"And he's no longer in a relationship with a lobster?"

"No . . . um . . . he broke up with the lobster after . . . ah." Iason's
expression was no longer friendly, and at long last, I clued in. "I don't
have a brother Haddrian, do I?"

"Lord Jubal of Oropat certainly doesn't," Iason said, his tone still
dangerously light. "Perhaps you do. Whoever you are."

An utter silence fell over the dining hall. There was just the barest *clink*
as Ariadne set down her spoon. There were no visible soldiers around, but
the tall servant at the back of the room was watching carefully, and his
hand had strayed to the back of his belt. A man as paranoid as Iason would
never be very far away from his bodyguards.

It was like that moment in a thunderstorm when the air itself seems
charged with electricity, an instant before the lightning hits.

My mind raced . . . or, more accurately, it tried to start running and fell
flat on its face. Plan, plan, I needed a plan, I needed someone who could
plan, I needed *Lynn*!

Lynn still hadn't looked up. She seemed half-dead, or drugged, as she
leaned against the wall with downcast eyes . . . and hell, maybe she was.
But if she could still talk, then she could still help me. I could just shout
out and ask her what to do. I could shout and I could ask and she would
tell me . . . she would tell me . . .

I knew exactly what she would tell me.

If you don't know what to do, Lynn used to say, *then do something.
Anything. If you stand around gaping like a stuffed dummy, everyone's
going to know that you don't have a plan. If you're doing something, as
long as you do it with a bang, everyone will think that it's what you meant
to do from the start. You'll look like the only person in the room who
knows what's going on.*

I did it all in one motion—threw back my chair and leapt up on the tabletop, kicking over a bowl of fruit and flowers on the way. Jubal's silly purple cape fluttered to the ground, and I ripped the longer of my knives from its sheath. There were a couple of shrieks around the table.

Nothing scares an opponent like confidence. You can never, never go into a fight thinking that you're going to lose. With every motion, every word, every gesture, tell your enemies that they don't have a chance. Make them believe it.

Iason was beginning to rise from his chair. I gave him a nasty, feral smile of warning. He hesitated, and that's when I kicked his wine goblet into his lap. It landed with a thud and a splash, soaking his pale blue hose, and he stumbled back into his seat.

You think that you can't be a hero, Lynn's imaginary voice ground on. *You think you're not good enough. But nobody's good enough. You, O my mistress, you are just decent and stubborn and stupid enough to keep trying to do the impossible. And that's why you got stuck with the hero gig, gods help you. But remember, you're not alone in this.*

"Who exactly *are* you?" Iason asked tightly, murder in his eyes.

"Me?" I said. "I'm the pirate queen."

I SAUNTERED UP and down the table once or twice, to make sure that no one was moving, and to give myself time to think. Sooner or later they would figure out that they could mob me, piling on top of me until I couldn't free my blade hand. But if I could scare them badly enough, then no one would want to be the first to move.

In the end, Iason broke the silence. "I heard you were in the area. One of your ships crashed on the reef the other night."

"Really?" I asked with mild interest. "Must have been one of my scouts. My *other* thirty ships are just fine, in case you were worried."

An icy smile flickered over Iason's face. "Where did you land?"

"On the north coast."

"You're lying. None of my watchmen reported a border attack."

"No. See, the thing is, watchmen have to be alive to report an attack. That's what we would call a loophole in your system."

Iason settled himself back in his chair. "Well, you've gone to great lengths to ruin a formal dinner, so you might as well tell me why you're here."

He was impressively calm. I was beginning to think that Lynn inherited her courage from her father, as well as her blonde hair and her sneakiness.

Before I answered Iason, I bent, speared an apple from the fruit bowl with my long dagger, brought it to my lips, and bit off a piece. This kind of thing always looks impressive, but it takes some serious leather to do it casually. I'm always scared that I'm going to cut my tongue in half. I chewed the fruit as I strode up and down, taking my time.

When I was good and ready, I said, "It's nothing big. Nothing dramatic. I'm not here to conquer Bero or take your throne. I'm not even planning to kill you, unless you piss me off. I'm just here to collect a piece of lost property." I waggled the apple in Lynn's direction.

Iason followed my line of sight, and his eyes narrowed to slits.

"I picked up that girl in a fishing town a couple of years back. She's nothing special, you understand, but she got to be a habit. Then she ran away *juuuuust* as I was getting her broken in. Talk about frustration." I took another cautious bite of apple, and spoke with my mouth full, spraying bits of pulp. "So if you'll just hand her over, then I'll get out of your way."

Iason's voice was thick with frost. "Why should I do that when I could simply nail you to a stake and have your throat cut?"

It was a valid question. I was still trying to think of a suitably piratical answer when there was a soft *whirr,* and then a *thud,* and a slim dagger was reverberating in the oak panelling to the right of Iason's head.

Latoya had a fine sense of timing, and even better aim. She stood in the doorway, filling it completely, half-a-dozen knives held loosely in her left fist and one in her right hand, ready to throw. She and Regon must have stopped off at the armoury before making their way upstairs. Regon was just behind Latoya, gripping two knives of his own. He was lousy at knife throwing, but Iason didn't need to know that.

Give Iason credit, he barely flinched. "If you harm anyone in this room, then you'll pray for death for months before it's granted to you."

I shrugged. "Duly noted. But you'll be dead first, and you don't want that. Besides, why are you making such a big deal out of this? I don't think I'm being unreasonable. All I want is the girl. A servant, a nothing. Why are you making such a fuss over her?"

There were murmurs at this. The others in the room, courtiers and the like, had no idea who Lynn was, and why Iason needed her. All they saw was pointy objects aimed at their heads. And Iason couldn't explain without blowing his secret wide open. I saw him realize it, saw his mouth open and shut twice before he thought of an answer.

"That girl is an orphan under my protection," he said. "I won't abandon her to the likes of you."

"*That girl,*" I corrected him, "is mine, and I really don't see the issue. Why are you making such a song and dance about a peasant slut who's no better than she ought to be? You could buy six wenches like that at the Freemarket for a jug of ale and a sack of onions. You really want to fight me for her? Really? When I've got knives aimed at your family?"

At that moment, Ariadne let out a snivelling kind of wail. She was quite the performer.

"And then there's your own pink hide," I went on. "I'm a pirate, Iason. Let's not forget that little detail. I can do things with a knife that they don't teach in any fencing academy. Maybe you're not afraid of the sight of blood, but most people don't deal with it so well when they get a close-up look at their own kidneys."

I kicked over another bowl of fruit. Ripe strawberries skittered along the table like tiny bleeding hearts.

I was beginning to feel almost good. Planting myself right in front of Iason, I sneered down at his frozen face. "What say we try to work out a civilized compromise? How would that be? Doesn't that sound better than having a hole drilled right between your eyes?"

Being the pirate queen, I should tell you, is a lot like being in a relationship. One minute everything is rattling along fine, then you take your eye off the ball and before you know it, everything's gone to shit.

Latoya didn't even have time to hurl another dagger—that was how fast it was. A hand snaked out at viper speed and grabbed me around the ankle. Melitta might not have been all *that* strong, but she was strong enough, and viciously determined besides. The yank that she gave threw me off balance. I took a few staggering steps, arms wheeling wildly. Then I fell off the table and landed flat on my face.

Pandemonium. Regon and Latoya were trying to fight their way inside, closer to me, as the panicking courtiers tried to fight their way out. Iason was on his feet, screaming to everyone and no one, "Kill her! Kill the bitch!"

It's always the same. Just once, I'd like someone to point at me and scream, "*Give her a foot massage! Give a foot massage to the bitch!*"

But no.

It took a few moments for me to scramble upright, with Regon's help. By that time, a group of grim-faced men had armed themselves—the generals and captains, the more muscular of the servants. Latoya snatched up a chair and swung furiously to keep them at bay while we backed into a corner. I drew Jubal's rapier, but it was a feeble, useless toy; I hurled it down again and grabbed my spare knife. Latoya's chair was a whistling hurricane, and Regon had the coachman's short sword. We could make a stand for a few minutes, but there were people streaming out the door. It wouldn't take long for them to fetch reinforcements.

And then I saw another pair on the move. Melitta had her arm around Lynn's shoulder, and Lynn was moving like a sleepwalker as she let herself be escorted away.

"Get away from her," I yelled. "Let go of her, *now!*"

Melitta was not going to be drawn into a debate, that much was clear. She cast a single dark glance at me, and then carried on with what she was doing—whispering softly, unceasingly, into Lynn's ear, as she backed the two of them towards the door.

I screamed in sheer fury and tried to charge, but a swinging mace nearly took the top off my skull, and I had to duck and retreat. "Lynn, get over here. Get clear of her, I'm right here!"

I couldn't get to Lynn, but she could get to me. It would be so simple. A hard stomp to Melitta's foot, enough to crack the smaller bones, a chop to the ribs, a backwards elbow into Melitta's face . . . I'd seen Lynn do that kind of thing dozens of times. Hundreds even. But not that day. She shuffled along dutifully where Melitta led. And now they were almost at the door.

"Lynn, I'm here! Please!"

Now bear in mind—I hadn't had a good night's sleep in almost two weeks, and I hadn't been eating enough to keep a rat alive. Nothing was really keeping me upright but anger and adrenalin. Bile burnt my throat. I know that doesn't excuse what I said next, but maybe it helps to explain it.

"Lynn, don't you *dare* ignore me. *Don't . . . you . . . dare*. You belong to *me*, girl, you do what *I* tell you, and I will tan your hide if you don't get over here *right now*! Lynn, *fight*. I am ordering you to fight!"

Lynn's head finally came up . . . and only then did I realize my mistake. There was total misery in her eyes, a darkness so deep that it burned. Humiliation, and shame, and an emptiness that I had never seen there before. She had nothing left, that was the bottom line. It didn't matter what I asked of her, because there was absolutely nothing there that she could give.

Lynn, I thought in a daze, *oh Lynn, what in hell have they done to you.*

I didn't say it out loud. Didn't have a chance. Melitta and her captive had slipped out the door. The next second, I became aware again of the chaos boiling around me, the fists and swords and boots. Regon was panting heavily, and even Latoya was slowing down. There was the telltale *tramp tramp* of hobnails from the hallway outside. Iason's soldiers were on their way, just as the last few drops of my energy ran out.

It was over. We had lost. Lynn had lost her only chance at a rescue, just as I realized how badly she needed one.

THEN CAME A shriek. A woman in silken skirts fluttered, wailing, into the centre of the wolf pack.

"Why haven't you killed her?" Ariadne asked hysterically. "Why haven't you killed her yet? Don't you know what that woman does? Did you hear how she defeated Mara of Namor?"

How she defeated Mara of Namor . . . I knew there was some kind of message there, but my brain was too numb to decode it. Luckily, Latoya and Regon were still awake. In unison, they grabbed Ariadne's arms and threw her into me. Startled, I tried to back away, but she grabbed my wrist and guided my knife into place against her own throat.

I gaped down at the top of her head. By then, I was so out of it that I wouldn't even have been able to pronounce the word *hostage*, let alone remember what to do with one. But I wasn't the only one in the room. One of our attackers (burly man with a tooled leather tunic; he looked important) pulled back immediately. "Keep back, watch for the princess."

They all leapt away from me, as if they were shards of iron, pulled by a lodestone. Weapons clattered down to the stone floor and hands were clasped behind heads.

Lord Iason was by the door; he'd been about to escape. Now he stared, hatred at war with panic in his face. I pressed the knife more tightly to Ariadne's neck, wondering whether this could possibly work. It wasn't Ariadne that the soldiers in the room were trying to protect—it was the House of Bain, the all-important royal line, which they thought was bound up in her blood. Unknown to them, it wasn't Ariadne but Lynn who really mattered. It might be worth Iason's while to let Ariadne die, if, by doing that, he could eliminate the threat to his descendants. That would be the brutally practical option.

Did Iason have some real affection for his oldest daughter? Would he at least decide that it was worthwhile to try to avoid the inconvenience of her death? I held my breath, while Ariadne's pulse ticked against my blade.

At last, Iason whispered, "Stand down."

Latoya and Regon didn't miss a beat. They each grabbed one of my shoulders and hurried me out of the room, past stock-still generals and wide-eyed servants, past Iason himself, my knife still quivering at Ariadne's throat.

Once we were halfway down the corridor, Ariadne ducked out and under my arm. "And now," she said, with dangerous calm, "we've got to run."

CHAPTER SEVENTEEN
Lynn
Evening, Day XII

IT HAD NEVER been so hard to make it up the tower steps. Melitta held me at her side, helping me up each one. Every time I wobbled, I clutched at her hard to keep myself from going over backwards.

"That's it," she kept repeating. "Almost there now, keep going. Good girl. Good girl, good girl."

When we reached her room, I was staggering, spent; my eyes had closed and I let her lead me.

"Sit. Sit down, Gwyneth, it's all right—"

It took a few seconds. My knees didn't seem to want to bend.

Melitta sat beside me; one arm encircled my shoulders, the other took my head, holding it softly against her. I relaxed into her, numbly; my mind was nothing but cobwebs and dust, her voice just kept going . . .

"It's all right now. Good girl. You did so well, so very well. That's right. *That's* right. Good girl. You're all right now . . ."

And I don't like to admit it, but it's true—the tears started rolling out of me, in choking sobs. Melitta held me tighter, stroking my head with great gentleness.

"That's my girl," she whispered, "there, that's the worst of it over. Everything will be better now, everything. Shhh, calm down, I'm here. There's nothing you need to do now. Just relax . . ."

She disentangled herself from me, carefully; the warmth of her was gone from my side and I felt a flutter of unreasoning fear. My eyes were still closed, but somewhere in the room there was a swishing sound, a heavy cloth being pulled back, and a door creaked open.

I knew what the sounds meant, somewhere in some dim part of me, but the broken bits of my mind could do nothing with the knowledge. I just sat, and breathed through the tears, and thought nothing at all until Melitta's hands were back, coaxing me up, leading me across the room.

"Nothing you need to do," she repeated. "You're safe, you're safe, I've got you, I'll take care of everything. All right, in you go. Now, sit. That's it, good girl. Just sit. I'll be back."

I slid to the stone floor of the closet. My back rested against one wall; my bare toes touched the other.

Melitta stroked my head, one last time, and then she took a step back, and closed the cupboard door on me. The key grated in the lock.

For a second, there were glimmers of light in there—a yellow spark from the keyhole and a shining line beneath the door. Then the tapestry swished back to its place in front of the closet, and even those winked out.

I put my hands on my knees and stared ahead into nothing.

Just sit, I repeated to myself. *Just sit. Just sit, just sit* . . .

CHAPTER EIGHTEEN
Darren, formerly of the House of Torasan (Pirate Queen)
Evening, Day XII

ARIADNE ALMOST FLEW as she led the way. The castle, like the lower city, was a maze of narrow passageways and hidden staircases and secret doors. I didn't even try to pay attention to where we were going, just jogged behind her numbly. There was no sound of pursuing feet behind us, so what she was doing seemed to be working much better than anything I had tried to do that night.

We charged through a bake house where the ovens still glowed red, down another short flight of stairs, and through a must-smelling wine cellar. Then there was a blast of cold air on our faces, and grit underfoot. We were outside, in the castle courtyard, our backs against the outer wall of the fortress. A stack of drying firewood the size of an average house stood in front of us, shielding us from view. There Ariadne ground to a halt, wheeled, and slapped me across the face with all her strength.

Regon leapt forward, but I waved him off, panting. The slap had felt almost good, waking me, focusing me, jump starting my thoughts. "It's all right—all right. I deserved that."

"Damn straight you deserved it," Ariadne said crisply. "You muffed that one good and proper, didn't you? And who do you think you *are*, talking to my sister that way?"

"It was a mistake," I said. "It was a stupid, idiotic mistake which I'm not about to repeat. But try to understand, I've never seen her that way before. Never."

"Haven't you?" Ariadne asked grimly. "I have."

She was contorting herself, reaching for the hooks that held her pale green gown closed at the back. It clearly wasn't working, because she stomped a small foot. "You—the terrifyingly enormous woman—help me get out of this thing. I can't move in it worth a damn."

Latoya froze, her face stiff with panic. Then she seemed to nerve herself, and she gingerly began to unhook Ariadne's bodice with her large, calloused hands. The princess angled to let her get on with it, and kept talking.

"You have to get her out. You have to get her out *now.*"

"Yes, that was the idea, thank you," I said testily. I was shrugging into my leather gambeson, which Regon had, mercifully, brought with him. I only wished he had brought my trousers as well. "I wouldn't mind a little help right around now. Where's Lynn? Where did they take her?"

"Hang on a second. Let me consult the crystal ball that tells me my sister's location at all times, including times when I can't keep an eye on her because I have to save her idiot *lover* from being crushed to death by a *mace* because her idiot *lover* can't maintain a disguise for a couple of hours without losing it and rambling about men who sleep with lobsters. Darren, I don't fucking know where she is. If they took her to the dungeons . . ."

"They didn't," Latoya said, breaking in suddenly. "Too far away and too risky. They'll put her in a place where they have total control."

Ariadne looked around with respect. "That's . . . that's true, actually. Would you mind hurrying up a bit, though?"

Latoya, seeming flustered, gave up on trying to extract Ariadne from her clothing in the traditional way. She grabbed the cloth of the bodice and gave a good yank. The hooks all popped free, seams splitting and thread tearing. Ariadne climbed out of the ruined gown. "Much better."

"Where does Lynn usually sleep?" I asked.

"On the floor outside my mother's room. But for the past few days, my mother's been keeping her locked in the room itself."

"And where's your mother's room?"

"Top floor of the high tower." Ariadne looked thoughtful. "Give me a boost, will you?"

With Latoya's help, Ariadne clambered up the woodpile until she reached a spot where there was a gap between the logs. She shaded her eyes, had a look, and then slipped back down to us.

"I thought so," she said. "Guards at the tower door. There are usually only five. Right now, it's more like thirty. And there could be more inside."

I hissed. "I can't take thirty."

"I don't think you have to. None of the guard houses face the back of the tower, so you might be able to climb it. Could you get up to that top window?"

I measured the distance with my eye and thumb. On an ordinary day, the answer to Ariadne's question would have been "No." Or, more accurately, "Hell, no!" with perhaps a hysterical laugh thrown in. But this wasn't an ordinary day.

"I'll need a rope and grapnel," I said in the end, evading the question itself. "Latoya, see what you can find."

She peeled off obediently, though she glanced backwards at the princess, who was shedding several layers of petticoats. Regon looked worried. "No rope on earth is going to reach to the top of that beast."

"Yeah, I know. I'll have to do it in stages." I tried to stay nonchalant. "You know . . . climb to each window in turn, and sit on each ledge while I throw the grapnel to the next floor. Nothing to it." I blew on my cold hands and tried desperately to persuade my dinner to get back down where it belonged.

"You won't be able to climb back down if the rope's too short."

"No. When I'm ready to come down, I'll throw a torch out the window. You'll have to create some kind of diversion to get the guards away from the door. Lynn and I will meet you at . . ."

"The pigsties," Ariadne suggested.

"The pigsties."

Regon nodded. "But what if Lynn isn't up there?"

"Then Darren will meet us at the pigsties all the same," Ariadne said. She had gotten rid of most of her underwear by then. Now she was left in a white linen sheath which still covered more skin than almost anything that Lynn liked to wear. "We'll have to find my mother and convince her to tell us where Lynn is."

"Convince her," I repeated. "I don't know if I want to have to convince that bitch of anything."

"We could always use the magic stick," Regon suggested, his bushy eyebrows twitching upwards.

"The magic stick?" Ariadne asked. "Is that some kind of pirate thing?"

I gave Regon a withering glare before I answered. "Um. Yes. It's not a magic stick so much as a normal stick which is . . . oh, how to explain . . . used in a non-traditional way."

"Does it *hurt*?"

"Um. Yes. A lot. Relax, I wouldn't do that to your mother."

Her eyes were flinty. "Why not? I would. As long as no sex was involved."

This wholly disturbing line of discussion was cut short when Latoya slipped back behind the stack of firewood, a long coil of grass rope draped over her shoulder and a metal object in her hand.

"That would be a crowbar, not a grappling hook," Ariadne observed. "I don't know if you understand exactly what we're trying to do here."

Latoya smiled halfway, then gripped both ends of the crowbar and flexed. In three seconds' time, the long metal bar was bent into a curve.

"I stand corrected," Ariadne admitted. Latoya twisted the other end of the crowbar into a loop and Regon lashed it to the rope with a long row of knots. I transferred the grapnel to my shoulder, picked up a handful of sand, and rubbed it into my palms to improve my grip.

"Remember, I'll need a diversion when I'm on the way down," I reminded Regon. "I am going to get very cranky if you decide to wander off and play skittles instead."

He smiled. "Diversion, captain. Aye. Anything else you need?"

A goat and a fishing net. "Just my girl. All right, I'm going."

Ariadne looked at me, then up at the tower. For the first time, it seemed to occur to her that there was an element of danger in crawling up a sheer surface for hundreds of yards while soldiers swarmed around below. "Can you do this?"

"That's the magnificent thing about not having a choice," I told her. "Whether you can do something or not, you do it anyway."

CHAPTER NINETEEN
Lynn
Evening, Day XII

FOR A LONG time, I floated, unthinking, in a place where I wasn't aware of anything, not hunger or cold or memory or pain. What tore me out of my beatific state was noise.

First there was a crash—glass breaking—and then a second one, as metal hit stone. In my sluggish state, it took me at least a minute to reach the obvious conclusion—*someone* had thrown *something* through the tower window. And by then I could hear something else, the scraping of boots against stone as someone climbed. Overlaying the scraping sound, nearby, and coming nearer, was a voice which spoke in short, breathless spurts. It sounded something like this:

"Stupid . . . *pant* . . ."

"Tower . . . *pant* . . ."

"Stupid . . . *pant* . . ."

"Slave . . . *pant* . . ."

"Oh . . . *pant* . . . sod . . . *pant* . . . this . . ."

"For . . . *pant* . . . a . . . *pant* . . . sodding . . . *pant* . . . game . . . *pant* . . . of . . . *pant* . . . soldiers . . ."

A final pant, a final scrape, and then, so far as I could tell, a gasping body flung itself over the windowsill. Then, once again, there came the sound of glass breaking. And a yelp.

"Blasted motherbollocking son of a *twat!*"

Darren had different curses for different occasions. That one meant that she had cut her finger. When she spoke again, it was muffled, and I knew she was sucking the wound.

"Lynn, are you there?"

I held my breath, said nothing, and waited, hoping the distraction would vanish. Nothing for five seconds, but Darren's voice just bored in again. "Lynn. Please. We need to move, fast. I know you're pissed at me, but we can deal with that once we're out of here. Where the hell are you?"

The voice was beginning to take on that edge of theatrical desperation. The one that meant that she had taken on more than she could handle. That was Darren. She would take all the problems of the world on herself, and then look around vaguely for a place to offload them.

"*Lynn. Please.* We have to . . . we need to . . ."

I closed my eyes tightly. She didn't get it. I couldn't save her. Not this time. And I wouldn't be able to bear her frustration and disappointment. She would ask me *why*. It should have been obvious *why.*

There were footsteps. Darren seemed to be turning in a small, bewildered circle.

"All right," she said, more softly. "All right. How about I just talk for a while? You can jump in any time you like."

Rope springs creaked as she sat down on Melitta's bed. I winced at the thought.

"I'm sorry that I wasn't here earlier," she began. "No excuses. I'm so sorry."

I pressed my face into the top of my knees, trying to control my breathing. But in my head, I answered her. *Kind of late for that now, pirate queen.*

"Melitta is the biggest bitch that I've ever encountered."

No shit.

"If I'd grown up with her, then I . . . I don't know what I would have done. I don't know if I would have made it."

This just made the nausea surge again. I bit my lip and rocked.

"I really hope that you can hear me, by the way. It's going to be bloody annoying if I have to go up and down the tower, repeating myself on every floor." She caught herself. "But whatever time it takes for this to happen, that's fine. Because this is *it*, you know. This is it. The most important thing. And nothing matters more. Nothing."

I heard her weight shift, and her boots touch the floor. She was beginning to prowl around the room, slowly. I could picture her bending to check under the furniture.

Melitta would be back soon.

You need to get out of here.

"You remember when we met? When I cold-clocked that thug Hasak, and then you challenged me to a duel and almost twisted my ear off?"

It was the tension, maybe, but I couldn't help it. I sniggered. I caught it almost at once, but Darren had heard; her feet were silent on the flagstones outside the closet. Then, very slowly, taking her time, she started to come nearer.

"At the time, I just figured you were insane."

Not so far from the truth.

"But these past few days, you know, I've been thinking."

Sounds painful.

"And I think I figured something out. I think I did. And I hope . . .

I hope that I'm right, because I kind of like to imagine that this is what happened."

Her voice was nearer, nearer . . . She was right on the other side of the door. Light prickled through the keyhole as she nudged the tapestry aside, and I stiffened, but she didn't touch the handle. Instead, she slowly let herself slide down until she was sitting on the other side of the wall.

That sent the panic surging. Iason's men would come charging up here while she was still crooning at me through a keyhole. *Melitta* would come back, and if she found Darren here, she would . . . I couldn't let myself picture it, but still, the idea hit my stomach so hard that I thought I'd been stabbed. My tongue still felt too thick to speak, but I thought the words at her harder. *You really need to go, you really, really need to go. Right fucking now.*

"So what I was thinking was . . . oh, by the way, I'm touching the door now. Right below the keyhole."

Darren could be stupidly mushy sometimes. What was I supposed to do? Touch the same spot on the door, only on the other side? Pretend that I could feel her through the wood? Embarrassingly soppy. I snorted. And touched the door anyway.

"So what I was thinking was this," she went on. "I think that, all through your childhood, you were completely powerless. Right? Getting thrashed whenever you spoke up. And you fought it as much as you could, because you're you, and you're the bravest person I've ever known. But there was no way you could win, in the end."

I closed my eyes. Her voice was as gentle as I'd ever heard it. I let my fingernails scritch against the wood.

"You were just a kid. They had all the power. There was no way you could win."

Then why do I feel so guilty?

"But when you met me, even that first day . . . well, you can tell me if I'm wrong here. I think, I believe, that you trusted me from the start. I think you felt safe with me from that very first moment." Her tone turned wry. "Or at least, you knew you could take me, any day of the week."

And twice on Tuesdays.

"You knew I would never hurt you."

You couldn't, *you stupid bint.*

"So you didn't have to be afraid of standing up to me. You could yell and scream and say that you were pissed off, and pound me and bite me, and still know that you were safe. You could twist my ear halfway off, slash at me with a cutlass, head butt me, threaten to sink my ship, and *still* know that I wouldn't hurt you. So what I'm trying to say is . . . thanks. Thanks for trusting me so much."

I licked my dry lips, my blood sounding painfully in my ears.

"So here's what I'm asking you for, Lynn—and I know it's a lot. Do you think you can trust me again? Here, now, today? Can you trust me to get you out of this fucking pisshole? I'll be doing the work this time, you know. It won't be your job to prop me up. You won't have to reassure me or cajole me or soothe me. You don't have to be the strong one. Not this time."

Silence, then, very quietly, "Lynn, please. Tell me to open this door."

Just sit, Melitta had said, *just sit, just sit.* I let the words slip out almost by accident. "If they catch us . . ."

There was no sign of surprise in Darren's voice. "Then horrible things will happen. I know."

"No, you don't," I said, harshly. "You don't, you can't. This is different, this is . . . you couldn't possibly understand."

A short pause, and a great effort. "All right. I guess I don't understand. Because I haven't lived what you've lived. But that's why I have to take the lead this time. That's why it's my turn."

"Do you have a *plan*?"

"Well . . . not a plan *as such*, no. We've been improvising. Things have worked out so far."

"Do you have a plan for escaping from the castle?"

"Um. It's in progress. Ariadne's helping. She's very bossy, you know."

"So you want me to charge blindly out of here, looking for an escape route that probably doesn't exist. Knowing that all of this will probably end with you dead, and me locked in a kennel somewhere, with stumps where my thumbs ought to be. How does that make sense, Darren? Tell me how."

"It doesn't make sense," Darren admitted softly. "You want to tell me what does make sense?"

What made sense was to give in, let Melitta carve me open and take what she wanted from me. But that wouldn't save Darren. Beautiful, heroic, idiotic Darren, who had as good as announced to my father that she knew too much to be allowed to live. I let my head fall forwards onto my hands.

"You know how I got here?" Darren asked suddenly. "I arrived at this island neither swimming nor sailing nor rowing, not accompanied and not alone, and neither by day or night. I came to the castle neither as a man or a woman, neither a guest nor an intruder, and not a noble or a peasant. And I gave your father a present which wasn't a present, by which I mean that I kicked a cup of wine into his lap. *I found another way, Lynn*. It's just how we work. We don't let the world define what's possible. We found a place together where the rules don't apply, and where we aren't anything except what we decide to be, from moment to moment. Damn right it doesn't make sense. But it's what we do. We do it every day. I learned from *you* how to do that."

I didn't answer. Light through the keyhole. Void roaring in me. The words, my keeper's last order, still ringing—*just sit, just sit, just sit, just sit . . .*

A scraping sound on the flagstones. Darren was sliding something under the door. I felt for it, picked it up. A small scalloped shape, ridged, with a sharp edge.

A shell.

I folded the thing in my palm. Squeezed it hard.

"Darren," I said, my voice oddly loud.

Tense now. "Yes?"

"What, you just happened to have a shell in your pocket?"

"Well . . . yes, as a matter of fact. Why, is there anything wrong with having a shell in your pocket? When I was a kid—"

"Darren," I interrupted her, "open this fucking door."

She was brought up short. "Did you say-"

"Open the door," I interrupted again. The small space was crashing in on me all of a sudden; the air was too warm and there wasn't enough of it. "Open the door, open the door, open this goddamned fucking door!"

She was already on her feet and light winked out in the keyhole; Darren had thrust a dagger-point in there, forcing the lock. The door was flung open. I was trying, awkwardly, to get to my feet, and expected Darren to reach into the closet and hoist me up by the front of my tunic. Instead, she bent, got an arm around my shoulders and another under my knees, and hefted me like a small child. Staggering a little under the weight, she made her way across the room and set me down on Melitta's bed as if I was a bruised peach. I forced down the instinct to jump straight back off of it.

Darren was doing her best not to blanch at the sight of my face, but it wasn't going well. She had that panicked, searching expression which she always wore when she was looking for a way to change the subject. The results were usually disastrous.

I waited for it.

Her eyes went wide, and she blurted, "I kissed your sister. With tongue."

I only smacked her six times for that. The other smacks were because she showed up so damn late.

CHAPTER TWENTY
Darren, formerly of the House of Torasan (Pirate Queen)
Night, Day XII

AFTER LYNN WAS finished venting her frustration, I rubbed my aching arms and took stock.

She looked far worse at close quarters, and I had to do my best not to stare. She knew, and her battered face was hot with embarrassment, but she tried to speak normally. "So, what's first?"

"First," I said, all business, "you need to strip."

I led the way myself, unlacing my leather gambeson and tossing it aside, then pulling off my shirt. Lynn watched me, forehead wrinkled.

"I'm happy to see you, and all," she said. "But is this really the moment?"

I shoved my shirt at her. "To change clothes? Yes, it is. Because I'm damned if you're going to wear something that bitch put you in for an instant longer than necessary."

I think I can say, that's the moment when I first honestly, seriously astonished her. A smile broke out on her bruised face; it looked like another wound.

"You had a good idea," she said, wonderingly. "When did you start having good ideas?"

In three-and-a-half seconds, she was out of her long respectable tunic and into my shirt. It hung down to her mid-thighs, and after she cinched it tight with Jubal's belt, it fit her well enough. Which is to say, it looked nowhere near respectable, and much more like Lynn. I pulled my gambeson back on over my bare skin, doing my best not to think about how badly I'd chafe the next day. One thing at a time. If I was alive tomorrow to do any chafing, then I would be doing pretty well.

As I was lacing up my armour, Lynn used her teeth to tear a long strip from her servant's tunic. She knotted it into a pouch with a few deft jerks. Then she toured the room as quickly as she could on her unsteady legs, filling the pouch with objects off the shelves and dressing table. There didn't seem to be any reason or pattern behind her choices. I saw her grab a snuff box, four small bottles of perfume, a little elephant carved of ivory, and a paperweight, among other things. But I wasn't about to argue. If Lynn wanted trophies, more power to her. I'd try to get her one of Melitta's fingers to add to the bag later on.

While she was at it, I retrieved the grappling hook and coiled the rope nearly. Then I ripped a reed torch off the wall, kindled it to glowing red in the fire, and threw it from the window, watching it descend like a falling star. Lynn and I finished at about the same time.

"Stairs, right?" Lynn asked. "You'd better let me carry that. You'll probably be fighting."

True enough. I handed the coil of rope off to her, unsheathed a dagger, and led the way out of the room.

Outside the bedchamber was a small alcove, where a straw pallet and crumpled blanket rested on the floor. From what Ariadne had said, this was where Lynn used to sleep, and the sight affected me more than I would have expected. It looked like a kennel; all that was missing was a water dish and a leash. I was beginning to realize that nothing in the way Lynn had been treated was simple neglect or cruelty. Every last aspect of her life was designed to keep her small, and shamed, and powerless.

Lynn very studiously didn't look in the direction of the alcove, so I didn't mention it, and we just hurried to the stairs.

"Damn," Lynn muttered before we got more than a few steps down.

I tensed. "What?"

"Listen. But keep moving."

I listened and I kept moving. It took three turns down the stairway before I heard what she had heard—the clicking of soldiers' hobnailed boots against the flagstones.

"Damn," I concurred wearily. Regon's diversion apparently hadn't been quite diverting enough. "Stay behind me. We've got the high ground, that's something."

Those old tower stairways are all designed the same way, to favour the defender. If you're coming down, you have free play for your sword; if you're coming up, you're hampered by the central post, slamming into it every time you swing.

It wasn't much but it was something, so when I saw shadows flickering on the stairs beneath us, I hurried to get past the landing. I wanted to meet them where they couldn't come at me at once.

There were only two in that first wave, and the first was stupid and eager enough to race up the stairs ahead of his comrade. I ducked under his blow and smashed the dagger hilt against his temple, and he dropped, rolling limply down the stairs. The next one gave me some more trouble— parrying a sword with a dagger is not a thing you want to do if you can avoid it—but while we were still clashing back and forth, a snuff box flew past my shoulder and struck him full on the forehead. It didn't put him out; he just staggered. Still, that gave me the chance to dive in fast and slice his inner thigh. Blood spurted. As he went down, I grabbed his sword from his limp hand.

"Thanks for that," I tossed back at Lynn.

"Don't mention it." She was already digging more ammunition out of her pouch.

There were three in the next cluster, and though they were all weak swordsmen, there were enough of them to give me a few very bad moments. Lynn had thrown the ivory elephant, and the paperweight, and several other items of bric-a-brac, before even the first of them dropped. But there was a lull in her throwing while I was battling the last one. It went on long enough that I almost forgot she was there, and focused on other things—my arm muscles, which felt like burning bits of string, and the sweat running into my eyes. Her shout burst out of nowhere, and it made me jump.

"You were *never supposed* to *see* me this *way!*"

Lynn punctuated this remark by throwing the perfume bottles. Three of them bounced off the luckless soldier's forehead, and the last smashed solidly into his crotch. He gurgled weakly as he crumpled.

"What way?" I asked, hopping over the body.

"You *know* what way!" Her voice was high-pitched, and I knew she was having trouble keeping it together. "I never wanted you to see me as some kind of victim—some *pathetic, mewling, helpless* little *kid.*"

Another few soldiers came charging up the stairs, and I tiredly raised my stolen sword again. "Is that why you never told me who you really were?"

Her response, when it came, was so soft that I barely heard it over the clanging swords. "Sort of. Maybe. I guess. I never wanted you to picture me like this."

"Lynn, you crackpot," I panted. "You really thought that I would respect you less because that bitch used to beat you?"

The last soldier was pressing me hard. I ducked; Lynn took the cue, and smashed the grappling hook into his face. He sagged, and we kept heading down.

"I didn't really think it over," she admitted. "I hoped that it would never matter, because I'd never be back here again, and I just wanted . . . I just wanted to leave it all behind."

"But you never even told me about your sister." More footsteps on the stairs. I transferred my sword from right hand to left hand and shook out aching fingers. "And you must have been missing her like mad."

"I know. I know. It's all so screwed up. But it was hard to think about her when I thought that I would never see her again."

"Just tell me this," I said. My sword pierced a man's shoulder, and I raised my voice over his scream. "Was it because of anything I did?"

"Was what because of anything you did?"

"That you couldn't tell me the truth." I got nicked along the ribs and flinched, but another paperweight came flying over my head, smashing my opponent's throat. His eyes bugged like a sick frog.

"No, it wasn't because of anything you did," Lynn said. "But I always kind of thought that you would get ten times as guilty and bashful if you knew. I thought you'd treat me like some kind of delicate flower, or like a kid who didn't know her own mind. And you'd get all Darren-knows-best and overprotective, and you'd think it was your duty not to exploit me, and you'd refuse to do anything in bed other than cuddle. Darren, hang on. Don't kill that one."

My sword point froze an inch from the soldier's throat. "Why not?"

"I know him from before. He carried some wood up the stairs for me, a few times. When I couldn't do it on my own. When my arm was broken."

It didn't seem like much, set against everything that had been done to Lynn in this castle, but oh well. I reversed the sword and smashed him with the pommel. Lynn bent and quickly tied his thumbs together with a strip of rawhide.

When she was done, I cupped her chin. "Look. I may be a slow learner, but there are two things that I've managed to figure out. One is that you're stronger than I'll ever be. And the other is that you *know* what you want. The two of us decide what goes on when the two of us are in our cabin. All the people who don't like it can go, collectively, to hell."

Her smile was pained, but it *was* a smile. "Thanks, Mistress."

"You're welcome."

"We're not getting out of this one, are we?"

I looked up. We'd left a trail of motionless or groaning bodies strewn along the stairs. I looked down. We were only a couple of turns of the staircase above the tower door. But even after we emerged, we were going to have to cut our way through the entire army of Bero to get out of the castle. Then we'd have to cut our way through the entire navy of Bero to get to neutral waters. Our odds of survival, objectively speaking, were crappy. But it was probably best not to think about that.

"We're not done yet," I told Lynn. "Who knows what could happen?"

"Stupid optimism," she noted, as we headed down the last few stairs. "See, I always said that you were the hero."

THIS NEXT PART, I admit, is a little confused in my memory. We emerged from the tower into a courtyard awash with acrid smoke and orange light. The giant woodpile was burning, the flames stretching up like the clawed fingers of some beast trying to scratch out heaven's eyes. Vaguely, through the smoke, I could see lines of soldiers passing buckets from hand to hand. Army drums pattered and trumpets howled. Lynn grabbed the back of my shirt and steered me through the chaos. It took about ten minutes to find our way to a row of low huts, built from the same white limestone as the castle itself.

We checked the pigsties quickly, one by one. They were all well built and scrupulously clean, and the thought occurred to me that Iason housed his pigs a damn sight better than his daughter. I decided not to mention that.

Ariadne, Regon, and Latoya were in the third hut along the row, with a bunch of yearling porkers destined to become bacon. They all seemed afraid of Latoya; they were huddled in a squealing pile at the far side of the pigsty, trying to stay away from her. I wondered, but did not ask, what she had done to keep them at a distance.

"Nice diversion," I told Regon.

"The great big fucking fire? You know me, I love a classic."

"Well, you did good."

At that point, I was knocked out of the way by Ariadne, who lunged across the sty towards her sister. Lynn caught Ariadne's arms, gave them a brief reassuring squeeze, then pushed her away. "I'm fine. Anyway, this isn't the time. We need a way out."

We all stared around at each other. It was then, in that momentary pause, that fatigue hit me like a fist, almost bending me double. I suddenly wondered whether I would be able to stand upright much longer, let alone fight and scheme and do the impossible. The others weren't much better off. Regon's shirt was badged with blood and from the way Latoya was blinking, she was practically asleep on her feet. Gods alone knew how Lynn was coping.

That left Ariadne, and I turned to her. "Quick. Think of a plan. Any plan. It doesn't have to be a good plan, it just has to be marginally better than cowering in a pigsty until the end of time. We need to use this moment while the fire's still burning and Iason has things other than us to worry about."

Ariadne made a desperate sound and pressed her hands to her head, as if she was trying to force out an idea. "I don't know, Darren. I've been trying to figure this out for years."

"Something. Anything!"

She looked around wildly—tile roof, stone floor, scuffling pigs.

"The guard house," she said at last. "Maybe we can find some spare armour and maybe we can dress up as soldiers and maybe we can blend in and maybe we can slip outside the gate that way."

Lynn's face twitched in a way that let me know this was a stupid plan . . . which was something that I could have figured out for myself. No matter how we dressed Lynn, there was no way to disguise her as anything but a very small woman. By now, Iason would have made it very clear to all his soldiers that horrible death would be visited on anyone who let a very small woman pass through the gates. I did tell Ariadne to come up with *something, anything,* though, so it was no good complaining. Maybe there was a way to make this work. Maybe I could hide Lynn in my own clothes and pretend to be a fat man. "All right. Fine. We'll do that."

At once, Ariadne looked like she wanted to take the words back. "The guard house is locked, though."

"Locks aren't a problem. We have Latoya."

"And some of the best swordsmen are there."

"Latoya! Now no more discussion. Only moving. Fast like bunnies. Ariadne in front. Regon, the rear. Move."

When we got outside, I knew we were in trouble. The fire was dying, the woodpile a sodden mess with a few glowing patches where there had been an inferno minutes before. The courtyard was swarming, and not just with soldiers. Stable boys thrust pitchforks into piles of hay; hostlers overturned wagons and barrels. Torches moved at a fast clip in the darkness; the tramp of soldiers' boots was everywhere. It was like the last part of a hunt, the seconds before the fox is torn apart or the stag is brought to its knees.

"Fuck," I heard myself saying meekly.

Ariadne suddenly veered off in a new direction. "The guardhouse is all the way on the other side of the courtyard. We'd never make it."

"So where are you taking us?"

"The root cellars. We . . . we can hide there until things cool down."

Brilliant, except that things were not going to cool down. We knew it, every one of us knew it, but we followed her into an outbuilding and down an earthy-smelling set of steps.

The air was close, stagnant. "Is there another exit from here?" I asked Lynn as we clambered down together.

"No." She sounded even more exhausted than I felt. "The words 'death trap' come to mind."

We jogged through a stone passage with bins of vegetables on either side, Ariadne still tramping along determinedly in front. I cast around for a topic of conversation other than our impending deaths, and thought of something. "By the way," I asked Lynn. "What was your mother like?"

Her mouth opened, but she never got a chance to answer. Torchlight suddenly blared behind us, and my stomach plunged to somewhere in the neighbourhood of my feet. I wheeled around and saw them—rows on rows of soldiers, choking the narrow passageway, the shadows of swords and spears along the wall. Too many of them to count, let alone fight.

In the front rank was a familiar face—the guard Lynn had asked me to spare, back in the tower. I thought I saw him give me an apologetic shrug.

Regon ripped his short sword from his sheath. "Lynn, they'll only come at you over our dead bodies."

"Thanks," Lynn said half-heartedly. "That's very comforting."

The rows of guardsmen parted as if split with a hot knife, and Iason and Melitta both walked through. Iason didn't look small now, not with fury pouring off of every square inch of his body, and Melitta looked anything but ordinary. Seeing her that moment, I got a tiny taste of what Lynn used to have to face every day, and I wondered all over again how she'd made it.

Ariadne leaned into me, her eyes suddenly liquid with false tears. "Father, you have to get back, you have to leave. They'll kill me, they've said that they'll kill me—"

"Ariadne," Iason said. "Do not ever again make the mistake of thinking that I am an idiot."

Somewhere nearby, water dripped from the ceiling.

Ariadne's voice was weakening. "But you don't understand—"

"Oh, darling," Iason said, but not as if he meant it. "I do understand. You've had a fit of what is hopefully temporary insanity, and you've decided to consort with criminals. Very well. We all commit acts of appalling stupidity now and then. I suppose you think that I wouldn't have you executed for treason. It's true that I'd rather avoid it. It would reflect badly on me if I had you burned to death in the village square. But I have no use for a child who can't be governed, and even less use for a child who lies. Now come here this minute."

"He's bluffing," Lynn said, immediately. "You know he can't kill you. Ariadne, don't move."

She sounded desperate and I knew why. Iason's two daughters were acting as human shields, keeping the soldiers from rushing us. We were dead as soon as they moved away. Ariadne knew this, she *must* have known it, but her face crumpled, and her strength along with it. Maybe she had given up hope, I thought. Or maybe she too, in her way, had been so badly hurt by Iason and Melitta that she couldn't resist them. Whatever the reason, she walked unsteadily over to her father. He snatched her wrist and swung her behind him, into the ranks of soldiers.

Lynn hissed, then pushed in front of Regon and Latoya and me, her wiry arms outstretched as if she could use them to block crossbow bolts. She spoke, not to her father, but to the soldiers surrounding him. "Do you want to know who I am? You want to know why he's hunting me?"

"Not one more word, Gwyneth, not one more word!" Iason's voice was a fang, a claw, a whip. "Those three savages with you are going to die, no matter what happens next. But you can control whether they die tonight, and die clean, or whether they die in the pits in three months' time. Do you want them eaten alive by rats? Do you want their faces peeled off, an inch at a time? Do you want them sawn in half with a length of rusty wire? If not, then hold your tongue!"

Lynn didn't say anything. Her chest heaved.

Water dripped. Drip . . . drip . . . drip . . .

"Good," Iason said at last, approvingly, as though Lynn was a student who had finally mastered the alphabet. "Now, Melitta, over to you."

Melitta smiled slightly, and her eyes focused on Lynn. "Gwyneth."

Lynn's hand found its way back to me, and I gripped it. It was all I could do.

"Gwyneth," Melitta said again. "It's time to end this."

"Don't listen," I said to Lynn, and she gave a quick sharp nod. Her eyes were tightly closed.

"Oh, Gwyneth," Melitta said, sounding hurt. "You know better than this, you truly do . . . You can't sacrifice yourself to save them. That's not how this works. They are going to die. You're not. This ends with you coming back upstairs with me."

The pulse in Lynn's wrist was a racing, skipping beat. She slowly shook her head. "If I were smart," she said to me, "I would ask you to cut my throat right now."

"But you're not going to, are you?"

"No. In spite of everything, it's still not my style."

"Just as well. I couldn't do it even if you did ask me to."

Melitta's face was darkening; her voice sharpened as the pitch soared higher. "Gwyneth, I'm only going to say this once more. Get. Over. Here. You've been very, very foolish. Now don't make it worse."

A funny thing happens when you realize you're about to die. Your life doesn't seem your own anymore, and you wonder whether it was ever really yours to begin with. When that happens, it makes perfect sense to spend what's left of it on some last, glorious hurrah, rather than trying to horde the last few drops.

I glanced questioningly from side to side, at both Regon and Latoya. They knew what I was asking. They nodded. I cleared my throat.

"Iason has dry withered balls!" I roared. "And his wife and daughter are both as barren as kiln bricks. Five-day fever, years ago. Gwyneth is Iason's bastard and his only hope of grandchildren. And now that you all know it, I'll have plenty of company when I'm dying in the pits!"

"It's a damn lie!" Iason shrieked, but all his smoothness was gone; his voice was too hysterical to convince. Soldiers shifted their grips on their weapons, suddenly uneasy.

"He'll kill you all!" I announced over Iason's screeching, pointing to each man in the front line. "He'll kill you, and you, and you, and you . . . he can't *not* do it. He would kill whole continents to keep people from finding out." A thought hit me, and I followed the thread. "He killed Gerard of Saupon, Ariadne's husband. Arranged that riding accident. Stuck a nettle under the horse's saddle or something like that. He didn't have a choice about that either. He couldn't have people asking why Ariadne wasn't getting pregnant, could he?"

Iason's face was turning purple, veins popping out all along his neck, but Melitta, unfortunately, was made of stronger stuff. "Men, you will ignore this woman's ravings. A bag of silver to the one who kills her. Two bags of silver to the one who captures her alive and removes her tongue. *Go!*"

They started forwards. Latoya snatched a barrel, hefted it, threw. It crashed into the front ranks, exploding into shards, and the soldiers flinched back. That gave us a few more seconds.

I gripped Lynn's hand, raised my sword, and addressed Melitta once more. "You're done, you hoary old bitch, and you don't even know it. Your sad little world is ending, and the new world is going to be one that this girl helped to design. She's turning the universe into a place that won't put up with people like you. *She builds heroes.* You kill me, she'll build another. And you can't starve or beat that out of her."

"Ah, well," Melitta said placidly. "I can try, anyway."

"Wrong," a voice said, halfway between a sob and a snarl, with an edge of desperation thrown in. "As always, *wrong.*"

I had seen this before—the flash of *something* in the air above Melitta's head, and, an instant later, a line drawing itself across the woman's throat as the cord was yanked tight. But it wasn't Lynn doing it this time. Lynn was beside me, gaping just as I did as Melitta gasped, white foam dribbling from between her lips. The soldiers to the left and right of her stood dumbstruck, and Iason stumbled backwards, while Melitta died. A strangling death isn't a pretty thing when it's being done by an amateur, and it seemed a long, long time, though it was just a few seconds really, before Melitta finally crashed to her knees. Behind her stood Ariadne, tear streaks in the dust down her face as she pulled the garrote still tighter.

Iason didn't exactly rush to Melitta's side, but he leaned towards the corpse, unbelieving. For once in my life, I didn't hesitate. I threw down my sword, grabbed a knife from the back of my belt, flipped it to grab the blade, and hurled it with all my might. Iason had just enough time to widen his eyes before the knife *thunked* solidly into the centre of his chest. His delicate white fingers splayed, then he wheezed, and folded on the floor of the tunnel. He wasn't done yet—his legs were still kicking in spastic jerks—but it was just a matter of time. Already, the dirt under him was melting into soft red-brown mud.

It had all happened too fast for the soldiers. For a whole five seconds, they didn't move, and the only sound was Iason's jerking feet as they drummed against a root bin. But then one of the soldiers lunged for Ariadne and twisted her arms behind her back, and more of them immediately followed suit. I suppose it seemed like the thing to do.

"They deserved it," Ariadne announced, her voice shaking mightily. "They deserved it, they deserved it, they asked for it fifty times over. They killed your mother, Lynn, did you know that?"

"I know," Lynn said, so softly.

"And then my husband, poor *stupid* Gerard. They *used* people, they broke them and bent them and tossed them away." She was getting properly hysterical now. "You don't understand. The things that they did to *my sister* . . . and I couldn't do anything but *watch!*"

She crumpled in the hands of the soldiers who held her, and she started crying. Not delicate maidenly blubbing, but full rolling sobs that made her entire chest shake. The soldiers looked bewildered again. Their lord was dead, his heir was a murderer . . . this was not a situation for which they had been trained, and they looked honestly confused about what should happen next.

But one of them rallied, a thought seeming to strike him. He raised his spear and levelled it at me. "Kill them all!"

Oh, no. Oh, fucking *fuck,* no. After everything we'd just survived, were we going to get murdered in a root cellar by a bunch of soldiers who didn't know what else to do with their day?

The troops started forwards, at first hesitant, but then with greater momentum. Latoya lifted another barrel, Regon raised his short sword, I screamed foul words and hefted my own blade. I could have sacrificed myself for Lynn with something like dignity, but *this* was just ridiculous, and I had no intention of being gracious about it. If I really had to die in such a stupid way, then I was going to perform *lots* of impromptu castrations before I went out.

But there was a soft touch on my wrist.

"It's all right, Mistress," Lynn said. "I've got this one."

Just four words, but her voice was her own again, really her own, and relief flooded me in a warm wave. Lynn, *my* Lynn, was back in control.

CHAPTER TWENTY-ONE
Lynn
Morning, Day XIII

"DROP YOUR WEAPONS. Do it now!"

Darren's sword, and Regon's, both hit the ground a second after I spoke. Latoya hesitated, but she, too, swung her barrel to the earth floor.

I moved in front of them, just in case, and sought and found the eyes of the man I needed—the guardsman I had asked Darren not to kill. "Captain Whytock, stand your men down. Just for a minute. Let's talk before the killing starts, or you'll make mistakes that you won't be able to fix."

Whytock's face, what I could see of it behind his helmet, was grim. He really had no stomach for this kind of thing. But he didn't sheathe his sword. "That woman murdered a Kilan lord. Our duty is plain."

"Your duty to what? The House of Bain? The House of Bain is bleeding out in a squelching pool of mud. Iason is dead, his line is finished, and before long, his generals and courtiers will start circling around Bero like jackals on a corpse. When that happens, you'll be in for a power struggle that'll make the war in the islands look like a chess match between neighbouring girls' schools. You'll all be swept into different factions and you'll spend the next ten years fighting pitched battles up and down Bero. Just about all of you will die, and what will your deaths purchase? At best, you'll have moved some idiot baron an inch closer to the throne of Bero. An idiot baron who doesn't deserve it. Most of the people who'll be fighting for the crown shouldn't be trusted with a puppy, let alone a kingdom. So if I were you, I would think a little less about your duty to the House of Bain, and a little more about your duty to yourselves and your families. You're the ones who are still alive."

I had been talking very fast; now I had to stop to breathe. The soldiers hadn't dropped their weapons, but they weren't attacking, either.

Whytock said something I didn't catch. "Sorry, what?"

"I said, what do you propose?"

"I'm going to tell you. Let me take care of my sister, first."

Ariadne was still bent double in a guardsman's grip. When I walked towards her, a few hands tightened on sword-hilts, but no one moved.

As I passed Melitta's body, I gingerly prodded her side with a bare toe. It wasn't meant to be an insult, I just had to know. No motion in the prone figure. No life in the purple-black face. It was strange that I didn't feel more.

The soldier holding Ariadne loosened his grip when I reached her. She leaned on me for the few steps it took to get back to the others.

"Take care of her, Latoya," I directed. The burly sailor blinked, nervous, but she bent over my sister, and, though she looked like an oak next to a sunflower, her hands were gentle as she took hold of Ariadne's shoulders. That was all it took. The next second, Ariadne flung herself, bawling, into the bosun's arms.

"What do you propose?" Whytock repeated, stiffly. "You know that the Lady Ariadne can't take the throne now. Under the law, she should be exiled, if not hanged."

"She couldn't take the throne even if she hadn't killed Melitta. She doesn't have an heir and she doesn't have any support among the army. She wouldn't last six months. You need someone else. You could elect one of your generals, but the runner-up will get sulky and declare himself lord as well. Same result. Civil war. Captain Whytock, would you take off your helmet, please?"

"What? Why?"

"Humour me. It's important."

His eyes flicked to my hands, looking for weapons. Unwillingly, he pulled his helmet off. I studied his hair. It was a sort of tawny straw colour. Yes, this would work.

"Do you have lemons?" I asked.

Whytock gaped. "*What?*"

"If we're going to do this, we'll need lemons. Lots of lemons. Rub the juice into your hair and then spend as much time as you can in the sun."

"If we're going to do *what*? What the hell are you suggesting? You're not going to propose this pirate as lady of Bero, are you?"

"No. Bero isn't ready for Darren. Ariadne wouldn't last six months, but Darren wouldn't even last three. There's only one man who can hold Bero together and rule it . . . and that's Iason's long-lost cousin."

"Lord Iason doesn't have a cousin."

"Not yet, he doesn't. Not until you've bleached your hair with lemon juice. But after that happens . . ." I let my words trail off enticingly.

There was a pregnant silence. It was almost a full minute before Whytock shook his head. "It'll never work. No one will ever believe it."

"People believe what they're told to believe, Whytock. There are people in every port in Kila who owe Darren favours. We'll draw up your lineage and make up a story about your childhood, and I'll have a man on every island who'll swear to every detail. Within a year, you'll be so solidly grounded that no one would *dare* to question where you come from. And these men?" I looked around, taking in each one of them. "These men will be your officers, your generals, your honour guard, well-paid and well-respected. They'll serve you loyally, because they'll be better off under your authority than under anyone else. And every single one of them will swear himself blue in the face at every opportunity that you're Iason's cousin, the rightful lord of the house of Bain."

More silence.

"Or you could just let Bero be ripped to shreds in a bloody and meaningless war. That's also an option."

Even *more* silence. Iason had stopped kicking. I stooped over, lifted his limp hand, and worked his signet ring off his finger. It took a minute, but nobody spoke. When the heavy gold loop finally came free, I held it out to Whytock.

I'm not the kind of person who believes in concepts like destiny. I think I'm in the world because my father was bored and needed an afternoon's entertainment, not because some cosmic power was directing events towards some ultimate goal. But if I'm wrong about that, if I owe my existence to some kindly god and not my father's urges, then this, I guess, is my purpose. To think the things that nobody else will think, to bend people's brains in directions they wouldn't take on their own, and to watch as their minds suddenly open. *Is it possible? Could it possibly be possible? But why shouldn't it be possible? Why shouldn't it?*

"Follow the rules, and you're doomed whatever you decide." I was talking both to Whytock, and the men who could raise him to the throne, if they only decided that they could. "Break the rules, and you have no idea just how good your life could get. You don't have to let this island fall apart. You can save yourselves, you can save *everyone,* but only if you're brave enough, and only if you have enough imagination. Whytock, think carefully before you answer this question. Does Iason have a cousin? Yes, or no?"

Slowly at first, then with greater conviction, Whytock reached out for the ring. He slid it onto his finger and closed his fist. The signet ruby sparkled in the torchlight.

"Well," he said. "Does anyone know where they keep the lemons?"

YOU WOULDN'T BELIEVE, unless you've been through it yourself, how suddenly freedom can happen. A day before, I'd been Melitta's captive servant, and an hour before, I'd been inches away from death. But in the faint glow of the pre-dawn, with Lord Whytock striding before us and ten new captains marching proudly on either side, we passed unchallenged through gate after gate.

Ariadne had a thing for poetry when we were still quite small. There was one that she would repeat to me endlessly—"in hope," she would always say. *Forgotten the fear that once held me in thrall*, it began. *And my bonds have become light as dreams* . . .

It used to make me roll my eyes. But as I walked through the walls that had shut me in for most of my lifetime, with Darren beside me, her face radiant in the pink light, all I could think was . . . well, exactly.

Ariadne had collected herself, more or less. She was talking to Whytock at high speed as we descended through the lower city. "You can keep the barons under control as long as you hold the tax coffers," she was saying. "Put your most trusted men in that department, and pay them well enough to keep them from taking bribes. And hire a different steward—the old one listens at doors. Remember, your mother's parents were named Demetrian and Iocosta and your father's parents were Teleager and Nerine . . ."

I watched Whytock out of the corner of my eye, trying to assess how he would do as lord of the most powerful state in Kila. I didn't know much about his brains or his talent. But he had taken a load of wood from me once, when I was too tired even to stagger. That was a straw in the wind.

"How are you doing?" Darren said, interrupting my thoughts.

I squinted up at her sideways. She looked exhausted. Her leather armour was slashed and crumpled. Threads of blood etched the right side of her face. She was beautiful.

"How do you think the Clever Lass felt when she left the castle?" I asked. "After she bested the wicked king?"

"After she hopped there with one leg on a goat? Sore. I'm going to say sore."

"I do, as it happens, feel a bit sore."

"As it happens, so do I. But I also feel fucking fantastic, so there's that."

A breeze wafted from the harbour—salt, fish, damp wood, seaweed. My knees almost buckled from sheer relief. We were so close to being *home*.

Darren's arm came around me, enveloped me. "Easy. Are you sure you can walk?"

Instead of answering her question, I announced, "I am *never* going to have children. Ever."

She shrugged. "Lynn, it's your damn body. Your choice. Besides, there's a war on, right? Orphans everywhere. If we ever decide that we want a kid, then we can pick up a slightly used toddler."

"Ha. Not for me. But Ariadne, maybe . . . she really does want to be a mother. Go figure."

Latoya was pacing alongside Ariadne, looking protective. Every so often, she would touch my sister's sleeve with a careful fingertip, as if reassuring herself that she was still real.

"I think my bosun is head over heels for your sister," Darren noted.

"Of course. Didn't you see it coming? My sister is a lady, Latoya is a gentleman. It's only natural."

Darren suddenly stiffened. "Oh . . . damn."

"What? You don't have a problem with this, do you? Latoya's been alone too long."

"No, it's not that. Hang on."

We sped up until we came abreast of Whytock. Darren coughed, and then spoke in the specially deep voice she used when she was scared of sounding desperate. "Whytock—I mean, *Lord* Whytock—can you lend us a ship? Nothing fancy, just something that'll get us off the island."

"A ship?" Whytock repeated, as though he'd never heard the word before. "Yes, I suppose so. There's a wreck that they pulled off the reefs a few nights back. They've just patched the hull. It isn't much. Bit of an old tub, I'm afraid. Called, uh . . . the *Badger*, or something like that. Do you think that'll do?"

DARREN DENIES IT, but I'll swear on a stack of gold royals *that* high that there were tears in her eyes as she caressed the *Badger's* gunwale.

"I swear, you love this ship more than me," I said.

"Do not," she said. "I sunk the damn thing so that I could come after you. Doesn't that tell you anything?"

"Just that you were getting randy. Let's face it, there are some things that ships *can't* do."

Regon gave me a sly wink as he brushed past with a barrel of pork over one shoulder. I nodded graciously back, accepting the tribute.

With Whytock there to lean on the dock master, we were allowed to take enough supplies for the trip back to friendly waters. Once we'd loaded them, and once Darren and Regon had crawled all around the patch on the *Badger's* hull to make sure it would last as long as it needed to last, we were ready to go. Only Ariadne was still on dry land. She and Whytock were standing with their heads close together, having what looked like a Very Serious Discussion. I was about to come after her when they broke apart. Whytock whispered something more, and then stood back politely. Ariadne approached the ship and stood with one foot on the gangplank and the other on the pier.

"What was that all about?" I asked warily.

Ariadne's face was pinched and grey. "He said that I can stay. He'll cover up the murder so that I can remain here as his advisor."

"Is 'advisor' the new secret code word for 'wife'?"

"No, he's married. Five sons. But he said that he could really use me, and if I want to be here, I'm welcome here."

"*Do* you want to be here?"

"I don't know," she said unhappily, with a glance back over her shoulder. "Let's face it, court intrigue is what I'm good at. It's where I really belong."

"That's total crap. You belong anywhere you want to be. Right now you belong on a pirate ship. I'm already figuring out where to put your hammock. I'm going to put ribbons on it and things."

"But I don't know a thing about sailing."

"Darren's *got* sailors," I pointed out. "What she doesn't have is a ship's surgeon."

"But I'm not—"

I looked at Darren. "She knows about herbs and specifics, she can bandage and split with the best of them, and she knows when to back off and let nature take its course. Plus, she can sew."

Darren cocked an eyebrow. "Did she ever stitch you up?"

"Well, not exactly . . . but she's done a hell of a lot of embroidery."

"It would be *nice* to have someone on the *Banshee* who could stitch wounds right," Darren said thoughtfully. "Spinner's been doing that, and he's got hands like . . . well, like a sailor."

Ariadne looked ragged and tired, with her face streaked with mud and streams of lace dripping from what was left of her underclothes. "But I know Bero. I could maybe ease the transition. Help Whytock with the deception. Stop some of the conflict. Don't I really have a duty to the people? To stay?"

The silence crawled, and then Darren rubbed her face fiercely. "It's what I would have done, if it were me. Ow. Lynn. Don't kick me, I wasn't going to stop there. I can't make this decision for you, Ariadne. All I can say is, duty is overrated. No matter where you go, there are people who need help. But you kind of have to take love wherever you find it."

Ariadne looked back at the castle.

And then back at me.

"The hell with it," she announced.

And in two great bounds, she was up the gangplank, taking me into a crushing embrace.

CHAPTER TWENTY-TWO
Darren, formerly of the House of Torasan (Pirate Queen)
Morning, Day XIII

THERE WAS A freshening wind from the south as we pulled out of the harbour. It would be a long trek to find the *Banshee*, but for once I didn't feel tired. It felt like the beginning of one of my early voyages, when every square inch of the ocean was new, and death was something that only happened to other people.

Regon had the tiller, and Lynn and I worked the sails. It was no good asking Ariadne and Latoya to do anything useful. They were huddled together by the side, Latoya's arm wrapped around the princess. Every now and then, she cast a sort of "how'm-I-doing?" glance over her shoulder, and I would give an encouraging nod in reply.

"So," I said to Lynn, "I've been thinking."

She peeked around the sail. Definitely concerned, if not panicked. "Have you?"

I clucked my tongue. "Ye of little faith. I've been thinking that we should revise our long-term plan."

"Revise what part of it?"

"The part that involves me becoming the High Lady of Kila after we're done with this whole civil war thing. I fret and panic enough when I'm in charge of twelve ships. I don't need an excuse to take all of the sins of the nation on my back."

She thought about that as she tied off a rope. "Hmm. You might have a point . . . and frankly, the whole 'ruling the world' business seems sort of labour intensive. I'm not interested in having you work twenty-two hours a day."

"Exactly. Besides, there's a better person for the job now."

She looked confused, and then her face cleared. "Ariadne?"

"That's the one."

"She wants to be a healer, you know. A mother too, gods help her."

"If she wants to be a healer, there's a whole damn country that needs healing. As for the mothering thing, we shove a few orphans in her direction and run away. Problem solved."

"So what about us? What'll we do after the war?"

For the time being, I let myself believe that the war would have an end, and that both Lynn and I would see the end of it. It wasn't even hard to believe on a day like today. I angled my head back and felt the sun on my face. "I thought that we could just keep doing this. Forever. Unless we get sick of it and decide to do something different."

Lynn studied me. "You know something? I think that is a well-conceived plan."

"Glad you agree. Now go and use your superhuman powers of persuasion on my lazy bosun. Get her to come over here and handle the sails. Because you and I are going down to the hold and we are not coming up until both of us are good and ready."

"You're going to ravish me *now*? Honestly?"

"Actually, I was thinking that we could both use a nap. But I'm open to other options, if you insist."

"We don't have a cabin down there."

"I'll build you one. Did it before. This one will be better. It may even have a pool."

"Because the ship's leaking."

"Because, as you say, the ship is leaking. But we don't need to dwell on little details like that, do we?"

"What if I refuse to go with you?"

"Well then, girl, I have my own powers of persuasion."

"Watch it, babe."

"Don't you mean 'Mistress'?"

"Don't push your luck. Now are you going to get your bony pirate arse below, or do I have to kick it down the stairs?"

I grinned. "Whatever you say, Lynn. As always, whatever you say."

EPILOGUE: SIX YEARS LATER

PEOPLE TALK ABOUT a time that seems as distant as a dream,
When the stars all spiralled backwards, and the rivers ran upstream,
In the middle of the war that brought our nation to the brink,
Back when nothing ever worked out in the way that you would think.

For they say there was a girl, back in the whirlwind of the war,
Who was whipped and shamed and tortured for the royal blood she
bore—
Yet as a nameless slave girl on a wild and wicked sea,
Bound and branded, lost and helpless, she found pride and dignity.

And her captor was an exile who had known a bitter time:
An unrepentant criminal, a kiss her only crime,
Who always stood the steadiest when tossing on the foam,
Who, had she not been banished, would have never found her home.

And they say a shining princess in a castle high above
Kissed her father out of hatred; killed her mother out of love.
And from that bloody murder, a new hope began to spring,
And a pirate and her slave girl were the source of everything.

You see, even murder heals sometimes, and even love can bleed;
A fruitful womb may bear no fruit; a barren one can breed.
What you see as devastation could be rescue in disguise,
If you let your blinkers fall away and open up your eyes.

Now I'm not much of a scholar, but it's clear to even fools
That sometimes there's no fairness 'til you start breaking the rules—
And it isn't really justice to treat everyone the same—
And if you've got no way to win, it's time to change the game.

And so we've come to twist the rules like bits of linen thread:
We'll bend each law all back to front, turn ethics on its head.
We'll be wiser than our parents, question everything they knew,
Hoping only that our children will be wiser than us, too.

For no matter what the jurists and philosophers assert
There is just one human duty: it's to help more than you hurt.
And the world must turn and change, whatever gloomy prophets say—
And if you can't accept that? Get the hell out of my way.

"Are you *ever* going to put out the lamp?"

Ariadne, formerly of the House of Bain, High Lady of Kila, laid her pen down on top of the completed poem and glanced out the window. White electric threads of lightning whipped across the purple sky, like cracks in a dark stone. "I'm worried about them."

"Don't be," Latoya said, propping herself up on one elbow in the canopied bed. "It'd take more than a summer thunderstorm to sink the *Banshee.*"

"I know, oh I know," Ariadne said. "But it might slow them down, and I'm going to have the biggest tantrum in the history of *time* if they're not here for the birth. Seriously, it'll be epic. You'll be able to sell tickets."

Latoya yawned and settled her head back down. "Is it raining like a bitch?"

"Yes."

"Are the waves whitecapped and horrible?"

"Yes."

"Does the whole sea look like a scene from a nightmare?"

"Yes."

"They'll be here tomorrow morning," Latoya predicted sleepily. "Doing the impossible is kind of what they do."

There was no denying that one. Ariadne stared at the frothing sea. Somewhere out there was a pirate ship, its red sails streaming water, and a storm-petrel flag streaking out against the sky. Darren would be on deck, bawling orders, and Lynn would be at her side, blonde hair plastered back with rain, eyes alive with delight. Or maybe they weren't on deck at all. Maybe Lynn's arms were aching in the damp weather, so they were down in their cabin, and Darren was rubbing the soreness out. Or maybe—

"Ariadne," Latoya groaned from behind the curtains.

After a last glance at the ocean, Ariadne blew out the lamp, kicked off her slippers, pulled off her robe, and slipped into bed. The coverlets were mounded over Latoya's bulging stomach. Ariadne touched the top of it gently. Right on cue, she felt a kick.

There's always *another way*, Ariadne thought, with drowsy happiness, and settled her head on Latoya's shoulder, her arm around the pregnant belly. Ten seconds later, they were both asleep.

About the Author

Benny Lawrence lives in Toronto, Canada, where she works as a lawyer while wondering just when in hell she grew up. Occasionally, she dons elaborate hats and sallies out after dark to solve crimes. There being no crimes lying around for her to solve, she mooches off home and eats cookies instead. She enjoys dead languages, not-dead cats, fizzy drinks, preparing for the apocalypse, and board games. She has been told that she takes her board games much too seriously. On a literature front, she is obsessed with mysteries, science fiction, and fantasy books, as long as they involve snappy dialogue and females who can deliver it.

Lightning Source UK Ltd.
Milton Keynes UK
UKHW011942290522
403692UK00001B/9